Here Lie the Dead

JD Kirk is the author of the multi-million bestselling DCI Logan series, set in the Highland s of Scotland . He also d oes not exist. Instead , JD is the pen name of former child ren's author and screenwriter, Barry Hutchison, who was born and raised in Fort William. He still lives in the Highland s with his wife and child ren. He has no id ea what the JD stand s for.

Also by JD Kirk

DCI Logan Crime Thrillers

JD KIRK

HERE LIE THE DEAD

CANELO CRIME

Penguin
Random
House

First published in the United Kingdom in 2022 by Zertex Crime

This edition published in the United Kingdom in 2025 by

Canelo, an imprint of
DK Publishing, a division of Penguin Random om House LLC
1745 Broadway, 20th Floor, New York, NY 10019

The authorized representative in the EEA is Dorling Kindersley Verlag GmbH. Arnulfstr. 124,
80636 Munich, Germany

ISBN 9798217269754

Look for more great books at
www.canelo.co | www.dk.com

–

154078558

Chapter 1

It had been the most perfect and magical day of Ellie Baker's life, right up until the moment the corpse turned up.

She had woken early, despite the late-night revelry of the evening before. Breakfast had been some avocado toast, washed down by a glass of icy-cold Buck's Fizz that helped take the edge off her hangover.

A shower had helped blast the rest of it away. She'd got clean, then just stood there for a while, eyes shut, letting the warm water cascade across her shoulders and down her back.

When she'd opened her eyes again, she saw that the steam had revealed writing on the glass door of the shower cubicle. A heart, her initials, and those of her soon-to-be-husband.

He must've drawn that and left it for her to find. She smiled —even giggled a little, though that was probably the champagne—then got out, got dried, wrapped herself in her plush white dressing gown, and presented herself to the whirlwind of friends and relatives all assembling in the hotel corridor outside her room.

From there, everything had been a bit of a blur. She'd been fussed over and bossed around in equal measures. But it had all been worth it. The hair, the makeup, the dress, it had all been perfect.

There had been tears shed —her mum, mostly, though a couple of bridesmaids, too—lots of talk about wishing granny was here to see her, and a barrage of remarks on just how beautiful she looked.

And she did, she knew. She bloody well should. She'd lost three stone for this and, as she'd made a point of telling anyone that would listen, that hadn't been easy. She'd shunned chocolate and takeaways, turned down nights out at the pub, and even taken up jogging.

Fucking *jogging*!

It had been hell, but it had been worth it. Ellie had been determined not to look fat in her wedding photos. No, more than determined, she had been *obsessed* with the idea.

Even if she put all the lost weight back on tomorrow, it wouldn't matter. She didn't care. She'd have today. She'd have o*perfect* day at her ideal weight, and that day would be captured forever from a variety of flattering angles by a trained professional, so that—years from now—she could open up the photo album and impress her future children with how good she had once looked.

Her choice of bridesmaids had not been accidental, either. She'd taken care to select some of her plumper friends, who she'd known would never have the willpower to stick to a diet. Next to those fat fucks—a term she used endearingly, although never to their faces—she was going to look like a supermodel.

In hindsight, though, she was starting to wish she'd pushed them a tiny bit harder on the diet and exercise front. She wanted them chunky for the photos, yes, but maybe not quite *this* chunky. Some of them looked a right bloody state. Bethan, in particular, looked like someone had stitched a baby hippo into what, on someone else, would've been an attractive dress.

Bethan was lovely, of course—they'd been friends since primary school, and Ellie wouldn't hear a word said against her—but by fuck, she looked a mess. Her makeup, clumsily applied as it was, was trying its best to conceal the shine on her enormous forehead, but it couldn't work miracles.

They'd just have to make sure she didn't stand in direct sunlight during the photos. Or, ideally, try to arrange it so she had her back to the camera.

Bless her.

Some more Buck's Fizz had been knocked back, then Ellie's dad had arrived to escort her to the waiting car. His throat had tightened at the sight of her in her flowing white gown, though he didn't quite cry. It took a lot to get a tear from him—he'd shed one or two when he'd been told the price of the dress, but seeing her wearing it clearly didn't have quite the same emotional impact.

Luckily, by that point, Ellie's mum had been crying enough for all of them.

They'd gone d ownstairs, and Ellie had been met with her first big surprise of the d ay. It was, she would later note, by far the better of the two.

Two white stallions stood waiting in the car park, a Disney-style carriage fastened behind them, all bling and silk ribbons.

It was her turn to come close to crying then, but she'd sucked them back up into the d ucts so she d id n't make a mess of her makeup. She'd air-hugged and air-kissed her father—she d id n't want to mess up her d ress, either—then allowed herself to be helped aboard the carriage by a short man in a tall hat who had appeared to curtsey at her approach.

The brid esmaid s had tried to climb in, too, but she'd quickly shot that d own in flames. There were only two horses, and given the size of Bethan—God love her—they'd be risking some sort of animal cruelty charge if they allowed her on board .

Not that Ellie would ever say such a thing out loud , of course. She'd never be so mean to her old est friend to tell her what she really thought of her.

She'd waved like the Queen to the peasants watching on the streets as the carriage had mad e its way through Kyle of Lochalsh, head ed for the wed d ing venue. Some of them had snapped off photos on their phones, and she'd tried not to worry too much about the unflattering angle. She'd never have to see them.

Tilting her head upward s to d isguise any excess chinnage, Ellie had quietly wished that Bethan had hauled herself aboard , after all.

Like the carriage, Eilean Donan Castle looked like something out of a fairytale when they clopped to a stop in front of it. It had been all d one up for their arrival. Bunting. Flowers. The works. The official photographer had been there waiting, and she'd been forced to pose for half a d ozen photos before she'd even got up from her seat.

The vid eo guy was there, too, though he lurked further back along the brid ge that led to the castle, and seemed content just to blend into the background .

Just as well, too. She'd picked up a bit of a creepy vibe off him d uring the booking process, and the last thing she wanted was him

3

appearing in any of the photos, with his slicked-down hair and sagging, acne-scarred jowls.

The ceremony had gone like clockwork. Gavin had been there waiting at the head of the aisle for her when she'd made her big entrance. Neither of them was religious, but Ellie had insisted that a minister carry out the service, because if they were getting married, then they were damn well doing it properly.

The minister, unlike the bride, groom, or any of the fifty-odd guests, was Scottish. Ellie had insisted on that. What was the point in coming all this way north to get married in a Scottish castle if you didn't get the funny accent?

She'd found herself wishing that he was *slightly less* Scottish at points, though, as some of the things he said were a nightmare to understand.

Still, they'd got through it. Vows and rings had been exchanged. A kiss had been shared. Confetti had been thrown, despite the castle's insistence that it wasn't allowed, and Bethan and the other bridesmaid had screeched and squealed like the sky was falling.

A young lad, camp as Christmas, with purple hair and a lot of piercings—she'd felt that shouldn't be allowed when handling food— had brought over a tray of drinks and canapés, and the first part of the afternoon celebration had got underway.

The intention was to mill around at the castle for a while, get the photos done, then return to the hotel for dinner, which would be followed by the evening reception. Forty or so more guests were coming for the knees-up part of the wedding day—work colleagues, Gavin's old Uni friends, and a few of the less palatable aunts and uncles who couldn't be trusted with a full-day invite.

That was the plan. Unfortunately, it all fell apart around quarter past three, while the newlyweds were kissing in an archway for the benefit of the photographer.

The scream had come from somewhere outside. It was Bethan, Ellie realised—she could recognise that bovine-like racket anywhere— and at first, she'd thought nothing of it. All the bridesmaids had been squealing since the service had ended, like kids on raging sugar highs.

4

Their cackling laughter had been echoing and bouncing off the castle's stone walls for the best part of the last hour, and Ellie just prayed that the creepy vid eo man had the good sense to put a music track over it. The last remind er she wanted of her special d ay was the sound of Bethan breathlessly grunting away like Jabba the Hutt having an angry wank.

It was only when the other screams rang out, and the shouting began, that Ellie realised something had gone terribly wrong. She'd mad e the photographer finish off the last few shots—she'd had to navigate a wind ing staircase to get to this spot, and she was buggered if she was coming back up again later. Then she had d ragged Gavin back d own the steps, through the labyrinth of rooms and corrid ors, and out to the back of the castle.

The back wall overlooked the point where Loch Duich and Loch Alsh flowed together. Around half of the wed d ing guests had assembled there now. They were staring d own at the water, pointing and babbling away to each other, their initial terrified reactions having d ampened d own by the time the brid e and groom arrived .

'What is it?' Ellie had d emand ed . She'd tried to keep her voice light, thinking this was befitting of a brid e on her big d ay, but the word s had come snapping sharply out of her.

Even then, though, nobod y had turned to look her way. Whatever was d own there—whatever was causing all the fuss—had well and truly stolen her thund er.

She hoiked up the train of her d ress and shoved her way to the front of the stramash, elbows powering her through the growing crowd like fleshy pistons.

'What's so interesting? What are we all looking at?' she asked , though she need n't have bothered .

She saw it for herself. A shock of orange in the water. A tangle of long, d ark hair moving with the ebb and flow of the tid e. A figure, limp, and pale, and broken.

'Oh, God . Oh, *God*,' Ellie whispered , her hand flying to her mouth. 'That's a d ead bod y. That's a girl's d ead bod y!'

Ellie's heart sank as a horrible realisation struck her. There was no escaping the fact. No d enying it. Years from now, d espite all her careful planning, and all the vast expense, when people talked about her wed d ing d ay, this would be the moment they talked about.

Not how beautiful her d ress was. Not her frankly staggering weight loss. This. Here. Now.

'Oh, God .' The tears she had so bravely fought back now returned with reinforcements. She sobbed . 'What the fuck have I ever d one to d eserve this…?'

Chapter 2

'We are, boss. I swear. I swear to God , we're going to d ie in here!'

Detective Chief Inspector Jack Logan rubbed a knuckle slowly up and d own the centre of his forehead . He was hoping to massage away the ache that had been rumbling there since he'd entered the room, and the d oor had locked behind him.

It was a d ecent-sized room, though the assortment of junk that filled the place—much of it Egyptian-themed —mad e it seem smaller and more claustrophobic.

This perhaps explained why Detective Constable Tyler Neish looked like he was two shallow breaths away from hyperventilating and passing out.

'For Christ's sake, calm d own, Tyler,' Logan said . 'Of course, we're not going to blood y d ie.' He gave a grunt. 'Well, I won't. But if you keep going on the way you're going, I'm not making any promises.'

When Logan's live-in girlfriend , Shona Maguire, had told him she'd arranged a special d ate for them, he had n't had any id ea what to expect. Shona was good at sorting out that sort of thing—much better than he was, anyway.

For him, the perfect d ate had always been d inner and a trip to the pictures. The big benefit of this was that you d id n't have a huge amount of time to talk, so there was less chance of him accid entally causing offence, or otherwise sticking his foot in his mouth.

Shona was much more ad venturous. For her, a d ate could be anything from a picnic on a rain-battered beach to a stroll through a street market, where she'd stop and smell all the cheeses, and take ad vantage of any free food samples that happened to be on the go.

7

She'd tried to book them a swimming-with-sharks experience a few months back, but Logan had managed to talk his way out of it, on the basis that he didn't like being underwater at the best of times, let alone when there was a bloody Great White circling around him.

Plus, it had been in Edinburgh, a city he'd always felt was far too full of its own importance. A Glasgow shark was one thing, but he'd be damned if he was having an Edinburgh shark swimming about while looking down its bastarding nose at him.

Of all the dates he hadn't been expecting, though, the one he'd ended up on today had perhaps been the most surprising of all.

It was a double date, for one thing. That had only been sprung on him at the last moment, of course. Shona had assumed —correctly— that he'd have called the whole thing off if he'd been informed in advance.

It was only when Tyler and his wife, Detective Constable Sinead Bell, had waved at them from a table in the corner of the cafe that Logan realised the terrible truth.

And it had all gone downhill from there.

Shona had booked them a place in an escape room experience that had temporarily set up in the Eastgate Shopping Centre. It was a competitive thing—two teams, head to head, in a race to see who escaped their room first.

Logan had assumed he'd be paired up with Shona. And that was fine, as it would've meant they were on a double date in name only, both couples kept apart by walls and puzzles, and so free to do their own thing.

He had assumed incorrectly. A 'girls against boys' structure had been adopted, and before Logan could voice his objections, he'd been shut in with DC Neish, who had soon proven himself even more irritating out of work than he was in it.

'None of it makes sense, boss!' Tyler chirped. He ran a hand down the smooth metal door, then slapped his palms against it like this might uncover some secret button or switch. 'I think it's broken.'

'You think what's broken?'

'I don't know!' Tyler fretted. 'Just, you know, whatever we're meant to be doing. The room in general. The whole thing. I think it must be broken.'

Logan sighed. 'Look, just keep the heid, son,' he said. 'We're detectives in the bloody polis, for God's sake. We can figure this out.'

Tyler looked back over his shoulder and gestured at the room around them. There was a hint of desperation to the way his hand moved. 'Fire on then, boss. Because I've tried everything.'

'My arse! In what way have you tried everything?' Logan shot back. 'You poked around at that pyramid, picked up the handset of that phone and listened to it for three seconds, then started hitting the door and shouting.'

'That's pretty much everything!' Tyler insisted.

Logan cast his gaze around the room. There were at least two hundred different items assembled on tables and shelves, or stacked up on the floor in the corners. That wasn't to mention all the pictures, newspaper cuttings, and paintings that hung on the wood-panelled walls, or the bookcase designed to look *just enough* like a door to keep you going back and trying to open it.

Logan wasn't going to fall for that trick, though. It was too obviously trying to look like a door to actually *be* a door.

Still, he tried pulling out a couple of books, just in case. Nothing clicked. Nothing creaked. Nothing swung inwards to reveal a secret exit.

'Aye, thought not,' Logan muttered, which drew the attention of DC Neish.

'Is that bookcase a door, boss?' he cried, rushing over to join the older detective.

Logan shook his head. 'No. Too obvious. I'm thinking it's just designed to make you wonder if it's…'

He left the sentence there, and watched in silence as Tyler frantically pulled volume after volume from the shelves.

Only when all the books lay scattered on the floor did the DC stop. He stepped back, hands on his hips, breath coming in squeaky wheezes, and shook his head.

'It's not a d oor,' he confirmed .

'No. I know. That's what I was in the mid d le of blood y telling you,' Logan said . He let out another sigh. He'd lost count of how many that was now since he'd entered the room. 'More likely, the ord er of the books was some sort of clue for us to follow.'

'The ord er of the books, boss?' Tyler asked . He looked d own. 'How are we meant to know that? They're all on the floor.'

'Aye, well, they are now,' Logan agreed .

'Can you remember what ord er they were in?'

'No, Tyler. Funnily enough, I d id n't get a chance to memorise the placement of a hund red d ifferent books before you chucked them all over the blood y place.'

Tyler winced , and there was a suggestion of reproach in his reply. 'That's a pity. That would 've really helped us out, boss,' he said , then he returned to the exit and tried to squeeze his fingertips into the one-millimetre gap between the d oor and the frame.

Logan groaned . What the hell was wrong with d inner and a trip to the pictures? A nice steak. Maybe a Bond film. There was usually one of them on the go.

But, no. Instead , he was trapped in a room with a man whose every word was bringing the DCI closer to an act of physical violence.

'Right. Look. It must be Egyptian-themed for a reason,' Logan d eclared , d etermined to get them out of here.

'Aye. Because we're going to d ie here and end up as mummified corpses,' Tyler said . He sound ed quite matter-of-fact about it now, like his earlier hysteria had been replaced by a sort of forlorn acceptance of his fate.

Logan d id n't d ignify the remark with a response. Instead , he crossed to the pyramid that sat on a table in the centre of the room and bent at the waist while he stud ied it.

The construction was around two feet tall, with some sand stuck to the outsid e and a rough brick pattern sprayed on with a stencil. Bits of the sand had scraped away, revealing thin plywood below.

The table was circular, and mad e of a highly polished wood that reflected the lights of the ceiling. Placed around the table, at regular intervals, were little symbols, painted onto parchment. There were eight of them. Presumably, this was significant, although Logan d id n't have the first id ea as to how.

'Right. Can you read hieroglyphics?' he asked , which d rew a squeak of d isbelief from Tyler.

'What d o you mean, boss? Of course I can't!'

Logan shook his head . He sighed . Again. 'No. Stupid question, I suppose. Forget I asked . Best you stick to mastering read ing English first, son.'

'They can't expect us to be able to read Ancient Egyptian, can they, boss?' Tyler asked , and the look on his face suggested he was outraged by the thought. 'I mean, how many people in Inverness can d o that? No bugger would ever get out!'

'Aye, bit specific, right enough,' Logan ad mitted .

'What if we set something on fire?' Tyler asked .

Logan raised his eyes from the pyramid and let them settle on the young d etective constable.

'Sorry?' he asked .

'Like, nothing major. Just something small,' Tyler said . 'They'd have to let us out then, would n't they?'

'We're not going to burn the blood y place to the ground so we can get out,' Logan replied .

'We'll have to d o something soon, boss,' Tyler said . 'I d on't know how much longer I can take this.'

'What are you talking about?' Logan asked . 'We've been in here...' He checked his watch. '...nine minutes.'

'I know! And we're not any closer to getting out than we were then! So, at this rate, we're never getting out,' Tyler reasoned . 'I'm telling you, boss, I've got a bad feeling about this. I d on't think we're going to get through it.'

Logan clenched his jaw and counted to ten. Or he tried to, anyway, but Tyler interrupted him before he'd mad e it halfway.

'Maybe we can kick the d oor d own?' the d etective constable suggested , and before Logan could stop him, Tyler lunged with a kick at the smooth metal.

The door did not budge. Not even when Tyler tried a second and a third time.

'Well, that didn't work,' the younger detective announced.

'You don't say,' Logan muttered.

'Wait! Forget that! I've got a better idea!' Tyler cried. He pointed to the door. *You* try kicking it, boss.'

'I'm not kicking the bloody door down, Tyler,' Logan snapped. 'This fucking game's for ages eight and up! If you'd just shut up for two bloody minutes, I can figure it out!'

It looked like Tyler was about to object, but then he nodded. 'Right, boss. I'll stop talking,' he said. 'Probably best, anyway. There's no saying how much oxygen's left in the room.'

'It's no' airtight, son. They're not going to suffocate us,' Logan said.

'Aye, well, I'd rather not take the chance,' Tyler said. He took a deep breath while he still could, then mimed zipping his lips shut.

Because he knew Tyler well, Logan waited a few seconds to make sure he wasn't going to immediately start speaking again, then turned his attention back to the pyramid on the table.

'Right. So. Where are we?' He quickly raised a hand in DC Neish's direction. 'Rhetorical question. Don't answer that.'

The pyramid was the obvious draw in the room, but maybe it was *too* obvious. Maybe it was there to distract from the real clues.

He looked back at the books on the floor. Might be something in one of those, but it would take hours to look through them all now.

He approached one of the framed newspaper clippings on the wall and scanned it. It was about some hidden chamber being discovered in one of the pyramids at Giza. In the fourth paragraph, there was what Logan assumed to be a pretty big hint. The hidden chamber had only been revealed when a shaft of sunlight was directed to a spot on some ancient scale model of the pyramid complex.

'Is that not the plot to *Raiders of the Lost Ark*?' asked Tyler from a foot behind Logan.

Logan added to his collection of weary sighs. 'I thought you were going to shut up?'

'I d id ,' Tyler said . 'But you d id n't seem to be getting anywhere, so I thought you might need a hand , boss. Two head s are better than one, and all that.'

Logan sighed . Again. 'It d epend s on the head , but fine,' he muttered .

He turned away from the cutting, and Tyler followed suit. They both stood in silence, taking in all the d etails of the room.

Logan ran a hand across his chin, his fingertips scraping through his stubble.

'Right,' he d eclared . 'I think I've worked out what we need to d o.'

–

Six minutes later, the d oor to the escape room was opened from the outsid e by Shona and Sinead . Then the pair of them just stood there in the d oorway, regard ing the room in shocked silence.

The books were still scattered on the floor, but now they'd been joined by the shattered remains of the pyramid , several framed pictures, and the contents of a large bag of marbles.

Empty boxes lay strewn around the place. The light fitting had been removed . Tyler, for reasons not yet clear, was missing a shoe.

'Um… having problems?' Shona asked .

'We're saved , boss!' Tyler cried .

'How the hell d id you two get out?' Logan d emand ed .

'We've been out for ages.'

'What d o you mean *you've been out for ages*? How the hell have you been out for ages?'

'We got the key from the secret chamber in the pyramid ,' Sinead explained .

Logan gestured angrily to the smashed -up triangular structure on the floor. 'Bollocks, you d id ! There's no secret chamber in the blood y pyramid . We looked !'

'See, boss? I *knew* our room was broken!'

'Eh, aye, sir. Not that pyramid ,' Sinead said . She pointed to the opposite wall. A mural of Giza was emblazoned on it in what Logan now realised was a series of interlocking tiles. 'That one.'

'Bastard !' Logan hissed .

'How d id you not see that, boss?' Tyler asked , and that hint of reproach was back in his voice again.

'You've got eyes, too, son!' the DCI pointed out.

'I see you two took a somewhat d ifferent approach,' Shona said , still taking in the mess. 'How was that working out for you?'

'We almost had it,' Logan grunted .

Tyler shook his head and hurried ly limped over to join the two women. 'No, we d id n't. I thought we were d one for. It was getting like the end of *Lord of the Flies*. Five more minutes, and we'd have been eating each other.'

'Where's your shoe?' Sinead asked .

'I d on't care,' Tyler said . 'Leave it. I just want to get far away from here in case they lock us in again.'

'Aye, well, you're in luck,' his wife replied .

'You're both going to get to put those obviously excellent problem-solving skills of yours to use again,' Shona ad d ed .

She held up two phones—hers and Logan's—and ad opted a gravelly accent that Logan guessed was meant to sound Glaswegian, but d id n't come anywhere close.

'Thurr's bin a muurd er!'

Chapter 3

Two hours later, Logan picked his way across the rocks in the shad ow of Eilean Donan Castle, head ed for a white sheet that had been d raped across an unmoving mound on the loch shore.

Geoff Palmer and his team of forensics experts were yet to arrive, but Logan wasn't overly concerned about compromising the scene. That ship had alread y sailed when half a d ozen wed d ing guests and castle staff members had gone blund ering into the water to d rag the bod y onto d ry land .

Their intentions had been good , he remind ed himself, though there was no saying what d amage they might have d one to the investigation. But then, what else could they have d one? Leave her at the mercy of the tid es?

No, they'd d one the right thing. He d oubted Palmer would have the same take on it, though.

Logan wasn't the first d etective on the scene. DS Hamza Khaled had got there fifteen minutes earlier, and had been d oing his best to keep things und er control when the others arrived . With fifty agitated wed d ing guests, twelve staff members, and only two local uniformed constables, though, he had his hand s full.

Tyler and Sinead were d ispatched to help him, while Logan and Shona mad e their way over to where the bod y lay patiently on the shore.

'I feel quite bad ,' Shona confessed , as they carefully progressed across the slippery, slime-coated rocks.

'About the d ouble d ate?' Logan asked .

'What? No!'

'Aye, well, you blood y should d o!'

'About the "there's been a murd er" thing,' Shona said .

'Oh, aye. The accent, you mean?'

'What? No! I thought the accent was good . The whole thing, I mean,' Shona said . 'It was a bit, you know, insensitive. Consid ering...'

She gestured to the sheet, which was now just a few carefully chosen steps ahead of them. Rain had been falling as a light mist on and off for an hour or two. Combined with the water seeping up from below, the sheet was d amp, and hugged the contours of the figure below.

'I would n't worry about it too much, I d oubt they'll mind ,' Logan replied , then he caught her by the arm when her foot slid on a smooth stone, and she almost went on her arse.

'Nice catch. Thanks,' Shona whispered , and she let him support her for the final few feet. 'And you're right, I'm probably overthinking it. Sure, for all we know, there's a Nazi und er there, or... I d on't know. Hannibal Lecter.'

Logan pulled back the sheet, and Shona let out a pained groan.

'Nope. Teenage girl. Great. Now I feel terrible.'

The young woman below the sheet could well have been a teenager, though the rigours of d eath mad e her age hard to d etermine. Mid -teens to mid -twenties, Logan guessed . Though, like Shona, he was leaning toward s the younger end of that range.

Her skin was a grey–white, with branching blue capillaries running just below the surface. Her eyes were closed , though this may have been d one by whoever had slung the bed sheet over her.

A wid e gash had opened the front of her skull, just above her left eyebrow, exposing a soup of blood , brain matter, and murky loch water.

Logan lifted the sheet a little further. She was still clothed . That would be of some vague comfort to someone somewhere.

'Looks quite recent,' Shona remarked from over his should er. 'It's possible she just fell and hit her head . Could be an accid ent.'

'Aye.' Logan looked along the shore, then up at the castle towering above everything. 'Maybe.'

He stood up, stood asid e, mad e room for the pathologist to d o her thing.

'I'm going to take a look around,' he announced . 'Give me a shout when you're d one.'

Shona replied with a nod and a smile, then set her bag d own on a rock near the bod y, and unfastened the clasp.

The rocks shoogled und erfoot as Logan mad e his way along the shore. It was certainly possible that she'd fallen, given how unstead y the ground was. But it would take quite a d unt to d o that much d amage to a skull, so she'd have to have fallen from quite a height.

His eyes climbed up to the castle ramparts again. A d ozen or more faces were peering d own over the wall. He could see a couple of phones in hand , too, pointing d ownward s, record ing away.

'You lot! Fuck off! Now!' he boomed , stabbing a finger in their d irection.

The faces quickly d isappeared , only to be replaced by a cap-wearing Uniform with a surprised expression.

'You. Make sure they d elete any vid eos and photos off their phones,' Logan shouted to him. 'Or I'll shove them so far up their arses they'll be shooting close-ups of their own blood y d igestive tract.'

The only reply was a nod and a thumbs-up, then the Uniform vanished out of sight again, hopefully to carry out Logan's ord ers.

'Blood y vultures,' the DCI muttered , then his thoughts returned to the d ead girl on the shore.

A fall from the castle would certainly be enough to inflict the sort of d amage her head had sustained .

Arguably, it was too high. Even if she'd land ed on a particularly pointy rock, there should be more trauma to the rest of the face. Not to mention a broken neck, which her position d id n't suggest she had .

She might have, of course—every bone in her bod y could be broken—but Logan had seen enough corpses in his time to be able to make some ed ucated guesses about this one, and his instincts told him that, asid e from the blow to the head , Shona was going to find very little d amage.

What his instincts were unfortunately keeping to themselves at the moment was whether they were looking at a tragic accid ent, a suicid e, or a murd er. Right now, it could be any of the three. He was hoping it was the first one, of course. He always d id . Still a tragic loss for some poor family somewhere, but perhaps a less painful one.

But then, since when had hope ever changed anything?

'Ho! What the blood y hell is all this?!'

The shout came floating d own from the castle above. Logan looked up, and his first thought was that someone had balanced four footballs on the wall. It was only when one of them spoke that he realised it was the white-hood ed head s of Geoff Palmer and some of his team.

'Who's been pissing about with the bod y?' Palmer d emand ed . Before Logan had a chance to reply, he shook his head and shouted again. 'Wait there. Don't blood y move. I'm just coming.'

One by one, the head s d isappeared .

One by one, they came right back.

'Here,' Palmer called . 'How the hell are we meant to get d own there?'

–

The brid e, they were all quick to conclud e, was an absolute night-mare. She'd sprung at Hamza as soon as he'd rocked up at the castle, d emand ing... well, it wasn't clear precisely what she was d emand ing, exactly, but she was d efinitely d emand ing something.

She went from insisting that she and the rest of the wed d ing party be allowed to leave and go back to the hotel, to d emand ing compens-ation, to telling him to get his finger out and 'clear that blood y thing away.'

The blood y thing in question, of course, being the lifeless corpse of another human being.

Ultimately, what she really seemed to want was for Hamza to wave some sort of magic wand that would rewind time and allow her big d ay to go smoothly. He wished he could , but since this was obviously impossible, he settled for curtly telling the brid e to go insid e and await further instructions, then he'd gone strid ing off to talk to the Uniforms while she'd seethed silently in his wake.

She must've eventually d one as asked , though, because she was there waiting in an enormous stone-walled room that had been set up as a function suite when Hamza, Tyler, and Sinead all entered together twenty minutes later.

Judging by the flowers, silver balloons, and the party poppers that remained unpopped on the tables, it was supposed to be a place of revelry and merriment. Unsurprisingly, though, nobody seemed to be in much of a mood to celebrate.

The members of the wedding party were mostly all sitting at tables, slouched forward, so they rested on their elbows, or slumped back in the wooden fold-out chairs. A Shania Twain song was playing from a speaker somewhere, turned down low. The upbeat melody was wasted on this shower of maudlin bastards, although they could hardly be blamed for that.

A photographer and videographer had gravitated together at a table in the far corner. They fiddled with their respective cameras, though both had the good sense not to be using them. Photographs of ashen-faced guests being held against their will by the polis were probably not the cherished memories the happy couple had been hoping to capture.

The detectives' arrival clearly triggered some sort of silent alarm in the bride's head. She was sitting with her back to them, but straightened in her chair when they entered the room, and turned so sharply to face them it appeared as if her head was rotating all the way around, *Exorcist*-style.

'Is this the bride?' Tyler asked, when she got to her feet and came racing over, the train of her ornate white dress dragging across the flagstone floor behind her.

'Aye. What gave it away?' Hamza muttered, then he flashed a smile and tried to defuse the situation before it could ignite. 'Hi. Sorry, didn't catch your name earlier, Miss...?'

'*Mrs*,' she retorted. 'It's *Mrs* Ellie Baker.' She hesitated, just for a moment, then begrudgingly spat out a correction. 'Tonks. Mrs Ellie Tonks.'

'Congratulations,' said Sinead, stepping between the DS and the bride, and offering Ellie a hand to shake.

The offer was not accepted.

'And just who the fuck are you, love?' Ellie asked with a sneer.

She stuck her hands on her hips as she looked Sinead up and down. Her gaze lingered a moment on the curve of the detective's belly. It was still relatively early days in the pregnancy, but it was hard to conceal twins for long.

'I'm Detective Constable Sinead Bell,' Sinead said, withdrawing her hand. 'But you can feel free to just call me Detective Constable Bell.'

'Are you pregnant?' Ellie asked, and it sounded like an accusation.

'I am. You?' Sinead said.

'No, I am not!' Ellie yelped. 'Are you saying I look fat? I lost three stone for this, I'll have you know! Three stone!' She turned to Hamza. 'Is she even allowed to ask me that?'

Hamza's eyes darted from the bride to Sinead and back again. The wedding guests had all turned in their chairs to watch the show now, though none of them appeared keen to get involved.

'Is she allowed to ask you what?'

'If I'm pregnant!'

Hamza blew out his cheeks. 'I mean, I don't see why not. I could go and check the rule book, if you like, but it might hold things up for a few more hours…'

'Forget it!' Ellie told him. 'I just want to get out of here. We all do. This was supposed to be my special day!'

'I appreciate that, Mrs Tonks,' Hamza began, but the bride was quick to shut him down.

'Oh, you appreciate it, do you? You *appreciate it*? Do you have any idea how much this wedding cost?'

'No,' Hamza admitted.

'Dad! How much did this wedding cost?' Ellie called back over her shoulder. When there was no response, she turned and shot daggers at an older man sitting slumped in the corner, an empty champagne flute upended on the table in front of him. 'Oh, for God's sake, *Dad!*'

'What is it now?' the older man asked, with a sense of weariness that permeated him right down to the bones.

'Tell him how much this wedding cost,' Ellie urged.

'I can't remember,' her father said . He sighed and shook his head . 'Too blood y much. Can we go back to the hotel yet?'

'Well?' Ellie asked , turning back to the d etectives. 'What d o you have to say to that?'

Sinead stepped in then, forcibly inserting herself back into the conversation before Hamza could try to placate the woman any further.

'Believe me, you d on't want to know what I have to say,' she said , fixing the other woman with a glare that could cut glass. 'Someone's d ied . People have lost a loved one. Now, I'm sorry your wed d ing's been spoiled ... in fact, you know what? I'm not. I d on't actually care. That's not my concern. So, how about you d o us all a favour, and go sit back d own until one of us d ecid es you're worth taking the time to talk to? All right?'

Ellie stared , open-mouthed . She was not the only one. Tyler and Hamza both ad opted the same slack-jawed expression, then watched in silence as the brid e huffily about-turned and marched back over to her table.

'Bit harsh, wasn't it?' Tyler whispered to his wife.

Sinead shrugged . 'I'm pregnant. You're allowed to say that sort of thing when you're pregnant.'

'I d on't know if you are,' Tyler ventured .

'You are. It's basically expected . I can get away with being a proper cow. I can say anything,' Sinead assured him.

Over at the table, Ellie was berating a glum-faced man in an ill-fitting kilt. Her new husband , presumably. Poor bugger.

'Besid es,' Sinead continued . 'I reckon it's probably high time some-bod y put her in place.'

'She *has* been a pain in the arse from the minute I arrived , right enough,' Hamza confirmed .

'There you go, then,' Sinead said , shrugging as if her point had been proven beyond all reasonable d oubt.

She looked around the room at all the anxious and forlorn faces, then turned back to Hamza.

'Right, then, Sarge. Where d o you want us to start?'

Chapter 4

Geoff Palmer was keeping his d istance, which suited Logan just fine. Given the choice, he'd never have to interact with the man again, but unfortunately their respective career choices meant they were locked into each other's orbits until one of them quit their job, moved elsewhere, or d ied .

The prospect of seeing that pud gy red face for the remain er of his d ays, Logan thought, perpetually encircled as it was by the elasticated band of the white paper hood , almost mad e the prospect of early retirement sound tempting.

But then, he'd tried that once before, and retirement had bored the arse off him. Thankfully, he'd been d ragged back in before the ted ium had killed him. So, like it or not, he was stuck looking at Geoff's coupon for the foreseeable.

'Stomach settled now, has it?' Palmer asked , his face contorted into a sneer even more punch-worthy than usual. From several feet away, his gaze flitted up and d own, sizing the DCI up. 'Not going to spontaneously chuck your guts up on me, are you?'

It had been almost six weeks since a bout of flu had led to Logan projectile vomiting onto the Scene of Crime man. In some ways, it had been one of the lowest points of Logan's career, but on the other hand , it was one of his fond est memories, and Geoff's look of mute horror was one that would keep the DCI warm at night for a very long time to come.

'No promises, Geoff,' Logan said . He had his hand s buried d eep in his pockets, the breeze blowing along the loch making the bottom of his overcoat swish around above the mossy rocks. 'What can I say? You must bring it out in me.'

Palmer raised a rubber-gloved finger and pointed accusingly. 'I could 've had you done for assault, you know?'

Logan shook his head. 'No. You could n't.'

'Well, shows what you know, because yes, I could, actually. I looked it up. You d eliberately aimed it at me, while you were knowingly ill. Therefore, it's assault.'

'OK. One, I d id n't aim it at you, Geoff. And two, you're boring the arse off me, so how about we just move on?' Logan nod d ed past him to where more white suits were picking their way along the shore. 'What have you got?'

Geoff prissily put his hand s on his hips. 'Well, not a blood y lot, thanks to all those d o-good ers trampling over the scene.'

'They were pulling the bod y out of the water,' Logan pointed out.

'Aye, but d id it take a blood y team of them to d o it? They might as well have run a herd of elephants around the place while they were at it. Or thrown a circus!'

Logan frowned. 'What?'

'Thrown a circus.'

'What d oes that mean?'

'Thrown a circus,' Palmer said, as if repeating it a third time might be enough of an explanation. 'As in, like, *throw a circus*. Put on a circus.'

'No one says "throw a circus", Geoff.'

'Aye, they d o!' Palmer insisted.

'They d on't. You can throw a party...'

'It's the same thing!' Geoff said, then he tutted and shook his head. His scowl puckered and red d ened further, until his face remind ed Logan of a blister waiting to be popped. 'Doesn't matter. The point is, they weren't careful. And as for the sheet. Was that necessary? Really?'

'I suppose they wanted to preserve the poor lassie's d ignity.'

'What d ignity? She's d ead! She's hard ly going to get a beamer from people seeing her now, is she?' Geoff cried. 'I'm sure she'd have much preferred her killer to be caught than for her so-called —' His rubber gloves squeaked as he mad e air quotes around the next word. '—"d ignity" to be protected.'

Logan sucked air in through his teeth. This time, it was his turn to look the other man up and down. 'God. Do you know what I've just realised, Geoff?'

Palmer's eyes narrowed. 'No. What?'

'You're an even bigger arsehole than I thought you were,' Logan said. 'And believe me, that's saying something. In fact, no. You're no' even an arsehole, you're an arse *cavern*. You're an arse *crevasse*. That's how big of an arsehole you are.'

Palmer didn't seem remotely put out or fazed by the insult. 'Aye, well, takes one to know one,' he said, then he looked annoyingly pleased with himself, like he'd just coined the phrase for the very first time.

Logan took a breath, swallowed back his dislike for the man, then tried to bring them back onto a more professional footing.

'You think she was murdered, then?' he asked.

'What?'

'You mentioned her killer. You're thinking it's murder?'

'Well, I mean, that's not for me to say, is it?' Palmer replied. 'You'll have to ask your *girlfriend* about that.' He paused just long enough to run his tongue across his yellowing teeth. 'Unless you two aren't together anymore…?'

Logan jabbed a thumb back over his shoulder. 'I'm going to go away now, Geoff.'

Palmer looked past him towards the castle, then beyond that to the road, where the two local Uniforms were directing traffic, which mostly involved waving at the rubberneckers to keep driving.

'Away where?' Geoff asked.

'Just away. Just away in general,' Logan said. 'Just somewhere where you're not. And, listen, do me a favour, will you? If you find anything—anything at all—don't tell me.'

Palmer looked confused. 'What?'

'Tell some other poor bastard, and they can pass it on to me.'

The Scene of Crime man shook his head in defiance. 'No. Oh, no, no. That's not how it works, I'm afraid. There are clear lines of communication, and it's my job to report to—'

Logan clutched at his stomach and blew out his cheeks like he was about to vomit. Palmer's objection end ed in a panicky squeal and some impressive cowering.

'Sorry, Geoff. Racing up that road played havoc with my guts. Best we stay out of each other's way. I would n't want to accid entally *assault* you again.' Logan thought for a moment. 'Well, no, I would actually quite enjoy that, but it's probably not in either of our best interests in the long run, so best we just keep our d istance, eh?'

And then, before Palmer could say anything more, the DCI about-turned , aimed himself at the castle, and set off at a march across the shore.

—

'Here, try one of these.'

Logan stole a glance around to make sure nobod y was watching, then opened his mouth to accept a canapé from Shona.

He chewed it up, his face contorting with each bite to show his d isapproval. It tasted a bit too salty, a bit too fishy, and with a sort of vinegary aftertaste that mad e him think of something left to ferment for far too long.

'Blood y horrible, isn't it?' Shona said .

'Jesus. Aye, you can say that again,' Logan said . He forced himself to swallow, then scraped his tongue with his top teeth, trying to make the taste go away. 'Why'd you make me eat it if you knew it tasted like that?'

Shona grinned . 'I d id n't want to suffer alone,' she said , then she popped another of the bite-sized snacks in her mouth. 'Although, I have to say, they're weird ly ad d ictive.'

The d etectives had taken over a small sid e room in the castle, and a member of staff had been good enough to snaffle them a plate of wed d ing snacks, and bring them some teas and coffees. Hamza, Sinead , and Tyler were all off talking to guests about the events of the d ay, and so Shona had taken it upon herself to work through the food while she waited .

'Aye, well, I'll take your word for that,' Logan said, turning his nose up at the rest of the plate.

He crossed to the room's only window—a tall, narrow thing that was probably ideal for firing arrows out through—and looked out over the loch. The bridge to Skye lay off in the distance, just a little too far away for him to be able to see.

Looking down, he could see Palmer and his team still busying around on the rocks. The girl's body was in the process of being bagged up, ready to be taken to Inverness for Shona to carry out the PM.

It was only then that he'd start getting the answers he needed. Still, no harm in asking the questions now.

'Well?' he said, turning away from the window.

Shona paused with a hand to her mouth, and hurriedly swallowed down another of the fermented fishy things before replying.

'Well, what?' she asked, then her eyes widened. 'Oh! You mean…? Right. Yeah. Sorry.' She picked up another canapé. 'Seriously, these things are like crack when you get going.'

Logan waited for her to throw that one back, too, then gave her a nod of encouragement.

'Right. Yeah. Sorry,' Shona said. She brushed her hands together, signalling that she was done with the food, then took three big paces away from the table to help avoid the temptation to go back for more. 'So, early days, obviously, none of this is gospel yet, but I'd say she's only been in the water for a few hours. Four, five, maybe. Certainly no more than ten.'

'The head wound killed her, I take it?'

'Well, it certainly didn't do her any favours,' Shona said. 'I'd say almost certainly that was the cause of death, yeah. No sign of plume around the mouth and nostrils that would indicate drowning, but the water could've washed that away, so I'll have to check the lungs. My instinct, though, is that she was dead before she went into the water.'

'So, someone killed her, then dumped her?'

Shona tilted her head from side to side, like she was weighing this up. 'Not necessarily. Could've fallen, cracked the old noggin on something on the way down, then landed in the water. Although, if that were the case, I'd expect to see more trauma to the rest of the body, and I'm not seeing that so far.'

Logan rocked on his heels, just a little, quietly pleased with himself for deducing the very same thing.

'But it could, in theory, still be an accident?' he pressed.

'In theory, yeah. Is it likely?' She shrugged. 'I honestly don't know. But I'll have more for you once I've had a proper look. What I would say, though, and it's probably going to sound a bit of a weird thing to say, you know, considering. But she didn't look well.'

'Beyond being dead, you mean?'

Shona smiled. 'Like I said, probably going to sound a bit weird. But she looked … I don't know. She's skinny. Too skinny. She looked a bit… malnourished, maybe. I don't know. Like I say, we'll know more soon. But you might want to check if there's any history of her having an eating disorder.'

'Right, aye. Will do. So, what's the plan? You heading back with the body?'

'Yeah. I'll go in the ambulance,' Shona confirmed. 'Don't forget the dog's in the car.'

'Oh, shite. Aye. I'll get Tyler to go take him for a walk. Keep him out of mischief.'

Shona smiled. 'Which one?'

'Both,' Logan replied.

He moved in closer, shuffling a little awkwardly. He hadn't quite mastered these goodbyes yet, even after all this time. Neither of them had, to be fair, so he couldn't take all the blame.

It had been simpler before they were an item. A respectful nod had been enough. A half-smile, and a wee wave. You knew where you stood.

Now, it was much more complicated. They were a couple, yes, but they were also professionals, and finding that balance was taking them longer than anticipated.

It could be two or three days before they saw each other again. More, maybe. A farewell kiss would be reasonable, wouldn't it? Professionals or not.

Aye, to hell with it. A kiss would be in order.

He had just taken another step closer when the door to the room was opened, and a smiling face appeared in the gap.

'Were my ears burning there, boss?' Tyler asked. 'Did I hear my name mentioned?'

Logan straightened. Stepped back. 'Jesus Christ, son, have you got sonar hearing or something?'

Tyler's smile remained fixed in place, but his eyebrows dipped in confusion. 'Boss?'

'Doesn't matter. Aye. Here.' He fished his car keys from his pocket and tossed them to the DC, who caught them in one hand.

'You giving me your car, boss? Very generous of you.'

'Haha. No,' Logan said, without a hint of genuine mirth. 'Taggart's in there. Go let him stretch his legs, will you?'

'No bother, boss,' Tyler said. He looked back over his shoulder, then turned to face the DCI again. 'But before I do, there's someone I think you're going to want to talk to.'

Logan shot Shona a sideways look. She had her bag on her shoulder, and was helping herself to a few more of the fishy hors d'oeuvres.

'Right, well, I, eh...' he started to say to her.

Then she nodded, and he half-smiled, and they gave each other wee farewell wave before duty pulled them in opposite directions, and Logan followed Tyler out through the arched stone doorway.

Chapter 5

Logan was led through the hall where most of the wed d ing guests were gathered , and felt all eyes on him as he followed Tyler toward s a narrow opening at the far end of the room.

As he passed the brid e, she started to get to her feet, but a warning look from the towering DCI quickly sat her back d own again, and the d etectives reached the passageway without further interruption.

'Christ Almighty, son, who are you taking me to see? Is it a Hobbit?' Logan asked , bend ing to peer into the tight corrid or Tyler had just started along.

'Sorry, boss. It's a bit narrow. Opens up in a sec, though,' Tyler assured him.

Grumbling, Logan lowered his head , stooped forward , and squeezed along the passageway, his should ers brushing against the round ed ceiling, his elbows scuffing against the rough stone walls on either sid e.

'I feel like you're taking me blood y potholing here,' he muttered .

Tyler stopped a few feet ahead of him. 'Shite. Sorry, boss, wrong way. We need to turn around .'

Logan almost choked . 'What?! Turn around ? I can't even fucking exhale. How am I meant to...?' He saw the grin spread ing across the younger man's face, and grunted . 'Very funny. Now, get a blood y move on before I hiccup and bring the whole roof d own on us.'

They pressed on, and to Logan's relief, the passageway soon opened out into a larger hallway, and to a d oor marked 'Staff Only'.

'He's through there,' Tyler said . 'It's like a wee sort of staff room. But I should warn you, he's a bit upset.'

'Who is it?' Logan asked . 'Who'm I meant to be talking to?'

'He's one of the guys who helped pull the bod y out of the water,' Tyler said , then he winced . 'Although, actually, I d on't know if "guys" is right. He might not be a guy.'

'What d o you mean?'

'Well, I mean, I assume he's a guy, because you d o, d on't you? But maybe that's wrong. I mean, who am I to say? You d on't know, d o you? In this d ay and age, I mean.'

'What are you on about, son?' Logan d emand ed .

'Remember that training they sent us on a few months back? About d ealing with people who, you know, id entify d ifferently?'

Logan remembered it well. Well enough that it elicited a low groan of d ismay. 'Aye. I remember.'

'Well, you might want to keep it in mind , boss. Because he just… he's a bit…' Tyler inhaled and sort of pursed his lips a bit, but elected not to finish that sentence. Instead , he gestured to the d oor with both hand s, like he was presenting it to the DCI. 'Maybe just best if you see it for yourself.' He flinched and quickly shook his head . 'I d on't mean "it" like he's an *it*. Though maybe he is an *it*. Or maybe she is. Because you can be an *it* now. If you want, like. Or a *they*. I d on't know. It's a total minefield , isn't it, boss?'

'All right, all right, just take a breath, Tyler,' Logan said . 'What the hell's wrong with you lately? You seem to be in a constant state of panic. Even more so than usual, I mean.'

'It's the babies, boss,' Tyler said . 'Got me a bit strung out.'

'They're no' going to be born for months,' Logan remind ed him.

'God . I know. And this is me now! Imagine what I'm going to be like when they're actually born!' Tyler squeaked . He pulled at the collar of his shirt, like the room was sud d enly far too hot. 'I mean, at least right now I know where they are. But what about when they start walking? Or *driving*, even. What then?'

'Jesus Christ, son. They're foetuses. I d on't think you need to worry about them getting their licence anytime soon,' Logan said .

'Well, not right now, maybe, but it's only a matter of time, isn't it?'

Logan sighed . There was no point in arguing. He'd learned it was best just to let the young DC burn himself out on this sort of thing.

'Aye. I suppose you're right.'

'Oh, great!' Tyler squeaked. He rubbed his forehead like this was the worst possible news he could 've been given. 'Thanks a lot, boss! You're supposed to be talking me down from stuff like this!'

With some reluctance, Logan put a hand on Tyler's shoulder. 'It's going to be fine, son,' he said. 'You'll get through it. There's really not a lot to it.'

'That's easy for you to say,' Tyler protested. 'But I want to be really involved with everything. I want to be a good dad, and ...'

The hand was withdrawn from his shoulder. Tyler had realised his mistake just a split second earlier, but it had taken him too long to pull the emergency brake on the sentence.

'Sorry, boss, I didn't mean... I wasn't saying that you weren't...'

'It's fine,' Logan told him. He jerked his head towards the door. 'Shall we?'

'Eh, aye. Aye,' Tyler said, still cringing so hard that his entire lower intestine had relocated upwards into his chest. 'And, eh, just—again—best keep that training in mind, boss.'

Logan reached for the handle, but felt the need to brace himself for a moment before pushing it down and opening the door.

When he did, he found himself outside a room barely bigger than a cupboard. There was one chair in it, currently occupied by a purple-haired teenager with a face covered with piercings, makeup, and snot, though not necessarily in that order.

'Hugo, this is Detective Chief Inspector Logan,' Tyler said. He side-eyed Logan. 'This is, eh, this is Hugo.'

'Nice to meet you, son,' Logan said.

He heard the sharp intake of breath from Tyler at that last word. Unlike the detective constable, though, he was choosing not to overthink things, and just offered out a hand to shake.

Hugo looked up at the hand, revealing that his thick purple eyeshadow had run down both cheeks. He placed his own hand in Logan's. It was a dead fish of a thing, with black-painted nails that had been picked around the base so often that the fingers were ridged with scar tissue.

'Hello. A pleasure to meet you, too,' he said , and Logan was sud d enly gripped by many of the same d oubts as Tyler.

Hugo's voice was higher than Logan had been expecting, and with an upper-class English purr that sound ed positively theatrical. It was the sort of accent that someone might affect to mock members of the aristocracy, but Hugo seemed to be genuinely trying to pass it off as his own.

It took Logan aback, and he found himself staring blankly at the teenager for what felt like quite a long time.

'Eh, boss?' Tyler prompted .

'Oh. Aye. Aye,' Logan said . He shook Hugo's hand , then released his grip. 'DC Neish tells me… well, actually, he hasn't told me a lot.'

'Hugo knows the victim, boss. Knew the victim, I mean.'

'Oh?' Logan's eyebrows rose. 'In what way?'

'She was a close personal friend of mine,' Hugo said .

'Right. I see. And who is she?'

Hugo inhaled a shaky breath before replying.

'Orla. Her name's Orla. She used to work here. We attend ed high school together.'

'What, you're local?' Logan asked .

'Yes,' he replied , in a voice straight out of a low-bud get Jane Austen film ad aptation. 'Why d o you ask?'

Logan shook his head . 'No reason. You were saying about Orla?'

'She was always… nice. To me, I mean.' Hugo shifted around in the chair and averted his gaze. 'Nicer than most of them, anyway.'

'Most of who?'

'Most of everyone,' Hugo replied . 'I'm sure you've noticed that I d on't exactly fit "the norm" around here.'

'Well, no. Aye. I mean…' Logan began, but then he just wrote the whole sentence off as a bad id ea, and gave what he hoped was a sympathetic sort of shrug, instead .

'Full name's Orla Coull, boss,' Tyler said , taking up the story. 'Age eighteen. Local girl. And get this—went missing just over six months ago.'

'Missing?'

'Aye, boss.'

'Vanished without a trace. Just... poof!' Hugo confirmed. 'You... I mean, the policemen that came. They believed she had left town of her own accord, but nobody around here believed that. Nobody who knew her, anyway. She wouldn't do that. Not to her mum. Not to me.'

'Were you two an item?' Logan asked.

'Eh, no,' Hugo said, and the note of sarcasm was hard to miss. 'I'm gay.'

'Oh. Right. Aye. Fair enough,' Logan said. He glanced at Tyler, who was biting down on his bottom lip like he was worried something was about to blow up in his face. 'But, eh, but you are... you are a man, aye?'

Hugo wiped a tear on the back of his hand, smearing it in watery eyeshadow. 'What's that got to do with anything?' he asked.

'Um... nothing, I suppose,' Logan admitted. 'No, I just... each to their own, and all that. Whatever floats your boat. I'm not going to judge. It's just... you know. Looking at you, it's not immediately clear what...'

'Boss?'

Logan shot another look at Tyler, who briefly closed his eyes and shook his head.

'No. Right. Aye. Maybe best not,' Logan muttered.

Hugo sighed. It was almost as theatrical sounding as his accent. 'Yes.'

'Yes, what?' Logan asked.

'I identify as male.'

'Right. Aye. Good,' Logan said.

Hugo's watery, purple panda eyes narrowed into slits. 'And why is that good?'

Logan hesitated, caught on the back foot. 'What?'

'Are you saying it would be bad if I identified differently?'

Logan could practically feel Tyler holding his breath. To be honest, though, he'd had enough of pussyfooting around the issue.

'Quite frankly, son, I d on't give a shite how you id entify,' Logan told him. 'You could be she, they, it, them, us, we… I d on't know. Whatever you like. No skin off my nose. What's "good " is me not having to tread on fucking eggshells for fear of offend ing or upsetting anyone, because, accord ing to recent training—and this came as news to me, let me tell you—apparently, that's frowned upon. And believe me, for a man who has based his entire career to d ate on upsetting people, it's all taking a bit of getting used to.

'So, you go ahead and be a man. Be a woman. Be a blood y Martian, if you want. Be whatever you blood y like. I d on't care. Just d on't piss me about. All right?'

Hugo's moment of d efiance had clearly passed . He quickly nod d ed and looked d own with hood ed eyes.

'Good . I'm glad we und erstand each other,' Logan said . 'So, the bod y. You're sure it was Orla?'

'Hund red percent,' Hugo replied . 'Definitely her. No question.' He stuck a painted thumbnail in his mouth and chewed on it. 'God !' he groaned . 'We need to tell her mum and d ad , d on't we? They're goin to be heartbroken. Do you want…? Should I d o that? I know them pretty well.'

'Thanks, but best if we hand le it,' Logan replied .

'But they'll be upset. *Really* upset.'

'Aye, they generally are,' Logan confirmed .

'And I know them,' Hugo insisted . 'They've been really nice to me. Maybe it should be me who tells them?'

'We've hand led this sort of thing before, Hugo,' Logan insisted . 'I appreciate the offer, but leave it to us.'

Hugo nod d ed , though he looked a little put out, like his thund er had been well and truly nicked .

'Well, whatever you think is best,' he said .

Logan passed him his notebook and pen, and had him write d own the names and ad d ress of Orla's parents. Hugo wrote slowly and neatly with his left hand , then passed the pad back.

'Right. Good . Thanks. Well, I'll leave you in DC Neish's hand s,' Logan said , either accid entally or d eliberately omitting the word 'capable'. 'He'll take a full statement, so if there's anything else that occurs to you, you be sure to let him know.'

'Like the top, you mean?' Hugo asked .

Both d etectives looked d own at him. He sat staring up, fid d ling nervously with one of the three metal rings that were through his bottom lip.

'The top?' Logan queried .

'The top. The one she was wearing. That horrible orange thing,' Hugo said . 'That wasn't hers. She would n't be seen d ead in that.'

Logan fired Tyler a look, warning him against making the obvious joke.

'That was a bad choice of word s,' Hugo muttered , his brain catching up with his mouth just a few second s too late. 'But, I mean, she'd never wear that. Not by choice. A bright orange hood ie? Not in a million years. That wasn't her top.'

'Right. That's useful. Thanks,' Logan said . He turned to the d oor, hesitated , then turned back. 'I d on't suppose you know whose top it is, d o you?'

Hugo sat back in the chair. He stopped fid d ling with his lip ring, and twirled a stud in his nose instead . 'Actually,' he said . 'I think maybe I d o.'

–

Taggart bounced out of Logan's BMW the moment the d oor was opened , hurtled onto the grass, and relieved himself against a rock without even bothering to have a cursory sniff around first.

Once d one, he gave the DCI quite a scathing look, then looked d own to the water and wagged his tail.

'Not right now,' Logan said . 'Maybe later.' He pointed in through the open back d oor of the car. 'Up you get. Come on.'

Taggart tilted his head and let his tongue loll out to its full, impressive length. He whined , but just subtly, like he d id n't want to come on too strong.

'Cut your shite,' Logan told him. 'In.'

With a final glance at the loch, Taggart sprang and sprachled his way up onto the back seats. He pressed his nose against the wind ow when Logan closed the d oor, gazing forlornly at the inviting stretch of water.

The DCI had just walked around to the d river's sid e when a shout mad e him look back along the brid ge toward s the castle.

'You want a hand , sir?' Sinead called . She strod e purposefully across the brid ge, actively trying to d isguise the early stages of a wad d le. 'Hamza and Tyler and one of the Uniforms have got everything in hand here.'

His instinct was to tell her to go and take a seat. Take the weight off a bit. But then, she'd only give him an ear-bashing for it. She was here to d o a job, she'd insist. She was pregnant, not d ying.

'Aye. Would you mind ?' Logan asked , and the relief on her face answered for her.

'If it means getting away from that arsehole of a woman in there, then it's a win in my book,' she said , and Taggart barked excited ly when she arrived at the passenger sid e of the SUV.

'What arsehole of a woman would that be?' Logan asked .

'That would be the brid e.'

'Oh. She causing problems?'

Sinead sighed . 'I mean, I can't really blame her for being upset, I suppose. Not the d ay she had planned , I'm sure.'

'Wed d ing planner would have a lot to fucking answer for, if it was.'

'Ha. Aye. Not sure "d ead bod y on the shore" is on the list of stand ard options you get to choose from,' Sinead replied . She opened the d oor and manoeuvred her way onto the front passenger seat. 'So, yeah, I get that she's upset, but there's no need to be…'

She wasn't quite sure how to finish the sentence, so Logan helped her out as he slid into the d river's seat. 'Such a pain in the arse about it?'

'Yes! Exactly! I mean, have a bit of empathy, for God 's sake.'

Logan closed his d oor, thrust a hand into the back to stop Taggart from trying to jump into his lap, then started the engine once the d og was settled .

'She local?'

'No. English.'

'Ah. *Tourists,*' said Logan, as if that explained everything.

'Whole wedding party's up from Essex.'

'Long way from home,' the DCI pointed out.

'Yeah. They apparently come up here a lot, though. Just the bride and groom, I mean. Not all of them en masse.'

Logan checked his mirrors. 'Are they no' all meant to be a shower of arseholes down there?' he asked, then he waved to catch the attention of the Uniform standing by the cordon tape. 'Essex, I mean.'

It took the young constable outside a moment or two to figure out what the signal was meant to convey, then he pointed to the tape and raised both eyebrows. Logan confirmed with a nod, and the constable set about unhooking the tape to let the BMW drive out.

'I don't know. Never been,' Sinead admitted.

'I'm sure there was some programme on the telly about them. Caught a bit of it once and wanted to murder every bastard in it.'

'The rest of the wedding party mostly seem OK, to be fair,' Sinead said. 'It's just the bride that's the problem. Although, it is quite fun watching her husband slowly coming to terms with the fact that he might've made a terrible mistake.'

'If only that body had washed up during the rehearsal, eh?' Logan said, pulling away from the side of the road. 'He might've been able to dodge a bullet.'

He reached into his pocket, pulled out his notepad, then handed it to Sinead.

'Right. Punch that address into the satnav, will you?' he said, his face settling into an expression even more sombre than his usual one. His fingers flexed, then wrapped themselves around the wheel again, and tightened until the leather creaked. 'And let's go ruin these poor bastards' lives.'

Chapter 6

Mrs Coull was at the wind ow when Logan pulled up. He could tell by the look on her face that she knew, even before he'd got out of the car. Not a huge surprise, of course. It was a small town, after all, and word travelled fast.

She d id n't react when they set off up the path. Did n't nod , d id n acknowled ge them, just watched them approaching with a blank look and red -ringed eyes.

The d oor opened before Logan had a chance to knock. The man that met them wore the same expression as his wife, only hard ened , like it'd had more time to set in place. He invited them in without a word , and they were ushered along the hallway in eerie silence.

'Mr and Mrs Coull?' Logan asked once they were all together in the living room. 'I'm DCI Jack Logan. This is my colleague, Detective Constable Bell.'

There was still no acknowled gement from either of the house's occupants. Mrs Coull had turned from the wind ow, but leaned back against the sill, her face as expressionless as it had been on their way up the gard en path.

She held a cigarette d own at her sid e, trembling lightly in her left hand . The light coming in through the wind ow picked out the tend rils of wispy white smoke that hugged her bod y like a shroud .

'I get the feeling you alread y know why we're here,' Logan said . He gestured to the large L-shaped couch that took up most of the space in the room. 'But it might be best if you both take a seat.'

'Just say it,' Mrs Coull urged , spitting out flecks of venom with each word . 'Just get it over with.'

Logan glanced from her to her husband. The man's eyes were looking back at him, but everything inside him was turned the other way. While his wife was desperate to hear the words, Mr Coull looked like he'd give anything not to have to.

Mrs Coull was right, though. It was better to get these things over and done with quickly.

'A body was found in the water near Eilean Donan Castle earlier,' Logan said. 'We believe it's that of your daughter, Orla.'

Mrs Coull's head jerked quickly up and down. A nod, Logan thought, but it could also be some sort of involuntary spasm. Her husband's legs seemed to give way beneath him, and he looked surprised when he found himself sitting at one end of the couch, his hands gripping his knees so hard that his knuckles were turning white.

Neither of them, Logan noted, made any move to comfort the other.

'We told you,' Mrs Coull hissed. She pointed at Logan and Sinead with the hand holding the cigarette, and the smoke became a halo around her head. 'We told you lot that she hadn't run away. We told you she'd never do that. But you didn't listen, did you?'

A shaking hand swiped at the ashtray on the windowsill. Grabbed it. Launched it across the room. It fell just short of smashing into the TV, and instead landed on the carpet with a solemn-sounding thud.

'Why didn't you listen?!' Mrs Coull demanded. It started as a shout, but collapsed into a sob by the end. 'We told you she wouldn't just leave. But you wouldn't listen to us. Nobody would listen to us.'

She turned away, shaking violently and sucking on her cigarette like it was the only thing sustaining her. Her husband sat limply on the couch, too wrapped in his own grief to be able to do anything about hers.

'Someone killed her, didn't they?' she asked. 'Someone murdered my wee girl.'

My Logan noted. Not *our*.

'We're not sure at the moment,' Logan admitted. 'But, given her disappearance, and the length of time she's been away, we can't rule it out at this stage.'

'God. You're just like all the rest,' spat the dead girl's mother. 'Aren't you? Wishy-washy, saying nothing, committing to nothing. Just full of shit, like all the rest!'

'I understand how upsetting this must be for you both,' Logan continued. 'I wasn't a part of the investigation into your daughter's disappearance—'

'*Investigation*,' the woman at the window snorted, not turning away from her view of the garden. 'Don't make me laugh.'

'But I give you my word that I—that we—are going to find out what happened to her. And, if there is someone who needs to be held responsible, we will make sure that happens.'

'Oh, how very generous of you,' Mrs Coull said. This time, there was no venom behind the words, just a flat resignation, like she didn't have enough energy left to be angry.

She took another puff of her cigarette, exhaled a bloom of smoke, then met the eye of Logan's reflection in the window.

'Get out,' she instructed.

Sinead stepped in before Logan could respond. 'Mrs Coull, I understand how horrible all this must be.'

'No, you don't,' Orla's mother snapped. She spun around, energised again by another wave of anger. 'Of course you don't! How could you? Look at you.' Mrs Coull glowered at Sinead's bump like it was some wretched, hateful thing. 'Coming in here. Like that. Saying you know. Saying you *understand*. You don't know anything. You don't have the first fucking clue what I'm feeling right now!'

The fire in her voice was dying again, her rage gradually being swallowed up by her grief.

'You've got a lifetime ahead with yours. A *lifetime*,' she continued. 'Or that's what you think, anyway. That's what we all think. You think you'll be gone long before they are. You think you'll get to see them grow up, get married, have kids. Have a life.'

She slapped a fist against her stomach, as if her daughter was still in there somewhere, not dead, just not yet born. Her sorrow once again tipped back into anger, and her words came out as a hiss through her clenched jaws.

40

'Where was my Orla's life? Hmm? Why didn't she get any of that? Why wasn't she allowed?' she demanded. 'Why wasn't she allowed that? Why weren't *we*?'

Sinead offered a sympathetic smile. 'I know. It's not fair. I wish I could —'

'Get out. Both of you.'

Logan gently cleared his throat. 'Mrs Coull, if we—'

She flew at him then, hands flailing, slapping, striking. Her eyes blazed, her face all knotted up in fury.

'Get out, get out, get out, *get out!*'

'Sarah, for God's sake!' her husband cried, getting up off the couch and catching her by the shoulders.

She spun around, and the crack of the slap she gave him rang out around the room. He cowered back, raising a hand like a shield, backing away from his wife's glare of red-hot rage.

'Don't you fucking touch me, Leonard, you *disgusting* little man!' she hissed at him.

And then, without another word or glance at the detectives, she ran from the room, and they listened to the thudding of her feet as she raced up the stairs and slammed a door somewhere above them.

Only then, only when he was sure she wasn't coming back, did Mr Coull lower his arm.

'You OK?' Sinead asked him.

'Hm? Oh. Yes. Fine. Fine,' he insisted. He tried to smile, but it was a misshapen runt of a thing that soon died on his lips. 'She's just upset. I mean, of course she is. Both of us. We both are. Upset, I mean.'

He prodded gingerly at the side of his face as he turned away. A red mark, vaguely hand-shaped if you used a bit of imagination, was becoming visible across a cheek and one side of his jaw. He winced as his fingers massaged the skin, then gestured to the door with his other hand.

'You should probably leave,' he suggested. 'Best to come back when she's calmed down.'

Sinead looked to Logan for his lead, but the DCI was looking around the room, and apparently not paying much attention.

'Right. Yes. That might be for the best,' Sinead agreed. She took a breath and braced herself before coming out with the next part. 'I'm afraid we'll need someone to come to Inverness and officially identify the body.'

Mr Coull frowned. 'I thought Hugo had done that?'

Logan suddenly found his focus again. 'Hugo?'

'Uh, yes. He called earlier to let me know what had happened.'

The DCI's voice was like the rumbling of distant thunder. 'Oh, he did, did he? When was this?'

Mr Coull's brow furrowed as he tried to recall. 'An hour ago, maybe. Bit less. He was very upset.'

'Aye, he's no' the only one,' Logan muttered, before Sinead jumped in again and took over.

'It's better if it's the next-of-kin,' she explained. 'But there's no rush. We can sort it out later. For now, it's important to take some time to grieve. The next few days and weeks are going to be difficult. It's vital that—'

'Why'd she call you that, Mr Coull?' Logan asked, cutting the younger detective short.

'I'm sorry?'

'She called you a "disgusting little man". Why was that?'

Mr Coull's lips formed a couple of different shapes, like they were trying on different replies for size. Eventually, they stumbled upon one that fit.

'Like I say, she's upset.'

'Aye, but why at you?' Logan asked. 'And why call you a "disgusting little man"? What did you do to deserve that?'

Mr Coull blinked rapidly, his eyes alive, like his brain was whizzing into top gear. 'I... I've got no idea. Nothing. I didn't do anything,' he insisted. 'She's just...'

'Upset,' Logan concluded.

'Exactly, yes. She's upset. We're both very upset.' He swallowed, brushed his fingers against the now-crimson mark on his face, and gestured to the door again. 'Please. If you could just...'

Logan looked down at the squirming man through eyes narrowed by curiosity. 'Right. Aye. We'll leave you to it,' he said. He looked around the room again, then nodded. 'But I want to make one thing very clear to you.'

'Oh?' The other man looked up just briefly, unable to hold eye contact for long. 'What's that?'

Logan buried his hands deep down in his pockets and leaned forwards a little, bringing his face a fraction closer to Mr Coull's.

'Whoever did this—whoever killed your daughter—they will be found. They will be caught. And they will be punished,' he said. And, without a lot of imagination, it almost sounded like a threat.

The other man's reply was accompanied by a series of clicking sounds, his mouth having suddenly gone dry. 'Good,' he said. 'I really hope you do.'

—

Logan and Sinead didn't speak until they were back in the BMW. Even then, Sinead waited for the DCI to calm the excited Taggart in the back before voicing her thoughts on everything that had just transpired.

'That was a bit intense, wasn't it?'

'I've seen worse.'

Sinead nodded. 'Aye, well, that's true.'

She'd seen a *lot* worse, in fact. She'd spent several months working as a liaison officer and had often been the first port of call for grieving parents and loved ones. She'd comforted people who'd been heart-broken to the point of self-harm. She'd called ambulances and watched stomachs being pumped clean of gobbled-down painkillers. She'd held mothers, and fathers, and daughters, and sons, all broken to pieces in her arms.

And she knew from first-hand experience just how deep the pit of grief could go.

'That in there, though—those two—that seemed different,' she declared. 'I mean, they were definitely upset and everything, not saying they weren't, it's just...' She turned in her seat to face the DCI.

'Did you notice that they didn't say anything to each other until he tried to pull her back? Like, literally not a word the whole time we were there.'

Logan had . Of course, he had .

'Don't think they even looked at each other,' he said .

'I know! And absolutely no physical contact, either,' Sinead continued .

'Besides the wallop to the face, you mean?'

'Aye, well, apart from that,' Sinead conceded . 'If I didn't already know, I wouldn't have pegged them as a couple at all.'

'I wouldn't even have put them down as casual acquaintances,' Logan agreed .

'Right? Glad it wasn't just me. And she was clearly upset. You'd think if there was anything between them—anything at all—he'd have given her a hug, or held her hand , or something.'

'You saw what happened when he did try and put his hands on her. Logan looked along the street to where the house stood . The curtains had been drawn in the downstairs front window now. *Disgusting little man*",' he muttered .

'What's that about, d 'you think?' Sinead asked .

'Dunno,' Logan said . He fired up the engine, pulled on his seatbelt, then turned to meet the DC's gaze. 'But we're bloody well going to find out.'

Chapter 7

It was almost seven when the wedding guests were finally given permission to leave the castle. Very few of them were in the mood to resume their celebrations, and so they mostly drifted back to their hotel rooms to start packing for home, despite the bride's increasingly vocal demands that they stay.

It took another ten minutes for Logan and the rest of the team to find the Kyle of Lochalsh Police Station. It was tucked up behind a block of council houses, with the entrance half-hidden by a row of wheelie bins.

The station looked like it had been tacked onto the rest of its block as an afterthought. It sprouted from the otherwise residential row like some gnarled and unwanted appendage, or a tumour crying out to be incised.

Logan liked it immediately. It felt like it was a part of the community, but a largely unwelcome and unwanted one. And that, as far as he was concerned, perfectly summed up the polis in general. Nobody in their right mind *wanted* the law to exist. It was just that you couldn't trust other people not to be a shower of bastards, so you needed someone there to help keep them in check.

And Logan pretty much agreed with every word of that. In an ideal world, they'd all be standing in an unemployment queue somewhere. But, given the current state of society, he reckoned their jobs were probably safe for the foreseeable.

If the outside of the station promised disappointment, then the inside more than delivered. It was made up of five rooms, including a small holding cell tucked away at the back that doubled as a cleaning cupboard when not fulfilling its designated purpose.

At the opposite end of the building, out front, the reception area was covered in old posters and flyers for safety campaigns that had long since run their course.

Tyler stopped for a moment beside a sun-faded picture of Dinny the Drink-Driving Squirrel, shuddered, then followed Logan and the others into an ill-equipped adjoining kitchen, where a familiar face was halfway through what looked to be his second Tunnock's Caramel Wafer.

'About bloody time, too!' announced Detective Inspector Ben Forde, spraying slivers of chocolate-coated biscuit from his mouth. 'Thought you buggers were never going to get here.'

'Aye, well, it's no' exactly the easiest building to find,' Logan pointed out. 'And we didn't know you were waiting for us, did we. Or we'd have taken longer.'

He glanced around until he spotted the kettle. Hamza, correctly picking up on the cue, started hunting around for some tea bags.

'What the hell are you doing here, anyway?' the DCI continued, shrugging off his coat and hooking it onto a hanger on the back of the door. 'It's no' like Mitchell to let you out of the office.'

It had been over a year since Ben's heart problems had seen him shunted into a more desk-based role on the team. His opportunities to get out and about in the field had been limited further, after the attack that had left him hospitalised six or seven weeks previously.

It usually took a lot of persuasion before Detective Superintendent Mitchell would relent and let him out to play. So, he'd been more than a little surprised when she'd come into the Incident Room at the Burnett Road station in Inverness, and all but turfed him out.

'I know. Very odd,' Ben agreed. 'She was absolutely adamant I should come, though.'

He realised he was hogging the only chair in the room, and quickly rose to his feet.

'What am I thinking? Here, you come and sit yourself down,' he said, beckoning Sinead over.

'What? Oh, no. I'm fine, sir. Honest,' she replied, but when it became clear that the DI wasn't going to take no for an answer, she graciously—if reluctantly—accepted.

'You think she was just sick of the sight of you, boss?' Tyler asked . 'The Super, I mean.'

'Very possibly, son,' Ben said . 'Although she can't be that sick of me, because she told me to come back tomorrow. I've just to "show face" up here tonight, then be back in the office in the morning.'

Logan frowned . 'Something's fishy there,' he remarked . 'I mean, at this point, we've all seen more than enough of your face. No need to see any more of it.'

'That's what I said ,' Ben agreed . 'No need for me to d rive two hours here and back just so you can ad mire my good looks. They've no' exactly changed since yesterd ay. But, no. She was ad amant. Come show face tonight, then back in the office tomorrow to help coord inate things from there.'

'Sound s to me like she wanted you out of the way,' Logan said . 'Which makes me think she's up to something.'

'Like what?' Sinead asked , looking up at the others.

She felt rid iculous being so low d own compared to the rest of them, but knew she'd be cajoled into sitting again if she tried to get back to her feet. Easier just to stay where she was, d espite how d etached from the conversation it mad e her feel.

'Not a clue,' Logan ad mitted . He nod d ed to Ben. 'But she's well aware he's a nosy, gossiping bastard , so whatever it is, it must be something she d oesn't want us getting wind of.'

'Sound s ominous, sir,' Hamza chipped in.

Logan ran his tongue across the back of his teeth. 'Maybe. We'll see. Might be nothing,' he said , then he turned , clapped his hand s together, and nod d ed to the kettle. 'Now, let's get some teas and coffees on the go. DI Ford e's biscuits are no' going to eat themselves.'

–

Eighty miles to the east, in her office in Burnett Road Police Station, Detective Superintend ent Mitchell checked her watch, tutted , then went back to glowering at the d oor. Her fingers d rummed a slow, stead y rhythm on her d esk, her neatly trimmed nails trip-trip-tripping against the polished wood .

It was a nice d esk. More importantly, it was *her* d esk. And she was d amn well sure that was how it was going to remain.

She'd had the call from reception to let her know that her 7PM appointment had arrived , so she knew the man she was being forced to meet with was located somewhere in the build ing.

Where he was not—and where he was meant to have been for the past three-and -a-half minutes—was sitting in the chair d irectly across from her.

Part of her, she had to ad mit, relished the d elay. She had been d read ing this meeting since it had first been inflicted upon her, and had tried everything in her power to get it called off.

But to no avail. It was happening. This whole d isaster-in-waiting was happening. In many ways, it had alread y happened , and this was all just part of the awful aftermath. The powers that be had alread y mad e their d ecision.

All she had to d o was learn to live with it.

Mitchell checked her watch again. Four minutes late. Unsurprising, but irritating all the same. Her urge to d elay things was quickly being supersed ed by her d esire to get the whole thing over and d one with. She d id n't appreciate being kept waiting.

But then, she d id n't appreciate any of this.

She'd thought it was a joke at first, albeit not a particularly funny one. It had seemed too absurd to be real. Too rid iculous to be true.

But the Chief Constable herself had spoken to Mitchell d irectly. She had explained the situation as best she could , while making it clear that the choice had not been hers to make. It had come from above. Government level, both at Westminster and Holyrood .

Pressure had been applied from somewhere on high, and while the Chief Constable was, of course, free to make her own d ecisions, it was mad e abund antly clear that, should that d ecision not be the correct one, she might not enjoy the consequences.

The same warning had been passed on to Detective Superintend ent Mitchell, too. It went without saying that she wasn't going to approve of the d ecision, but that was irrelevant. She d id n't have to approve. She d id n't have to like it. She just had to suck it up, and d o what she was told .

Five minutes late.

Trip-trip-trip went her fingernails on the desk.

And then, from along the corridor, she heard swing doors being flung inwards. He'd taken the stairs. Probably wandered around for a bit first, poking his nose in where it wasn't welcome.

Mitchell stopped drumming her fingers and interlocked them in front of her instead. She cleared her throat, sat up straighter, and arranged her facial features into a look of utter contempt just as the door to her office was opened from outside.

The bastard didn't even bother to knock.

Detective Superintendent Mitchell regarded the unshaven gentleman standing in her doorway, and somehow fought the urge to throw something at him.

'You all right there, Suki?' Bob Hoon boomed. He frowned when he saw the expression she wore. 'And why the fuck do you have a face like a camel eating sherbet? It's almost as if you're no' pleased to see me...'

–

While they drank their teas and coffees, Logan and the others continued on through to a slightly larger room that was only accessible through a door at the back of the kitchen. It was an office, in as much as it had a couple of desks and a filing cabinet in it.

An ancient computer was squatting on the desk closest to the corner, the weight of the big CRT monitor bowing the wood beneath it.

There were four chairs in total, three of them basic plastic office chairs with a swivel base, and one folding wooden deckchair-type affair that would almost certainly play havoc on the arse. If they claimed the one from the kitchen, that meant they'd at least all have somewhere to sit, though the Uniforms would be shit out of luck.

'They've got a Big Board!' Sinead cried as they entered, then she looked a little embarrassed by her enthusiastic outburst over the rectangle of corkboard on the back wall.

Right now, it was partially covered by more safety campaign leaflets and flyers like those out front, plus a couple of copies of a 'MISSING' poster showing a smiling teenage girl.

'That's her, isn't it?' Tyler said, plucking one of the posters from where it had been pinned. The name in smaller print below the photo sealed it. 'That's Orla Coull.'

'Aye, that's her,' Logan confirmed. He motioned to the board. 'Sinead, d'you want to clear this off and get it set up for us?'

'Will do, sir,' Sinead said, trying to downplay her excitement.

Tyler sometimes made fun of her for it, but she'd grown to love her role as Keeper of the Board —a title her husband had jokingly bestowed on her a year or so back. She'd protested, of course, but had secretly quite liked the name.

'Tyler, since you're already holding that poster—'

'I can put it down, boss,' Tyler countered, fearing what might be coming next.

Logan just talked right over the protest, shutting it down. 'Go and talk to those two Uniforms based here. See what they can tell us about Orla's disappearance.'

'They'll have community insight, too,' Ben added. 'Local knowledge. We'll want to quiz them on that, as well.'

Logan nodded. 'Aye. Hamza, maybe best you go with him.'

'Good idea, sir,' DS Khaled agreed. 'No way he's remembering to do two different things on his own.'

'Here, I heard that,' Tyler objected. 'I can remember two things!'

Hamza smirked. 'All right. What were they?'

Tyler glanced around at the others, who were all watching him now, then he shrugged. 'I mean, I suppose it won't do any harm if you tag along…'

Ben took the opportunity to claim his seat. There was no chance he was subjecting his backside to the wooden chair, but nor did he want to be sitting too close to the computer, in case everyone took leave of their senses and asked him to operate it.

The chair next to the Big Board had Sinead's name written all over it, which left just one option. It was risky, as it was very close to where

Logan was standing, and was likely the one the DCI would 've chosen for himself. Ben approached it slowly, and succeeded in sitting down without drawing any unwanted attention to himself.

Or so he thought.

'Aye, you can get that idea right out of your head,' Logan told him. 'I want you on the phone to CID back in Inverness. Find out what went on with the original investigation. Did they follow it up? If not, why not?'

'I can do that sitting here,' Ben pointed out, rolling the chair as close to the desk as it would go and sandwiching his midsection between them like this might secure him in place.

He quickly threw out a distraction before Logan could insist he shifted his arse.

'Are we all stopping over tonight?' the DI asked. 'Someone'll need to sort out accommodation, if we are.'

'Not too bad a drive home,' Hamza said. 'I might head back, if that's all right with everyone? Want to get back in time for bed time story.'

'Thought you'd have grown out of that by now, mate,' Tyler joked, drawing a half-smile from Hamza.

'You know me and *The Gruffalo*,' the DS replied. 'Can't get enough of the big hairy bastard.'

'Right, fine, once you two have spoken to Uniform, you can shoot off,' Logan told him. 'But I want you back here sharp. And get hold of Dave Davidson. I want him up here, too.'

'OK, but we're taking my car back up,' Hamza replied. 'He drives like a lunatic.'

'It's mental, isn't it?' Tyler nodded. 'It's like being a passenger in a Scalextric car. You keep thinking you're going to shoot straight off the track at the bends.'

'Fine. Whatever,' Logan said. 'So, Hamza's heading back. Sinead? Tyler? What about you pair?'

Both detective constables looked at each other and shrugged in near-perfect unison.

'We just sort of assumed we'd be staying over,' Sinead said. 'Harris is all set up over at our aunt's house.'

'And I don't really fancy that road again tonight, boss,' Tyler added a hand slipping onto his stomach like he was feeling for something kicking in there. 'So, if we can get a place to kip for the night, that would be better.'

Sinead took out her phone, opened a web browser, and began tapping away at the on-screen keyboard with her thumbs. 'I can try and sort us somewhere if you like?' she said, glancing up at Logan. 'Not exactly got a lot to stick on the board yet, so that'll only take me a couple of minutes.'

The DCI gave her the nod. 'Aye. Go for it, then. Try and get three rooms for tonight, then four for the rest of the week. With any luck, we'll no' be here very long, but I'd rather have a base sorted out in case we are.'

'Hotels look full,' Sinead said, swiping at her screen. 'I'll try the bed and breakfasts.'

A grin nearly split Tyler's head clean in two. 'Here, boss. Mind that time we had to share a room in that B&B on Canna?'

A pained expression stretched out the lines of Logan's face. 'Aye,' he said, with the dead-eyed stare of a man still struggling with the associated Post Traumatic Stress Disorder. 'How could I forget?'

'That was a laugh, wasn't it?'

'What, the murder investigation of my old girlfriend, you mean?' Logan asked, raising an eyebrow. 'Oh aye, laugh a bloody minute.'

Tyler's face paled. 'No, I didn't mean that... I just... you know, with...?' He swallowed, then looked over at Hamza and tilted his head back towards the door. 'We should probably go talk to them Uniforms, eh?'

'Yeah,' Hamza agreed, resisting the urge to grin. 'Maybe best for your sake if we do...'

Chapter 8

Ben sat at the d esk, pen scratching across the top page of his notepad , muttering the latest in a series of uh-huhs into the phone. The mobile was jammed between his ear and his should er. This left a hand free to surreptitiously unwrap the last caramel wafer, which he'd pocketed when nobod y else was looking.

Only Taggart was aware of what he was up to. The d og had explored the room when Logan had brought him in, then settled und er Ben's d esk the moment the biscuit's foil wrapper had given its first crinkle.

'Uh-huh,' the DI said , pen working its way d own the page. 'Uh-huh. Got you. Got you. Uh-huh.'

Over at the d esk with the computer, Logan turned and shot a glare back over his should er. Ben d id n't shift his own gaze from his notebook, but positioned his hand to fully conceal the caramel wafer from view.

'I see. Uh-huh. Uh-huh. Right. Uh-huh. Uh-huh. Uh-huh.'

There was a long pause. Logan started to turn back to the d esk he was stationed at.

'Uh-huh. Uh-huh,' Ben said , pen still writing away. 'Interesting. Uh-huh. Uh-huh.'

'For fuck's sake,' Logan muttered , rising to his feet. He clicked his fingers to get the DI's attention, then pointed to the d oor. 'I'm going next d oor until you shut up.'

'Uh-huh,' Ben said , and it wasn't entirely clear who he was respond ing to.

Logan whistled through his teeth to summon Taggart, but the d og was too invested in the biscuit in Ben's hand to move.

'Suit yourself,' Logan remarked, then he head ed through to the kitchen and clicked on the kettle.

While waiting for it to boil, he heard voices coming from out front, and followed them through into the reception area.

Tyler was sitting up on the reception counter, but quickly slid back d own to ground level next to Hamza when the DCI appeared. The two Uniforms who'd helped out at the castle—a male constable and a female sergeant—stood facing them, so they formed four points of a square.

'All right, boss?' Tyler said. 'Just having a chat with...' He paused for a moment, collecting his thoughts, then pointed to both officers in turn. 'Sand ra and Gareth. That's right, isn't it?'

'It is,' Sand ra confirmed. 'Sergeant Sand ra MacGeachan.'

She was in her mid -to-late forties, and of below-average height. She had an air about her that mad e Logan suspect she would use this to her ad vantage, though, and he found himself fearing for the goolies and kneecaps of anyone who tried to mess with her.

She gave Logan a nod and a thin smile. It was respectful, yet relaxed, acknowled ging his higher rank, but not kowtowing to it.

'Sir,' she said, then she gave the younger man besid e her a nud ge with a pointy elbow.

'What? Oh!' Gareth spluttered. 'Hello. Hi. Sir. I mean. Hello, sir.'

Unlike his sergeant, he practically bowed when Logan came over to join them, and averted his gaze through the rest of the conversation like he was scared of d rawing the ire of some cruel and temperamental god.

'Sergeant. Constable,' Logan said, acknowled ging them both in as few word s as possible.

'Sand ra and Gareth are both quite new to the area, sir,' Hamza revealed. 'Neither was stationed here when Orla Coull went missing.'

'Oh. Right,' Logan said, not bothering to hid e his d isappointment. He turned to the uniformed sergeant. 'Who was here, then?'

'It was a Constable Williams, I believe,' Sand ra said.

'On his own?'

'Yes, sir.'

She wasn't giving much away, Logan noted. 'And?' he asked, prompting her to continue.

Sandra hesitated before responding. 'And what, sir?'

'And where is he now?'

'Not sure, sir,' the sergeant admitted. 'Not here, anyway. He moved on.'

Logan shot a look to Hamza, who nodded and made a note to follow up with HQ on the constable's current whereabouts.

'And now there are two of you,' Logan said. His gaze tick-tocked from the straight-backed sergeant to the cowed constable, and back again. 'Why's that? What changed?'

'Couple of reasons. There was a bit of... unrest, sir,' Sandra explained. 'Following Orla's disappearance. Some of the locals became a bit hostile towards Gareth here, and it was felt a temporary increase in visibility might be of benefit until things had calmed down.'

'And have they?' Logan asked.

Sandra nodded, but then followed it up with a shrug. 'I mean, nobody's exactly inviting us out for drinks, but they're not hurling abuse at us either. So, you know. That's progress.'

'Locals didn't approve of the way the investigation was run, I take it?' Logan asked.

'You could say that, sir, yes,' Sandra confirmed. 'They say there wasn't one. From what I can gather, they think the whole thing was swept under the carpet. A lot of them blame Constable Williams.'

Logan dismissed the suggestion with a grunt. 'It was a CID case. He wouldn't have had any say in it.'

'No, sir...' Sandra said. For a moment, it looked like there was more to follow, but then she snapped her mouth shut and gave an almost imperceptible shake of her head.

There was no way Logan was letting that just slip by.

'Out with it, Sergeant,' he ordered. 'What were you going to say?'

'Nothing, sir,' she insisted.

Logan stared. Waited.

It didn't take long.

'Just… they claim he refused to escalate it at first. Did n't take it seriously. She was missing almost three d ays before CID got involved . Some people think that, if he'd moved quicker, things might have been d ifferent.'

'Any id ea why he d id n't call it in earlier?' Logan asked .

'None. I d id n't meet him.'

Logan turned his attention to the constable. He had positioned himself slightly behind the sergeant now, like a child hid ing behind his mother.

'What about you? Gary, was it?'

'Yes. I mean, no. Sir. No, it's Gareth,' the junior officer replied . 'But… Gary's fine. You can call me Gary, if you prefer.'

He was young. Stupid ly young. One of those recruited straight from high school types, by the looks of him, all bum fluff and plooks.

He had a long scar running d own the left sid e of his face, half an inch in front of his ear, which could 've been from an attack or some sort of operation. It had healed to a d ull pink, so it looked old . Old er somehow, than the lad himself.

'I'm no' going to call you by the wrong name for my own conveni-ence, son,' Logan assured him. 'What about you, *Gareth*? You meet this Constable Williams?'

'Yes.'

Logan gave the constable the benefit of the d oubt, and assumed he was going to follow up with more information.

He d id not.

'Well?' the DCI pressed . 'What was he like?'

Gareth had a wid e-eyed look of panic about him now, like a school pupil who'd just been asked a question on a topic he had n't bothered his arse to stud y.

He raised a hand to somewhere just above the level of his head . 'Well, he was about that height, and —'

'I d on't mean, "what d id he look like?"' Logan said , cutting him off. 'I mean, what was he like? What d id you make of him?'

Gareth shifted his weight from one foot to the other, and fid d led with his fingers. 'Oh. Right. Yeah. I mean… I only really said hello to him in passing. He seemed normal enough, I suppose. He was a bit old er than me.'

'Aye, well, to be fair to him, I'm sure I've probably got socks old er than you, son,' the DCI said . 'What about a hand over? Did he no' d o one of them with you?'

Gareth shook his head . 'No. A sergeant from Portree came over to d o that. Drove me round for half an hour, showed me where the fuse box for this place was, then pretty much left me to it.'

'He tell you why your pred ecessor wasn't giving you the tour? That'd be the usual in a hand over like this, would n't it?'

'Not always, boss,' Tyler said . 'I got d ropped into a few places back when I was on the beat where I was just left to get on with it.'

Logan tutted . Back in his d ay, there'd have been a full hand over, even for one-man stations like this. *Especially* for one-man stations like this. It would last a week or more. The outgoing officer would show the incoming one the ropes, introd uce him to the locals, make him aware of which of the bastard s to keep a close eye on. That sort of thing.

There would often be some time spent in the pub after the shift end ed , too, where more nuggets of wisd om could be given and gleaned , and the new arrival could be ingratiated into the community over a few games of pool and half a d ozen cold pints.

Granted , it d id n't always work out that way. If the vacating officer was leaving d ue to illness, or und er a cloud of some sort, then often the hand over was a bit makeshift and cobbled together. But that wasn't the norm.

Or it d id n't used to be, at any rate.

Bloody cutbacks.

'You said there were two reasons,' Hamza said , ad d ressing his fellow sergeant. 'For you being shipped in as backup.'

'I d id . There was,' Sand ra confirmed . 'There's a guy. Stephen Boyd . Goes by "Camd en Steve", though God knows why, because he's originally from Tain. Lives over near the brid ge. He's got a caravan. I mean, he lives in the caravan full time. It's not parked on his d riveway or anything. He was… having some trouble.'

'In what way?' Logan asked .

'He's got previous, sir,' the sergeant explained . 'Statutory rape. Young girl. Did a two-year stretch for it a d ecad e ago. He's on the register.'

Logan could guess the rest. 'And locals got word of that?'

'They d id . Blamed him for Orla going missing. He's been attacked a couple of times. Quite bad ly, in one instance. We believe that time was Orla's father, though Mr Boyd refused to confirm or d eny.'

Logan consid ered what he knew of Leonard Coull, Orla's d ad . H d id n't seem like the violent type, but it was possible that he'd snapped .

'Did he move on?' Hamza asked . 'Boyd , I mean?'

'No,' Sand ra replied . 'We sort of suggested that it might be a good id ea, but he said this is his home, and he wasn't going to be d riven out of it.'

'He lives in a caravan,' Tyler remind ed everyone. 'Is that not the whole point? That your home d rives around with you?'

'You'd think, but he's not up for shifting,' Sand ra said . 'Things seemed to have calmed d own for a while, but Christ knows what's going to happen now.'

'You think it's all going to kick off again?' Hamza asked .

And then, as if it had been waiting in the wings for just the *perfect* moment to arrive, a brick came through the front wind ow, showering the reception area in fragments of flying glass.

'Oh, God ! Oh, God !' Gareth wailed , d ucking and covering hi head with his hand s, even as Logan and Sand ra raced each other to the front d oor.

They arrived to the sound of squealing tyres, and the bang of a car backfiring. The vehicle itself was out of sight, hid d en by the houses at the front of the station. Tyler clattered through the d oor, then went sprinting past both senior officers, giving chase. From the fad ing roar of the engine, though, Logan knew he'd be too late to catch so much as a glimpse of a number plate.

'In answer to that last question,' Sand ra said , glancing back at the broken wind ow, and the uniformed constable still keeping his head d own insid e. 'I think there's a very good chance that it's all going to kick off again, yes.'

Chapter 9

'What the hell's all the racket out here?' demanded DI Forde, hurrying through to reception.

When he spotted the carpet of broken glass, he grabbed for Taggart, who had been trotting along just ahead of him. He caught the dog by the collar before he could make a mad dash for Logan, and tear his paws to pieces in the process.

With a bit of effort, he steered the excited mutt back into the kitchen and closed the door, shutting him safely out of harm's way.

Hamza was squatting in the middle of it all, staring down at a broken brick that lay in two pieces on the floor while he wriggled his fingers into a thin pair of rubber gloves. A Uniform whom Ben had n't met before was standing over in the corner, well away from the window, both hands clutching his head like he was stopping it from falling off.

'What's the story?' Ben asked.

'Well, this,' Hamza said, indicating the brick, then nodding up at the broken window, 'came through there.'

'What, you mean someone threw it?'

Logan ducked through the doorway as he returned inside. 'Well, I doubt it bloody jumped,' he replied. 'Car sped away right after. Tyler's in pursuit.'

Hamza looked up in surprise. 'Tyler's in a car chase?'

'Christ, no,' Logan said. 'Can you imagine? No, he's on foot. Not got a chance of catching it, mind. We'll see how long it takes him to work that out for himself.'

Sandra appeared at the other side of the broken window. 'If you're all all right here, I'm going to go take a drive around,' she said. 'Never know, might see someone with a big box of bricks in the passenger seat.'

'Keep us posted ,' Logan told her, then he jabbed a finger at Gareth. 'You. Go with her.'

'Me?' chirped the constable, then the look on the DCI's face started him scurrying for the d oor. 'Yes, sir. Going now, sir.'

The d etectives all waited for the Uniforms to leave. It was Ben who finally broke the silence.

'Good grief, how old was that lad ? Ten?'

'Might as blood y well be, I think,' said Logan. He looked d own at Hamza, who had now picked up one half of the wind ow-shattering project, and was carefully turning it over in his hand s. 'What have we got?'

'Well, I'm not an expert on these things, sir, but I'd say it's a big brick,' the DS replied . 'No markings or notes attached , or anything like that. It's just a brick. Must've broken on impact.'

'Bollocks,' Logan muttered .

The brick was a red d ish mix of clay and aggregate, and far too rough to have any hope of getting fingerprints from. If they were very lucky, it would turn out to be a special kind of brick only prod uced by one local manufacturer, who kept a hand y list of all those people he'd ever supplied .

That was how it would happen in the movies, at least. Here in the real world , however, Logan fully expected it to be a bog-stand ard , mass–prod uced , read ily available to all and sund ry, brick.

Which meant that, unless the Uniforms miraculously stumbled upon the answer, they only had one chance of find ing out who had thrown it through the wind ow.

And that chance was almost no chance at all.

–

Tyler ran.

Again.

Running was rapidly becoming his thing, he thought. Whenever someone needed to be chased, he would be the one sent to do the chasing.

It made sense, of course. He was the youngest and the fastest of the team. Well, Sinead was actually faster, but they couldn't exactly send her sprinting after a fleeing suspect. Especially not now. Not in her condition.

That was a point, actually. He was going to be a father now. He had responsibilities. He couldn't be expected to go racing headlong into danger all the time. It was only a matter of time before he got hurt. Or killed. Or worse!

OK, probably not worse. *Killed* would be pretty much as bad as it could realistically get.

But he couldn't afford to get killed. Not with a young family to support.

To be fair, not all of his running was *towards* danger. He spent quite a lot of time running *away* from danger, too—the oncoming Jacobite Steam Train being a particularly memorable incident, but there were others, too. A couple of big dogs. Several angry Russian men. His own wedding. Tyler had run full-tilt away from them all.

At least that last one he'd had the sense to turn back for.

Now his shoes smacked flatly on the pavement as he raced down the hill in pursuit of what had already become just the rumble of distant traffic. He wasn't even sure the car he was chasing was still anywhere within earshot. Certainly, the roaring of its engine was no longer the headline story it was just a few moments before.

Could it have already got away? Or had the driver just pulled off the road somewhere in an attempt to hide?

'Not a bloody clue,' he wheezed out loud, but he did his job and kept running, his tie trailing behind him, dark spots of sweat already appearing on his light blue shirt.

It wasn't until he reached the bottom of the slope and clattered onto the road between two parked cars that something occurred to him. Nobody had actually asked him to run anywhere this time. He'd thrown himself into the chase without anyone telling him to.

Shite.

What had he been thinking? He could still be back at the station, just standing around, looking disapprovingly at the mess of broken glass on the reception floor. Maybe even occasionally tutting, or shaking his head.

They probably had the kettle on. That was the default response to any unexpected setbacks or moments of stress—a quick cup of tea while they all pulled themselves together, before getting down to work.

He could be sitting waiting for the water to come to the boil right now. What's more, after getting the accommodation booked, Sinead had headed off to the Chinese takeaway along the road to fetch them some grub. She'd be back soon, if she wasn't already, and the fried rice would almost certainly be getting cold.

Tyler came to the conclusion that this running malarkey was a big waste of time. Whoever had lobbed the brick through the window was either long gone, or in hiding. Either way, it was pointless him running around like a headless chicken.

Not when there was a cup of tea and some sweet and sour pork with his name on it waiting back at the station.

Slowing to a stop was made more difficult by the way the road sloped, and it took him several seconds to wind his speed all the way down.

He came to a breathless halt at a junction where the road he was running along forked off to the left and right.

It was then that he heard the thunder of an engine.

Close.

Getting closer.

He only saw it from the corner of his eye, too briefly to be able to fully grasp any of the details or the shape.

Big, he thought.

Metal, he thought.

Solid, he thought.

Brakes screamed. Rubber burned.

And then a tonne-and-a-half of motor vehicle slammed sideways into DC Tyler Neish.

Chapter 10

This meeting was not going the way Detective Superintend ent Mitchell had hoped . It was, however, going more or less exactly as she had expected .

The man was incorrigible, intolerable, and insufferable, all at once. And , though she took no pleasure in lowering herself to his level, he was also an arsehole.

Even the way he sat in the chair across from her was irritating. He d id n't just slouch, he *sprawled*, one arm hooked over the back, one foot pressed against the front of her d esk, like he might at any moment try to kick it—and her—out through the wind ow at her back.

That wasn't actually possible, of course. He could n't *actually* d o it.

And yet, some nagging, unreasonable d oubt told her that maybe he could . Something about Robert Hoon had changed . The last time she'd seen him, he'd been a mess—cowed , broken, and bord ering on suicid al.

Granted , he was still a mess now—still as scruffy-looking, at any rate—but the shape of him had changed . This was her office. She was a senior officer in Police Scotland . And yet, everything about his d emeanour suggested he was the one in charge.

Fortunately, in this instance, his d emeanour was wholly incorrect. She just had to keep remind ing herself of that fact.

'People aren't going to like it. This whole thing. You d o appreciate that, yes?' she said . She was sitting poised and upright in her chair, her fingers clasped tightly together, like she was wringing some tiny version of his neck.

'And what fucking people is that?' Hoon asked .

'Just people,' Mitchell told him. 'All people in general. The ones who work in this station. The ones who work further afield.' Her gaze flitted up and d own, taking him in. 'People who believe that wrongd oing should not go unpunished.'

'See, that's where you're wrong, Suki—'

'Detective Superintend ent Mitchell.'

'—people are going to be high as fucking kites when they hear the good news. They'll be shiteing themselves insid e out with joy. Aye, literally.'

The image d istracted the female officer for a moment. She shook her head to d ismiss the question that had started forming there, then got back to business.

'There are a few things we need to clarify,' she told him. 'Firstly, you d o not work here. You are not a police officer. You have no authority beyond that which I allow you, and I intend to allow you this much.'

She held up a hand , forefinger and thumb touching to form a 'zero', and held it there until she was sure he'd got the message.

'You better be careful, Suki—'

'Detective Superintend ent Mitchell.'

'—is that "OK" sign no' a racist symbol now?' Hoon crossed his arms and shook his head d isapprovingly. 'I mean, I hear about all the institutional racism in the force these d ays, but you're the last person I'd have pegged as a fucking white supremacist. With you being a fucking Detective Superintend ent, I mean.'

She counted silently in her head , anticipating the upcoming punch-line.

'And , you know, black.'

And there it was.

Mitchell had her hand s clasped again, palms squeezing together. Her chair creaked as she shifted her weight forward until her forearms were fully resting on the d esk.

'Some people might find your remarks amusing, Robert. Your little rants, and outbursts, and whatnot. Some people might get a kick out of you *saying the unsayable*. But me?' She shook her head . 'I'm unmoved by it. In fact, no. That's not true. I'm actively unimpressed . I'm bored rigid by your whole act, in fact.'

64

'Don't you fucking hold back to spare my feelings, Suki,' Hoon said .

'Detective Superintend ent Mitchell.'

'Just you go ahead and call it as you fucking see it. I can take it.'

The corners of Mitchell's mouth pulled fractionally upward s into something the shape of a smile. It was not a real smile, though. Not even close.

'Fine. Thank you. In that case, I'll d o just that,' she said . 'I d on't know who you've threatened , blackmailed , bribed , or perhaps slept with, to bring this whole rid iculous situation about. I d on't want to know. I have been told that you are being mad e available as *consultant*.'

Those last couple of word s caused her some visible d ifficulties. She ejected them with the air of a cat hacking up a hairball.

'I've gone on record to say that I d on't approve, but it appears you have friend s in high places. Quite how that has happened , I have no id ea. Having spent some time in your company over the years, I'm surprised you've got friend s in *low* places, let alone anywhere else.'

'Bit fucking harsh,' Hoon protested .

Mitchell ignored him and continued with her speech. She'd started workshopping it from the moment she'd stepped out of the meeting with the Chief Constable, where the news had first been broken to her.

'But I have my ord ers. And I will carry them out to the best of my ability,' she continued . 'Because, unlike you, I respect the job I'm in. I respect the people I work with, and I respect the office I inhabit.'

Hoon glanced around the room. She cut him off before he could make some snid e remark or other.

'Not the physical office. The metaphorical one.'

'Aye, I was going to fucking say,' Hoon said , conclud ing his look around with a d isapproving scowl. 'This place looked way better when I was in it. It had a wee basketball net over the bin. Any id ea what the fuck happened to that, by the way? I'd quite like it back.'

Mitchell somehow found the strength to lock her fingers together even more tightly, until the bones let out little aud ible groans of d istress. She forced them to relax again, annoyed with herself. She was letting him get to her. She was allowing herself to be wound up by him.

And the worst of it was, she didn't think he was even trying to annoy her. This was just his default setting. A lot of people had found themselves on Mitchell's bad side over the years. Hoon had been the first person to do so simply by existing.

'As I was saying,' she continued. 'I accept that you are to be available to us as a consultant. Begrudgingly, but I accept it.' Her smile crept up another millimetre or two. 'That does not, however, put me under any obligation whatsoever to *consult*. Nor does it grant you any access to crime scenes, to case files, or to any of my officers.'

'Can I come in and use the coffee machine?'

'No,' she replied. 'No, you cannot.'

Hoon sniffed, then ran the back of his hand across his nose, wiping it. 'Thank fuck for that. The coffee here's like a jakey's piss. And no' in a fucking good way.'

'Here's what's going to happen now, Robert,' Mitchell began. 'You're going to leave this office—my office—and you're going to go and do... whatever it is you do. Drink. Fight. Fornicate. I'm sure you've got plenty to keep you occupied. At least, I hope you do, because there will be nothing here for you. Ever. You can go home and wait on my call, but I'm telling you now, that call will never come.

'And why? Because you're not a police officer, Robert. Honestly? I don't think you ever were. You're not a team player. You're not a rule follower. You're a violent, destructive force, deeply unreasonable, and in possession of a range of personality disorders as long as my arm.'

'Bloody hell.' Hoon grinned as he got to his feet. 'Are you trying to make me fucking blush there, or something? Cheers, Suki. You're no' so bad yourself.'

One of Mitchell's eyes twitched, just once.

'It's Detective Superintendent Mitchell,' she corrected for the umpteenth time, and this time, the words barely squeezed out through her pursed lips. She glanced at the chair he had just vacated. 'And I didn't excuse you.'

'Aye, well, like you said, I'm no' one of your wee fucking drones. I don't work here, and I've no' broken any laws.'

'You're currently und er investigation for everything that took place out near Mallaig,' Mitchell said .

Hoon's smile grew wid er. 'No. I'm not,' he said .

Her molars ground together. That had been the other outcome of her meeting with the Chief Constable, and she'd found that one even more of a bitter pill to swallow. He should 've been locked up for what had gone on out there, regard less of the outcome.

But the Chief Constable—reluctantly, granted , and through teeth even more gritted than Mitchell's were now—had painted him as a hero. He'd broken up a sex trafficking ring, not just once, but twice. He'd risked his life to bring a squad of cop killers to justice. There was even some talk of giving the bastard a med al.

Friend s in high places. It mad e her sick.

Hoon threw a thumb backward s over his should er in the d irection of the d oor. 'So, I'm just going to fuck off. Lovely as it's been to catch up. You take care of yourself, sweetheart, because you're looking a bit rough. But then, I get that. It's a shite job. Don't you let the bastard s get you d own, all right?'

He turned away as if to leave, then continued all the way around until he was facing her again.

'Here, I had a half-bottle of *Grouse* in that bottom d rawer there. Don't suppose—'

'Good bye, Robert,' Mitchell said . 'Good bye, and good ...' She started to say 'rid d ance' but her professionalism took over and she d iverted to 'luck' at the last possible moment.

This d id not go unnoticed by Hoon, whose grin only stretched further up his cheeks. He winked , pointed to her, then turned and left the room, leaving the d oor wid e open behind him.

Mitchell sighed , ran a hand d own her face, then rose from her chair to go and shut the d oor. She was halfway across the room when Hoon reappeared out in the corrid or.

'Here, is Jack around ? Want to tell him the good news.'

'What good news? There is no good news to tell him,' Mitchell replied , her tone one of clipped irritation. 'Nothing has changed . Nothing is d ifferent. You are still not a part of life in this station.'

'Aye, well, we'll just have to fucking agree to d isagree there.'

'No!' Mitchell insisted . 'No, we won't!'

'Whatever. Is he around ?'

'No. He isn't.'

'He at home?'

There was a moment—just a fractional, fleeting one—of hesitation on Mitchell's part. She cursed herself for it. 'I would n't know.'

Hoon's eyes narrowed . 'He off on a case?'

Mitchell said nothing. But that, in turn, said it all.

'It's nothing to d o with you,' she insisted . 'Go anywhere near it, interfere with the investigation in any way, and I'll have you arrested . I mean that.'

'Interfere? Come on, Suki,' Hoon replied . He held his arms out at his sid es, like he was presenting himself as a prize. 'Since when have I ever caused any bother to anyone?'

Chapter 11

Detective Constable Tyler Neish was d ead .

He was sure of it.

He had to be.

He tried to run back over the events of his final moments.

There had been the running, of course. The thrill of the chase.

Well, 'thrill' was probably stretching it.

But there had d efinitely been running.

And then the sound of a car coming up quickly on his right. The squeal of brakes. The fluttering of panic in his chest when he realised — when he *knew*—what was about to happen.

The impact had followed .

A moment of flight—brief, but od d ly euphoric—had come right after that.

And then, what?

Death?

No. Pavement.

Then d eath.

Yeah. He reckoned that felt about right.

He wond ered how Sinead was going to take the news. She'd be a single mother, bringing up their babies alone. Tyler would never get to meet his own—

'You all right, mate?'

An eyelid peeled open. An eye swam. Tyler babbled out a sound that no one on Earth had ever mad e before, then concentrated until a concerned , kind ly face came into a vague sort of focus. It was a man, he thought. He was leaning over Tyler's corpse, smiling with benevolent concern.

'Are you Jesus?' Tyler mumbled.

The other man's face collapsed into a frown. 'Eh, no,' he said. 'It's Gareth. PC Coleman. From the station.'

It occurred to Tyler then that he probably wasn't dead. He blinked a few times, clearing his head, then allowed himself to be helped up into a sitting position by the young constable.

A small silver hatchback stood sideways on the road, the engine still running, a small dent in the back door the only indication of the impact that had occurred. The other Uniform—the sergeant—was holding someone by the arm, like she was worried he might run off.

'Oh, thank God!' squeaked the man Tyler guessed must have been driving the car. It was Hugo, Tyler realised. He stood fiddling with his face piercings, his purple hair tufting back and forth on the breeze. 'You're alive!'

DC Tyler Neish, it turned out, was not dead, after all.

That was a welcome turn-up for the books.

With the aid of the constable, he got to his feet, dusted himself down, and straightened his tie.

'Cheers,' he said, and his skull vibrated with the echo of the word. 'How long was I out for?'

'About... I don't know.' Gareth looked back at Sandra, who shrugged. 'Eight seconds, maybe?'

'Eight seconds?!' Tyler ejected. 'No way it was eight seconds. It must've been longer than that! How could you two get here in eight seconds?'

'We were driving down the hill when he hit you,' Sandra said.

'We saw the whole thing,' Gareth confirmed.

'Oh. Oh. Right.' Tyler considered this for a full two seconds longer than he had been unconscious. 'Must've looked pretty dramatic,' he said, almost hopefully.

'Not really,' said Sandra, wrinkling her nose.

'You just sort of fell over,' Gareth added.

'I nearly managed to stop,' Hugo said.

'Oh, well, good for you,' said Tyler, limping over to him. He wasn't in any particular pain, but he felt that, having recently been struck by a speed ing vehicle, he'd earned the right to a sympathy limp. 'As long as you *nearly* stopped , that's what matters, isn't it? That'll be some consolation to my wife at my funeral, eh? "Don't you worry, Mrs Neish, he *nearly* wasn't d ead ."'

'But... you're not d ead ,' Hugo pointed out.

Tyler hesitated . The guy, he had to ad mit, had a point.

'Aye, well, no thanks to you,' he said , jabbing a finger at him for ad d ed emphasis. He turned away, then turned back. 'Wait. Were you the one I was chasing?'

Hugo fid d led with his eyebrow ring. 'What?'

'Were you in a car?' Tyler asked , then he answered the question himself before anyone could point out the glaring flaw in it. 'Obviously, you were in a car. Was it that car?'

Hugo followed Tyler's outstretched finger to the silver hatchback with the d ent in the d oor.

'Was I d riving that car?'

'He was,' Sand ra confirmed .

'We saw him,' ad d ed Gareth.

Tyler shook his head , both d ismissing the replies and trying to arrange his thoughts into some sort of coherent ord er.

'Was that the car I was chasing?' he asked .

'Not that I know of,' Hugo said .

'Did you put a brick through the wind ow?' Tyler d emand ed .

Hugo glanced at the sergeant besid e him like he was looking for a bit of support. 'Of the car?'

'No! Of course not, the... the car d oesn't have...' Tyler sighed and gestured back up the hill. 'Did you put a brick through the wind ow of the police station?'

'What? Oh. No. No, I d id n't,' Hugo insisted .

Tyler stepped in closer. He d id n't have the height to loom like Logan d id , but he had an inch or two ad vantage over the younger man, and he milked it for all it was worth. 'Why d on't I believe you?' he asked .

Hugo's eyes searched the d etective constable's face. 'Because you've recently had a head injury?'

Tyler flicked a look in PC Coleman's direction. 'Take him in for questioning.'

'Well... we were going to take him in for driving without a licence,' Gareth replied.

'Oh. Right. Fair enough,' Tyler said, deflating a little.

They all stood in uncomfortable silence for a few moments, until Sandra took charge.

'Right, well, I'll get Hugo up to the station. Gareth, you can follow me up in his car, will you?'

'Will do, Sarge,' the constable confirmed.

Both officers regarded Tyler with a sort of awkward curiosity.

'You, eh, you want a lift?' Sandra asked.

'What, to the hospital?' Tyler asked.

Both Uniforms looked him up and down. So, too, did Hugo.

'I meant to the station,' Sandra replied. 'I didn't think you'd need the hospital.'

Tyler looked down at himself, blew out his cheeks, then shrugged. Aside from a dull ache in his right hip, some light grazing to both hands, and the suggestion of a lump above one ear, he appeared to be in pretty good shape.

'Probably not,' he admitted.

'Right, then. Good,' Sandra said. She opened the back door of the police car, and guided Hugo inside. 'So... you want a lift, then?'

Tyler looked past her, up the slope towards the station. 'I'll, um, I'll probably just walk, actually,' he decided.

'Fine,' Sandra said. 'Maybe try and watch where you're going this time, though, eh? And maybe best you don't stand around in the middle of the road.'

'I was chasing him!' Tyler protested.

'No you weren't!' came the muffled reply from the back of the squad car. 'It wasn't me. This is a stitch-up.'

'Shut it, Hugo,' Sandra warned. She gave Tyler a nod. 'Right, well, I suppose we'll see you back at the station, then.'

'Aye.'

Tyler waved, then put his hands in his pockets, and set off up the hill.

Then, when he realised quite how steep it was, he opened the front passenger door of Sandra's car, and climbed in beside her.

'Actually, I think I'll take that lift, after all,' he said, smiling sheepishly. 'Don't want to get back and find out my dinner's gone cold.'

—

Logan looked up from his chicken chow mein as the door to the kitchen was opened. His gaze locked on the purple-haired young man with the face full of metal, and he sucked up a noodle with a long, deliberate slurp.

'Aha!' the DCI announced. 'There's just the big-mouthed wee bastard I've been looking for.'

'I didn't mean it,' Hugo announced.

Logan poked at his dinner in its tinfoil tray. 'You didn't mean what?'

Hugo's eyes darted from side to side. The other three detectives were all staring back at him, each paused, mid-munch.

'Nothing. Anything.' Hugo gave a quick, furtive shake of his head. 'I don't know.'

Sandra started guiding him towards the door at the back of the kitchen, but Logan stepped into her path. 'Hold on. Where are you going?' he asked.

'I was taking him through the back,' Sandra replied. 'It's where we do the interviews.'

Logan shook his head. 'That's the Incident Room. There's sensitive information in there,' he said. 'You'll need to stick him somewhere else until we're ready for him.'

'I was going to talk to him about a driving offence,' the sergeant explained, which earned some raised eyebrows from Logan.

'Is that a fact?' he asked, glowering down at Hugo far more effectively than Tyler had been able to. 'Driving offences, breaking windows, interfering with an investigation. You've been busy, Hugo.'

'I didn't break that window!' the young man protested, his voice becoming shriller. 'You can't pin that on me.'

'He knocked me down, though!' announced Tyler, shuffling into the room.

'What, with a car?' asked Ben, looking up from where he stood hunched over his foil tray of food.

'Aye, boss,' Tyler confirmed. 'Ploughed right into me.'

Ben regarded him in silence for a moment. 'You're looking well for it.'

'I don't know if I'd say "ploughed" exactly,' Sandra said. 'He more *tapped* right into you.'

'It was more than a tap! I went flying!' Tyler insisted.

'You fell over,' Sandra said.

'I nearly stopped,' Hugo reminded everyone.

'Will you quit it with the "nearly"?' Tyler cried. 'You might've nearly stopped, but you didn't stop. That's all that matters.'

Sinead, who had once again been given the room's only chair, sat down her dinner and got quickly to her feet. 'You all right?' she asked Tyler.

He squared his shoulders. Set his jaw. Dismissed her concerns with a suitably manly wave. 'Don't worry about me. I'm fine. It was nothing I couldn't handle,' he said. 'I just shrugged it off.'

'You seemed to be under the impression that you'd died,' said Gareth, who had appeared at the back of the room.

'What? No, I wasn't,' Tyler insisted.

'You asked me if I was Jesus.'

'Well, aye, but...' Tyler began, but it quickly became apparent that he had nothing else to offer.

Logan, for once, decided to put him out of his misery.

'I've got an idea where we can put Hugo until we've finished up here,' he said to Sandra. 'Am I right in thinking there's a cell through the back?'

'There is, sir, yes,' Sandra confirmed. 'Though it's got a Hoover in it at the moment.'

Logan nodded. 'Good. There we go, then. Stick him in the cell.' He shot a stern look at the boy with the purple hair. 'But don't you get too comfortable in there, Hugo. Because you and I are going to have ourselves a *very* serious conversation.'

Chapter 12

Shona Maguire had watched on in respectful silence while the bag containing Orla Coull's remains were d umped , quite unceremoniously, onto the mortuary slab. She had signed for the d elivery like it was an Amazon parcel, then had exchanged some pleasantries with the paramed ics, before ushering them out the d oor.

Then she'd had some coffee. Strong stuff, too. Since Jack and Taggart were both away, she d id n't relish the thought of returning to the empty house. Better to throw herself into work for a few hours. Get ahead of things a bit. Make some progress.

Because, for reasons she d id n't choose to d well on, being in here with a d ead bod y for company felt far less d aunting a thought than spend ing the night alone.

She finished the coffee, poured herself another one, and was in the process of snapping on her rubber gloves when she heard the squeak of a footstep out in the corrid or. The mortuary was tucked away in a remote corner of Raigmore Hospital, well off the beaten track. Nobod y came this way except to see her, and at this time of night, she certainly wasn't expecting visitors.

Another footstep. Closer this time. A man, she thought, though that might have been the fear talking.

She tried to remain calm, but the message d id n't reach her pulse, which raced , or her lungs, which tightened , squeezing all the air out of her bod y in one shrill gasp.

Not too long ago, keeping calm would n't have been an issue. Not too long ago, she would n't have batted an eyelid at hearing someone wand ering around out there at this time of night.

Not too long ago, she had felt safe.

But after some of the things that had happened in the past year—some of the things she'd been put through—she didn't know if she'd ever truly feel safe again. Not on her own, anyway. Not without Jack.

Still, woe betide any bastard who tried to get the jump on her. She'd be ready for them. She'd be prepared.

Not like the last time.

There were two small pairs of scissors in her desk drawer. She slipped her fingers through the holes of each, then clenched her fists so the blades stuck up like pointed claws.

'Right, you creeping bastard,' she whispered, tiptoeing over to stand behind the door. 'Let's be having you.'

She waited there. Lurked there. Held her breath and froze like a statue as the person on the other side of the door gave it an experimental prod, swinging it inwards just enough for them to peek through.

Shona's fists tightened further, curling the blades of the scissors inwards a little.

Maybe whoever was out there would go away. Maybe they'd think the place was empty. Maybe they'd think she'd already left for the night.

Her gaze fell on the coffee cup on her desk, steam rising slowly from the hot, freshly poured liquid within.

Feck!

The door gave a creak. Inched inwards.

Shona pressed herself against the wall like she was trying to merge with the paintwork. She continued to hold her breath as an unfamiliar man came creeping into the room, his shoulders stooped, his head shifting left and right as he scanned for any signs of life.

The door swung closed behind him. Any second now, he was going to turn. He was going to turn, and he was going to see her, and then God alone knew what he was going to do.

No. No, he wasn't. He wasn't, because she wasn't going to let him.

'Piss off, I've got scissors!' she screeched, leaping from the shadows and brandishing her bladed fists like the deadly weapons they were.

'Jesus fuck!' cried the intrud er, staggering out of stabbing range with his hand s raised in surrend er. 'What the fuck are you trying to d o, give me a bastard ing heart attack?'

'What d o you want?' Shona d emand ed , still waving her fists around like she was a boxer from the early 19th century.

'Well, no' getting scissored through the fucking eye sockets is higher on my list of priorities than it was five second s ago, I'll tell you that much!'

Shona narrowed her gaze, sizing him up. 'Who are you?' she d emand ed , though based on the man's responses so far, she had a pretty d ecent id ea.

'I'm Bob. Bob Hoon. I'm sure Jack's told you all about me.'

He had . Many times. Very little of what he'd said had been in any way complimentary, and a lot of it had mad e him quite angry.

'He's mentioned you,' Shona conced ed . She started to lower the scissors, then thought better of it, and raised them again. 'Why are you here?'

'Jesus. Cool your tits, sweetheart,' Hoon urged , turning his raised hand s into a calming gesture. 'I'm no' here to fucking murd er you or anything. You d on't need to go all fucking *Nightmare on Elm Street* on me. I'm just looking for Jack. He around ?'

Shona consid ered the blad es of the scissors for a moment like she wasn't quite sure how they'd got there. She let her hand s d rop to her sid es, and tried to pretend none of what had just happened had just happened .

'Uh, no. No. He's not here,' she said , trying to remove her fingers from the hand les of the scissors. Unfortunately, the rubber of her gloves had become wed ged , which was severely hampering the extraction process.

'Where is he?' Hoon asked .

'He's over at, um...' She twisted and fid geted . 'What's it called ? Where the Skye brid ge goes?'

'Skye?' Hoon guessed .

Shona tutted . 'No. Coming the other way.'

'Oh, right. Aye. Because I was going to say, clue's in the fucking name,' Hoon replied . 'Kyle of Lochalsh?'

'That's the one,' Shona said . The rubber of her gloves squeaked and creaked , but the circular and oblong holes in the scissors had her fingers trapped tight.

'You, eh, you want a hand there?' Hoon asked .

Shona shook her head . 'Ah, you're grand . I'm fine.'

'Right.' Hoon watched her continue to struggle for a few second s. 'It's just, from where I'm stand ing, you look like you've got both hand s stuck in a couple of pairs of scissors.'

'Yes, well. I can see how it might look that way,' Shona conced ed , still trying to maintain some sort of air of professionalism. Or, if not that, then at least a sense of general competence.

Eventually, having come to the conclusion that those ships had both now sailed , however, she offered out her hand s and sighed .

'Fine. Can you take them off for me?'

Hoon took hold of the scissors on Shona's right hand and wiggled them from sid e to sid e while she pulled her hand in the opposite d irection.

'Top fucking marks for improvisation, by the way,' Hoon muttered , as they shimmied her fingers out of the holes. 'Thank fuck you d id n't let rip with these.'

Shona felt herself blushing. 'It was silly. Got carried away.'

'No, fuck that. Quite right,' Hoon said . 'No saying what sort of bastard s are wand ering around . Scissor through the face first, ask question later, that's my fucking motto!'

Shona felt herself smiling. 'That's quite a specific motto.'

Her right hand sprang free of the scissors, but left her glove behind , so the now empty fingers were stuck tangled through the holes.

'Aye. I suppose it is,' Hoon agreed . He tossed the scissors onto the d esk, then nod d ed at her other hand . 'You all right with them ones?'

'Yeah, I can d o these,' Shona confirmed . Now that she had one hand free, getting the other one loose was significantly less complic-ated .

While she worked her fingers free, Hoon wand ered over to the swing d oors that led through into the business part of the mortuary, and peered in through one of the wind ows. Orla Coull's bod y was on the table, but covered by a sheet.

'You here on your own?' he asked , glancing back over his should er.

Shona hesitated with the scissors still partly on. 'Uh, yes. I mean, no. I mean... there are people around . Doctors and nurses. Porters. It's always busy. There's always someone.'

'Again, relax. I'm no' here to murd er you... Shona, isn't it?'

Shona nod d ed . 'Yeah.'

'Aye. Jack's told me a lot about you.'

'Has he?' Shona asked .

Hoon blew out his cheeks. 'Actually, no' really,' he ad mitted . He shook his head . 'Dunno what you fucking see in him, to be honest, but each to their own. And listen, you d on't have to worry. I'm one of the good guys. I'm just making conversation, that's all.' He looked through the glass again. 'That the victim, is it?'

'Yes!' Shona cheered , as her fingers finally boinged free of the scissors. She caught the frown from Hoon, cleared her throat, and tried again. 'I mean, yes. Yes, that's the victim.'

'What happened ?'

'Don't know yet. I was about to start the PM.'

Hoon checked his watch. 'Fuck's sake. At this time of night? Jack turned into a slave d river these d ays, or something?'

Shona shook her head . 'No. Just thought I'd get it out of the way.'

Hoon stud ied her curiously, like he suspected her of hid ing some-thing.

Eventually, he shrugged . 'Fair enough. Is it no' a bit creepy being here so late all on your tod , though?'

'You're never alone with a corpse!' Shona replied . 'That's my motto!'

Hoon grunted out the first note of a laugh. 'That's quite a specific motto,' he said . His forehead creased , just momentarily. 'And a bit fucking weird .'

Shona smiled . 'Yes,' she replied . 'I suppose it is.'

'Aye, well, I'd better shoot off. You make sure you have a lovely time with...' Hoon gestured to the swing d oors, and to the lifeless shape beneath the sheet. 'Whoever your new pal is und er there.' He rocked on his heels, clicked his tongue against the roof of his mouth, then gave a nod that suggested he'd come to a d ecision. 'Kyle of Lochalsh, you say?'

'Uh, yes,' Shona said , and she sud d enly realised her mistake. 'Bu he's got a lot going on. You know, with the case, and everything? He probably won't want you—or, not just you, anyone, really—turning up unannounced . He probably would n't like that.'

'Oh, God , I know,' Hoon said . He grinned as he backed into the office d oor and nud ged it outward s into the corrid or. 'He's going t be absolutely fucking raging!'

Chapter 13

There were two narrow bed s in the cell that d oubled as benches d uring the d ay. They were fixed to walls across from one another, with a scuffed metal toilet stand ing in the no-man's-land between them.

Hugo sat perched on the ed ge of one bench, his elbows on his knees, his head resting in his hand s. Every part of him was jiggling as his right leg bounced nervously, the heel of his shoe tapping against the smooth stone floor. The repetitive movement mad e some of his piercings ting together.

Logan sat on the other bench, straight-backed to emphasise his massive size ad vantage over the younger man. They might be on opposite sid es of the room, but the cell was small enough that no point of it lay beyond the DCI's reach, least of all Hugo himself.

The Hoover and other cleaning equipment that had been stowed away in the cell, were nowhere to be seen.

'So, we spoke to Orla's parents,' Logan said . They were the first word s he had spoken since entering the cell, and he let them hang there in the space between them for a while before ad d ing more. 'We went to tell them what had happened , but they seemed remarkably informed alread y. Any id ea why that might be?'

Hugo's leg stopped bouncing, then started again with even more urgency.

'Well, you see, the thing is, I'd alread y sent them a message before speaking with you,' he said , sticking with his faux aristocratic d rawl. 'Obviously, had we had our conversation earlier, I would n't have said anything.'

'You sent them a message?'

'Uh, yeah.'

Logan masked his surprise well. 'A text? You told them that their daughter was dead,' Logan intoned. 'By *text*?'

'I always talk to people by text,' Hugo countered. 'I mean, who phones people these days?'

'That's not the point, is it? The point is, you should n't have been blood y contacting them at all. It's not your job.'

Hugo's movements became small. Furtive. He picked at the base of his black-painted nails, ad d ing to the scarring there.

'Well… it is, though, isn't it?' he ventured.

Logan's face d arkened. The bench beneath him groaned like it was trying to warn the boy to get out, to run, to get away. But the d oor to the cell was closed, and there was nowhere for him to go.

'And just how d o you figure that out?' the DCI d emand ed.

'Well, because I'm a friend, aren't I? Of the family. They've been worried sick about Orla for months now. When I knew what had happened to her, I felt it was my responsibility—no, my d uty—to share the news.'

'Oh. I see. You thought it was "your d uty", d id you? Well, while we're on the subject, let me tell you about my d uty, shall I? It's my d uty to investigate Orla's d eath. It's my d uty to d etermine if she was murd ered, and, if so, then it becomes my d uty to find out who killed her,' Logan explained.

He leaned a little closer and lowered his voice, like he was sharing some insid er secret.

'And here's a wee trick of the trad e, son. What helps immensely with that is seeing how people react when you break the news to them. Are they shocked? Are they ind ifferent? Are they hid ing anything? You can work out a lot from those first few moments.'

He let the boy d well on that for a short while before following up with the killer blow.

'Assuming, of course, that nobod y buggers it up for you by breaking the news to them in ad vance.'

Hugo said nothing, just increased the ferocity with which he was picking at his nail bed s.

'Speaking of reactions, what was yours?' Logan asked. 'When you saw her? When you realised it was Orla? If I'd been watching you then, what would you have done?'

There was no hesitation on Hugo's part. He launched straight into it, placing a hand in the middle of his chest and drawing in a gasp that would've seemed over the top in a high school production of *Gone With the Wind*.

'Aye, well, I'd have seen through that performance right away,' Logan said.

'Too hammy?' Hugo asked, disappointed. 'Yeah. Orla always said I went too big on stuff like that.'

'What do you mean?'

Across on the other bench, the lad suddenly looked embarrassed. 'Nothing.'

'Look, if you've got something to say, son, I recommend you say it,' Logan urged. 'Because, right now, you are *not* in my good books. If there's anything you can do to endear yourself to me, I strongly suggest you seize that opportunity with both hands.'

Hugo shifted around, trying to get comfortable. An impossible task, given the thinness of the bench's padding.

'No, I mean, it's nothing really. Honestly. We just… we were both into drama.' He raised his eyes to meet the detective's. 'You know? Acting.'

'I know what drama is.'

'Right, yes. Of course. Well, we used to do these little sort of skits. Just improv stuff, mostly. I'd give her a character to perform, and she'd give me one, and we'd act it out.'

The redness of his cheeks was really setting off the purple in his hair. He looked down again and shrugged, and there was less flamboyance to the movement this time.

'Stupid, I know.'

Logan grunted. 'Aye. Well. We've all got to start somewhere, I suppose.' He looked at his watch, then tutted. Time was getting on. 'Was it just her parents you told? Or did you feel it was "your duty" to tell anyone else?'

83

'No,' Hugo said.

'No to which one?' Logan pressed.

'Um, well, I mean... I felt Ayesha should know.' He quickly raised his hand s, like he was afraid Logan was going to make a grab for him. 'Just Ayesha, that's it. Nobod y else.'

'Who the hell is Ayesha?' Logan d emand ed.

'A friend. A mutual friend. Well, mostly Orla's. They were like—I mean, seriously—they were like sisters. Oh my God. You should 've seen them. Totally obsessed with each other. But not, like, in a gay way, just in a BFF way.'

Logan let out a long, weary sigh that seemed to d rag on forever.

'Right. I see. And what d id you say to her?'

'Oh, nothing really. Just, like, *oh my god, Orla's dead.* Or word s to that effect.'

'By text?'

'Yes.'

'You d id n't call her?'

Hugo baulked at the suggestion. 'Nobod y ever calls.'

'Fine. Give me her name.'

'Uh, it's Ayesha. A-Y—'

'Her surname,' Logan said, cutting short the spelling lesson.

'Oh. Yes, sorry. It's Fulton. Ayesha Fulton. Lives with her gran. Well, her gran and her gran's utterly revolting car crash of a boyfriend. A boyfriend! Can you imagine? At their age! And someone like him, especially.'

'Why? What's wrong with him?'

'You mean, "what's right with him?" He's just... ugh.' Hugo shud d ered. 'Go meet him. See for yourself. I can't d o him justice. Stephen King could n't d o him justice. You know, the horror author?'

'I know who Stephen King is, aye.'

Hugo looked surprised by this, and even a little impressed.

'They live just a few d oors from here, actually. Have you seen that house with the gnomes in the gard en?'

'No.'

'Ah. Right. Well, when you d o see it, it's that one.'

'Fine. And what did she have to say about it, this Ayesha?' Logan pressed.

'Nothing,' Hugo said. 'She didn't reply. I mean, maybe she has now, but they took my phone off me. I could try her again, if you like?'

'That won't be necessary,' Logan said, rising to his feet. 'I'm going to hand you over to Sergeant...' He realised he'd forgotten what Sandra's last name was. 'To the sergeant here.'

'MacGeachan,' Hugo said. 'It's Sergeant MacGeachan. She and I have had ... dealings before.'

'Fine. Well, she wants to talk to you about the driving offence.'

'I didn't mean to hit that policeman. I tried to stop,' Hugo said, the words rushing out of him. 'And I didn't break the window. Honest.'

Logan gave the appeal his momentary consideration, then nodded. 'Aye, well, you be sure to let the sergeant know all that.'

He thumped a fist on the metal door, and listened to the sound of keys jangling along the corridor. While he waited, he turned back and asked the prisoner one last question.

'And you definitely texted? Hugo's parents, I mean?'

Hugo nodded. 'Yeah. Yes. Definitely. I can show you my phone.' He glanced at the door, just as a key was rattled into the lock on the other side. 'If they ever give me it back.'

'I'll hold you to that,' Logan told him. The door was opened to reveal Sandra standing on the other side, her cap on her head, a clipboard pressed tightly under one arm. 'Sergeant,' he said, stepping past her. 'He's all yours.'

Chapter 14

By the time Logan gathered with the others in their makeshift Incid ent Room, the Big Board was starting to take shape. Sinead was putting the finishing touches to the current version, tacking up some hand - written notes, and using lines of string to start laying out a rough timeline of events.

Usually, there would be photos of the victim and of any potential suspects pinned up there somewhere, but most of those were currently notable by their absence.

The only photograph was a blurry photocopied black-and -white image that had been taken from one of the 'MISSING' posters d ating back to Orla's d isappearance.

'Can't get the printer working, boss,' Tyler explained , read ing the DCI's mind , or perhaps just his expression. 'We're having to write everything out by hand .'

'What, can Hamza no' fix it?' Logan asked .

He looked around the room and noted that, like most of the photos, the team's resid ent tech expert was nowhere to be seen.

'He had a bash,' Ben explained . 'Reckons it's jiggered , though. He's going to bring one back with him tomorrow morning, along with the internet.'

Logan turned to the DI. Ben was sitting in the chair he had claimed earlier, stroking Taggart, who had managed to scramble up onto his lap and fall asleep.

'What d o you mean, "along with the internet"?'

'He's bringing the internet,' Ben said .

'What are you on about?' Logan asked . 'How can he be *bringing the internet*?'

Ben stopped patting the dog just long enough to wave a hand at the ancient computer, as if this explained everything. Taggart opened one eye until the hand resumed its stroking duties on his head, then went back to sleep.

Logan concluded that this was about as much information as he was likely to get from the older detective, so he turned to Tyler and Sinead. 'Can someone translate?'

'There's no WiFi,' Sinead explained. 'That PC's connected by cable. Ham's going to bring a new router back with him that'll let us get the laptops hooked up.'

'Exactly. That's what I said,' Ben insisted, sounding a little put-out. 'He's bringing the internet.'

Logan decided it was best to let the comment go. Clearly, Ben had no understanding of how the internet worked. But then, to be fair, Logan was pretty sketchy on the details himself.

He approached the board and studied what was there so far. He'd made himself a coffee while passing through the kitchen on the way back to this room, and sipped it while he scanned the information they had pulled together so far.

Given the short amount of time and the lack of resources, the team had done well. There were statements—abbreviated, admittedly—from witnesses and suspects taken around the time of Orla's original disappearance, extracts from the locally held case notes, an account of her known movements before vanishing, and some other bits and bobs about her relationships with folks both in town and further afield.

Details of today's events—the who, where, and when of the body being discovered, accounts from those who had found her, and some snippets of the statements given by the wedding party—had also been carefully written out and pinned in place.

'Ben, you spoke to CID,' Logan said, turning back to face the room. 'Who handled the original case?'

'DS Kevin Ness,' Ben said.

Logan gave the name some thought, but drew a blank. 'Do I know him?'

'You'll have seen him around, I'm sure,' Ben said. 'Skinny lad. Dark hair. Had a wee moustache for a while.'

Logan shook his head , his expression blank.

'Bit seed y. Oily,' Ben continued . 'Like, I d on't know, sort of shiny. Like a slug. That sound s a bit harsh, but honestly, it's the best way to d escribe him. Like he's got a film of grease on him.'

'Oh! I know the guy you're talking about, boss. That's Buttersoap!' Tyler looked around at the others, grinning. 'You know? Because he looks like someone swapped his bar of soap for a block of butter.'

'He d oes!' Ben agreed , chuckling. 'He blood y d oes, too.'

'Wait, is that the one that looks like a pound shop Errol Flynn?' Logan asked , d ragging the memory of the man up from the d eepest, d arkest recesses of his brain.

'That's him!' Ben said .

'Haven't seen him around in a while, I d on't think.'

'No, he transferred across to Aberd een a couple of months back,' Ben said . 'Snecky's patch.'

Ben gave an involuntary shud d er at the thought of his old boss. Snecky had been a liability lead ing the Major Investigations Team d uring his time in Inverness, and was likely just as much of a d isaster head ing up CID across on the northeast.

Fortunately, the fact he had transferred out and been replaced by Logan meant Ben no longer had to clean up after him.

'DS Ness was sent up here to investigate when Orla went missing,' the DI continued . 'He conclud ed that she'd just run away, though.'

'How old was she at the time?' Logan asked .

'Seventeen. She'd be eighteen now,' replied Ben. 'Parents insisted she'd been abd ucted , but turns out she went home and packed a bag first. Even left them a note saying she was going away for a while, and not to worry.'

'Typed or hand written?'

'Hand written,' Ben said . 'Hand writing was confirmed as hers, but her parents—the mother, mostly—says someone must've been making her write it. Refuses to believe she d id it herself.'

'She blaming anyone in particular?' Logan asked .

'A few people, aye,' Ben said . 'But mainly…'

The name escaped him, so he shot a look across the room to where Sinead stood by the Big Board.

'Stephen Boyd, sir,' DC Bell said, catching the pass and running with it. 'Known locally as—'

'Camden Steve,' Logan concluded, recalling his conversation with the Uniforms earlier.

'Oh, he wishes, boss!' Tyler said. 'That's what he calls himself. Probably just hoping it'll catch on, but no luck. Everyone else calls him Paedo Steve.'

Logan winced. 'Aye, I can see why he'd be less keen on that one, right enough.'

'You certainly wouldn't want it on a name badge, no,' Ben said.

'CID speak with him at the time?'

'They did, sir, yeah,' Sinead confirmed. 'He had an alibi for the day she went missing, which DS...'

She glanced down at her notes, searching for the name. Fortunately, her husband was on hand to help her out.

'Buttersoap.'

'...Ness,' Sinead said, shooting Tyler a glare. 'DS Ness looked into the alibi, and it checked out, so he didn't feel the need to investigate Mr Boyd any further.'

'So, if Paedo Steve was the killer, then you might say he slipped through Buttersoap's fingers,' Tyler announced. He looked quite proud of the comment, but the look it earned him from his wife and both bosses soon knocked that out of him. 'Sorry,' he mumbled. 'I'll shut up now.'

'Thank Christ for that,' Logan said. 'And, do you think we might be able to refrain from calling the man "Paedo Steve"? Whatever he has or hasn't done, we treat him with professionalism and respect.' He took another sip of his coffee and turned back to the board. 'Even if he is a nonce.'

Although the Big Board was filling up, there were a couple of key elements missing. This was understandable, of course, given that Logan was yet to pass those particular nuggets of information on.

In his defence, there was one bit of it that he'd only just received. And very interesting it was, too.

But he'd get to that in a moment.

'The top Orla was wearing,' he began.

'Orange hood ie,' Sinead recalled .

'Hugo in there reckons it belonged to Orla's boyfriend . Or ex-boyfriend now, I suppose. Some lad called … Christ, what was it?'

He fished in his coat pocket until he found his notebook, took it out, and ad justed the d istance between it and his eyes until his scribbled writing came into focus.

'Ronnie Donlon.'

Sinead 's head jerked in his d irection. 'Donlon?'

'Aye. Why?' Logan asked .

'Um, not sure, sir. Might be an issue.' She took out her phone and started tapping. 'Give me a minute.'

'I knew a Ronnie Donlon once,' Ben said . 'Years back.'

'On the job?' Logan asked .

'Aye. Back on the beat. He retired yonks ago, mind you, so unless the lassie had a taste for old men, I would n't imagine we're looking at the same fella.'

'They were in high school together, so highly d oubt it, no.' Logan watched Sinead typing away for a moment, then continued . 'Accord ing to Hugo, Ronnie and Orla were a couple since second year. Not constantly, but more on than off.'

'Were they winching when she went missing?' asked Ben.

'So he says.'

With some d ifficulty, Tyler got to his feet and limped his way to the board , d ragging a foot behind him.

'What the hell's wrong with you?' Logan asked , watching him heave himself across the floor.

'I was hit by that car, boss,' Tyler remind ed him. 'Remember?'

'They said it barely touched you.'

'Aye, well, they weren't the ones on the receiving end of it, to be fair,' Tyler pointed out. 'They d id n't experience it first-hand like I d id .

'You weren't limping when you came in, were you?' asked Ben.

'And you weren't limping when you were helping me stick stuff on the board earlier,' Sinead ad d ed .

Tyler stopped halfway across the room. He sighed, tutted, then shook his head, all more or less at the same time. 'Fine. I just thought, you know, a wee bit of sympathy would n't go amiss,' he said. He walked normally the rest of the way over to the board, muttering, 'Consid ering I *was* hit by an actual car.'

'Anyone brought a wee violin?' Logan asked. When it was clear that nobod y had, he shrugged. 'Sorry, son, wish we could help.'

Tyler stopped at the board and put his hand s on his hips, searching the hand written text.

'What is it?' Logan asked, joining him. 'You got something?'

'Just thinking, boss.'

He left a gap for the inevitable 'first time for everything' type comment. But, to his surprise, none came.

'The boyfriend,' he continued. 'Ronnie Donlon, you said ?'

'Aye. What about him?'

Tyler gestured to the board. 'Where is he?' He looked back over his should er. 'I d on't know about anyone else, but I d id n't see that name coming up anywhere when we were pulling this stuff together.'

'What, not even in the original report?' Logan asked.

Tyler shook his head. 'Don't think so, boss, no. You'd think, if they were a couple at the time she vanished, he'd be high on the list of suspects. Or, at least have been questioned as a potential witness.'

'Aye,' Logan agreed. He flicked through the small bund le of longhand pages pinned to the board that summarised the original investigation. 'You'd think.'

He turned to Sinead just as she looked up from her phone. The raising of his eyebrows asked the question for him.

'Um, no, d id n't see him in the reports, sir, but the name Donlon d id come up somewhere else.'

'Where?'

'It was here, sir.' Sinead held up her phone. It showed a reservation for a room at a local bed and breakfast in Logan's name. 'I think I might've booked you in to stay at his mum and d ad 's house tonight. Should I change it?'

'No. Could be interesting,' Logan replied after some thought. 'And speaking of which, when I was chatting with Hugo through there, he told me something *very* interesting.'

'Was it that he hit me with his car, boss?' Tyler asked.

Logan dismissed the remark with a roll of his eyes. 'No, he thought he'd leave that for you to bang on about every five minutes,' the DCI said. 'Hugo admitted he'd been in touch with Orla Coull's parents earlier, to let them know about the body being found.'

'We knew that already, though, didn't we?' asked Sinead.

'We did. But he says he texted.'

Sinead blinked. 'Texted? But Orla's dad said —'

'He called, aye. Was quite specific, too. Said he sounded upset.'

'So, one of them's lying,' DI Forde chipped in. Taggart stirred in his lap, and Ben lowered his voice before continuing. 'But why?'

'And which one?' Tyler wondered.

'Hugo said we can check his phone and see the text for ourselves,' Logan told them.

'He could've deleted the call from his history,' Sinead pointed out.

'Aye, so we'll get the number, run a check, see if any calls were made. Tyler, you can get on that first thing.'

'Will do, boss,' the DC replied. 'But, eh, what are we hoping to find out? What will it tell us if there was a call?'

'It'll tell us for sure which one of them is trying to fill us with shite,' Logan said. 'Whichever one it is, they must have a reason for lying. Pick away at that thread, and there's no saying where it might lead us.'

'Anything you want me to crack on with in the morning, Jack?' asked Ben. 'You've not got me long before I have to shoot off back down the road. Can't hang around, got to keep Herself happy.'

He mimed cracking a whip, which made Logan shudder.

'Herself? What, your... fancy woman?' the DCI asked, and he winced at the thought of it.

It had been almost two months since he'd first found out about DI Forde's clandestine relationship with Moira Corson, the wasp-faced old dragon who manned the front desk at the polis station down in Fort William, but he was still unable to wrap his head around the idea.

She had always struck Logan as a right hard-nosed, unpleasant bastard, whose only joy in life seemed to come from the misery and suffering of others. Moira wasn't just a stickler for paperwork, she was fanatical about it. She was *militant*. If there had been a paperwork division of the Third Reich, one of her ancestors was almost certainly in charge of it.

Or, given that nobody could quite determine her age, possibly even Moira herself.

If the paperwork wasn't completed to her standards, you could kiss goodbye your chances of being allowed through the security door and into the main station. And, when it came to filling out forms, her standards were excruciatingly high.

'No! Mitchell, I mean,' Ben said, to Logan's immediate relief. 'And she's not my "fancy woman". We're just...'

He shifted in his chair, which earned him a raised ear and a huffy sigh from Taggart until he stilled again.

'We're friends, that's all. No need for any of that hanky-panky business at our age. All we're interested in is a bit of companionship, no' to be bloody...' He waved a hand, like the rest of the sentence was way on the other side of the room, and he was trying to draw their attention to it. '...rolling around on each other like a couple of past their best sausages in a pan, or, I don't know, slapping against one another like lumps of room temperature corned beef.'

A long, horrified silence fell, as the three other detectives all tried to keep either of those images from taking root in their heads.

None of them were successful.

Even Taggart, who had until now seemed content to remain there forever in Ben's lap, jumped down and retreated under one of the desks.

'Jesus. Well, that was hauntingly descriptive,' Logan muttered.

'And oddly meat-based,' Sinead pointed out.

Logan nodded slowly. 'Aye,' he agreed, ashen-faced. 'Aye, very much meat-based.'

'I feel a bit sick now,' Tyler added.

'All right, all right, shut up. My point is,' Ben began, but his brow creased into a frown before he continued. 'I forget what my point is.

Forget it. Doesn't matter.' He stood up and brushed some of the dog hair off him. 'Is anyone else hungry all of a sud d en?'

'Definitely not, boss,' Tyler said , still unsuccessfully trying to block out all those sexually charged , meat-based mental pictures. 'What's the opposite of hungry? Because whatever it is, I'm that.'

From out front there came the shrill buzzing of a power saw being started up, as one of the local joiners set about covering the broken wind ow. There was going to be a fair amount of racket for the next while, and Logan could alread y feel a head ache beginning to stretch and warm up on the sid elines.

He glanced at his watch, then reached for his coat on the back of his chair. 'Right. Not a lot else we can d o tonight. Might as well get some kip and get back here early, and we'll see where we are then. Should have the first PM results by early afternoon, and we'll have a clearer id ea of what we're working with at that point.'

'What you leaning toward s, sir?' asked Sinead . 'You thinking murd er or accid ent?'

Logan regard ed the Big Board as he pulled his coat on. As soon as the coat had been picked up, Taggart had emerged from below the table and was sitting upright like the *goodest* of boys, his tail thumping excited ly on the floor.

'I'm not ruling it out yet, and I hope I'm wrong, but I d on't think it's an accid ent,' Logan announced . 'She can't have been hid ing herself away for six months, only to slip and fall on her return. Someone had to have been hid ing her.'

'At her request, or against her will?' asked Ben.

'That I d on't know,' Logan ad mitted . 'But we'll figure it out tomorrow. We all in d ifferent B&Bs?'

'We are, sir, yes. Could n't get us together anywhere,' Sinead confirmed .

'Fine. We'll meet back here in the morning.'

'One thing I was going to suggest, sir,' replied Sinead . 'The place Tyler and I are staying, it's actually across the brid ge in Skye.'

'And ?'

Sinead gestured at the board . 'And , well, accord ing to the info d ug up, we need to pass Stephen Boyd 's caravan on the way.'

'What, Paed o Steve?' her husband cried. 'You booked us in next door to Paed o Steve?!'

'Not next door, obviously. We just pass it on the way.'

'Where is it we're staying?' Tyler asked. 'The Jimmy Savile Lodge?'

Sinead sighed. 'I just thought, since we were passing...'

Logan looked unconvinced. 'You shouldn't be overdoing it.'

The comment, though well-meaning, made Sinead's mouth become a thin and puckered thing.

Out front, the buzzing of a saw became the thacking of a hammer.

'Here we go. What, you mean *in my condition*?' Sinead asked.

The DCI had not reached his position without learning to read body language, and all his instincts were suddenly warning him of danger.

'Well, that wasn't exactly what I was...' he began.

'I think we should leave it for tonight,' Tyler said, but then Sinead shot to her feet, silencing him before he could continue.

'Fine, I'll go in myself,' she insisted.

'You can't go yourself!' Tyler shot back.

'Why not?' Sinead demanded.

'Well, because...' Tyler looked to the two senior detectives for support, but it was clear from their expressions that they weren't going to get involved. 'He's a paedophile.'

'I'm twenty-six,' his wife reminded him. 'I don't think I'm his target demographic.'

'Aye, well, suppose you've got a point there,' Tyler admitted, but he soon found his resolve again. 'But, no. No way you're going on your own. I'm coming with you. Unless, you know, you think otherwise, boss...?'

Tyler nodded encouragingly at Logan, but the DCI failed once again to come to the rescue.

'If you're up to it, go ahead,' he told Sinead. 'Just... for God's sake, be careful. If there's any sign of trouble, get out of there. In fact, no. Throw this bastard into his path first, then get out of there,' he suggested, pointing at Tyler.

'Cheers for that, boss,' Tyler grumbled.

'Right. That's settled , then,' Logan said . He turned to the d oor, and Taggart bound ed after him. 'Now, let's get out of here before all that hammering d oes my blood y nut in.'

Chapter 15

Shona drummed her fingers on the underside of the clipboard, tapping along to the beat of Blondie's *One Way Or Another* while she ticked off the check boxes on her top sheet, and scribbled a signature at the bottom.

The office door was now locked, so she'd have no more unexpected visitors dropping by. She'd asked her smart speaker to play hits from the eighties, and had been surprised when this song had been the first to come blasting out, given that it was released at the tail end of the seventies.

Still, it was an absolute banger, so she wasn't going to complain.

The body of Orla Coull lay naked and exposed on the table before her, waiting patiently for her to begin. They were always patient, the dead. That was one of the things Shona liked about them. They were never in a rush, didn't require awkward small talk, and were generally far more accommodating than their still-living counterparts.

It wasn't that she didn't like the living, of course. Some of them were all right. Many of the people she liked most in the world were alive, in fact. Well, currently alive, anyway. She was all-too-aware that it was never a permanent state.

So, she didn't *dis*like the living. It was just that, in general, alive people were much harder work than dead ones. The living were driven by goals and ambitions, and worked endlessly to further their own purposes.

They had motives. *Ulterior* motives, in some cases. They planned. They schemed. They required careful consideration and constant second-guessing.

The d ead , on the other hand , hid nothing. Asked nothing. Hur
nothing.

However they had been in life—whether they'd been an absolute
saint, or a heartless monster—that stuff was all gone by the time they
wound up here on Shona's slab. The actions of their life were all just
backstory, irrelevant to the tale that unfold ed beneath her blad es.

And tonight would be no d ifferent.

Debbie Harry was singing about a supermarket checkout when the
clipboard was hooked onto the end of the bed , and Shona turned he
attention to her latest patient.

'Now, then,' she said in a voice like a warm hug. 'I'm sorry you've
end ed up here. It's not fair. Especially you being so young, and all. But
it is what it is. We're here now, and we might as well make the most
of it.

'And I'm sorry, too, about some of the things I have to d o to you.
They're not pleasant. I know, if the shoe was on the other foot, I
would n't want anyone d oing them to me. But it's important that we
d o them, so we can find out what happened to you, and …'

While talking, she'd started to pace around the bod y, looking it
over for any obvious marks or signs of d amage. One thing had quickly
caught her eye, and her word s fell away into silence as her brain raced
to consid er the implications.

It d id n't take her long to come to a conclusion.

'Oh, God , no,' she whispered , then she took the girl's cold hand
in her own, squeezed it, and offered the lifeless shell a smile that was
lined with heartbreak. 'Oh, Orla. I am so,*so* sorry.'

Chapter 16

'It's a nicer caravan than I was expecting,' Tyler said , as he pulled the car up at the sid e of the road .

Sinead looked ahead through the rain-slicked wind screen. The caravan was small, d ated , and propped up at both end s by uneven stacks of bricks. The one tyre visible on this sid e was completely d eflated , a wound in the rubber suggesting that someone had taken a knife to it at some point.

Very possibly the same person who had scratched the incorrectly spelled *PEEDO HOUSE'* above the d oor, like it was the name of some cosy country pub.

'Jesus. What d id you think it was going to be like?' Sinead wond ered .

'I d on't know,' Tyler ad mitted . 'I just had low expectations.'

'What, lower than *that*?' Sinead asked , incred ulously.

'You should 've seen the last caravan I was in. This one's a luxury villa, compared to that one,' Tyler said , shutting off the engine and unclipping his belt. 'God , I hope this one d oesn't smell. That one I was in with Hamza really stunk.'

'And then it went on fire, if I remember rightly,' Sinead teased .

'Aye. That was unfortunate, but probably for the best in the long run,' Tyler replied , then they both opened their d oors and approached the caravan.

It sat in a layby d own near the ed ge of the loch, just before the road rose to become the brid ge across to Skye. It was shad ed by a couple of trees, but otherwise pretty out in the open and easy to find . If he was having trouble with the locals, he wasn't exactly hid ing from it.

A somewhat dinged-up Ford Focus was parked in front of the caravan, though it was impossible to tell from their angle of approach if they were hooked up together.

'How do you want to play it?' asked Tyler, as they made their way towards the narrow door of the caravan. 'You want to do the talking, or will I?'

'Depends,' Sinead replied.

'On what?'

'On which one of us is more likely to accidentally call him "Paedo Steve" to his face.'

Tyler ran through the possibilities, then nodded. 'Maybe best if you do the talking.'

'Aye, maybe,' Sinead agreed, and she smiled. 'How are you feeling, anyway?'

'What, about this?' Tyler asked, indicating the caravan.

'After being hit by that car.'

'Oh. That? Nah, I'm fine. Like I say, shrugged it off.'

Sinead planted a peck on his cheek. 'My hero,' she said, then she ran a hand down her face, wiping the smile away, and raised a hand to knock on the door. 'You ready?'

Before Tyler could answer, the door was yanked open from the inside, revealing a man quite unlike the one either detective had been bracing themselves for.

He was in his late-twenties—no older than thirty, anyway—with a full head of wavy black hair, and matching coloured stubble that hugged the angled lines of his jaw. His eyes were a striking shade of blue that shone like gemstones in the half-darkness.

He was dressed for bed in a pair of pyjama shorts and a pale blue T-shirt that suggested the rippling of abdominal muscles below. A long brown dressing-gown hung open from his shoulders and swished around at his knees, giving him the look of a boxer about to head down the aisle to ringside.

'Fuck off! I'm filming you, you know? I'm recording everything.'

Sinead and Tyler exchanged glances.

'Sorry?' Sinead asked.

He reached out of the caravan and tapped the wind ow that was closest to the d oor. The rattle it mad e sound ed plastic.

There, between the wind ow and the curtains, sat a small white box with two black circles on the front, one larger than the other.

'Camera. It's all being record ed . Started as soon as you pulled up, so I d on't want any trouble. I'm not in the mood . Not tonight.'

His accent was local to the Highland s, without so much as a suggestion of inner Lond on about it that might have justified the 'Camd en Steve' moniker. That said , it was entirely possible that this wasn't the man they were looking for, and that he had some gnarled , sweaty-palmed creepy uncle lurking insid e.

'We're not here to cause anyone any trouble,' Sinead assured him. She prod uced her warrant card , and he squinted at it with suspicion. 'I'm Detective Constable Bell. This is my husb— I mean, this is my colleague, DC Neish.'

'All right?' Tyler said , but his usual cheerful d emeanour was nowhere to be seen.

'We're looking for Stephen Boyd ,' Sinead continued , returning her ID wallet to her pocket.

The man in the d oorway glanced into the caravan, like he was looking at someone else sitting insid e, perhaps seeking their approval.

'What for?' he asked once he'd turned back.

'We'd just like to ask him a few questions,' Sinead promised .

'About what?'

Sinead smiled . 'Nothing too onerous, I promise.' Her gaze d arted in the same d irection the man had looked a moment before. 'Is he in?'

'Uh, yes. Yes. So, I suppose…' He gave a little sigh of resignation, then stepped asid e. 'Come in if you must. It's a bit of a mess, though. If I'd known you were coming, I'd have tid ied up.'

'That's not a problem,' Sinead said , climbing the two metal steps and squeezing through the caravan d oor.

It led straight into the living area, and the first thing she noticed was that the place wasn't really all that messy, at all. Dated , yes—the upholstery was a blend of browns and burgund ies, and the worktop in the small kitchen area was mad e of scratched Formica in a zig-zag pattern that made her eyes cross—but it was clean, and it was tidy. Arguably, far more so than their own kitchen at home.

In fact, not even arguably. It just was.

There was a sitting area in the far corner—although, given the compact size of the place, 'far' was something of a misnomer. A couple of padded benches that most likely turned into a bed, framed two sid of a small dining table. A laptop sat open on it, angled away from the door so she couldn't see what was on it.

The other thing she noticed about the caravan was that there was nobody else in there but the three of them.

Which meant...

'Oh!' she said, unable to hide her surprise. She caught herself looking him up and down. 'So are you...?'

'Am I who? Am I Paedo Steve?' The man in the dressing gown shifted his gaze slowly from one detective to the other, like he was assessing a threat. 'Is that what you're wanting to ask?'

'What? No,' Sinead said, half-laughing the question off.

'Are you?' Tyler asked.

The man in the dressing gown tutted. 'Yes. Aye. Yes, I am. That's me. Well done. You found me. So, what are you here for? What is it that I'm meant to have done this time?'

'You mind if we take a seat?' Sinead asked. She put a hand on her lower back and grimaced to suggest the weight of her swollen belly was taking its toll.

Stephen's gaze moved down to her stomach, and Tyler felt himself bristling at the thought of what might be going around in this sick bastard's head.

'Fine. No. Go ahead,' Stephen replied, but Sinead was already on the move, playing up her waddling walk, before plopping herself down on the longer side of the L-shaped bench.

She started to shuffle her way along, making room for Tyler to sit. Stephen hurried over to the table and snapped the lid of his laptop shut before she could see what was on the screen.

'OK. So... what?' he demanded, once Sinead had settled into position. 'What do you want?'

Tyler now stood beside the table, but had n't yet moved to sit down. Stephen was half a head taller than him, and he did n't want to give the man any further height advantage.

'I'm not sure if you've heard the news, Mr Boyd,' Sinead began, before he immediately cut her off.

'Oh. Great. It's "Mr Boyd", is it?' he spat. 'Now I know I'm in trouble.'

Sinead smiled. 'Would you prefer me to call you Stephen?'

'Whatever. I really don't care. Just get on with it. Get it over with. Why are you here?'

Sinead side-eyed Tyler to make sure he was taking note of the other man's reaction, then laid it all out.

'I'm sure you're aware of Orla Coull's disappearance a few months back,' she said.

'Aware?' Stephen snorted. It was a bitter, angry sound, full of resentment. 'Aye. You could say I was made aware, right enough. Repeatedly, in fact. But I told you lot then the same as I'll tell you now, I don't know anything about her. I don't know who she is, and I don't know where she is.'

'She turned up today,' Sinead continued.

'Did she?' Stephen said, his voice climbing in pitch, his sentence punctuated by a sharp laugh of relief. There was a note of hysteria about it. 'Well, about bloody time, too. Still, good for her, I'm glad to hear it. Maybe I'll stop getting dog shit hurled at my windows now, and won't have as many people gobbing at me on the street.'

'I'm afraid she's dead, Stephen.'

His rejoicing stopped. The laughter curled up and died in his throat. He stared at Sinead —or in her general direction, anyway, his focus having shifted to somewhere far behind her, beyond the caravan wall.

'She's what?' he asked.

His voice was a flat monotone. His Adam's apple sunk all the way to his chest, then bobbed back up again. His eyes swam, then pulled focus on the detective sitting on the bench.

'She's dead?' he said.

'I'm afraid so, yes. Her body was found today, in the loch near the castle,' Sinead explained.

'Oh, God . Oh, Christ!'

Stephen sat d own heavily on the ed ge of the bench, at the furthest end of the L-shape. His head d ropped into his hand s, and he perched there with his back to the officers, babbling below his breath too quietly for them to make out any of the word s.

Sinead stole a glance at the closed laptop on the table between them. What had he been up to on it? There was something he was hid ing. Was that why he'd looked back into the caravan before inviting them in, to check there was nothing d amning on d isplay?

And why the rush to close it over before she could see?

'What happened to her?' Stephen asked , not turning to look at them.

'We're not sure yet,' Sinead ad mitted .

He d id turn then, his eyes wet with tears, his face an open wind ow into the emotional turmoil currently bubbling away insid e him.

'Well, was it an accid ent, or d id someone…?'

He stood up sud d enly, and regard ed the d etectives like he was only now seeing them for the first time. Like he was only just realising the d anger they posed .

'Jesus. Hold on. You're going to try and pin this on me, aren't you? That's what you're here for. That's why you came. You think I d id this. You think I killed her!'

Sinead shook her head . 'That's not why—'

'I d id n't! I d id n't touch her! I d on't even know who she is, beyond what I read in the papers at the time,' Stephen insisted , and as he spoke, more tears bubbled to the surface, then mad e a break for it d own his cheeks.

He marched to the wind ow—this only required him to take one-and -a-half steps, so it probably wasn't as d ramatic a gesture as he'd have liked —and stabbed a finger at the curtains.

'Them, out there, that lot, they all think I'm a d irty fucking child -molester,' he cried . 'Because that's how the tabloid s framed it at the time, after they came round , d igging for d irt. They pointed fingers at me because I've got a record . Because I'm on the *register*.'

'Because you had sex with a child,' Tyler added, then he straightened as Paedo Steve spun to face him, preparing to defend himself from an attack that didn't come.

'Yes,' Stephen admitted, his voice hoarse and dry. 'I did. She was fifteen. A couple of weeks away from turning sixteen. I was less than thirteen months older. *Thirteen months*! We'd been together for over three fucking years! It was her idea to do it! I didn't grab someone off the street or… or lure them into a van with a box of fucking puppies! I, having just turned seventeen, had consensual sex with my nearly sixteen-year-old, long-term girlfriend, who I was in love with.'

His gaze flitted from one detective to the other, eyes wide and desperate, like he was pleading for some sort of salvation from them. For them to absolve him of his sins.

'Should I be punished for that for the rest of my life?' he cried. 'Shunned, and victimised, and attacked in my own home? Is that fair? Is that right?'

Tyler felt there was a moral high ground waiting to be claimed here. After all, everyone had their excuses for breaking the law. Everyone had their reasons for doing terrible things. The only way that most of the population managed to sleep at night was because nobody ever liked to think of themselves as the bad guy.

So, Paedo Steve was no different in that regard to any other criminal attempting to justify their crimes. In this instance, however—and to his annoyance—Tyler actually found himself feeling sort of sorry for the guy. The punishment, in this instance—especially the one being dealt by the public—didn't seem to fit the crime.

'You were attacked?' Sinead asked, and it was clear from the softening of her voice that she shared at least some of her husband's feelings on the matter.

Stephen turned away, and ran his arm across his eyes, wiping tears and snot onto the sleeve of his dressing-gown. 'It's fine. It was a while ago. It doesn't matter now,' he said.

His voice cracked, mid-sentence, and he hurried to a half-width door at the other end of the caravan, which presumably housed the toilet.

'Excuse me,' he said, then he sidled inside, shut the door behind him, and slid the bolt-lock into place on the other side.

To Tyler's horror, Sinead immediately opened the lid of Stephen's laptop and tapped repeatedly on the touchpad to wake it up.

'What are you doing?' Tyler whispered.

'I'm just having a look,' Sinead replied, glancing furtively from the computer to the bathroom door.

The laptop's fan started to whirr, and the hard drive let out a series of irregular clicks, but the screen remained dark.

'You can't just mess with his stuff! We could get into deep shit for that,' Tyler pointed out.

'I know. But I think there's something he doesn't want us to see.' Sinead frantically swiped her finger across the touchpad, trying to rouse the screen from its slumber.

From inside the bathroom came the trickling sound of a cassette toilet being flushed.

'Come on, come on, come on,' Sinead chanted below her breath.

'He's coming out!' Tyler squeaked. 'Close it over!'

The laptop screen illuminated. For a moment, Sinead wasn't sure what she was looking at, then the realisation hit her just as the lock of the bathroom door was slid aside.

She shut the laptop lid, turned it back so it was in roughly the same position it had been when she'd started to snoop, then hurriedly shuffled her way along to the end of the bench.

'Thanks for your time, Mr Boyd,' she said, squeezing herself out of the gap between the bench and the table. 'Especially with us turning up unannounced this late in the evening. We appreciate you taking the time to talk to us.'

Boyd looked surprised by the apology, or perhaps by their sudden desire to leave. He looked first at the female detective, and then at her husband. Something about Tyler's expression—the way he was avoiding all eye contact, and *definitely not* looking at the table—made the caravan owner glance at his laptop.

He lingered over it for a few seconds, before fixing on a smile and opening the door.

'No problem. Thank you for coming over and telling me the sad news. I appreciate you keeping me up to d ate,' he said .

'No bother,' Tyler told him, hanging back insid e until Sinead had d escend ed the two shoogly steps. 'And , eh, if you have any more bother with the locals, you give us a shout,' the DC told him. 'We'll d o what we can to help.'

'Thank you. I appreciate the sentiment,' Stephen said . He waited until Tyler had climbed d own the steps and back onto solid ground . 'But I'll believe it when I see it,' he said , then he quietly but firmly shut the d oor.

Tyler turned to his wife. 'Well, I d on't know about you, but he wasn't what I was expecting at all. I thought he'd be more… I d on't know. Clammy.'

'Car. Now,' Sinead urged , setting off toward s the vehicle at a rate of knots.

Tyler was grateful she was lad en d own by the baby bump, because without it he reckoned she'd have broken into a sprint.

She still got to the car before him, and was alread y impatiently tapping her hand s on the steering wheel when he got into the passenger seat besid e her.

Back at the caravan, the light in the living area went out, plunging the whole place into d arkness.

'What's the big rush to get out all of a sud d en?' Tyler asked . 'Did you see something on his computer?'

Sinead nod d ed . 'I think I d id , yeah. Just a glimpse. Just for a second .'

Tyler flinched . 'God . Wasn't some weird o porn thing, was it?'

'No. Nothing like that,' Sinead said . She turned to her husband . 'He was looking at a Facebook page.'

'Nothing strange about that,' Tyler said .

'It was Orla Coull's Facebook page,' Sinead revealed .

'Oh!' Tyler sat up so straight and so sud d enly that the back of his head thumped against the car seat's head rest. 'Oh, shit! Are you sure?'

'No,' Sinead ad mitted .

Tyler's should ers sloped d own again. 'No?'

'I mean, I think it was, but I can't be certain. It was scrolled down, so I could n't see the name, but it was d efinitely a Facebook page, and it had photos of Orla on it.'

'We should ask him,' Tyler said . 'Confront him with it. See what he says.'

The look from Sinead only confirmed what he alread y knew. Without a warrant, they should n't have been looking at the laptop in the first place. Confront him, and he'd know they had . They could get into serious trouble for that sort of thing. And , more importantly, it could jeopard ise the whole investigation.

'Bollocks,' Tyler muttered . 'We can tell the boss, though, right?'

Sinead hesitated , but only for a moment, then she nod d ed . Tyler relaxed into his seat.

'Good . The boss'll know what to d o,' he said . 'The boss *always* knows what to d o.'

Chapter 17

Logan was at a complete loss. Sinead had assured him that the B&B she'd booked him into was easy to find . 'Impossible to miss', had been her exact word s. And yet, here he was backtracking along the same street for the third time, the strap of his battered leather hold all d igging d eeper and d eeper into his should er.

As he walked , he stopped at each gate and peered along the d arkened paths, checking the names on the signs fixed to the walls of each house. Find ing the one he was looking for should have been easy, given that the name—*Off the Beaten Track*—was so rid iculously long it would require a sign at least twice as big as any of the others.

But, no. Try as he might, his accommod ation for the evening continued to remain elusive.

Salvation came in the form of a young couple who came strolling around the corner, the fiery tips of their cigarettes glowing in the d arkness.

They were in their late teens, he thought, as he got up close. One half of the d uo was a tousled -haired young man shivering in a T-shirt and jeans. The girl with him was taller, but looked younger, with a bob of silver-blond e hair, and enough common sense to be wearing a jacket.

They both looked startled —a little bit terrified , even—when he summoned them with a 'Haw! You pair!'

They were also both quick to throw their cigarettes on the ground and stamp them out beneath their heels, like they were afraid of being caught in the act by their parents.

'Who, us?' asked the lad .

'Well, I d on't see any other bugger around here,' Logan pointed out, stopping in front of them. The pavement wasn't particularly narrow, but the sheer scale of him meant he almost completely blocked their path. 'I'm looking for somewhere.'

The girl slipped in behind her male companion, her wid e eyes looking away, clearly happy to let him d o all the talking.

'Well d one, then,' the lad said . He gestured around , all bluff an bluster. 'You found somewhere.'

One of Logan's eyes twitched , just once, as he got the measure of the lad . Mouthy wee arsehole. Showing off in front of his girlfriend , but probably shiteing himself below the surface.

If he wasn't, he soon blood y would be.

'Aye, very good , son. You must've been workshopping that one for a while. Name's Detective Chief Inspector Jack Logan, by the way,' he said , then he pointed to the ground between them. 'You know there's an eighty-quid fixed penalty charge for that, aye?'

Both teenagers followed his finger. 'For what?' the young man asked .

'Littering. That's eighty quid per d og-end , by the way. So, that'll be hund red -and -sixty quid between you.'

He let them consid er that for a few moments, then pointed again.

'Well, pick them up, then,' he barked , in a voice like an army sergeant major of the old -school variety.

They both jumped into action, almost knocking head s together in their rush to bend over and retrieve their d iscard ed ciggies.

'Jesus Christ, son,' Logan said . 'Be a fucking gentleman and pick up your girlfriend 's while you're d own there.'

'I'm not his girlfriend ,' the lassie said . She was quick to say it, too, like she wanted it firmly established upfront.

Despite Logan's suggestion that her companion d o it, she picked up her own d og-end , looked around for something to d o with it, ther slipped it into her jacket pocket.

'I d on't care,' Logan told them. 'I'm looking for a bed and breakfast.'

'There's load s,' the lad fired back.

'Hold your bloody horses,' Logan told him. 'A *specific* bed and breakfast. *Off the Beaten Track.*'

The young woman shot a look at her friend. He missed it completely, but Logan didn't. There was surprise and anxiety in that look. A hint of panic, too, maybe.

Logan looked the boy standing before him up and down, his eyes narrowing. 'You Ronnie?' he asked. 'Ronnie Donlon?'

'Um...' The sound of the lad swallowing would've been answer enough, but he continued. 'Yeah. Yes. I am. How do you...? How did you know that?'

Logan leaned forward, bringing his face a few inches closer to Ronnie's. 'Because I know everything, son,' he said. 'Except where to find this bloody house of yours. So, how about you wave goodbye to your wee friend here, and you can take me there yourself?'

'Well, but—'

Logan raised a finger to silence him. He held it close to the young man's face, forcing him to go cross-eyed as he tried to keep the digit in focus.

'I appreciate that what I just said to you there might have sounded like a question,' the DCI said. 'But I assure you, it very much was not.'

He held Ronnie's gaze until any and all thoughts of resisting left the young man's head, then turned his attention to the young woman.

'Where do you live, sweetheart?' he asked.

The girl glanced back over her shoulder at a house on the corner of the street. Logan had walked past it twice while searching for the B&B.

'That you there?' he asked, and she gave a furtive little nod of confirmation. 'Good. Then you piss off home,' Logan instructed.

The girl looked uncomfortable with the suggestion. 'I'm, eh, I'm meant to wait for someone.'

'I don't care. I'm changing your plans,' Logan told her. 'Go home. Now.'

He slapped a hand down on Ronnie's shoulder, and his fingers tightened like they might crush the boy's bones to dust.

'Your wee friend and I are going to have ourselves a little chat while we walk.'

Their 'wee chat' d id n't come to much, as the B&B turned out to be just half a d ozen yard s d own an alleyway between two other houses, and it took them less than a minute to reach it.

Ronnie picked up the pace as they head ed up the path, and practically ran in through the front d oor, calling for his d ad .

'Here, here, I'm here, there's no need to fucking shout,' came a snarl from along the hall.

The hallway was a grand , two-storey affair, with a curving staircase that led to a mezzanine level above. The d ecor was a bit on the d ated sid e, with a lot of varnished pine on d isplay, and a couple of skanky-looking d eer antlers mounted above a d oor marked 'Guest Lounge' but it was nice enough, and better than the relatively boxy exterior of the build ing had suggested .

A man stepped into the hallway from an ad joining room that had been marked as 'Private' by a small brass plaque on the d oor. He wore a look of near contempt on his face, which was wiped clean just a split second too late once Logan came clumping in through the front d oor, hot on Ronnie's heels.

The guy was in his late fifties, Logan guessed , but trim and fit-looking, like he ran half-marathons on the regular, and d id his share of weight training. He was the proud owner of a thick, voluminous head of d ark hair, and *Magnum P.I.* style moustache, both of which he clearly d evoted a lot of care and attention to the grooming of.

He carried a big hard back atlas in the crook of his arm so it was pinned against his chest, and after regard ing the DCI over the rim of his wire-frame glasses for a moment, his face lit up in a welcoming smile.

'Well, good evening! Are you Jack?' he asked , with none of the viciousness that had been d irected at his son. 'Are you Jack Logan?'

'Aye, that's me,' Logan confirmed .

He let his bag slip off his should er and onto the varnished wood en floor, then shook the hand that was offered to him. The grip of the other man's hand shake confirmed his suspicions.

It had taken him roughly half a second after seeing him to come to the conclusion that this was the same Ronnie Donlon that Ben had known. This man was ex-polis, no two ways about it. Cut the bastard in half and, once the screaming had stopped, you'd see 'Police Scotland' running through him like the lettering in a stick of rock.

It wasn't just the overly assertive hand shake that was a thinly veiled attempt at asserting his authority. You could tell by the way he carried himself, by the way he moved, like wherever he was, whatever was happening, he believed himself to be the one in charge.

Logan could easily have developed the same swagger over the years, but had consciously worked against it. Now, seeing how much of an arsehole it made this guy look, he was glad he'd invested all that time and effort.

'Am I right in thinking you're Ronnie?' Logan asked.

He didn't so much as bat an eyelid as the host attempted to squeeze his hand into some form of submission. Instead, he tightened his own much larger and stronger fingers, and enjoyed the fleeting moment of shock on the other man's face.

'Uh, yes. Yes, I am,' came the confirmation, followed by a hasty withdrawal of the hand. 'Well, I go by Ronald. My son's Ronnie.'

He glanced around the hall, like he'd suddenly remembered the lad's existence. Ronnie Jr. had already scarpered, though, so he turned his attention back to Logan.

'How did you know my name?' he asked.

Direct to the point of borderline rudeness. Definitely a copper.

'I think you used to work with a colleague of mine. Ben Forde.'

Ronald let out a single barked 'Ha!' that echoed around the high-ceilinged room. 'Mustang? How the hell is he?'

Logan didn't hear the second part of the question, due to still being hung up on the first bit. 'Mustang?'

'Yes. You know. Like the car? Ford Mustang.'

'Ben's nickname was *Mustang*?'

Logan conjured up a picture of the detective inspector in his head. There was nothing Mustangy about him. A knackered old Sierra maybe. An early model Focus before they ironed out the quirks. But a *Mustang*? He couldn't see it.

'Oh, yes. Very much so,' Ronald said. 'Suited him to a tee. Fast, muscular, a hit with the ladies…'

'I think you must be talking about a different Ben Forde,' Logan said. 'I've known him for twenty years, and he's never fit that description.'

'Yes, well, I'm talking twice as long ago as that,' Ronald said, and something a bit wistful moved in like a fog behind his eyes. 'He was a few years ahead of me, age-wise, but we walked the beat together back in the eighties. Proper fanny magnet, he was. Good for me, since I got to bask a bit in that reflected glory, if you know what I mean?'

'A fanny magnet?'

Logan pulled up that mental picture of Ben again, and tried to make that phrase apply. Granted, the DI had changed a bit in the two decades since he and Logan had first met, but at no point during that time could the words 'fanny' and 'magnet' be used to describe him.

Well, maybe the first one, but never in tandem with the second.

'*Ben* Forde?' Logan said. 'You sure you're definitely thinking of *Ben* Forde, and not some other guy?'

Ronald chuckled. 'We all change, son. None of us is who we were forty years ago, much as we might wish otherwise. What is it he's doing with himself these days? Work-wise, I mean?'

'Still the same.'

A beat was missed. His eyes widened, just a fraction. Just enough for Logan to notice.

'Oh. Oh, so you're…?'

'With the polis, aye. Detective Chief Inspector.'

'A DCI? Goodness.' Ronald saluted. It was limp and relaxed, and there was something almost mocking about it. 'Well, I'll be sure to be on my best behaviour, sir! What brings you up this way, if you don't mind me asking?'

'You haven't heard?'

Ronald's eyebrows bunched together, and he gave a single shake of his head. 'Heard what?'

Logan considered his reply. Small town like this, gossip would already be running wild. Nothing to gain from keeping it secret now. Might as well get a look at the man's face when he first heard the news.

'Orla Coull. The girl who went missing a few months back?'

Ronald didn't turn to look in the direction his son had gone. Logan noted the mental effort that this took.

'What about her?'

'She was found dead today.'

Still no movement of the eyes. Nor, for that matter, the rest of Ronald's face. He was holding it all steady, holding it all together.

'Oh, no,' he said.

'Oh *yes*, I'm afraid,' Logan replied.

'Damn. Oh. That's awful. Just... horrible. Always hoped she'd turn up someday, full of stories,' Ronald said. His face suddenly looked like it was thinning, the skin hugging his skull like shrink-wrap. 'Never believed it, of course. Not really. Not deep down. Once you've seen a few of these things, you know how they usually play out.'

'Aye,' Logan agreed. 'Usually.'

'Was she buried somewhere?'

'No.'

'No? What, so...?' His eyes darted around, searching the detective's face. 'She was just left out all this time?'

'She hasn't been dead long,' Logan told him, and if the look of shock on Ronald's face wasn't genuine, then he had some serious acting chops.

'Oh. Right.' The other man continued to stare at Logan for a few seconds. 'Well, that blows my theory out of the water. I assumed she was killed back when she was abducted.'

'Who said she was abducted?' Logan asked.

'Well, it's a reasonable conclusion to draw, isn't it?' Ronald ventured. 'Especially now, given her body turning up like it has.'

Logan was about to press the topic, when the first few bars of Gloria Gaynor's *I Will Survive* came piping up from nowhere. Both men frowned, each expecting the other to take responsibility for the sudden arrival of the music, which was clearly coming from one of them.

It was only Ronald's failure to react that made Logan reach a hand into his coat pocket. He felt the vibrations of his phone right away, and when he took it out, Shona's name was emblazoned across the screen, along with a photo of her wearing a beard mad e of tinfoil.

'The hell…?' Logan muttered , then he remembered where he was, and quickly silenced the mobile. 'Sorry, I'd better take this. Could be important.'

'Right. Yes, of course. Of course. The siren call of d uty must not—*cannot*—be resisted !' Ronald said , and he laughed like he'd sa something funny.

If he had , Logan had clearly missed it.

Ronald reached into a box mounted on the wall besid e the d oo and prod uced an enormous d iamond -shaped key ring with a tiny Ya key d angling from it. 'If you'd like to follow me, I'll take you to your room.'

'Great. Cheers,' Logan said . He hesitated , not yet following. 'And the person who booked me in, she said you take d ogs?'

'We d o, yes. Assuming they're well-behaved and house-trained ,' Ronald replied .

'He is, aye,' Logan said , leaving off the 'mostly' and 'sometimes' he should technically have followed up with.

'And is he…? Are we talking canine unit?'

Logan snorted . 'Christ, no. This one can barely find his own arse, never mind anything else.' He met the other man's eye. 'Why? You're not worried about anything, are you, Ronald ?'

'Haha. No. Only my carpets, I assure you,' Ronald replied , then he continued across the hallway. 'Now, I'll show you your room, then you can go bring the mutt in, and take your phone call.' He smiled back over his should er. Once again, there was something sarcastic about it. 'Far be it from me to get in your way.'

He stopped sud d enly, and Logan almost walked right up the back of him.

'Oh, but while you're here, you must d o me a favour.'

'And what's that?' Logan asked .

'Bring Mustang round some time. Let's all have a d rink. Set the world to rights, like only old polismen can.'

Logan nod d ed . 'Aye,' he said . 'I'll see what I can d o.'

Five minutes later, as Taggart set off to explore the bed room with his nose, Logan returned Shona's call. Before he got onto the reason for her phoning him, though, he quickly wanted to clear a few things up.

'Did you change my ringtone?' he asked, once the usual greetings and niceties were taken care of.

'What? Oh, yeah. I d id!' came the reply d own the line, and there was something joyous sound ing in her voice. 'It's just for when I phone, though. Changed it to *I Will Survive*. You know, the Gloria Gaynor song?'

'Oh, I know. It just rang when I was talking to the guy who owns this guest house,' he told her, and he heard her stifling a giggle.

'Well, I'm sure he enjoyed it. It's a big gay anthem.'

'He d id n't strike me as a big gay anthem sort of a guy, so I'm no' sure he was a fan,' Logan said.

'His loss.'

'You ad d ed a photo, too,' Logan continued. 'When it rings, I mean. A photo comes up. Of you.'

'Oh. Yeah. Yeah, I d id that,' she confirmed, sound ing even more pleased with herself about that one.

'Right. I mean, good. I like the id ea. It's just…'

'Just what?'

'Did you make yourself a beard out of tinfoil just for that photo?'

'No! What? No, God! Of course not,' Shona laughed. 'No *just* for that photo. I mad e it so I could pretend I was a space wizard.'

The way she said the word s suggested that was explanation enough. And, it probably should 've been, Logan knew, yet he felt compelled to d ig further.

'Why?'

'Just for a laugh,' Shona said. Clearly, for her, that was all the reason she need ed, and so who was he to argue? 'I d id n't have it on for long, like,' she insisted. 'I'm not mental. And I can take it off again, if you want? The photo, I mean, not the beard. I'm not currently wearing the beard. Or *am* I…?'

'Just you blood y try and take it off. I like it. It suits you,' Logan replied , and he was sure he heard her smiling at that. 'Anyway, what's up? You just calling for a chat, or—'

'Shite! No! Not a social call, I'm afraid . Work stuff. Are you some-where private?'

'I am, aye.'

'Oh yeah? *How* private?' she teased , then he heard her pulling herself together. 'No. Sorry. Be professional, Shona, for God 's sake. This is serious stuff.'

There was a thwack from d own the line.

'Did you just slap yourself in the face?' Logan asked .

'Only lightly,' Shona assured him. 'And it was for my own good . Anyway, are you sitting d own?'

Logan was stand ing in the mid d le of the rented bed room, the phone held to his ear, and Taggart weaving between his legs.

'Yes,' he lied . 'What's up?'

'Right, so, OK. So, I'm d oing the PM—oh, you had a visitor a little while ago, by the way.'

'A visitor? What, at home?'

'Sure, why would I be d oing the post-mortem at home? Where would I even d o it, the kitchen table?' Shona asked . 'No, it was here. I'm still at the hospital.'

'At this time of night?'

She glossed right over that and went back to her point. 'Your man was here.'

'My man?' Logan's mind raced . He d id n't, as far as he was aware, have a man. 'What man?'

'Bob Hoon.'

Logan felt all his muscles tensing at once. 'Hoon? Hoon was there?'

'Large as life.'

Logan groaned . 'What the hell d id he want?'

'Dunno. Just said he was looking for you.'

'He hasn't tried calling,' Logan said . 'You d id n't tell him where I was, d id you?'

Her hesitation gave her away. 'Define 'tell him,' ' she said .

'Does he know where I am?'

'He *might* d o, yes. That's d efinitely a possibility,' the pathologist confirmed . 'But that's not why I called , either. That's not the big news. Are you read y for the big news?'

'I'm read y,' Logan confirmed .

'I know you're not sitting d own, by the way. I can tell by your voice,' Shona said with a note of reproach. 'But, anyway, if you fall d own, you fall d own. On your own head be it.'

'I'm sure I'll cope.'

'Fair enough. Right, so I'm about to start the post-mortem. I'm just getting my head into the zone, and all that, and then I spot something. Just spot something there, right off the bat.'

'What?' Logan asked . 'What d id you spot?'

'Stretch marks,' Shona replied .

'Stretch marks? What d o you mean?'

'Like… I mean, she had stretch marks. I'm not talking in cod e. It's not a cryptic clue or anything. She had actual stretch marks, is what I'm saying. On her stomach.'

'Like she's lost weight?'

'No. Yes. Well, I suppose, sort of,' Shona said . 'I mean, like she was pregnant.'

'Jesus,' Logan said , and he d id sit d own then, planting his arse on the end of the bed . Taggart sprang up and sprawled out on the d uvet besid e him, belly up, his rid iculous tongue lolling sid eways out of his mouth. 'What, you mean she was pregnant when she d ied ?'

'No. I d on't mean that. I'm not saying that she's pregnant *now*, I'm saying that she *was* pregnant. Past tense,' Shona said . 'I'm saying that, at some point in the last couple of weeks, Orla Coull had a baby.'

Chapter 18

Logan awoke to the smell of bacon. Or, more accurately, he awoke to the sound of Taggart getting excited by the smell of bacon. The dog sat by the bedroom door, making little guttural noises and whining to draw his owner's attention to all the deliciousness that was currently taking place somewhere on the other side.

'Aye. All right. Hold your bloody horses,' Logan said, shuffling up onto his elbows.

He checked his watch. Not yet seven. Someone was early on the go.

He tormented the dog by having a shower before finally opening the bedroom door. Taggart forced himself through the gap before the door was even technically ajar, then went racing along the hallway and skidding around a corner out of sight.

'Taggart!' Logan hissed, hurrying after him. 'Come here, ye wee bastard!'

Too late. A cry of shock went up. Something clattered onto a tiled floor.

'Fuck,' Logan whispered, then he was full of apologies when he arrived at the kitchen, where a forty-something woman with a tartan pinny and a shocked expression was waving a spatula like it was a deadly weapon.

And, considering the vigour with which she was waving it, it might well be.

Taggart, for his part, was having a whale of a time, running from side to side and barking, his tail going like the clappers. The metal tray that had fallen onto the floor had been empty, so there was no spilled food for him to pounce on, which was some small mercy, Logan thought.

'I'm really sorry,' Logan said, hurrying over and hoisting the dog aloft by the scruff of the neck. Taggart's legs continued to flail around, like he could run in mid-air. 'He clearly likes the smell of your cooking.'

The woman in the pinny looked up.

And up.

And *up*.

Her expression became one of wonder as she craned back to take in Logan's full, impressive height.

'Clearly,' she agreed, then she wiped her hands on a tea towel that was the same tartan as her apron, and picked the tray up off the floor. 'He's a cheeky one,' she said, drawing the dog a dirty look that suggested she could think of a few other things to call him, too. 'You must be Mr...?'

'Logan. Jack. I arrived last night. I met your...' He realised he was making assumptions. 'Ronald.'

'My Ronald.' She smiled at that. 'Yes, he mentioned he'd checked you in,' she replied, giving nothing away, then she fired another look at Taggart. 'And that you had a dog with you. You saw the notice, yes?'

'Notice?'

'About no dogs on the bed?'

Taggart, sensing he was in trouble, wriggled his way out of Logan's grip, sprawled on the floor, then contorted himself so it looked as if he was trying to take cover behind his own legs.

'Oh. Aye. That one. I saw that notice, aye,' Logan said, lying through his teeth. He made a mental note to get the worst of the dog hair off the duvet before he left for the day, then rapidly changed the subject. 'Are you... I mean, I'm assuming you work here?'

'Oh, I work here all right! Twenty-four-seven, it feels like. Sorry. Where are my manners?' she asked, setting the tray down next to the oven.

The bacon that he and Taggart had smelled —or maybe some ancestor of it, given the ten minutes Logan had spent getting showered and dressed —was sizzling away in a big cast-iron frying pan, along with a slice of square sausage, a hockey puck of black pudding, and a thick wedge of soon-to-be-fried bread.

Logan was able to tear his eyes from it long enough to shake the hand that the woman held out to him, after she gave it a quick wipe on her apron.

'My name's Merry.'

'Mary,' Logan acknowledged.

'No, no. Merry. With an E. Like at Christmas.'

'Oh. Right. Aye, sorry,' Logan said.

Merry broke off the handshake and dismissed his apology. 'Don't worry about it, everyone does it. I answer to both, but Merry's my name.'

'Merry by name, merry by nature, is it?'

'Oh, no. I'm a right crabbit cow. You ask anyone,' she replied, then she smiled, winked, and turned her attention back to her pan of delights.

'So you're married to Ronald, then?' Logan asked, still not entirely sure this assumption was correct.

If they were married, then she was considerably younger than her husband. A good fifteen years, at least. Twenty, maybe. Like him, she was in good shape, with a trim frame and toned muscles that suggested the fry-up wasn't for herself.

'I am. For my sins,' Merry said, then she laughed the comment off. 'No. I joke. We're honestly very happy.'

It was the 'honestly' that was most telling, Logan thought.

'Right. Good. Well… I'm glad to hear it,' he said, then his hunger got the better of him. 'Is, eh, is that for me?' he asked, practically salivating over the pan.

The reply hit Logan like a sucker punch out of nowhere.

'Oh. No. Sorry. I don't do cooked breakfasts anymore.'

'What?' Logan asked, and there was a note of desperation to it that drew further apology from the woman with the frying pan.

'Oh, I'm really sorry. Wasn't that made clear when you booked?' she asked. 'I haven't done them for about a year now. Continental, yes, I make up little packs, but I don't do cooked.'

'Why not?' Logan asked .

'Well… I can't guarantee I'm going to be in,' she explained . 'My mum passed just over a year ago. We've been sorting out her house. Slowly. A few bits here and there. Boxing stuff up—bin, keep, charity shop. Working through the memories, sort of thing.'

The thought of her late mother, and the sorting of her possessions, took its toll on Merry. Her expression, which had been relatively cheerful a moment before, now became solemn, and Logan got the impression that tears might not be far away.

Which was why, when replaying the conversation later, he'd conced e that his next question was a touch insensitive.

But then, he *was* quite hungry.

'Well, who's that for, then?' he asked , pointing to the pan.

Merry frowned , looked him up and d own like she could n't quite believe the cheek of him, but then replied . 'This is for my son.'

'Would that be Ronnie junior?' Logan asked . When he caught the look of suspicion from the woman, he quickly clarified . 'I bumped into him with some lassie outsid e last night. He showed me in.'

'A lassie? What lassie?' Merry asked .

'No id ea,' Logan ad mitted .

Merry looked concerned for a moment, then rolled her eyes. 'Boys,' she said and quickly turned back to the hob and gave the pan a jiggle. 'But, yes, this is for him. Ronald —his d ad , my husband , that is—is off out for the d ay.'

'Oh? He off working somewhere?'

'Ha. No. Working? No. Not since he left the police. Fishing tod ay, I think, but could be golf. He's always up at the crack of d awn, always off d oing something or other.'

'So he's not taking it easy in his retirement, then?'

'Definitely not. Quite the opposite. Still, it gets him out from und er my feet, which is good . If he's stuck in the house too long he gets…' She poked at the fried bread with the tip of a spatula. '…frustrated .'

'Does he?' Logan asked . 'In what way?'

A bit of square sausage sizzled as she flipped it over.

'Just, you know, a bit grumpy. *Antsy*,' Merry explained, still not looking at him. 'That's all.'

'Right. Aye, I'd probably be the same,' Logan replied, deciding not to probe any further. Not yet, anyway. 'How did you meet? If you don't mind me asking?'

She looked at him, and there was that hint of suspicion again.

'It's just that the job doesn't make it easy to meet people. Well, not people you'd generally want to meet,' Logan replied. 'I'm always interested in how people get past that.'

Merry went back to poking around in the pan. 'We met through my brother, actually. He knew Ronnie through work.'

'Ah! Runs in the family,' Logan said.

Merry smiled at him in reply, but left it there. She flipped over the black pudding and pushed it down with the back of the spatula. The smell it gave off almost made him groan out loud.

'And that's all for your son?' he asked, gazing longingly at the pan. 'Bit early in the day for a teenager, isn't it?'

Merry, who had just started to move the other components of the breakfast around the pan with the spatula, stopped.

'He's got work. And, well, he didn't sleep much last night. You know... with everything.'

'But he's still going to work?' Logan asked.

Merry sighed in a way that suggested she didn't approve. 'His dad says it'll help keep his mind off things,' she said.

'Right. Aye. Well, it might do, right enough. It must all be a shock for him, though,' Logan said, working to draw as much information from her as he could.

'It is, yes,' Merry replied. 'For all of us.' She went back to flipping the bacon. It hissed when the other side hit the hot pan. 'It has been for a while, since she... left. Went missing. Whatever. We were just starting to get back on an even keel, and now... God.'

She turned towards him, her voice lowering to a whisper, her eyes shimmering as tears pooled atop the lower lids.

'It's been so hard on him. Ronnie. Since Orla went, he's been... distant. Sort of detached, you know? And there was gossip, of course.

124

The usual tittle-tattle, but he wasn't even here when she went missing. He was in Manchester. He didn't even know she had gone missing until he got back. The police checked everything out, and cleared him as a suspect immediately. They were very good. But, of course, that doesn't stop the gossips, does it? No. They still spread their poison around town.'

'Aye, they're the same everywhere. It must've been rough for him,' Logan said.

He couldn't help himself. He had to ask.

'What was it he was doing down in Manchester?'

'It was a music trip. Pipe band,' Merry explained.

'He plays the pipes?'

'I bloody wish. I mean, they're a racket, but at least they make a tune. No, Ronnie plays the snare drum.'

'Ouch.' Logan winced.

Merry chuckled. 'Aye, you can say that again. Lost count on the number of headaches I've been given by all the rat-a-tat-tatting over the years.' She shrugged, then sighed. It was the sound of a woman who had long since come to terms with her lot. 'But, you do your best by your kids, don't you?'

The question dragged Logan back fifteen years, to missed school concerts and days on end spent away from home.

'Aye. You do your best,' he agreed.

'Mum, how long until…?'

Ronnie Donlon was halfway into the kitchen when he spotted Logan standing there. Taggart, who had been fixated on the smell coming from the pan, gave a little yelp of fright, then turned to the boy and barked until Logan silenced him with a nudge of a foot.

'Sorry, didn't know anyone was in,' the lad said. He shifted his gaze from his mum to the detective, before it finally settled on the dog.

Taggart seemed pleased by the attention, and his stumpy tail started helicoptering so fast he looked like he might take off and go whizzing around the kitchen.

Ronnie was dressed in a long-sleeved shirt that was untucked on one side. The cuffs and top two buttons were undone, and the collar stuck up like the points of Dracula's cape.

'Don't mind me, son,' Logan said.

'It'll just be a couple of minutes,' Merry said. She pointed with a spatula at a small, unfussy-looking table with three chairs that was tucked up against the back wall of the kitchen. 'Go. Take a seat.'

Ronnie considered the suggestion, though not for long.

'Actually, it's fine,' he said, crossing the kitchen and opening a cupboard a few feet away on Logan's right. 'I'll just grab a breakfast biscuit.'

There was a rustling of cardboard and foil, then the cupboard was closed again. Ronnie tore into the wrapper, and as he did, Logan caught a glimpse of three red lines on the inside of the lad's forearm.

Scratches. Recent, too.

'Well, what am I meant to do with this lot?' Merry demanded, holding the pan out to him.

'Give it to the dog?' Ronnie suggested.

He crossed the room again, passing Logan on the way to the door. Through the open collar of the boy's shirt, Logan thought he saw a flash of another mark. A bruise this time, on the side of his neck.

But then, before the DCI could say anything, he was gone.

'Looks like it's your lucky day, Mr Logan,' Merry announced.

The detective continued watching the door for a moment, deep in thought, then turned to the woman standing over the stove.

'Sorry, what was that?' he asked.

Merry shoogled the frying pan, and the smell of all its many delights filled Logan's nostrils.

'If you're still fancying breakfast, this one's all yours.'

Logan looked over at the door, then down at the pan of food.

'That's great!' he said. 'Just give me two minutes, while I take the dog out for a pee...'

—

'Ronnie!'

Ronald Donlon Jr. stopped at the garden gate, sighed, then turned back to the door.

'What?' he asked.

'You all right, son?'

'I'm fine,' Ronnie replied. 'Why?'

'No reason,' Logan said. 'I just noticed that you had some scratches and bruises.'

Ronnie fiddled with his sleeve and his collar. 'So?'

'So, I wanted to make sure you were all right,' Logan reiterated. He held the boy's gaze, while Taggart went sniffing around the garden. 'Are you?'

Ronnie shrugged, then nodded. 'Fine.'

'Did someone do that to you? Your injuries, I mean?'

'You mean did Orla do it while I was murdering her?' Ronnie asked. He scowled. 'That's what you're really asking, isn't it? That's what you think.'

'Well, now that you mention it...' Logan said, but then he shook his head. 'Wasn't what I was asking though, son. If someone's hurting you, you can tell us. Tell me.'

'Nobody's hurting me, all right?' Ronnie told him. 'And I didn't kill Orla. I've got nothing to do with it.'

'I'm told that hoodie she was wearing when they found her was yours,' Logan said.

'So? She used to borrow my stuff all the time. Hoodies, jackets, T-shirts.' He almost smiled at the thought of it. Logan could see it there, hidden beneath the surface of his anger and grief. 'She always said she'd give me it back, but she never did. So, yeah, she might've been wearing my hoodie. She might've been wearing my pants. I still didn't kill her.' He put a hand on the gate. 'So, is that it? Are we done?'

'For now,' Logan told him.

'Good.'

Ronnie unclipped the latch, left the garden, then slammed the gate closed behind him again. He took a step away, but just one, before looking back over his shoulder.

'You'll find who did it, won't you?' he said. 'You'll find who did this.'

'Aye,' Logan told him. 'We will.'

Ronnie Jr. took a d eep breath in through his nose, blew it out slowly through his mouth, then nod d ed .

'You'd better,' he said .

And with that, he was gone.

Chapter 19

After breakfast, Logan returned to his room and availed himself of the free WiFi to make a video call to Shona. She was yawning when she answered, so wide-mouthed that, for a moment, he thought he'd caught her in the act of trying to eat the phone.

He waited for the noise—like a Wookie having a particularly thorough colonoscopy—to stop, then greeted her with a 'Morning.'

'Howdy,' Shona replied, picking sleep from the corners of her eyes.

'Did I wake you up?'

'Only in a literal sense,' Shona said, then she yawned again.

At the sound of her voice, Taggart had sprung up from the floor, and was now running in circles, trying to find where she was hiding. From past experience, Logan knew this would keep him occupied for the entire duration of the call.

'You're going to want to wipe that drool from the side of your mouth before you see anyone else,' he told Shona, before realising that the room behind her was not the bedroom he'd been expecting to see. 'Hang on, are you still at work?'

'What? Oh!' Shona glanced around guiltily. 'Yeah. Might be.'

'Have you not been home?'

'I wanted to crack on with the PM,' she said, half-deflecting the question. The picture on-screen lurched as she rose from her chair, holding the phone. 'Uncovered some stuff you're going to find interesting.'

Logan would like to have talked more about her spending all night in the office, but his curiosity got the better of him. 'How interesting are we talking?'

'Oh, up there,' Shona said. She wiped the sid e of her mouth on her sleeve, rid d ing herself of the trail of d rool. 'I mean, not as interesting as her having had a baby, or anything, but not a kick in the backsid e off it.'

While speaking, she'd been approaching the d oor to the theatre where she carried out all the various post-mortem proced ures. Logan heard the creak as she pushed it open, but then she stopped.

'Have you had your breakfast yet?'

'I have, aye,' Logan confirmed. 'Why? Should n't I have?'

Shona took a moment to think about her reply, then shrugged. 'You're grand. I'll just be careful where I point the camera,' she promised, then she continued on into the mortuary.

The live-streamed footage jerked around as Shona crossed the room, then became still again when she set the phone d own, afford ing Logan a rock-stead y view of the mortuary's ceiling tiles. He heard a zip being und one, and thought he could just make out the sound of Shona whispering 'Good morning' to the corpse on the slab.

Then her face appeared on-screen, looking d own at the camera, fully masked up.

'Right, hello!' she said, and she gave him a little wave like she was seeing him for the first time in ages.

The greeting set Taggart off with renewed purpose, and he began trying to burrow und er the bed in search of her.

'Cut it out, you d aft bugger,' Logan spat. Then, when he saw the look of confusion on Shona's face, quickly ad d ed, 'The d og, not you.'

'Ah. Right. Good,' she replied. 'Now, I'm going start by answering the question I know you're going to ask me.'

Logan went ahead and asked it, anyway. 'Was she murd ered?'

'That's the one. And, actually, I lied. I can't fully answer it, but I'm going to half answer it. Because I can't say *definitively* that she was murd ered,' Shona ad mitted, her voice slightly muffled by the protective mask. 'But what I *can* say, is that she had a pretty rough time of it over the past few months. We're looking at multiple fractures— wrist, three ribs, couple of fingers, eye socket, left heel, and ... actually, I think that's the lot.'

'Sound s like more than enough.'

'Yeah, rough time of it, like I say. They were at various stages of knitting together, so they d id n't all happen at once. I d on't know if that makes it better or worse for the poor girl, mind you, but I'm leaning heavily toward s worse.'

'How far back d o they go?' Logan asked .

'I'd say five or six months, so around the time she d isappeared .'

'So, d o we think she was being beaten?'

'Well, sure, either that or she was a right clumsy bastard ,' Shona said . 'But you'd have to really go some to be that accid ent prone, so yes. I'd say she was beaten. Repeated ly, and pretty savagely, too.'

'Someone was hold ing her against her will, then,' Logan reasoned .

'I'd say that's likely, yes,' Shona agreed . She picked up the phone and the image on-screen lurched sud d enly. 'And look, I'm going to show you something.'

Logan braced himself. He'd seen enough d ead bod ies over the years that he was comfortable enough d ealing with them—especially remotely, where the filter of a screen and the lack of smell mad e it easier to imagine them as not quite real.

But the younger ones still got to him. And while Orla Coull was technically an ad ult, he wasn't relishing the thought of seeing whatever Shona had to show him.

She tilted her phone d own. Logan saw a flash of the d ead girl's face, silent and sombre, then the image settled on her throat.

'Can you see that?' Shona asked .

'It's a bit blurry,' Logan told her, and she moved back and forth a little until the image sharpened .

'Better?'

'Much,' the DCI confirmed .

'Right, OK. Can you see those marks?'

Logan brought his phone closer and peered at it. He tried pinch-zooming the image, only to d iscover that vid eo calls d id n't work the same way as photographs, and so nothing happened .

'What am I looking at?' he asked . 'Not seeing much on this screen.'

'Right. OK. Well, you see these?'

The tip of a pencil appeared from the right and hovered above a series of tiny, irregularly spaced d ots on the front of the victim's throat. There were d ifferent shad es of red , some d arker than others. More old wound s, Logan assumed , though he could n't explain what they were.

'Aye, I see them,' he said . 'What d id that? Mid ges?'

'Not unless they were armed ,' Shona said . 'It took me a minute or two to figure it out. Longer, actually, but I think I got there. Hang on, I'll give you a clue.'

The pencil was withd rawn. The image shook as Shona moved around , and then a shiny blad e entered the frame from the same sid e the pencil had .

'A scalpel?'

'Well, probably not a scalpel, no, but a knife of some kind ,' Shona replied . 'Pointy end pressed against the throat on several d ifferent occasions. Like, to threaten her, maybe. Or to keep her quiet.'

The bed Logan was sitting on creaked as he shifted his weight around . He could feel the first stirrings of anger in his gut now.

'Or to control her,' he said . 'To make her d o… something she d id n't want to d o.'

Shona d id n't say anything to that. The picture on-screen showed the speckled wound s, and the curve of Orla's chin, still plump with baby fat.

'Anything und er the fingernails?' Logan asked . 'Any sign that she'd scratched her attacker?'

'Afraid not,' Shona said . 'Could n't really get any samples. She had n't been in the water that long, but she'd been in it long enough.'

'Right. Fair enough,' Logan said .

Nothing to suggest, then, that Orla had been the one to give Ronnie Jr. those scratches on his arm, but nothing to rule it out, either.

'Anything else?' the DCI asked .

'Uh, yeah. Few things,' Shona said . 'Holes in her feet for one thing.'

'Holes in her feet?'

'Little ones. Like she'd been stand ing on d rawing pins, or something, but close together.'

'Jesus.' Logan stood up and looked around the room. 'Hang on, I'll get a pen and write all this d own.'

'Grand ,' said Shona. She turned the camera back to herself, and this time she was the one left with a view of the ceiling as Logan went off to search his coat pockets for his notebook. 'Nice lightshad e,' she remarked . 'Is that glass?'

Logan glanced up at it. 'Um, aye? I d on't know,' he ad mitted , rummaging in the pockets of the coat that hung on the back of the bed room d oor.

'We should get one of those for the top hall. Oh! How was your breakfast, by the way?' Shona asked from where she'd been aband oned on the bed . 'Have anything nice?'

'Got you, ye bastard ,' Logan said , fishing his notebook and pen from the last of his pockets. He returned to the bed , sat d own, and picked up the phone again. 'Sorry, what was that?'

'Your breakfast. How was it?' Shona asked .

'Eh, all right, why?'

Shona shrugged . 'I just thought that's probably the sort of conver-sation normal couples have when one of them's away. "How was breakfast?" "How d id you sleep?" That sort of thing.' She smirked at him from a hund red miles away. 'But then, I d on't suppose we qualify as a normal couple, d o we?'

Logan fired the smile right back at her. 'Christ, no. Not by a long shot,' he ad mitted . 'But then, who the hell wants to be normal, anyway?'

Then he clicked the button on his pen, opened his pad , and listened to everything she had to say.

Chapter 20

Hamza sat in his car, d rinking coffee from a slim Thermos flask, and watching the comings and goings in the Burnett Road Police Station car park. He'd arranged to meet Dave David son at quarter past six, and while it was just a few minutes past that time, he was impatient to get on the road and get ahead of the morning rush.

If they left soon, they'd get to Kyle of Lochalsh just before eight, assuming the traffic behaved itself. The router that would bring WiFi to the station was in the boot, alongsid e a new printer, and his overnight bag, which he'd packed with enough clothes for a couple of d ays.

Amira and Kamila had both been asleep when he got home last night, and given how little time it felt like he'd spent in bed , d riving home felt like it had been a largely pointless exercise.

Especially consid ering how little he'd actually slept after d iscovering the email that had arrived earlier in the d ay. He'd been too busy to notice it until he got home, and found it tucked between some news of an upcoming training course, and the preliminary find ings from Geoff Palmer's team, which had been sent to the MIT's shared inbox and copied to all the ind ivid ual members.

He'd read the email three or four times in its entirety. Not that this took long, given the relative brevity of the message.

After that, he thought about d eleting it.

Then he thought about replying.

Eventually, he d ecid ed to hang fire. To let the contents of the message bed in a bit. No point being too hasty about it. No point rushing into anything.

While he waited in the car, he took out his phone, opened the email app, and read it again. Nothing about it had changed . Of course, it had n't. Why would it have?

Even now, in the cold light of d ay, the d ecision it was asking him to make was not any easier.

He put the phone away again, checked his mirrors for any sign of Dave's car, then tapped his fingers on the wheel in time with the music playing from the rad io. It was tuned to a local station, Moray Firth Rad io, and the lassie hosting the show seemed particularly energetic this morning. He'd hoped he might be able to absorb some of that d rive and enthusiasm for himself, but instead the relentlessness of it was starting to grate on him, and he was relieved when she finally shut up and played a track.

Nothing against the woman, of course. She had a job to d o, and he was sure she was very good at it. It was just that, at this time of the morning, after turning in late, getting up early, and having very little sleep in between, everything about her irritated the shit out of him.

Hamza was just taking another sip from his flask when a Peugeot hatchback screeched into the space besid e him on the left, tyres prac- tically belching out smoke as the engine coughed and spluttered its way into an exhausted silence.

He wiped some spilled coffee from his tie, and was met by a nod and a thumbs-up from the new arrival.

'Open your d oor,' Dave mouthed , pointing to the passenger sid e of the DS's car.

Hamza stretched across and pulled the hand le, then watched as Dave opened the d oor of his own car, and hauled himself effortlessly across the gap like a monkey on a climbing frame.

'All right?' he asked , his broad face d rawing up into a grin. He was wearing his stand ard issue shirt and tie, but looked like he'd fallen into both of them from a height. 'Do us a favour and grab my chair out of my car, will you?' he asked , gesturing to his own vehicle with a thumb. 'I'd d o it, but your legs work, so you'll be quicker.'

Hamza screwed the lid back on his flask, then stretched behind them and tucked it into the pocket in the back of Dave's seat.

'Sure,' he said, opening his door. 'Give me a minute.'

He got out, walked around to the back of Dave's car, then wrestled the folded-up wheelchair free. With some difficulty, he managed to transfer it into the boot of his car next to all the other stuff, then closed the lid, dusted off his hands, and returned to the driver's seat.

He had just planted his backside in it when the passenger door behind him was pulled open from outside. Hamza and Dave both jerked their heads around in time to see Hoon sliding into the middle of the rear bench seats. He placed his feet on either side of the bump that ran the length of the floor, so his legs were in full manspread mode.

'All right, ya pair of fuds?' he asked.

It took Hamza a few seconds to formulate a response. Even then, it wasn't worth the wait.

'Umm...' he said.

'You're fucking whatshisname, aren't you?' Hoon said, flicking an index finger in Dave's direction. 'You're that, eh, what's it again? The wheelchair lad.'

Dave's wide brow furrowed. 'Actually, Wheelchair Lad's my super-hero alter ego. Most people just call me Dave.'

'Dave!' Hoon struck the back of both front seats, bumping the occupants forward and back. 'That's it! Dave. Should've got that, too. He looks like a fucking Dave, doesn't he? You've got a Dave face.'

'A Dave face?'

'Aye. A face like a Dave,' Hoon clarified. 'Getting real fucking Dave vibes off you from back here.'

It wasn't clear if this was an insult, a compliment, or merely an observation, so Dave wasn't quite sure how to react. In the end, he settled for a half-shrug, and a mumbled 'Cheers', which seemed to satisfy the man in the back.

'Right, we hitting the fucking road then or what?' Hoon asked. 'Because if we don't get a shifty on, I'm going to need to stop for a shite.'

Hamza adjusted himself so he could turn a little further in his seat. 'What do you mean?' he asked.

136

Hoon stared back at him, his face lined with an irritable sort of confusion. 'Well, you don't want me shiteing in your car, I'm assuming?'

'No. I mean... why are you here?' Hamza asked, fighting the instinct to add, 'sir,' at the end of the question. 'Why are we "hitting the road"?'

'Well, because I can't exactly take my own fucking car, can I?' Hoon scoffed, like this was the most absurd thing he'd ever heard. 'Sister's using it. Well, I say she's using it, daft bastard reversed it into a fucking wall a couple of days ago. New fucking car, too!'

He sniffed and crossed his arms over his chest.

'Well, I mean, obviously it's no' a *new* new car, I'm no' a fucking mug, but it's new to me. Decent, too. Or it was until she arse-ended it into that fucking wall. Daft bint's no' even got a licence. So, was she insured? Was she fuck.'

Hamza looked across the gap at Dave Davidson. The constable, sensibly, was leaving this one to the more senior officer, and the only assistance he offered was a shrug and a raised eyebrow.

From the radio, the morning presenter launched into another burst of excited half-gibberish.

'I'm sorry to hear that,' Hamza told Hoon, choosing to completely ignore all the reported criminality in the former Detective Superintendent's outburst. 'But I meant, why are you here in a sort of... broader sense?'

'What are you asking me here, son, the fucking meaning of life or something?'

'Well, no. Not that broad,' Hamza said. 'Just... what are you doing here? Now, I mean. Why are you in my car?'

'Same as you,' Hoon said. 'Heading across to Kyle.'

'Right. Got you,' Hamza said. He glanced at Dave again, but didn't even get any moral support this time. 'It's just... why?'

Hoon sat back and spread both arms out along the top of the rear seats, like he was claiming them for his own. He winked, grinned, and nodded ahead towards the car park entrance.

'All will be revealed, son,' he said. 'All will be fucking revealed soon enough. For now, my churning guts reckon you should get a move on before they make a mess of your upholstery back here. Oh, and turn that fucking rad io off. I d on't know who's talking, but she sound s like a hummingbird having a fucking panic attack.'

Hamza came to the conclusion that Dave was right, and that d ealing with Hoon was above both their pay grad es. Best to bring him to Logan. He'd know how to hand le the man. He's had more practice at it than most.

The DS turned off the rad io, as instructed , and had just started th engine when he heard the little cheer of d elight from behind him.

'Oh, fucking *magic!*' Hoon said , unscrewing the lid of the flask he'd taken from the back of Dave's seat. 'Someone's even mad e me a coffee!'

Chapter 21

'Right, well, I just thought I'd pop in and say cheerio before I head back to Inverness,' said Ben, appearing in the makeshift Incident Room with his overnight bag on his shoulder.

He had a look about him of a man who had not only enjoyed a lovely sleep, but a hearty breakfast, too. Such breakfasts were supposed to be off the menu, thanks to his heart condition, but Logan knew Ben well enough to know that he wouldn't have settled for the continental option, especially not if both options were included at the same price point.

He could almost hear the DI justifying it to himself now. 'No point in me subsidising some other bugger's fry-up by sticking to the bloody cornflakes. Where's the sense in that?'

'Morning, Ben,' Logan told him. 'And you're not heading anywhere. Change of plan. Plant your arse, you're staying here.'

Ben frowned, confused. Tyler and Sinead were yet to arrive, so he and Logan were the only two people in the room, assuming you didn't count the snoozing Taggart.

'But Mitchell was pretty clear about me heading back across.'

'I'll worry about Mitchell,' Logan assured him. 'I need old Mustang on this case.'

Ben winced, sucked air in through his teeth, then surrendered to a laugh. 'God. There's a blast from the past. How did you...?' The penny suddenly dropped. 'Wait. Not Ronnie Donlon?'

'Aye.'

Ben leaned a hand on a desk, supporting himself. 'Ronnie Donlon was at it with the victim?'

'Jesus, no! Ronnie junior was. Ronnie senior is his father. Speaks very highly of you.'

'Does he?' Ben asked, and he sounded surprised by that. 'Well, that's good. He was always a nice enough fella.'

'I don't trust him,' Logan said.

'No?' Ben asked. He dumped his overnight bag next to the chair he had sat in for most of the day before, claiming it for himself once again. 'Why? What did he have to say for himself?'

'Nothing specific. Just a feeling I got,' Logan said. 'We can go over it when the rest of them get here.'

'Did you see his boy, then? Orla's ex?'

'Aye. Don't think I like him, either,' Logan said. 'We'll go over that, too, when everyone else...'

Both detectives turned to the Incident Room door as it was opened from the other side. A stooped, bleary-eyed Sinead came through first, her face pale, her eyes ringed with circles of black. Tyler shuffled along behind, trying to guide her by an elbow, which she looked one wrong word away from smashing into his face.

'Morning,' she croaked.

She carried a half-empty bottle of water—and it was definitely half-*empty* judging by the look of her, and not half-full. She took a big swig of it as she flopped down onto the first available chair. It was the hard wooden seat that everyone had tried to avoid the day before, but she didn't seem to care.

'Jesus Christ, what's the matter with you?' Logan asked.

'Morning sickness, boss,' Tyler explained. He whispered it, like just hearing the words spoken out loud might somehow make his wife feel worse.

Apparently, he was not wrong. She groaned and leaned forward so she was looking down at the floor between her feet, her forearms resting on her knees.

'You sure it's no' morning Ebola?' Logan pressed. 'I mean, no offence, Sinead, but you look like a half-chewed sausage.'

Sinead made a dry retching sound, and Tyler darted over, opening plastic carrier bag and presenting it like he was ready to catch anything that might come tumbling out of her mouth.

'I'm fine,' she wheezed. 'There's nothing left. Just... can we not mention food?'

'Aye. Aye, of course,' Logan said. 'Sorry.'

'No bother, pet,' Ben agreed.

Both men were a little disappointed, though, as this meant they'd have to wait until later to swap notes on their respective breakfasts.

'Still, they say it's a wondrous, magical thing, pregnancy, don't they?' Ben ventured.

'Who? Who says that?' Sinead demanded, her head snapping up. 'Men. It must be men. It's got to have been a bloody man who said that.'

Ben crept his chair backwards across the floor a few inches, and decided it might be in his best interests to change the subject.

'What time do we think Hamza's going to get here?' he asked.

'Eight-ish, he reckoned,' Logan replied.

'You not shooting back across, boss?' Tyler asked Ben.

'Apparently not,' the DI said. 'Jack wants me to stick around.'

Sinead, who had let her head drop down again, now raised it once more. From the moan this drew from her, it clearly required quite a lot of effort. 'Does that mean I need to sort out another room?'

'Um...' Ben looked around at the team, and did some mental maths. 'Not sure. We've got... what? How many? There's four of us here.'

'Three, boss,' Tyler corrected.

Ben stared at the DC like he'd lost his mind, then pointed at them all in turn. 'One, two, three, four.'

'Aye, but rooms-wise, I meant,' Tyler explained. 'Me and Sinead share. That's three rooms.'

'Jesus. Don't complicate things, son. This is hard enough as it is,' Ben told him. 'Four of us.'

'He's right. For once. Easier just to say three,' Logan chimed in.

Ben tutted. 'God Almighty. Fine. *Three* of us, then. Plus Hamza and Dave. That's five.' He turned to Sinead. 'How many rooms do we have booked?'

'Four,' she croaked.

'Ah. Shite, then yes,' Ben said . 'We'll need a fifth room for Dave.'

'Have to be wheelchair friend ly, too,' Tyler ad d ed .

He had d irected the comment at Sinead , like he was expecting her to make a note of it. One look at her, however, told him that the team's accommod ation issues were way d own her current list of priorities.

'Tell you what, I'll get on that now and see if I can sort something out for us,' Tyler said .

Logan held a hand up to stop him. 'Don't be d aft, son,' he said .

Ben shook his head . 'Aye, Jack's right. We can't be having an officer of your calibre d oing that,' he agreed .

Both men pointed to the d oor at Tyler's back, but it was Logan who d id the talking.

'Tea first.'

–

Both of the station's resid ent Uniforms were in the kitchen when Tyler entered . Spying an opportunity, he d ecid ed to chance his luck.

'Eh, d o one of you two fancy making a round of teas and coffees?' he asked .

The Uniforms exchanged looks, then they both shrugged . Their timing was near-perfect, like they'd been rehearsing.

'Not really, no,' said Gareth.

'Absolutely no chance whatsoever,' Sand ra agreed .

Tyler sighed . 'Worth a try,' he muttered , then he crossed to the kettle and began sorting out the mugs, which had been aband oned on the worktop the night before.

'How you feeling this morning?' asked the sergeant. 'No lasting d amage?'

'Just to my prid e,' Tyler said , giving the mugs a wee skoosh und er the tap to rinse out any remnants of yesterd ay's beverages. 'And , you know, my knees, my elbows, and my arse.'

'Well, you'll be pleased to know we're charging Mr Hend erson with d angerous d riving,' Sand ra revealed . 'Plus, d riving without a licence or insurance.'

'What's the story there?' Tyler asked, looking back over his should er.

'He's a wee prick, is the story,' Sand ra replied. 'Nice enough lad, no malice in him, but just blood y d aft. Always in trouble for something, but usually just gets off with a warning.'

'What sort of stuff d oes he get up to?'

'He d raws a lot of d icks on things,' said Gareth. The constable stared blankly out the wind ow for a moment, like he was lost in a d ifferent time and place. 'A *lot* of d icks.'

'Chained himself to a tour boat a few weeks ago to protest... oh, God knows,' Sand ra continued. 'Something or other he d ecid ed was worth attaching himself to a boat for.'

'Aye?' Tyler asked. 'What happened?'

'He nearly d rowned,' the sergeant said. 'The d aft wee bastard.'

'Sound s like hard work,' the d etective constable ventured, finishing up with the mugs and laying them out in a row on the countertop.

'Aye. Of late, anyway,' Gareth said. 'Just seems to have been since I arrived, mind. I'm trying not to take it personally.'

Tyler clicked the kettle on, then turned to face both Uniforms. He leaned against the kitchen counter, arms fold ed. 'So... what are you saying? He's just become an arsehole in the last few months?'

'Since my pred ecessor moved on, aye. I'm told that's when he started with all the piercings, too.'

'Right.' Tyler chewed on his bottom lip as he thought this through. 'So, that was about the same time as Orla went missing, then?'

The uniformed sergeant looked to the constable for confirmation.

'Yeah. Yeah, suppose that would be about right,' he said.

'That's interesting,' Tyler remarked.

'You think it might mean something?' Sand ra asked.

Tyler realised that both officers were watching him with a look of... maybe not quite ad miration, but d efinitely respect. They seemed to be waiting for him to say something profound. Something clever, and befitting of a d etective in the Major Investigations Team.

Unfortunately, he was d rawing a total blank. 'Christ knows,' he ad mitted.

He turned back to the kettle, silently berating himself for wasting one of his few genuine opportunities to impress. He started fishing around, searching for another chance.

'What about the window? Did he own up to doing that?'

'No, he's denying that completely,' Sandra said. 'And I'm inclined to believe him, too. He tends to own up to most things he's done. He's an arsehole, but he's not sleekit about it.'

'I don't think it was him, either,' Tyler agreed. 'I had a wee look at the road layout on the way to the B&B last night. Can't see how he could've been coming that direction if he'd been speeding away from the station.'

He'd hoped that might impress them both a bit, but they didn't exactly look blown away when he glanced back over his shoulder.

'So, someone else did it, then?' the detective constable asked.

'Well, as DCI Logan said, "the brick didn't jump through the window itself", Gareth,' his sergeant replied.

Gareth shrugged. 'I mean… you do see some strange things in this job, don't you?'

'Aye, but not that strange. We're Police Scotland, Gareth, not *The X-Files*,' Sandra told him. She turned back to Tyler. 'We're going to knock on a few doors this morning, see if anyone saw someone chucking the brick through or driving off. It's a residential area, so we might get lucky.'

'Aye, well, keep us posted, will you?' Tyler urged.

'Sure. Do you think it's related to your case?'

There was that tone again—curiosity, mixed with a very slight suggestion of deference, like a keen pupil hoping to learn at the feet of a master.

Now, he thought, was his chance to really shine.

The kettle clicked off, and Tyler sloshed the boiling water into each of the mugs in turn, while he frantically grasped for some words of wisdom to impart. He had a very narrow window of opportunity, though, and his mouth started moving before he'd fully thought anything through.

'Aye, well, you know what they say,' he began.

The Uniforms continued to stare at him. He could sense them.

'No. What is it they say?' Sandra asked.

Tyler set the kettle down, but kept holding it by the hand le *Bollocks.* What had he gone and said that for? What was he meant to say now?

'Well, eh, you know...' he said, scrabbling even more desperately for those words of wisdom. For some nugget of insight that would make him look learned and wise. 'Eh, one man's case is another man's...'

It was a decent start, he thought. As openers went, it was solid, and had his mind not gone completely blank again at that point, he might well have been onto something.

As it was, the only word he could think of—the only word coming to mind, and perhaps the only word currently in existence—was 'custard', and he could hardly use that.

Largely, because it made absolutely no sense whatsoever.

And yet, what other words were there? None. None that were coming to mind, anyway.

But he couldn't say, *'One man's case is another man's custard,'* could he?

No.

Or could he? Was it just the sort of cryptic-sounding bullshit that they might just swallow?

Again, no.

His hands were suddenly sweating. He wiped them on his trousers, then picked up all four mugs, two in each hand, by slotting his fingers through the handles. Then, fully laden, he turned back to face the Uniforms. They were watching him with what seemed to be quite a high level of expectation now, waiting for him to finish dropping his pearl of wisdom.

Don't say custard, don't say custard, he thought. And then—thank God—another word finally popped into his head. In his relief, he immediately seized on it.

A half-second later, Tyler heard himself saying, 'Cucumber' out loud.

Shit.

How was that better?!

He watched the confusion creeping across their faces. They would have questions. Of course they would . The main one almost certainly being, 'What the fuck's that supposed to mean?'

Tyler d id n't intend to be around to answer any of them.

'So, yeah, you know. Food for thought,' he said , with an air of what he hoped was mystery.

Then he nod d ed at them both, and with four mugs of tea all lightly scald ing the backs of his hand s, he scarpered as quickly as he could out of the kitchen and back to the relative safety of the Incid ent Room.

Chapter 22

Hamza hurtled along the A890, keen to offload his unexpected cargo as soon as was humanly possible. Right now, in the car, he was the senior officer, which meant Hoon was his responsibility. As soon as they reached the station at Kyle of Lochalsh, though, he became Logan's problem.

Of course, Logan might have a few things to say about the DS having brought Hoon along to the scene of an active investigation in the first place, but Hamza could deal with an ear-bashing from the DCI. Give him that any day, in fact, over a mouthful from the man currently lying across his back seats.

It was fair to say that conversation had been quite one-sided so far. Hoon had been loudly and fiercely critical of everything from the Inverness roads planning department to 'bike-riding arseholes who think they're the second fucking coming of Christ.'

He'd been particularly disparaging about a family of ducks that had wandered across the road just a few minutes outside the city, after Hamza had stopped to let them cross. They had kept their heads high and taken their time, despite the onslaught of personal abuse they'd received from one of the car's back windows.

After forty minutes or so, he'd fallen silent. While this was a treat for Hamza's ears, it set the rest of him on edge. If Hoon wasn't talking, then he was probably thinking, and something about that idea made the DS very uneasy.

What did a man like Hoon sit and contemplate? Probably nothing that would bode well for Hamza.

'Nice that, isn't it?' said Dave, nodding out to the stretch of water on their left.

147

He had n't spoken much d uring the d rive so far—he had n't had the chance—and the fact he was saying anything now told Hamza the uncomfortable silence had been getting to him, too.

Hamza stole a quick glance out of the passenger sid e wind ow. One of the d ownsid es of living in the Highland s was that you quickly became acclimatised to the sheer majesty of the place.

Back when Hamza had first moved across from Aberd een, trips like these had blown his mind . He'd spent most journeys with his jaw in his lap, just marvelling at the sights surround ing him—the rugged , snow-capped mountains, the vast and sweeping lochs.

After a while, though, you stopped seeing it as anything special. The scenery just fad ed into the background .

'Aye, it's nice,' he said , and silence fell again.

'What loch's that, any id ea?' Dave asked .

Hamza was forced to ad mit that he d id not. He glanced into his rearview mirror to check if Hoon was about to offer an answer, but the former Detective Superintend ent was just staring ahead , and not apparently listening.

'Hang on, I'll check my maps app,' Dave said .

He leaned over in his seat and began trying to fish his phone out of his trouser pocket. The pockets were quite d eep, though, and the phone was shoved well d own. It took almost a full minute of d igging and teasing for him to finally lure the mobile out.

He tapped the screen, opened the app, then tutted .

'No signal,' he announced , before beginning the process of returning the phone to the same pocket he'd taken it from.

Hamza checked the mirror again. Hoon had n't moved , and was still looking out at the road ahead . He was scowling, like he was annoyed at something. But then, as Hamza had long ago learned , that was just Hoon's face at rest.

The man's silence was getting unnerving now. Hamza could n't take it any longer.

'How's your sister d oing?' he asked , raising his voice and turning his head a little to make it very clear who the question was aimed at.

Hoon grunted . 'How's she d oing what? How's she d oing at getting on my fucking nerves? She's top of the fucking class. She's fucking excelling herself, thanks for asking.'

'She settling in all right?'

'Aye, like an outbreak of mould , infecting the whole house. Spraying her spores into every fucking nook and cranny.'

'Right,' said Hamza, alread y wishing he had n't asked . 'I see. Well, I suppose it takes a bit of time to settle into these things.'

He hoped that would be the end of it, and that silence would now return to the car. He missed the silence. The silence had been nice.

No such luck. Hoon swung his legs d own so he was sitting upright, and leaned forward through the gap in the front seats.

'So, this case, then? What's the fucking score with it?'

Hamza glanced in his rearview mirror again, but with Hoon leaning forward , all the DS could see was the top of his forehead . Up close, he realised he could smell alcohol on his breath, too. Not a lot, and given the tolerance the former d etective superintend ent had no d oubt built up over the years, probably nowhere near enough to impair him in any way.

But, still. At this time in the morning?

'I'm afraid I can't give you that information,' Hamza said .

'How the fuck not?' Hoon d emand ed .

'You, eh, you know why not, sir,' Hamza said . He winced a bit when that last word slipped out, but he could n't exactly take it back, so he let it slid e.

'Is it because I'm no' polis anymore?' Hoon asked .

Hamza turned just enough that he could shoot him a sid eways look. 'Well… aye.'

The man in the back seat grinned . This, Hamza had long ago conclud ed , was never a good sign. He faced front again as Hoon returned to his reclining position.

'Aye, well,' the old er man said . 'I guess we'll just have to fucking see about that.'

Chapter 23

As soon as Tyler came scuttling through to the Incident Room, he was forced to jump out of the way, clearing a path for Sinead to go racing past.

He recognised the look on her face. It was the same one she'd had most mornings lately, and it didn't take a detective to know what that look—green around the gills, eyes wide, hand clamped over the mouth—translated to.

'Is she going to be all right?' asked Ben.

'Eh, aye, boss,' said Tyler, watching the door thud against the wall in the kitchen, then swing shut again. 'She's just a bit... pukey. It passes by about half-nine.'

'How the hell has the human race continued for this long?' Ben wondered. 'I mean, there's no way I'd go through all that for nine months. Let alone the actual pushing it out part. I don't even want to bloody think about that bit.'

Judging by the way his face screwed up and he crossed his legs, though, he did think about it, and in some detail.

Logan was sitting at the other desk, his phone to his ear, the faint cling-clang of hold music drifting from the speaker. He nodded in the direction that Sinead had run.

'Should you no' be going to make sure she's all right?' he asked. 'Holding her hair, or rubbing her back, or something?'

Tyler adamantly shook his head. 'No way, boss. Tried that before, and she nearly stabbed me in the throat with a toothbrush. She prefers to handle it on her own.'

He passed each of the senior detectives a mug of tea, then took a quick sip of his own.

'Suits me fine, too, if I'm honest. Being around someone who's throwing up totally sets me off, too,' he announced. 'I've actually got a bit of a weak stomach.'

'You don't say?' Logan muttered, having experienced just *how* weak Tyler's stomach was on a number of separate occasions.

He was about to say something else when the hold music stopped and a voice took over. Mitchell already sounded annoyed, even before Logan had said a word. This was not going to be a pleasant conversation.

'Mitchell. What is it?' the detective superintendent asked.

'Morning, ma'am,' Logan began, then he was immediately shut down.

'Yes, yes, Jack. It's quarter to eight. You're not calling for a chat. What's the issue?'

'Not really an issue, ma'am,' Logan said. Once again, she interrupted him.

'You want DI Forde to stay. No. I want him back here,' she said.

Logan hesitated, impressed by Mitchell's apparent mind-reading powers.

She seized on the silence and filled it.

'That was the arrangement. Given Ben's health issues, we all agreed he'd be based at his desk, not out in the field.'

Ben, who was sitting close enough to hear both sides of the conversation, pointed to his mug and the desk he was sitting at. 'Tell her I'm no' in the field.' He clicked his fingers to get the DCI's attention. 'Jack? *Jack!* Tell her I'm no'... tell her I'm no' in the field.'

Logan pressed the phone to his shoulder. 'Will you fucking shut up for a minute so I can hear?' he whispered, then he put the phone back to his ear and addressed the detective superintendent. 'Something's come up in the case, ma'am. A connection with DI Forde.'

It was Mitchell's turn to pause. 'What sort of connection?'

'The victim's boyfriend. His dad's an ex-copper. Worked the beat with Ben back in the day. I think we can use that relationship to build rapport. Might lead us somewhere.'

He heard Mitchell's fingers drumming on her desk, and the squeak of air being drawn in through her pursed lips.

'We can bring him to Inverness. Ben can talk to him here,' she suggested . 'I'm not comfortable with him being in the field .'

'I'm no' in the field . Tell her!' Ben whispered , earning himself another glare from the DCI.

Logan d ecid ed to throw caution to the wind . 'You were comfortable enough to send him last night, when you wanted him out of the way, ma'am.'

Ben and Tyler both froze, bracing themselves for the reply.

When Mitchell's reply rolled out of the phone's speaker, it practically d elivered a blast of cold air with it.

'I beg your pard on?'

Logan should have backed d own. That would 've been the sensible move, he knew. He'd mad e his point. She was actually d oing him a favour by pretend ing she had n't heard . She was offering him that lifeline. A way to avoid what might otherwise come next.

In truth, they both knew what he'd said , but in those four word s, she'd mad e it clear that he could avoid any further escalation by not saying it again.

Aye, well, if she thought that was happening, she could away and shite.

'I said you were comfortable enough send ing him across here last night, ma'am. Driving up that road on his own. And now you're expecting him to d rive back solo, too?'

'I can d rive a car, I'm no' a blood y invalid ,' Ben whispered , but Logan waved him into silence.

'I appreciate that you're worried about his welfare, ma'am. We all are. Given his ad vanced years.'

'Cheeky bastard !' Ben mouthed .

Logan smirked , then continued . 'He'll be d esk-based here. He's alread y planted his arse in the comfiest chair, and by the looks of him, he's got no intentions of moving. So, if he was fit enough to be sent on what would seem to be a pointless journey across here and back, then he's fit enough to sit d rinking tea and running the Incid ent Room.'

He d eliberately left it a few moments, before ad d ing, 'Ma'am', like it was something of an afterthought.

Mitchell d id not sound pleased , but she d id n't waste her time trying to argue with him.

'OK, you win, Jack. Congratulations. DI Ford e can stay there with you,' she said . 'But, if I get so much as a sniff of him being out in the field , you and I are going to have some very serious word s, one of which will be "you're" and another being "fired ". Is that clear?'

'Could n't be clearer, ma'am,' Logan said . 'Thank you for your und erstand ing, and your time.'

'Jack.'

He'd been about to hang up, but brought the phone back to his ear. She'd said his name more quietly than the rest of the conversation, and yet there was an urgency to it that intrigued him.

'Ma'am?'

She d id n't say anything right away, and Logan got the impression she was trying to formulate her next sentence before saying it out loud .

'Have you heard from Hoon lately?' she asked .

Logan d ecid ed not to mention what Shona had told him about her surprise visitor the night before.

'Hoon? No, ma'am,' he replied . 'Why? What makes you ask?'

There was a groan. Just a suggestion of one, and Logan imagined the senior officer sitting there rubbing her forehead in d espair.

'Doesn't matter. We'll d iscuss it when you're back,' Mitchell said . 'But if he tries to contact you, I want to know about it. Und erstood ?'

'Und erstood ,' Logan confirmed .

Then, before he could ask anything more, he heard the *clunk* of the d etective superintend ent hanging up her d esk phone, and the line went silent.

This silence, however, d id not last long.

'All right, ya bag of fannies?'

They all turned to find the man Logan had just been d iscussing stand ing in the Incid ent Room d oorway, his arms spread wid e like Christ on the cross.

'Who fucking missed me?'

Taggart, startled by the sud d en arrival of this total stranger, ran at him, barking furiously, the fur on his collar stand ing on end .

He lost his nerve as he got closer, though, when it became clear that the stranger wasn't about to back off.

His paws skidded on the floor, his back end dropped, and he slid on his backside for a couple of feet, before coming to a stop right in front of the newcomer.

Taggart looked up to find Hoon scowling down at him.

'Aye, well, you can fuck off for a start,' Hoon snarled.

Ejecting a single high-pitched warning bark, Taggart turned and, mustering as much dignity as possible, went straight back to hiding under the desk.

'Whose fucking dug is that?' Hoon asked.

'He's mine,' Logan replied, with a sigh of exasperation.

'Looks a bit daft,' Hoon said.

'What the hell are you doing here, Bob?'

'What am I doing here? My fucking job, sunshine, that's what!' Hoon announced. He pointed to DI Forde, winked, and fired clicking sound out of one side of his mouth. 'Benjamin. Good to see you're still this side of the ground, although just fucking barely by the looks of you.'

'Eh... thanks,' Ben said, though the rising inflection at the end made it sound like he was asking a question.

'Jack, look at you, you've no' changed a fucking bit,' Hoon told him.

Logan frowned. 'Aye, well, you saw me less than a month ago,' he said. 'So short of an industrial accident of some kind, it's unlikely I'd look much different.'

Hoon turned to Tyler, who was about eighty percent successful in his attempts not to flinch.

'And who the fuck do we have here?' the ex-detective superintendent asked. 'This a new guy?'

Logan sighed. 'You know full bloody well who it is. And I'd ask that you treat DC Neish with the respect he deserves.'

'Aye, I'm pretty sure I just fucking did,' Hoon smirked.

'He, unlike you, is a member of this team,' Logan continued. 'I mean... what are you doing here, Bob? How did you even get here?'

'You can blame this arsehole for that,' Hoon said, nodding to the doorway just as Dave rolled his way into view.

Dave blinked in surprise, then looked around at the others. 'Eh? How am I an arsehole?' he wondered. 'What did I do?'

'Shite, no. Not him, the other one,' Hoon said. He pointed when Hamza appeared behind Dave's chair. 'Him. He brought me.'

Logan, Ben, and Tyler all turned to Hamza and glowered at him like he'd betrayed each and every one of them.

'He didn't exactly give me much choice!' DS Khaled protested.

'There's always a fucking choice, son,' Hoon told him. 'It's no' like I siphoned off all your free will when you weren't looking. I'm no' a fucking warlock.'

Hamza knew that Hoon was right, of course. The DC had been under no obligation to bring him along for the ride. He could, in theory, have simply told him to get out of the car.

And yet, realistically, such a thought hadn't once crossed his mind.

'Oh, great. That's all I need,' muttered Sinead, shuffling into the room. 'What's he doing here?'

Her face was white, yet shiny with a thin film of sweat. She acknowledged Hamza and Dave with just the most fleeting of nods, then planted herself in the first available chair and wrapped her arms across her stomach.

'Well, that's fucking charming, that is,' Hoon said.

'Don't,' Sinead warned him, holding up a hand. 'I'm really not in the mood for your shit.'

Hoon studied her in silence for a few seconds, then nodded. 'Christ, aye,' he muttered. 'She *is* fucking pregnant, isn't she? What's up, morning sickness, is it?'

She had neither the energy nor the inclination to reply to him.

'Have you tried dry toast?' he asked.

Sinead stared back at him. 'What?'

'Dry toast. Supposed to help,' Hoon said. 'And ginger. I'm told you want to get as much of that in you as possible.'

Ben almost choked on his cup of tea. 'Ginger? I don't see how that's going to bloody help matters!'

Hoon ignored the DI's interruption and continued ad d ressing the slightly vomit-tainted d etective constable. 'You should try them,' he said , then he shrugged d ismissively. 'Or, you know, d on't. I could n' give a shite.'

He wheeled around to face the rest of the room, and raised his voice like he was a ringmaster ad d ressing the aud ience in the big top.

'So, you not going to ask why the fuck I'm here, then?'

'I d id ,' Logan remind ed him. 'Twice.'

'Did you? Fuck. Clearly wasn't listening. Which I blame you for, by the way,' Hoon said , with an accusatory glare. 'Maybe try being less fucking boring in future, and folk might start paying more attention.'

Without looking, he stabbed a finger in Dave's d irection.

'You. Wond er Wheels!' he began. 'Drumroll, please.'

'Just get on with it, Bob,' Logan barked . 'Not sure if you've noticed , but we're a bit busy here.'

'Aye, well, count your lucky fucking stars, Jack. Because I'm here to lend a hand .'

Logan regard ed the other man's broad smile and raised eyebrows for a few moments, then fixed him with a look that wasn't *entirely* unkind .

'Maybe it's slipped your mind , Bob, but you're not in the polis anymore,' he said .

Hoon's smile grew wid er. 'Well, there's a fucking funny thing, Jack,' he said , after stealing an exaggerated glance around the room like he was checking for foreign spies. 'Because I am.'

'You are what?' Logan asked .

'In the polis,' Hoon said .

'You're not.'

'I fucking well am.'

'What are you saying?' the DCI d emand ed . 'What d o you mean?'

'I mean, after proving myself so hand y over the past few months— saving all them women, bringing a team of cop-killers to justice, to name just a couple of my more notable fucking achievements—some of the big boys upstairs d ecid ed to give me a second chance.'

'My arse,' Ben called from over by the d esk. 'No way they let you back onto the force.'

'Well, no' on the actual payroll, as such,' Hoon admitted. 'But my contacts pulled a few strings, and got me a cosy wee fucking consulting number.'

Logan groaned. He didn't like how this was going. Not one bit.

'Your contacts? We're talking about your dodgy secret service mate, are we?'

'He's no' dodgy,' Hoon said. 'He's about the least dodgy guy I know, and considering I'm surrounded by you fucking stiffs right now, that's quite a fucking claim.'

Logan picked up his phone and tapped to open up his contacts list.

'What the fuck are you doing?' Hoon asked.

'Calling Mitchell.'

'What? What for?'

'Because I don't believe you,' Logan told him.

'You don't believe me?' Hoon looked momentarily hurt. 'Fuck's sake. That is upsetting, Jack. That has fucking wounded me, that has. After everything we've been through?'

'Aye. Exactly. After all that,' Logan confirmed, then he hit Mitchell's name and put the phone to his ear.

Hoon looked around at the others, dejected. 'I have to say, this isn't the glorious fucking celebration of my return that I was expecting. I thought we'd all been fucking oiling ourselves up and high-fiving each other by now, like that bit in *Top Gun*. But, oh no. There's you going and fucking checking up on me. I have to say, I find this lack of trust a bit upsetting, Jack. There's absolutely no fucking need for this. None whatsoever.'

'Aye. Ma'am. Sorry, me again,' Logan said into his phone. He kept his eyes locked on Hoon, who stared back at him, shaking his head in disgust. 'Quick question. You mentioned Bob Hoon, earlier. Is he meant to be here now?'

The reply wasn't meant for anyone else's ears, but thanks to the sudden increase in volume and sharpness of tone, they all got the gist of it.

'No. No, I thought that, right enough,' Logan said, nodding while he continued to stare Hoon down.

'Fuck's sake. I mean, what d oes she know?' Hoon muttered .

'He's come in here saying something about…'

Logan stopped talking as he listened to the woman on the other end of the line. His face went through a range of expressions, from surprise to horror, to a sort of grim, thin-lipped acceptance.

'Und erstood , ma'am,' he eventually said . 'But, for clarity, he has absolutely no authority whatsoever, has no actual right to be here unless requested , and we can tell him to piss off at any time?'

'Oh, that is fucking charming,' Hoon grumbled .

'Great. Thanks, ma'am. Will d o, ma'am,' Logan said , then he end ed the call and returned the phone to his pocket. 'I'm sure I d on't have to tell you how that went, Bob.'

'Sound ed to me like it went pretty fucking well from my perspective,' Hoon insisted . 'Did she, or d id she fucking not, confirm what I told you?'

Logan looked around at the rest of the team. They were all watching him, waiting to hear the full story.

'She said that, d espite her many,*many* objections, you're now available to consult with, yes,' Logan ad mitted .

Hoon clapped his hand s together, then raised them above his head , fists clenched in victory. 'There we fucking go, then. What d id I tell you? The Big Bad Hoon's back in fucking toon!'

'She also said she has no intention of consulting with you at any point, and we're to arrest you if you insist on sticking your—and , I'm going to quote here—"pug-like nose" into the case.'

'Pug-like? How the fuck's my nose pug-like?' Hoon barked . He turned to Tyler, then pointed to his own face. 'Does that look fucking pug-like to you?'

Tyler swallowed and shook his head . 'Not really.'

'No' *really*? But a bit? Is that what you're fucking saying?'

'Bob.' Logan's voice was a firm snap of authority. 'You need to leave. You can't be here.'

Hoon sneered . 'Why? Because your fucking boss said so?'

'No. Because I said so,' Logan shot back. 'This is my investigation. My Incid ent Room. And I'm not having you compromising either of them. So, thanks for stopping by. Keep in touch—though, maybe not too often, eh? And d on't let the d oor hit you on the arse on the way out.'

The others braced themselves. Tyler practically took cover behind a d esk.

To their surprise, though, there was no big eruption. No outburst. No fireworks. Instead , Hoon just ran his tongue across the front of his teeth, clicked it lightly against the roof of his mouth, then nod d ed .

'Right. Fair enough,' he said . 'Your loss. I'm no' going to stay where I'm no' welcome, like a shite on a coffee table.'

'Good . So you're head ing back to Inverness, then?'

'Am I fuck,' Hoon said .

Then he raised both mid d le fingers, waved them around for a few second s to make sure everyone got their share, and went storming out of the Incid ent Room.

Chapter 24

With Hoon out of the way—and once they were absolutely certain he had left the build ing—Logan and the others got d own to business He started with the big revelation first, and watched the various looks of surprise and shock registering on the faces of the other officers.

Sinead , fittingly, was the first to reply. 'She was pregnant?'

'No. I mean, aye. She was, but not when she d ied . She'd alread y given birth by that point. A week or two back, Shona reckons.'

'Oh God . That's… that's horrible.'

This big reveal suggested a very obvious question, of course. Nobod y seemed to want to voice it, until Tyler eventually threw himself into the firing line.

'So, where's the baby, then?'

'I d read to think,' Logan said . 'Right now, we've got nothing to help us on that. We have no id ea where Orla was in the months since she d isappeared , so we can't even guess at where the baby might be, if it's even still alive.'

'Jesus,' Ben muttered . 'Someone must've been with her, though, aye? For her to have gone to term and actually had the baby, someone must've been looking after her.'

Logan grunted . 'I'm not sure "looking after" is the right choice of word s,' he said . 'Take a look at the summary of the PM Shona sent through, once we're all online. Orla's last few months were not pleasant ones. There's a list of historical injuries that show she was bad ly beaten on a number of occasions. She had multiple fractures in various bod y parts, all at d ifferent stages of healing, and it looks like she had a knife held to her throat on several occasions, too.'

Sinead d rew in a breath. 'God . That poor girl.'

'Aye. You can say that again,' Logan agreed. 'No sign of drug use in the PM, though full toxicology won't be with us for a while yet. No track marks or similar, though, and initial bloods are clean. She was malnourished, though. Wherever she was, whoever had her, they weren't feeding her well.'

Tyler, who hadn't said much during the meeting, now piped up. 'So... hang on, boss,' he said. His lips moved, and he tapped an index finger against the tips of the fingers on the opposite hand, counting silently. 'So, if she just had the baby, and assuming it wasn't early, she must've been about two or three months' pregnant when she disappeared.' He looked to Sinead, seeking confirmation. 'Right?'

Sinead checked Tyler's sums in a fraction of the time it had taken him to do them. 'Yeah, that's about right. If she went to full term.'

'So could that be why she left?' Tyler wondered.

'By the sounds of it, she didn't "leave", though, did she?' Hamza pointed out. 'Someone took her.'

'No. She left,' Tyler said. 'Or that's what CID reckoned, anyway.'

Logan turned to him. 'When did you speak to CID?'

'Oh. No, I didn't, boss. I mean, Ben—DI Forde mentioned it yesterday, didn't he? And I just... well, I've been practising for when the babies get here. *Our* babies, I mean,' he said, then he clarified further with, 'aye... me and Sinead's,' just in case anyone thought that he and Logan were having children together.

'What do you mean you've been practising?' asked Sinead. Clearly, this was all news to her.

Tyler looked a little embarrassed, like he knew what he was about to say was going to sound insane. As usual, he went ahead and said it all, anyway.

'Well, like, I've been getting up during the night for a while. Just sort of sitting up, and that. Just for an hour or so.'

Sinead blinked, clearly confused. 'Have you?'

'What the hell are you doing that for, son?' asked Ben.

'Well, I mean, it's not fair on you to have to do it all the time, is it?' he said to Sinead. 'Not with two of them to deal with. You'll need to rest, so I want to, you know, like, be ready. To help. And, like, do my bit, and that. So, I've been training for it.'

'Seriously?' Sinead asked. 'You've been doing that?'

'Eh, aye. Aye. Probably daft, really. Should be getting as much sleep as we can now, I suppose.'

Despite her raging hormones, physical exhaustion, and overwhelming urge to vomit, Sinead put a hand on his arm and smiled.

'Aye,' she agreed. 'It's completely demented.' Her smile widened 'But thank you.'

Logan allowed the moment to linger for almost three full seconds before loudly clearing his throat. 'You were saying, Tyler?'

Tyler tore his eyes away from his wife and aimed them in the DCI's direction. 'Eh, aye. It just seems unfair, like I said, that Sinead should have to—'

'About the case, Detective Constable,' Logan interrupted. 'What were you saying about the case?'

'Oh! Aye, sorry, boss,' Tyler said. 'So, I pulled up the CID case files. It's like DI Forde said, the night Orla went missing, she went home, packed a bag, and left a note saying she was going away for a while.'

'Aye. We know this,' Logan said.

'Yeah, boss. But, according to the notes, on the afternoon of the day she left, she took all her money out of her bank account. In branch, not at a machine. Bank staff said she walked in on her own, and seemed happy enough.'

'I'd like to talk to the staff and have them confirm that,' Logan said.

'Bit tricky that,' Tyler told him. 'They're closed. They shut down the week after Orla went missing.'

'What, out of the blue?' asked Ben.

'No, boss. Been in the pipeline for months before that. Community was pretty unhappy about it, but there were half a dozen branches closed around the same time. Cutbacks, and that.'

'Christ. Typical,' Logan muttered. 'Presumably the staff must still exist somewhere, though?'

'Relocated to different branches. Might be able to track them down, though their statements were all taken at the time.'

It probably wasn't worth the bother to go looking for them, Logan conceded. He doubted that now, six months after the fact, they'd have any new information to share.

'How much d id she have in the account?' Hamza wond ered .

'Just over three hund red quid , I think. Not a huge amount, but d ecent. Cleared the account out, though.'

'Did she shut it?'

Tyler's brow furrowed in concentration. 'Eh... not sure, boss.'

'The main bank'll have that information. Find out if she shut the account or left it open,' Logan instructed . 'Might help us figure out what her plans were.'

'Will d o, boss.'

'Did they see where she went? After taking the money out, I mean?' asked DI Ford e. 'Did they see which d irection she went?'

'No, boss. But when CID looked at the bank's camera footage later, they reckoned there was a car waiting for her out front.'

Logan perked up at that. 'A car? They get any d etails?'

'Afraid not, boss. Bad angle. All they got was the colour—silver— and the last two characters off the plate. W and O. They thought it could be a Vauxhall, but could n't say for sure. Engine seemed to be running, though.'

'That mean anything to anyone at the time?'

'Not from what I gathered , boss, no,' Tyler said . 'Not a local plate, far as CID was able to tell. And there's no saying she even went away in the car. It sat there for about five minutes after she left, before it pulled away.'

Logan tutted . Worth making a note of, but probably a d ead end .

'What about her phone? Any sign of her using that after she left?' Hamza asked .

'Not sure,' Tyler ad mitted . 'I d id n't really look.'

'Hang on, hang on!' Ben called . He set d own his mug and started flipping through his notebook. 'I asked about the phone when I spoke to CID yesterd ay. Hang on.'

They all waited while he continued to peel his way through the pages, lips moving silently as he read over his scrawled hand writing.

'Hang on,' he told them, sensing their growing impatience. 'Got it here somewhere.'

More pages were turned . From und er the d esk, Taggart let out a long sigh.

'Got it!' Ben announced , with more triumph than was necessarily appropriate. 'No.'

'No?' said Logan.

'No, she d id n't use her phone after she went missing.'

'Well, that was worth the blood y wait,' the DCI muttered . 'So it's possible that Orla d id set out to leave on her own steam, but either she went away in a car with someone, or someone else intervened at some point and grabbed her. Do we have a copy of the note she left?'

'It's in the files,' said Ben. 'I'm sure we can get that printed off tod ay.'

'Good . Hamza, get on that, soon as you can.' Logan turned to Tyler and Sinead . 'Did you two manage to swing by Stephen Boyd 's last night?'

'Paed o Steve? Aye, boss,' Tyler said . 'We saw something pretty interesting, too.' He caught the look from his wife, then hastily corrected that last statement. 'Well, Sinead d id . I d id n't.'

'Oh? What d id you see?' Logan asked .

'It could be absolutely nothing, sir,' Sinead stressed . 'And , well, I technically should n't have been snooping, but when he nipped to the bathroom, I checked his laptop.'

'Right. Well, glossing over the legality of that for the moment, what d id you see?' the DCI asked .

Sinead screwed her face up a little. 'I'm not... I can't be a hund red percent sure, but I think he had Orla Coull's Facebook page open.'

'But you're not sure?' Logan pressed .

'No. Sorry. I only saw it for a second ,' Sinead ad mitted .

Hamza sat forward s on the uncomfortable wood en chair he'd been sad d led with. His arse cheeks thanked him for the change of position.

'We could call up her profile and go through it,' he suggested . 'See if it looks familiar. Might ring some bells.'

'Alread y tried that,' Sinead said . 'We looked through it back at the B&B. Word has obviously got out, because it was full of messages from people who knew her.'

'Messages?' asked Ben. 'Like what?'

'Just condolences and stuff, boss,' Tyler told him. *Sorry you're dead*, sort of thing. But, here's the thing. Paedo Steve—Stephen Boyd, I mean, sorry. He acted surprised when we told him she was dead. Acted like he didn't already know. But if that was her Facebook page...'

'Then he was lying to you,' Logan concluded.

'It would seem like it, boss, aye.'

'*If* it was her page,' Sinead stressed. 'I only got a glance at it. And, honestly? He did seem genuinely surprised when we broke the news.'

'Right. Well, we'll sort out a proper interview room and bring him in later today,' Logan said. He very deliberately didn't look at Sinead when saying the next part. 'We should get all this up on the board. Any volunteers?'

Dave, who had been sitting quietly, but could now sense where this might be going, was quick to pipe up.

'Aw, God. I'd love to, but I can't reach,' he said, tapping the arms of his wheelchair, and shooting his legs a dirty look.

Tyler's gaze shifted from Dave to the board, then back again. 'Actually, I'm pretty sure you probably could reach.'

'Well, maybe, aye,' Dave conceded. 'But...' He tried to come up with an alternative excuse, but couldn't settle on one in time. 'I don't want to.'

Tyler sprang to his feet. 'Fair enough. No worries. I'll do it, boss! Leave it to me.'

'Jesus, no!' Sinead said, grabbing him by the arm. She used it to haul herself upright. 'I'll do it. I'm not having any of you lot making a mess of it.'

'You sure you can manage?' asked Ben.

'I'm sure I can somehow summon the strength to stick bits of paper to a wall, sir, aye,' Sinead said, and the sarcasm was so cutting it almost drew blood. She sighed, then forced a smile. 'Sorry. I'm fine, sir. It's not a problem.'

'Right. Good. Well, crack on, then,' Ben told her. 'And no need to apologise. It's not your fault you're feeling rough.' He pointed to Tyler. 'It's his fault.'

'Eh? Me, boss? How is it my fault?'

Ben raised an eyebrow and glared at him until the penny dropped.

'Oh. Right, aye. I suppose it is a bit my fault,' the DC conceded.

'Dirty bastard,' Ben said, shaking his head in disapproval.

Logan clapped his hands together to silence the chatter and get them back on track.

'Right. Hamza, get the new router up and running. I want everyone connected. Sinead'll need access to the mailbox and the printer going so she can get the board up to date.'

'Will do, sir,' Hamza said.

He thought about the email that was sitting there on his phone. Waiting. Biding its time, yet demanding an answer. He'd have to talk to Logan about it at some point, of course. He wasn't relishing the conversation, but it had to happen soon.

Soon, but not now. Not yet.

'Ben, you're running the room,' Logan announced. 'Tyler—God help me—that means you're with me.'

'No worries, boss,' Tyler said. 'But, eh, where are we off to?'

Logan rose to his feet and picked up his coat. 'We're going to start with Orla Coull's parents. Then, assuming we survive that in one piece, we'll see where we are.' He looked back over his shoulder at Tyler. 'You going to be all right dealing with a couple of grieving parents?'

Tyler smiled broadly. 'You know me, boss!'

Logan groaned. 'Aye. I do. That's a good point,' he said. 'So, for God's sake, son, just you keep your mouth shut and leave all the talking to me.'

Chapter 25

It was Orla's father who answered the door, all puffy-eyed and pale. He didn't bother asking them why they were there, and instead just shuffled aside to allow them to enter.

Logan retraced his steps from the day before, until he arrived in the living room. There was a half-eaten pizza on the coffee table, grease soaking through the box onto the wood below. A couple of empty bottles of cider stood on either side of it like guards, and an overflowing ashtray was balanced on the arm of the couch closest to where the food had been abandoned.

'Sorry. Bit of a mess,' Mr Coull said, entering the room behind the detectives.

He was dressed in a pair of brown pyjamas, with white piping around the collar and cuffs. A couple of stains had dried on the front of the button-up top, suggesting he'd been a bit clumsy with the pizza the night before.

'That's quite all right, Mr Coull,' Logan said. 'We understand.'

'Leonard. It's... just call me Leonard.'

Logan nodded. 'Leonard. Thanks. I'm not sure you caught it yesterday, but I'm Jack. This is another colleague of mine, DC Tyler Neish.'

'All right?' Tyler said, offering out a hand. 'Really sorry for your loss.'

Leonard wiped his hands on the trousers of his pyjamas before shaking the extended hand. 'Thanks. Nice to meet you,' he said, then he turned his attention back to the DCI. 'And I'm sorry about yesterday. Sarah, she's... she can be...'

'Again, all perfectly und erstand able,' Logan assured him. He glanced around the room, then upward s to the ceiling. 'She around ?'

Leonard shook his head . There was something almost shameful about the look that settled on his face. 'No. She's, um, she's gone to Inverness. To... well, to id entify Orla's... to see...'

'Right. Aye. Of course,' Logan said , with a softness so uncharacteristic that Tyler shot him a sid eways look to check he was OK. 'Did she... is she away on her own?'

'Yes. She insisted . Said it d id n't need the two of us, and tha someone has to watch the cat.'

Behind Logan, Tyler looked around for any sign of a cat, but found none.

'I see. Is she going to be OK? It's a big thing to go through on your own.'

Leonard sat d own heavily on the couch. The movement sent the ashtray slid ing off the arm and toward s the floor. He scrambled d esper- ately to catch it, then resigned himself to d efeat just before it clunked onto the carpet.

For a moment, it looked like this might be the final straw. The thing that broke him completely. He just sat there, motionless, tears welling up, breath rattling hoarsely in his chest.

But then he swallowed , gave himself a shake, and moved on like nothing had happened .

'She's mad e of strong stuff, Sarah,' he said . 'She'll be fine.'

'And what about you?' Logan asked . 'Did you not want to be there?'

Leonard mad e a sound that might have been mistaken for laughter, were it not for the pained expression twisting his features.

'Like that matters,' he said , then he pressed his hand s together, pinned them between his knees, and looked up at the d etectives with a pained smile painted across his mouth. 'Anyway! What can I d o for you?'

'We just wanted to fill you in on the latest d evelopments,' Logan told him. 'And ask you a couple of questions, if that's all right?'

'Right. OK,' Leonard said , though he d id n't sound sure about it. 'I'm, um, I'm sure that'll be fine.'

He stole a glance at the door. Logan could n't tell if he was hoping his wife would walk back in, or was terrified that she might.

'Great. Thank you,' Logan said.

So far, Mr Coull was proving to be far more accommodating than his wife. If she returned, there was no saying the detectives would n't immediately be turfed out again.

And that made it important to prioritise things.

'Before we do that, though, Leonard,' Logan said, and his eyes flitted back to the ceiling above his head. 'I wonder if we might get a wee look around in Orla's bedroom?'

–

Leonard did n't follow them up. He could n't, he told them. Not yet.

He'd been in and out of his daughter's bedroom regularly in the months since she disappeared. He'd sit on the end of her bed, looking out of her window, praying he'd see her striding along the road with a big smile on her face and a skip in her step.

Now that he knew his daughter wasn't coming back, he could n't even contemplate setting foot in the place. He could n't face going in there again, knowing that she never would.

He'd slept on the couch last night. But then, Logan got the impression that sleeping on the couch was not particularly unusual for the man.

All the upstairs doors were closed, but Orla's was marked with a colourful Plaster of Paris nameplate that had likely been there since much earlier in her childhood. It looked to have been lovingly hand-made, though the varnish had cracked over the years, so it had lost some of its lustre.

The room felt cold when they entered. The window had been left partway open, as if Orla's parents had been hoping she might sneak back in one night and —just like her father with the ashtray incident— they'd carry on as if nothing had happened.

The whole room had that feel about it, in fact, of a place waiting to be occupied. The bed was ready and made up with a pink and green d uvet, and a couple of fluffy cushions acting like bod yguard s to the plump, welcoming pillows.

An assortment of soft toys stood assembled around the cushions like a welcoming committee who had n't yet been told that their services were no longer required .

At the far end of the room, below the wind ow, stood a bookcase, its shelves lad en with what looked like the d ead girl's whole life in literary form. The bottom shelf—the tallest—held a couple of d ozen picture books, their narrow spines creased from regular read ing.

Above those was a row of early-read er-style chapter books, which gave way in turn to a shelf full of *Percy Jackson*s, *Harry Potter*s, and some sort of child ren's horror series about evil imaginary friend s.

The final row held *Twilight*s, and *Vampire Academy*s, and a couple of *Hunger Games* books.

The very top of the bookcase was clear of clutter. There were no more books stacked up there, nor anything else. Prime storage real estate, just going to waste.

Interesting, that, since almost every other surface, from the bed sid e table to the computer d esk, was covered in what Logan could gener-ously d escribe as 'shite'.

There were d ozens of chubby wee plastic figures stand ing around everywhere, all based on characters from films, and games, and God knew what else.

Between those were d otted a whole army of smaller characters. These looked like animals, albeit severely mutated versions. They all had big eyes and swollen head s, and while this was presumably meant to make them look cute, Logan found them all to be horrifying wee bastard s.

Ad d to that the cans of d eod orant and bottles of perfume, the hairbrushes, the art supplies, the magazines, and all the other bits and bobs that lay in a sort of well-organised d isarray around the room, and the empty top shelf of the bookcase was even more intriguing.

Unless they really had been expecting her to climb back in the wind ow, of course. In which case, the shelf would make a perfect step.

'You can't imagine, can you, boss?' Tyler said.

Logan was still taking in the room, and his reply sounded distracted. 'Imagine what?'

'Losing a child,' Tyler said. 'As a parent, I mean. You can't imagine it.'

Logan shot him a look, thought once again about questioning him on his definition of the word 'parent' but decided to let it go.

'No,' he agreed. 'No, you can't.'

Producing a pair of thin rubber gloves from his pocket, Logan approached the chest of drawers. He pulled them on with a snap, then slid open the top drawer to reveal dense bundles of sports socks and colourful underwear. He rifled through them, one-handed, feeling around for anything else that might be in there.

'Should we really be rummaging around in a dead girl's pants, boss?' Tyler asked.

'I'm not *rummaging*.'

'You look like you're rummaging.'

'I'm *searching*, Detective Constable.'

Tyler's gaze flitted to the hand in the drawer. 'Searching for what, boss?'

'Well, I don't bloody know, do I? I'll know if I find it. Right now, I'm just searching.'

He ran his hand all the way around the base of the drawer, then withdrew it.

'There,' he said, slamming the drawer closed. 'Happy now?'

Tyler watched as the DCI pulled open the next drawer down, revealing a stack of clumsily folded T-shirts.

'Would CID not have checked all this already, boss?'

Logan grunted. 'You read the report. Did it sound to you like they'd bothered their arse to check anything?'

Tyler had to concede that no, it didn't.

'Well, then.' Logan pointed to a bedside table with a cupboard and two smaller drawers in it. 'Get your gloves on and go look in there. See if anything jumps out.' He started to turn back to the T-shirts, then thought better of it, and ad d ed a final instruction. 'And mayb d on't smash the place to pieces this time in panic.'

'Boss?'

'The pyramid .'

'Oh! Right. Aye. No, boss. Long as we're not going to be locked in and forced to solve rid d les, you can count on me.'

They both set to work. Logan checked between each fold ed garment in the d rawer, while Tyler yanked open the little cupboard and began poking around at the contents.

'Not much here, boss,' the DC announced . 'Phone chargers, pair of head phones, some jewellery...'

'It's no' *The Generation Game*, son. You d on't have to list off everything you've seen.'

Tyler glanced back at him. 'What's *The Generation Game*, boss?'

Logan muttered something low and unsavoury below his breath. He sometimes forgot just how young the DC was. 'Forget it. Keep looking.'

'Right, boss,' Tyler said . 'And it was just for, like, anything interesting, aye?'

'Aye.'

'Like a d iary, say?'

Logan turned quickly, thinking Tyler had hit the jackpot. The DC had his back to him, though, and was still searching through the cupboard .

'Well, aye. A d iary would be id eal, but let's not get our hopes up,' Logan said , closing the T-shirt d rawer and moving on to the one below.

A d iary was the d ream, of course. A journal of Orla's innermost thoughts and feelings in the run-up to her d isappearance? That would be just the very d ab right now.

Such a find would be far too convenient, though. Too *neat*. Cases like this one were many things, but 'neat' was rarely one of them.

'Looks like Orla and her boyfriend were pretty serious, boss,' Tyler announced .

He held up a necklace with a chunky locket in the shape of a heart hanging from the bottom. There were no photos insid e it, just the couple's names carefully engraved , Orla's on the left, Ronnie's on the right.

'I think it's gold . Aye, like, proper gold . Got the wee marks on it, and everything,' Tyler said . 'Must've saved up his pocket money for years.'

'I know he's working somewhere,' Logan said .

'What as, boss, the head of ICI?' Tyler asked . He pointed to a little gemstone set into the front of the heart. 'Is that a d iamond ? That can't be a d iamond . Can it?'

'I d oubt it. Take pictures, though. In fact, bag it up, and we'll check it out. If you're right, then Ronnie Donlon got a whack of cash from somewhere to pay for it,' Logan said . 'Good find , son.'

'Cheers, boss!' Tyler chirped , then he searched his pockets for an evid ence bag in which to store the locket.

Logan returned to his own search. The next d rawer was the third of four. Pulling it out d ragged the one below out an inch or two, suggesting something in the bottom d rawer was snagging. He'd get to that in a moment.

He'd just started to search through some jeans and skirts when Tyler piped up again. The DC was hesitant. Nervous sound ing.

'Eh, boss?'

'What now, Tyler?'

'I just... I just wanted to apologise.'

Logan continued to poke around between the clothes. 'For anything in particular, or just in general?'

'For, eh, for that stuff I said yesterd ay. In the castle. About wanting to be a good d ad . I d id n't mean... I wasn't saying...'

'Don't worry about it,' Logan said . Both men still had their backs to one another, busying themselves with their respective searches. 'You weren't wrong.'

'Nah. I'm sure you were a great d ad , boss.'

'No. God , no. Not even close,' Logan said . He stopped looking through the clothing, just for a moment. 'I mean, d on't get me wrong, I wanted to be. There were times I even thought I was. But I wasn't. Not really. And not often enough.'

Tyler turned on his haunches so he was half-facing the DCI. 'You must have some ad vice, though, boss. Some word s of wisd om you can pass on.'

'Christ, no. I'm the last person you want to be taking parenting tips from.'

Tyler's smile was equal parts hopeful and terrified . 'I've a feeling I'll need all the help I can get, boss.'

Logan aband oned his search. He had knelt d own to check the lower d rawers, and remained there on his knees while he consid ered his response.

'All I'd really say is… d on't wish it away,' he said . His word s came out slowly. Hesitantly. His usual boom of authority notable by its absence. 'You spend so much time wishing they could talk. Wishing they could walk. Always wishing for that next milestone, instead of just making the most of the stage they're at.

'And then, next thing you know, they're up and they're off, and you find yourself looking back at old photos, mourning for all those d ifferent versions you'll never get to meet again. Grieving for the two-year-old , and the four-year-old , and the ten-year-old . Tearing up over all those other kid s who're now gone—lost—forever.'

A silence hung there in the room between them, while Tyler contemplated everything Logan had said .

'Jesus. That's a bit d epressing, boss,' the DC finally said . He turned back to the bed sid e cabinet and resumed his search. 'Sort of wishing I had n't asked now.'

Logan chuckled , although just the once. 'Aye, well, I d id try and warn you.'

He conclud ed that there was nothing of interest in the third d rawer, and moved on to the fourth. It opened smoothly to reveal a couple of pairs of pyjamas, and not a whole lot else.

Od d .

He closed the d rawer again, and opened the one above. The fourth d rawer snagged , was d ragged out an inch or two, then stopped as the upper d rawer pulled free.

'That's weird ,' he muttered .

'What's weird , boss?' Tyler asked , looking back over his shoulder.

'Not sure yet,' Logan replied .

He tried to pull the third drawer all the way out of the unit, but something *thumped* against the frame, preventing its removal.

The bottom drawer slid out easily, though. Logan set it to one side, then reached into the space it had occupied , and began feeling around the underside of the drawer above.

His fingers brushed against something almost immediately. He traced the straight edges until he found a trailing corner of tape. It tore off easily, allowing him to withdraw a slim hardback notebook not much larger than the palm of his hand .

On the front, on a rectangle of white paper held on with tape, was the word 'DIARY'.

'Well, now,' Logan remarked , holding the book up for Tyler to see. 'Isn't that convenient?'

Chapter 26

Once they'd finished in the room, Logan and Tyler came downstairs to find Leonard Coull carrying a teapot in one hand, and a cafetière in the other.

'I didn't know if you'd want tea or coffee, so I made both,' he said 'Or there's lemonade.' He looked back into the kitchen, like there was some terrible secret hiding back there. 'Might be a bit flat by now, though.'

'Much appreciated, but not necessary, Mr Coull,' Logan told him. He held out a hand, and Tyler passed him both the diary and the necklace, both now sealed in plastic evidence bags. 'Would you mind taking a look at these for me? See if they're familiar.'

Leonard looked around for somewhere to set the hot drinks down then finally settled on the top of a bookcase. He patted himself down until he found his reading glasses, and looked over the pendant first.

'No. Don't think I've seen this before,' he said. He pulled his glasses down just enough for him to peer at the detectives over the bridge. 'Should I have?'

'We found it in Orla's room,' Logan explained. 'We'd like to take it away so we can have a look at it. This, too.'

He handed over the journal. Once again, there was no flicker of recognition from the victim's father.

'Were you aware that Orla kept a diary?'

'No,' Leonard admitted. His grip tightened on the book, and he pulled it in against his chest, like holding it would let him keep his daughter with him.

Or keep her secrets to himself.

'I mean, she was always writing something. Letters, mostly. She wrote a lot of letters. By hand , I mean, not email. She was quite old - fashioned like that,' Orla's father continued . 'But other stuff, too. Lots of things. Stories. Film scripts. A musical, one time.'

'A musical?' Tyler asked . 'What about?'

Leonard crossed his arms over the book. He looked to the ceiling, eyes filling with tears.

'I d on't know,' he ad mitted .

'Oh right. Did she not tell you about it?'

'Oh, she told me!' Leonard said , and his voice cracked into a hoarse chuckle. 'She told me *all* about it. In great d etail, too.' His jaw clenched , and the word s that followed had to struggle out through his tightening throat. 'But I was too busy. Always too busy to listen to her. To really listen to her, I mean. There was always something else that seemed so much more important at the time. But d o you know what? Right here and now, I can't even remember what any of those things were.'

Logan reached out a hand , palm open, fingers curving upward s.

'We'll bring you the d iary back when we're d one with it, of course,' he said , making it very clear that the book currently clutched in Leonard 's arms would be leaving with them.

Leonard struggled with that id ea for a second or two, but then relented and hand ed the bagged book over. 'Maybe you'll d o better than I d id . Maybe you'll pay attention where I d id n't,' he said , his eyes lingering on it before flicking up to meet Logan's. 'Please take care of it, won't you?'

'We will,' Logan promised , taking the d iary.

He passed the book back to Tyler, who was alread y hold ing onto the necklace. Before he could take up Leonard 's offer of tea and sit d own with him for a long-overd ue conversation, his phone buzzed in his pocket.

'Excuse me a moment,' he said , when he saw Ben's name on the screen.

'Of course.'

Logan retreated out into the hallway to take the call.

'Ben? What's up?'

'We've had a bit of a d evelopment, Jack,' Ben said . 'How soon can you get back to the station?'

Logan glanced back at the living room d oor.

'I was about to talk to Orla's father,' he said .

'I'd postpone and come back,' Ben told him. 'There's someone else you're going to want to talk to first.'

–

Hamza—of course—had worked wond ers by the time Logan and Tyler returned to their makeshift Incid ent Room at the station, and all their technological prayers had been answered .

Sinead was in the process of pinning up some freshly printed d ocuments, still warm from the new printer. Ben, meanwhile, was sitting in front of his laptop, chatting away to a man on the screen.

Hamza himself was nowhere to be seen, though the fact that Taggart had n't come bound ing out to greet Logan when he returned suggested they were both off for *walkies* somewhere.

Logan hung up his coat and crossed the room toward s where Ben sat. The snippets of conversation he picked up d id n't seem to be about anything particularly interesting. The weather, mostly, and some general, low-level grumbling about the state of the world at large.

It was only when Logan d rew closer that the DI turned to him and gestured to the man on-screen. 'Jack. This is Campbell.'

'Hello there,' Logan said , grabbing a chair by the back and wheeling it over to sit next to Ben. 'DCI Jack Logan.'

'Campbell was the constable stationed here,' Ben explained . 'When Orla went missing.'

Logan's eyes wid ened a fraction. 'I see. PC… Williams, wasn't it?'

'It was, yes,' the man on-screen replied .

He was sitting in what looked like a storage cupboard , with pipes running upward s behind him that someone had painted the same puke green as the walls themselves. It had been a while ago, jud ging by the way they were scuffed and flaking.

He wore a black sweater that he'd spilled half of his dinner down. Either that, or it was stained with a range of different substances, all of different colours and textures. Paints, varnishes, oils—that sort of thing.

'Dave managed to track Campbell down for us,' Ben said, and from the corner of his eye, Logan saw Dave David son raise both clenched fists above his head in triumph.

'Good stuff,' Logan said. His eyes searched the frame of the video for a moment. 'Where is it you're stationed now?'

'Oh, I'm not,' Campbell replied. 'I'm not on the job anymore. I've got a job at a wee school in Ullapool. I'm the jannie.'

'Right. I see,' Logan said.

'I enjoy it,' Campbell insisted, unprompted. 'Everyone's nice. Kids are fun. It's good.'

'Do you mind telling Jack here what you told me, son?' Ben said.

On-screen, Campbell checked his watch, and they watched him doing some mental maths before he nodded. 'Aye. OK. Should have time before the next bell. Where do you want me to start?'

'The day Orla Coull disappeared,' Logan prompted.

The former constable blew out his cheeks. He nodded again. And then he began.

The call had come in from her parents, he explained. Her mother had found the note on her bed saying that she was going away for a while, and telling her not to worry. She insisted in it that she was fine and just needed some space to clear her head.

The instruction not to worry, of course, had made her parents start worrying immediately.

Campbell had gone round to the house, spoken to the parents, and then had a look around in Orla's bedroom. A couple of her drawers were open, and it had looked like she'd packed some clothes. Her parents couldn't be sure, but a holdall was missing, and they'd agreed that it was likely she'd taken at least a few things with her.

'So they agreed then that she'd run away?' asked Logan, interrupting.

'Half and half,' Campbell replied . 'Her d ad , yes. Her mum was less convinced . She would only agree that it*ooked* like she'd run away, not that she had .'

'Right. And what then?' Logan asked .

The ex-policeman continued with the story. He'd taken statements from the parents, taken note of Orla's mobile number, got a copy of one of her old bank statements that her d ad had found in a kitchen d rawer, along with a list of her friend s.

She had n't had a particularly wid e social circle—two close friend s and an on-off boyfriend —so he'd gone round to check if any of them had seen or heard from her.

'To be honest, I thought she might be with one of them,' Campbell said . 'The boyfriend , most likely, but no such luck. He was actually away in Manchester with some music thing.'

'You checked she wasn't there, though, aye?' Logan said .

'Yeah. Spoke to one of the band lead ers. They'd been d own a couple of d ays by that point, and she'd have been going some to get d own there that d ay, consid ering one of her mates had seen her in the afternoon, and she'd been to the bank after that,' Campbell explained .

'Which friend ?' Logan asked .

'The girl. Forgot her name.'

'Ayesha?'

'That's her. I remember thinking—without being racist, I mean— that it was quite a black name. But she wasn't. Black, I mean. Or mixed , or anything.'

'Right,' Logan said , not particularly concerned with the girl's back-story.

'Yes, so, anyway. It's not easy to get from Kyle to anywhere by public transport come the evening, let alone all the way d own to Manchester. There's a bus around seven that goes to Inverness, but she wasn't on that. We checked . And the boyfriend came back up the road early next morning, so if she d id head d own that way, she'd have missed him.'

'Would n't necessarily have to be public transport,' Logan pointed out. 'She could 've hitched .'

'Yeah. We asked, though, and nobody saw her. It's a small community, so if she'd been hitching anywhere near the village, someone would have recognised her.'

DI Forde chimed in. 'And none of her friends knew she was planning this? She hadn't told them she was planning on running away?'

'No. Not a cheep. Or not that they told me, at least,' Campbell said. 'The only thing that came out was from the girl—Ayesha. She said when they'd met earlier in the day, Orla had told her she had some exciting news. Wouldn't say what it was, though, just told her she was going to "freak out" about it, or words to that effect.'

'She didn't give any hints as to what the news was?' Logan asked, though he suspected he already knew.

'No. But she did say that this sort of thing wasn't unusual for her. For Orla, I mean. She was a bit of a... she didn't use the word "fantasist", but that was the impression I got. She liked a bit of drama. Literally—she wanted to be an actor—but figuratively, too.'

'The other friend you spoke to—the boy—was that Hugo?'

'Aye. That's the one,' Campbell confirmed. 'Nice enough lad. Seemed happy enough to answer questions, and do what he could to help. He was maybe a bit...'

He made a face not all that dissimilar to the one Tyler had made while trying to describe the lad to Logan. A sort of pursing of the lips and suggestive raising of the eyebrows.

'I mean, it's not that he's gay—although, he must be, surely? No, it's not that. That's fine. Whatever. It's just, he's maybe a bit...' Campbell winced. 'I don't want to say *too gay*...'

'Aye. Best you don't,' Logan told him.

'No. No, you're right. Of course,' the former constable agreed. 'Each to their own, and all that.' He hesitated, before carrying on. 'But I did think that it must be exhausting.'

'What must be?' asked Ben.

'Being him. Being like that. All the time. Because it's a perform-ance, isn't it? His parents don't talk like that. Like they're aristocrats from the nineteenth century. They've got no idea where he gets it from. He just puts it all on, like a, I don't know, like a daft wee act.'

'Or a shield ,' Logan suggested . 'I can't imagine it's easy being him in a small town like this. Maybe easier to have people jud ge the act than the person hid ing behind it.'

On-screen, Campbell scratched at his chin. 'Yeah,' he conced ed . 'Yeah, that makes sense. And , no, I suppose he probably d id n't have the best time of it. Kid s can be pretty cruel and jud gmental about stuff like that, even in these... *enlightened times.*'

'Not just kid s,' Logan replied , then he pressed on. 'The boyfriend . That was Ronnie Donlon, yes?'

Campbell stopped scratching his chin, and let both hand s fall into a clasp in front of him. He shifted his weight from one foot to the other, and glanced at his watch again, before finally replying.

'Yes.'

Logan gave him a moment, then gave him a nud ge.

'And ? What can you tell us about him?'

'Well, I mean... not a lot. He wasn't there, was he? I alread y said , he was in Manchester.'

'But they were a couple,' Logan said . 'That makes him of interest. Had she confid ed in him that she was thinking of leaving? Was he the reason she left? Was she scared of him?'

'No,' Campbell said .

'To which one?'

'All of them. She d id n't... he said she had n't said a thing to him about leaving. He was performing all d ay and had n't heard from her since that morning. He showed me his phone when he got back. The text was just a "good luck" sort of thing. She said she missed him, could n't wait for him to get home, and then signed it off with a kiss. Well, an x.'

'And that's it? Presumably, you questioned him further.'

Ben nod d ed to the screen. 'Go on, son,' he urged . 'Tell him what you told me.'

On-screen, Campbell checked his watch, then looked up and to the left, presumably d ouble-checking the time on a clock elsewhere in the room.

'I need to get off soon,' he said . His movements were stilted , his gaze averted from the camera.

'Just tell him, Campbell. Best coming from you,' Ben said .

There was a pause.

There was a sigh.

When the ex-copper lifted his gaze to the camera again, there was a heaviness to them that had n't been there a moment before.

'Ronnie said not to worry about it too much.'

'What d o you mean?' Logan asked . 'Since when d oes a missing girl's boyfriend get to d ecid e the course of a blood y investigation?'

'Senior, I mean. Ronnie senior. Ronald ,' Campbell clarified . 'He was my Inspector when I started my probation. Helped me a lot. Got me the job up here, though he'd retired by then. He still kept in touch, though. Offered ad vice. That sort of thing.'

'Ad vice on cases?' Logan asked .

Campbell laughed d rily. 'I think "cases" is maybe stretching it,' he said . 'Biggest issues I was used to d ealing with was people speed ing, the occasional d omestic, and the od d fight outsid e the Nor-West on a Frid ay night.'

'The Nor-West?'

'The pub. In the hotel. Nice place. Generally no bother, but you'd sometimes get some knob or other having a few too many and getting himself a slap.'

'Right, aye,' Logan said .

'But I d id n't have *cases*. It was community policing. Ronnie— Ronald , sorry—he knows the community. If I need ed , like, guid ance on how to d eal with an issue, he was good at offering it.'

Logan sat forward in his chair, just a little. 'And he offered guid ance when Orla went missing?'

Another pause, followed this time by a long d rawing in of breath.

'Aye.'

'And what was that guid ance, exactly?'

'He, eh, he said she'd turn up,' Campbell replied . 'Said not to worry. She was an ad ult. She'd left a note. She'd clearly left of her own free will. He said just to leave it, and she'd come back in a d ay or two.'

'He told you that? Ronald Donlon told you to "leave it", d id he?' Logan asked .

'Sorry, I'm really going to have to run,' the man on the screen said , looking at his watch once again. 'The bell here's still on a manual system, so if I d on't ring it…'

He sighed . He closed his eyes, screwed them tight, then opened them again and stared straight d own the camera lens at the d etectives

'But, yes. Ronald told me not to investigate. Even the next d ay, and the d ay after that, he told me not to worry. Even when her parents were coming into the station and shouting at me. I told him on the third d ay that I d id n't have a choice. I had to report it.'

'And what d id he say to that?' Logan asked .

'He, eh, he wasn't happy,' Campbell said . 'Told me I was being stupid , that it was all a waste of time and resources. But he said I should d o what I felt was right. He just… he just asked me for one thing.'

'Which was?' Logan asked .

Campbell swallowed . His gaze flitted away again, like he could n't hold the camera's bead ily insistent eye any longer. 'He asked me to help keep his son's name out of it.'

Chapter 27

The call with the former Constable Campbell Williams came to an end soon after his revelations about Ronald Donlon's interference. He didn't have much to say about the CID investigation, other than that Ronald was only too eager to volunteer his services to the detective leading the case, too.

Lunch was still an hour or so away, so when Hamza returned with a joyous, somewhat mud-stained Taggart, the team gathered around for some pre-lunch tea and biscuits, and went over all the morning's findings together.

Someone from Geoff Palmer's team—Logan prayed to God it wouldn't be Geoff himself—was summoned to come check Orla's diary and jewellery for prints, while Logan dished out instructions for the rest of the afternoon.

'Tyler, Hamza, I want you two keeping an eye on Ronald Donlon.'

Ben shifted around in his chair. 'I don't know if that's really necessary, Jack,' he said. 'Ronnie's a decent guy. I know what the PC said, but... I just don't think he'd be involved. Not in murder.'

'I hope you're right,' Logan said. He turned back to Hamza and Tyler. 'Park up near his house, keep watch, and see if he comes or goes,' he told them. 'And try not to let him see you.'

'How come we're just watching him, boss?' Tyler asked. 'You not going to pull him in for questioning?'

'Not yet, no. I want to get more on the bastard first. He'll know his stuff, so no point us going in half-baked on it. When we pull him in, I want us to have something more concrete.'

'Makes sense, sir,' Hamza said, knocking back what was left of his tea in one big gulp. 'Should we shoot off now?'

'No time like the present, Sergeant,' Logan told him. 'And for God's sake, be careful,' he reminded them both. 'I don't want him getting wind of you watching him.'

'Don't you worry, boss. We'll be like a couple of ninjas,' Tyler promised, then a better idea occurred to him. 'No. Wait. We'll be like ghosts!'

His eyes widened in excitement. His mouth began to open.

'If you're about to say that you'll be ghost ninjas, Detective Constable, I urge you to reconsider,' Logan warned.

Tyler deflated. 'Eh, no, boss. Wasn't going to say that, actually.'

Sinead smirked. 'Ninja ghosts?'

'Maybe,' Tyler conceded. 'Maybe it was that.'

'Right, go. He's not going to stakeout himself,' Logan told them.

Both detectives got up and grabbed their jackets. Just before they left, Logan asked one final question of the whole team.

'Anyone seen or heard from Hoon, by the way?'

Nobody had. Logan wasn't sure whether to be relieved about that, or concerned.

'He's probably gone back home by now,' Ben suggested.

Logan's 'hmm' hummed with scepticism. 'We'll see,' he said, then he waved a hand, dismissing Tyler and Hamza.

He waited for them both to leave the Incident Room, then turned his attention to DC Bell.

'Sinead. How you feeling now?'

'Fine, sir,' Sinead assured him. She looked a better colour, too. A human colour.

'Good. In that case, once Scene of Crime's checked it for prints, I want you going through the diary. See if you can find anything she wrote in the run-up to leaving.'

'Will do, sir.'

'It might not be easy, though,' Logan told her. 'Had a quick flick through it back at the house, and can't see any dates or anything. You might need to wade through a lot of waffle before you get to the good stuff.'

Sinead smiled at him. 'You're remembering who I'm married to, sir, aye?'

'Good point. You'll be fine,' Logan told her, then he turned his attention to Dave Davidson, who was studying Orla's necklace through the clear plastic of the evidence bag. 'Dave, get that stuff checked in, will you?'

'No bother,' Dave said. He scrunched up his nose, screwed up his eyes, and brought the bag closer, really studying the jewellery. 'This wasn't cheap.'

'No, that's what we thought,' Logan said. 'One of the reasons we brought it in, actually. Want to get an idea of its value.'

'Want me to send a picture to my mate?' Dave asked.

Logan frowned. 'I don't know. Depends who your mate is.'

'He's a jeweller in Banff,' Dave said. 'Well, I say he's a mate, he's not. He's a mate of a mate. Well, a mate of a guy I know. Well, not really a *mate* of his, just a guy he knows.'

Ben tried to unravel that. 'He's a guy who knows a guy that you know?'

'Bang on,' Dave said. 'But he knows his stuff. About jewellery, and that, I mean. Fucking clueless about everything else. So my mate says, anyway. Well, not my mate. He's not my mate. That guy.'

'Fine,' said Logan, who was already much deeper into this conversation than he'd ideally like to be. 'Send him a picture, see if he can tell us anything. But ask around and see if there's anyone local with a bit of knowledge who might be able to take a look up close.'

'On it like a car bonnet,' Dave announced.

Logan got to his feet. 'Ben, the room's yours,' he announced.

He reached for his coat, then urged Taggart to stay when the dog started hurrying towards the door. The dog stood facing the door, pretending not to understand the command, and only relented when Logan picked him up, turned him the other way, then set him back down again.

'Where you off to, Jack?' Ben asked.

'Orla's mate, Ayesha Fulton. As far as we know, she was the last person in town to see Orla before she left. Which means that, for all intents and purposes, she was the last one to see her alive,' Logan explained .

He pulled on his coat, smoothed d own the collar, then shoved his hand s d eep in the pockets.

'I think it's time that she and I had a little chat.'

'You bringing her in, sir?' Sinead asked . 'Want me there, if so? Young girl on her own, and all that...'

'If it comes to that, maybe, aye,' Logan said . 'Right now, I'm just planning catching her at home.'

He looked around the Incid ent Room. As looks went, it was quite a d isparaging one. The station wasn't the smallest one he'd ever been in, and yet it felt more ill-equipped for the business of policing than most.

'Besid es, we haven't even got room for Paed o... I mean, for Stephen Boyd , if we bring him in. No way we can accommod ate both of them.'

Ben sat up straighter. 'Oh! That remind s me, I might just have an id ea about that. Our space problem, I mean.'

'Aye? What sort of id ea?' Logan prompted , but Ben shook his head .

'I'm not sure it's possible yet. I'm still working on it,' the DI said . He tapped the sid e of his nose. 'So, all in good time, Jack. All in good time...'

–

It wasn't until Logan was almost there that he realised which house the ad d ress from the file had been lead ing him to. It should 've clicked before then. It was, after all, just d own the road from where he was staying.

It was the house of the girl he'd seen with Ronnie Donlon the night before.

At night, in the d ark, the house had looked much like the others on the street. Here in the cold light of d ay, though, it reeked of neglect.

A fence ran all the way along the front of the row of four terraced houses. Three of the fence sections had been painted . One had not, and the Highland weather had greyed and rotted the wood so it looked like a strong breeze would make the whole thing fall outward s.

None of the four gard ens was much to write home about—d rab squares of gravel and slabs. The d ifference being that the occupants of the other three had mad e an effort to keep on top of weed ing.

The occupants of the house Logan was attend ing, however, had n't bothered their arse, and there was almost as much jaggy, und esirable greenery as there was stone.

The curtains were shut both upstairs and d own, and Logan mad e sure to hammer hard on the d oor, in case those insid e were in need of rousing.

On the other sid e of the d oor, a frenzy of barking erupted and quickly grew loud er as a d og came charging along the hall. It was not like the slightly shrill, excited bark of Taggart. This one was d eeper and more guttural—a low, resonating sound that evolution had worked hard to make as terrifying as possible.

Had Tyler been there, Logan knew, he'd alread y be vaulting the gate and running for his life. As it was, even Logan took a step back, and braced himself for whatever sort of creature might explod e through the d oor the moment it was opening.

'Fucking shut up, you prick!'

The voice that rasped out the command was a bit of a mystery. It wasn't local, and while Logan could n't quite tell if it was male or female, he recognised the accent. It wasn't local, but was instead from one of the less affluent areas of Glasgow. You could take your pick as to which. Heavy smoker, too, jud ging by the way the word s rattled around in the throat.

The command d id nothing to calm the d og. The barking intensified, and Logan found himself taking a second step backward when the d oor thumped against the frame, as the animal hurled itself at it like it might knock it d own.

And , jud ging by the way the whole thing was shaking, there was a very real possibility that it might.

'Aitchy? Gonnae fucking get this bastard oot the road !' the voice bellowed .

Another voice replied from further back in the house. It sounded similar to the first, but more nasal. It spoke with the slow, brain-addled drawl he'd heard a thousand times before. A junkie. He'd put money on it.

'How can you no' fucking do it?'

'Cos the prick'll have my fucking hands off, that's how!'

If there was a reply, Logan couldn't hear it over the dog's demented fury. Instead, he heard the rattling of a security chain being slid into place on the other side of the door. By the sounds of things, it took a few attempts.

And then, the door pulled open a couple of inches. A pair of slavering jaws were forced through the gap about two feet from the floor. Thankfully, that was as much of the dog as was able to fit.

Three feet above that, half of a woman's face appeared in the space between the door and the frame. Based on what Logan could see of her, he'd put her in her early sixties. She looked older than that, but he felt confident that she'd spent a chunk of her life pumping herself full of illicit substances, none of which were exactly renowned for their powers of preservation.

Her hair was short. Probably grey, though she'd attempted a dye job recently, and it was currently as black as pitch, while the top of her forehead and the bit of her scalp he could see at the front were stained in a rainbow of charcoal hues.

'What are you wanting?' she all but coughed at him. 'If you're selling something, I'm no' fucking wanting it.'

Logan didn't say anything. Not yet. For now, he was content to let his warrant card do the talking.

She peered at it for several seconds, then recognition dawned, and she ejected a single, raw-sounding, 'Fuck.'

The dog, meanwhile, was so adamant that it could squeeze its way through a space a fraction of its own width that it must surely have been causing itself physical harm. If it was, though, the pain was doing nothing to diminish its killer instinct.

If anything, it was making it worse.

'Right, first thing's first,' Logan said. He pointed to the dog. 'Get that to fuck.'

'It's no' my d ug,' the woman replied .

'I'm not asking whose d ug it is,' Logan told her. 'I d on't care whose d ug it is. I'm telling you to lock it away.'

'Oh, aye? And where am I meant to fucking lock him, like?' she d emand ed .

'I d on't know. Kitchen?' Logan suggested .

She stared at him for a moment, like this had never occurred to her before.

'Give us a minute,' she said .

Then, with some effort, a few panicky yelps, and a lot of swearing, she was able to pull the d og back enough to let her shut the d oor. By the sound s of things, it wasn't happy about that, and the incessant barking became punctuated by a few low, menacing growls.

Logan watched the hand le closely, and listened for any sign that she was und oing the chain so she could release the hound on him.

Thankfully, his fears were unfound ed , and after a bit more shouting and a lot more barking, he heard the firm thud of a d oor being closed along the hallway, then the shuffling of footsteps—human ones—coming closer.

The d oor was opened again, though the chain still blocked access. He was able to see a little more of the woman on the other sid e this time, now that she presumably d id n't have to lean over the d og to see out.

The d og was still going d emented , but it was now far enough away that Logan could at least hear himself think.

'You're the polis?' the woman in the d oorway asked .

'Aye. Well, I'm not all of it,' Logan told her. 'But, aye. DCI Jack Logan. Are you Ayesha's gran?'

'We've no' d one nothing,' the woman shot back.

'I never said you had ,' Logan told her. 'Although, I'd be lying if I said I d id n't have a few suspicions.'

'Is there someone at the d oor?' called the man's voice from insid e.

'God . Nothing gets past him, I see,' Logan noted . 'I'd like a quick word with Ayesha, if you d on't mind ?'

The woman chewed her bottom lip, clearly uncomfortable with this suggestion.

'Have you got a 'hing?'

'A 'hing?' Logan asked . 'What sort of 'hing would that be?'

'Just, like, you know? A 'hing. For getting into hooses, an' that.'

'What, a key, you mean?'

This appeared to confuse the shit out of her, and she frowned like she was doing some complex mathematical equations.

'What? Naw. You know, like… just… A 'hing,' she insisted . 'I've no' got to let you in unless you've got—'

'She means a fucking warrant,' drawled the man's voice.

It was louder now. Closer. A face—long, gaunt, and with eyes so sunken they looked like they'd been fired halfway to the back of his skull with a rivet gun—appeared above the woman's, and peered out at him.

'You can't come in withoot a warrant,' the man said , his brain so mushed , and his words so dragged out he sounded like he was talkin in slow motion. 'I know my fucking rights, I do.'

'I don't want to come in,' Logan replied . 'In fact, off the top of my head , I can't think of much I'd like to do less. Is Ayesha in?'

'Ayesha?' the man said , and from the note of confusion in his voice, Logan started to wonder if he had come to the wrong house.

Unfortunately, it soon became clear that he had not.

'How come is it are you wanting to speak to her for?' the woman asked , in what felt to Logan like two different sentences both trying to co-exist at the same point in space and time.

'That's not your concern, sweetheart,' Logan told her. 'Is she in?'

Her male friend jumped in to answer for her. Albeit very slowly. 'And how the fuck are we meant to know that?'

Logan returned to the top step. Though the occupants of the building were still a step higher, they were forced to look up to meet his eye.

'Because she lives in your fucking house, pal,' Logan intoned . 'Now, I suggest you go and get her while I'm still in a half-decent mood . Otherwise, the only 'hing I'm going to use to gain access is a bloody big battering ram. And either I'm going to find a whole range of illegal substances in there, or you're going to manage to flush them away just in the nick of time. Either way, you'll be saying good bye to your stash.'

He let them stew on that for a moment, waited for them to finish exchanging their furtive glances, then continued .

'So. Ayesha. Go and fucking get her. Now. I won't ask you again.'

Despite his reactions und oubted ly being the slower of the two, it was the man who spoke first. He gave the woman a d unt with an elbow, then pointed upward s.

'You'd better go get her, eh?'

'Fuck's sake,' the woman muttered . She vanished from the gap in the d oor, walked a couple of steps at most, then screeched , 'Ayesha! Door!' so loud ly that even the d og stopped barking.

Although, unfortunately, not for long.

When no answer came from upstairs, Logan listened to the thud - d ing of footsteps head ing upward s, accompanied by a sound track of muttering and grumbling from Ayesha's granny.

'Mind if I ask you something?' the man in the d oorway slurred .

Logan blew out his cheeks. 'Aye,' he said . 'But go on.'

'What's it like, being in the polis? Is it all right, an' that?'

'Well, I mean, it's been going d ownhill fast for the last few minutes,' Logan replied . 'But, aye, otherwise it's a barrel of laughs.'

'I wanted to be in the polis,' the man said .

Logan had n't been prepared for this ad mission. 'Aye?'

'Aye. But they would n't let me, but. I've got flat feet,' the man said . The one should er Logan could see twitched in a little shrug. 'An' I was in the jail at the time, which I was told later that they d on't like.'

'No. No, that's generally frowned upon, right enough,' Logan said . He ran a hand d own his face, muttered a 'Jesus Christ' then listened to the sound of footsteps returning back d own the stairs.

A moment later, the woman appeared again. 'She's no' in.'

Logan sighed . 'Great. Do you know where she is?'

'Naw. She's no' been home, by the looks o' it.'

'What? What d o you mean?' Logan asked . 'Since when?'

'Since yesterd ay. Her bed 's still mad e. Or, like, sort of. She's no' been in it.'

'No,' Logan said . 'I saw her last night. I sent her home. To here.'

'I d on't remember her coming in,' the man mumbled .

'Aye, well, I d oubt you can remember your own name, pal, so I'm not going to pin my hopes on your memory,' Logan told him.

'He's right, though,' Ayesha's gran insisted . 'I mind , last night, thinking that she was late getting in. She's usually in early. Hid es away upstairs, like she's no' wanting to sit with us.'

'I wond er why that could be?' Logan asked .

'Fuck knows. She's a snobby wee cow,' the woman said , completely missing the sarcasm. 'But I d id n't hear her coming in.'

Logan turned and looked back along the street. In the d istance, beyond the little alleyway lead ing to his B&B, he could just see one head light of Hamza's car. The DS and Tyler would be sitting in the vehicle, watching for any movement from the Donlons' house.

The stakeout was unlikely to come to anything, Logan knew, but there was always a chance of getting lucky with these things.

From his current vantage point, Logan could also see the spot where he'd been stand ing when he sent the girl he now knew to be Ayesha back home.

She'd set off in this d irection. He'd seen her go.

He had n't, however, seen her arrive.

So what the hell had happened to her along the way?

'Right, I want to look in her room,' he announced , turning back to the zombie-like pair on the other sid e of the d oor.

Neither of them looked remotely keen on that id ea. Their eyes narrowed and their mouths moved , like they were searching for some reason to stop him entering.

'What about that 'hing?' the granny asked .

'Fuck the 'hing, sweetheart,' Logan spat. 'Ayesha could be in d anger. Something could 've happened to her. So either you let me look at her room—just me, just that room—or I arrange for twenty heavy-set bastard s with battering rams and batons to come round here and turn this whole house upsid e d own.'

Once again, he gave their d rug-ad d led brains a few moments to process what he'd said . Then he took out his mobile, and held his thumb over the little green phone icon.

'So,' he said , glowering at both of them in turn. 'What's it to be?'

Chapter 28

Hamza and Tyler sat in Hamza's car, sipping on takeaway coffees as they watched the house that Logan had directed them to.

It was still early days, but as of yet, nothing of note had happened. Nothing, that is, aside from the eating of the doughnuts that Tyler had insisted they pick up on the way over.

After all, was a stakeout even a stakeout if there weren't coffee and doughnuts involved?

Between them, they'd gone through all six of the deliciously jammy wee bastards, albeit at an uneven four-to-two split.

'I think I'm getting a sugar rush coming on,' Tyler announced, putting a finger to his wrist as he checked his pulse.

'Is it a sugar rush?' Hamza asked. 'Or is it Type Two Diabetes?'

'You're one to talk, mate!' Tyler protested. 'You ate two!'

'Aye. Which is half as many as you ate,' Hamza countered.

'Yeah, well, I need to store up energy, don't I?' Tyler said. 'For when the babies come.'

'Of course. Yes. Because that's the ideal way to get in shape, isn't it? Hoovering up four doughnuts one after the other.'

'Aye, but you need energy reserves, is my point,' Tyler said. He patted his stomach, and the little smile he gave the DS suggested he felt the argument had been well and truly won.

'I suppose that's fair enough,' Hamza admitted. 'I mean, as we all know, if there's anyone with energy to spare, it's the morbidly obese.'

Tyler stopped patting his stomach, looked down at it, then shifted around in his seat.

'I'll burn it off quick,' he concluded. 'No doubt someone'll have me chasing some bugger at some point.' He looked out of the side wind ow and lowered his voice to a mumble. 'Even if I was recently hit by a car.'

'Were you? I d on't think I heard that,' Hamza replied . 'You must not have mentioned it.'

They both sipped their coffees through the little slots in the takeaway cup lid s.

'I Spy?' Tyler asked .

'Best to save that for later, I reckon,' Hamza said . 'We're not that d esperate yet.'

'No,' Tyler agreed . 'We'll maybe give it ten minutes.'

They took another swig of coffee, and watched the house for a while.

'How's Sinead d oing? With the pregnancy, and everything?' Hamza asked . 'She seems to be struggling a bit.'

'Mostly just the mornings,' Tyler said . 'Though, she's more... how can I put it? *Emotional* than normal.'

'Sad ?'

'More... angry.'

'Oh.'

Tyler ad justed himself, turning in his seat so he was facing the d etective sergeant. 'She had a full-on go at the postie the other d ay. Properly shouting at him.'

'How come?'

'He kept knocking for ages. I was sleeping, Sinead was up being sick,' Tyler said . 'When she answered the d oor, it turned out the parcel was for the neighbours. He'd come to the wrong house.'

'To be fair, I would n't have been happy with that, either,' Hamza reasoned .

'Aye, but she nearly punched him through the fence! And she's having these weird cravings.'

Hamza chuckled . 'Aye, that happens. Amira was obsessed with pickled beetroot when she was pregnant with Kamila. Went through jars of the stuff. What's Sinead craving?'

'Jam,' Tyler said , and there was a note of trepid ation in his voice.

'Jam? Oh, well, that's not too bad ,' Hamza said . 'I mean, you hear people craving all sorts when they're—'

'Tuna jam.'

A silence fell. Hamza's eyebrows twitched d ownward s.

'Tuna jam?' he said . 'As in… the fish?'

Tyler nod d ed as he slurped some more of his coffee.

'I d id n't know that was a thing.'

'It isn't, thank Christ. I mean, can you imagine?' Tyler said . 'When she said that's what she wanted , I thought she was taking the piss. But, no. She must be the only pregnant woman in history to have cravings for something that d oesn't even exist.'

'That's… I mean, that's…'

'Weird . I know,' Tyler said . He chewed his lip and shot Hamza a furtive look, like he wasn't sure whether to say the next part. 'I tried making her some.'

'You tried *making her some*?' the DS practically yelped . 'You tried making her tuna jam?'

'Aye.'

'Blood y Hell, Tyler.' Hamza stared blankly into space for a moment, trying to process all of this information. 'What was it like?'

Tyler shrugged . 'Pretty much what you'd expect.'

'What, utterly fucking horrifying?'

'Bang on,' Tyler confirmed .

'Did she try it?'

'No. One look at it, and she came to her senses,' Tyler said . 'I think she thought I'd lost my mind , though.' He knocked back more of his coffee. 'House still stinks of it.'

'Nice,' Hamza said .

They watched the house in silence for a little longer. Nobod y left or arrived .

'I could go some more of them d oughnuts,' Tyler said .

'You're an animal,' Hamza told him.

The DS sipped from his takeaway cup, sid e-eyed the younger officer in the passenger seat besid e him, then came to a d ecision.

'Can I tell you something?' he asked . 'But it's got to stay a secret.'

'You're d ying, aren't you?'

'What? No!'

'Oh, right. Good . Phew.'

'Why would I be d ying?' Hamza d emand ed .

'What? Oh. No reason. Just thought you were looking a bit...'
Tyler shook his head . 'Nothing. Forget it. You look fine. What's the
secret?'

Hamza checked his reflection in the rearview mirror. When he was
reassured that he d id n't look terminal, he turned back to the DC.

'Right, so—'

'Are you gay?' Tyler guessed . 'Is that it?'

'Just shut up for a minute and I'll blood y tell you!' Hamza snapped .
He shifted around in his seat, d rummed his fingers on the sid es of his
coffee cup, then came out with it. 'I've been offered a job.'

'You've got a job,' Tyler pointed out.

'Aye, but I've been offered a d ifferent one,' Hamza said .

Tyler stared at him, like he was waiting for a punchline that d id n't
appear to be coming.

'What d o you mean? What are you saying?' he d emand ed . 'Are you
quitting the polis?'

'No. It's still on the force. Well, alongsid e it. I would n't be an
officer.'

'What would you be?'

'Tech support,' Hamza said . 'But quite high-level stuff. Installing
software and hard ware. Interesting work.'

'It d oesn't sound interesting,' Tyler countered .

'It's what I spend half my time d oing now, anyway!' Hamza pointed
out. 'It's a wee bit of a d rop in wages, but it's office hours. Mond ay to
Frid ay, maybe one weekend in four.'

'Blimey,' Tyler said .

'Just, you know, with Kamila… being away so much. Working late.
It's… hard .'

'Aye. Aye, I bet,' Tyler said . He sucked in his bottom lip, then spat
it back out again. 'What's Amira saying?'

'Nothing yet. I haven't told her,' Hamza said .

'I'd imagine she'd jump at it.'

Hamza nodded. 'I'd imagine so, aye.'

'So, does that mean you're taking it, then?' Tyler asked.

The DS sighed and smiled at the same time. 'Honestly, mate? I wish I knew,' he said. 'Haven't decided yet. Still thinking it over.'

'You said anything to the boss yet?'

'Of course I bloody haven't!' Hamza replied. 'And don't you go saying anything, either. All right? It's our secret.'

Tyler winced. Keeping his mouth shut was not exactly his strong point.

'I'll do my best,' he said. 'And, you know, if it means anything, I don't want you to go. But obviously, you've got to do what you think's right for you and the family.' He broke into a broad, beaming grin. 'That's good advice, isn't it? That's, like, proper fatherly advice! Like what a dad would say.'

Hamza rolled his eyes, but smiled back at the junior detective. 'Aye,' he said. 'Aye, I suppose it was.'

Chapter 29

The smell of cannabis had permeated the fabric of the house. Upstairs, though, away from where Ayesha's grand mother and her boyfriend seemed to d o all their smoking, it was notably less pungent.

The d oor to Ayesha's bed room had been left open. Logan had been left to explore upstairs himself, while the other two human occupants of the house—and the head case of a d og—waited d own below.

Logan could hear the man and woman hard at work now, frantically hid ing their stash, and trying to clear away all evid ence of their d rug use.

Right now, he d id n't care. Right now, his only concern was the girl who should 've been there in that bed room.

Jud ging by what little he'd seen of the rest of the place, Ayesha's room was, he imagined, the neatest one in the house. It was sparsely furnished, and everything was a bit of a mish-mash, like it had been cobbled together over a number of years, but it was clean, and it was tid y, and it looked like it had been well cared for.

The bed was a single, and was tucked away in one corner of the room. The bed covers were pink with thin green stripes running through them, and while it was unlikely to impress an army d rill sergeant or a hospital matron, the bed had been mad e up to a reasonably high stand ard .

Down at the foot of the bed , a d ressing table d oubled as a d esk. There was no chair for it—anyone using it would have to sit on the end of the bed and hope their back held out—and the workspace on top was limited .

Still, it looked to be well used . An old , thick as a doorstop, laptop computer sat on top of it, surround ed by cans of deod orant, bottles of cheap perfume, and a selection of flavoured ChapSticks and lip glosses.

Logan got d own on his hunkers and checked und er the bed . Ther were some boxes there, a small suitcase, and a couple of pairs of shoes. No Ayesha, though. Not that he really expected there to be.

There was a built–in ward robe on the other sid e of the room from the bed . The slid ing d oor was a bastard to get open, and turned ou not to have been worth the effort. Clothes on hangers, some more shoes in a pile on the ward robe floor.

Otherwise? Nothing.

Ayesha could 've gone to stay with a friend , of course. She could be having a high old time to herself somewhere right now. There was no saying that anything was wrong. There was no saying that anything had happened to her.

And yet…

She was supposed to wait for someone. That's what she'd said when he told her to go home. She was supposed to wait for someone.

But who?

He walked out of the room, returned to the top of the stairs, and summoned the resid ents with a bellowed , 'Haw! You pair!'

There was some muttered d ebate from d ownstairs about who should respond . The barking, which had temporarily subsid ed a little returned with renewed vigour and volume.

It was Ayesha's grand mother who eventually appeared at the foot of the staircase.

'Were you shouting?' she asked .

'Aye, I was shouting,' Logan confirmed . 'What's your name, by the way?'

She looked back into the living room. 'He's asking what my name is.'

'What d oes he want to know your name for?' d rawled her boyfriend .

She turned her attention back to Logan and mangled another couple of sentences together. 'How come is it are you wanting to know my name for?'

Logan tutted . 'Well, because I can't keep thinking of you as "that arsehole of a woman d ownstairs", can I?' he said . 'Name. What is it?'

'Don't fucking tell him, Kathleen,' the guy in the living room urged .

There was a pause, then the voice came again.

'Shite.'

'Kathleen. Right. Good ,' Logan said . 'Get on the phone. Call Ayesha.'

'Call her? What for?'

'Because she's not here. And because I'm telling you to,' Logan said . 'Call her. Now.'

She grumbled a bit, but then went shuffling off, shouting to her boyfriend to find the phone.

As he returned to the bed room, Logan consid ered the possibility that Ayesha had just run away. From all this. From *them*. Who could blame her, if she had ? Not him, certainly. If anything, he'd be cheering the poor bugger on.

Legally, he had absolutely no right to look at her laptop, but he looked at it anyway.

Password protected . Of course it was. One for Hamza to d eal with.

He continued to poke around . The room wasn't as nice as Orla's, and not as cluttered with toys and collectables. Unlike the mini library in Orla's room, Ayesha had just seven or eight books on a single, ever-so-slightly slanted shelf, their spines so creased and fold ed that the titles and author names were barely legible.

A chest of d rawers that stood in the corner looked like it had been lovingly crafted in the fifties, then wilfully neglected ever since. The wood was tarnished , the varnish cracking and scuffed . A curved glass top had survived the d ecad es in one piece, but had picked up so many scratches that it was now only barely transparent.

Logan pulled one of the metal d rawer hand les, which immed iately came off in his hand . He jammed it back in place, angled it so the bolt d ug into the wood , then d ragged the d rawer open enough that he could get a grip on the front and pull it the rest of the way.

Und erwear. Good job Tyler wasn't here, he'd be starting to think this was a habit.

He checked through the garments, found nothing of interest, then closed the d rawer and moved on to the next. The hand le on thi one was fixed more solid ly in position, but the contents were just as uninteresting.

He turned his attention, instead , to another piece of furniture that sat und er the wind ow. If the chest of d rawers looked old , the d ressin table was positively antiquated .

Not an antique, exactly—that word implied a certain amount of value, and it was clear at first glance that this thing would only be of interest to the wood worm who'd had a blood y good go at it over the years.

It was a solid bod y, mad e up of three d rawers—two narrow but d eep ones on either sid e, and a wid e, shallow one that ran between them. The legs were curved , spind ly things, that looked like they were struggling to bear the weight of the rest of it, and the whole thing almost cowped over toward s him when he jiggled open the long mid d le d rawer.

At first, he thought he was looking at a lot of rand om junk. And , for the most part, he was. The d rawer contained toenail clippers, eyelash curlers, a scattering of cotton bud s, about three quid in loose change, several d ozen paperclips, some pens, a couple of Clipper lighters, and a stramash of other bits and bobs.

It was only when he inched it open a little further that he found the letters.

There were a d ozen of them—more, maybe—all neatly written on both sid es of plain, cream-coloured paper, that had been fold ed in half d own the mid d le.

Roughly a third of them were still in envelopes, albeit with a tear along the top to ind icate they'd all been opened and read . On the front of each envelope, and somewhere near the top of each letter, was the same name.

Ay-Ay.

Presumably, it was the send er's pet name for Ayesha. A glance at the end of one of the letters confirmed what he alread y suspected from the hand writing, which he recognised from his flick through the journal—the author of the letters was Orla Coull.

'She's not answering.'

Kathleen's voice came out of nowhere, and yet from so close behind him that he almost punched her to the ground through sheer instinct. He settled for barking a 'Jesus!' at her, which seemed to wash right over her.

'It's going to her 'hing,' the old er woman continued. She seemed even more out of the game than she'd been d ownstairs, like she'd taken a wee bump of something to get her through the stress of having the polis in the house.

'Do you mean her voicemail?' Logan asked. 'Is that what you're trying to say? It's going to her voicemail.'

'Aye. 's what I said,' Kathleen insisted.

'Keep trying,' Logan urged. 'And give me her number.'

Ayesha's gran's bushy eyebrows knotted together, like two caterpillars in a head -butting contest. 'Her phone number?'

'Naw, her *lucky* number.'

'What? How'm I meant to—'

'Aye, her phone number,' Logan spat. 'Of course her fucking phone number!'

'I'm not sure I should be giving that out,' Kathleen slurred. 'Without her say-so, an' that.'

Logan set the pile of letters d own on top of the d ressing table, then turned back to the much smaller woman. He leaned in, bringing his face closer to hers. It wasn't threatening—it wasn't meant to be, anyway—he just wanted to make certain that the message was received and und erstood.

'Listen to me, Kathleen,' he told her.

'All right. I'm listening.'

'Well, you're not. You're talking. So shut your mouth a minute,' Logan replied.

'Right,' she muttered, and he d ecid ed to let that one go.

'A girl is d ead. Orla Coull—Ayesha's best friend —is d ead. Murd ered. They're close pals. Both the same age. Both no d oubt mixing in the same circles,' Logan said. 'And one of them is d ead.

And now, the other one—Ayesha, your grand daughter—is missing, and has been all night.'

He watched her intently, hoping to see some flicker of und erstand ing there on her face, but her expression continued to hang slack with confusion.

'Are you getting where I'm going with this, Kathleen?' he asked . To make sure she d id , he spelled it out in the clearest possible terms. 'There's a chance that whoever took Orla—whoever killed her—has taken Ayesha, too. There's a chance that her life might be in d anger. So I need to find her.*We* need to find her. You and me. And that's going to start with you giving me her phone number. All right?'

Nothing changed about her face. Nothing of her expression altered . Not a muscle flickered .

Logan sighed , hung his head , and was about to try a d ifferent approach when she held her phone out to him in one gnarled , shaking hand .

He took it, and her fingers tightened around his for a moment.

'I d on't want nothing to happen to her,' Kathleen said .

There wasn't a lot of emotion behind the word s, but then it was likely that her brain had been too fried for too long to experience such things. Or at least to successfully convey them to others.

Logan took the phone, and after taking a bit of time to remind himself how these non-touchscreen d evices worked , he managed to find his way to the contacts list, and took a copy of Ayesha's number.

'Right. Keep trying her,' he instructed , passing the mobile back. 'If you know of any friend s of hers, try them, too. Ronnie Donlon. You got his number?'

'Donlon?' Kathleen said , screwing up her face. 'What, the old polis d ick? No offence. What would he know?'

'Not him, his son. I saw them together last night,' Logan said , then he was struck again by the state of the woman in front of him, and shook his head . 'Forget it. Doesn't matter. Don't bother. Just keep trying Ayesha. If you get through to her, get her to call me.'

'What, get her to phone you on the polis number?' Kathleen asked . 'Like, on nine-nine…' She frowned , searching the jumbled mush of her brain for that missing last d igit.

'For Christ's sake,' Logan muttered. 'It's nine. But, no. Here.' He took a business card from his pocket and forced it into her hand. 'My number's on there. If you get her, tell her to call me. And you call me, too, to be on the safe side.'

Kathleen studied the card up close. Far too close to focus on, Logan would 've thought.

'Won't it be engaged?' she asked.

'Won't what be engaged?'

'Your phone. If we both call you at the same time. Her and me, like. Will that not make it engaged?'

Logan tutted. 'I just want you to let me know you've spoken to her,' he explained. 'In case she doesn't call.'

'How will I know if she doesn't call, but?' Kathleen asked.

'It doesn't matter,' Logan snapped, his patience wearing so thin it was now a nanosheath, just an atom thick. 'Just phone me if you speak to her, all right?'

'Aye. God. Keep your hair on. I'm no' thick,' Kathleen said. She pursed her dry, cracked lips. 'Is it that dirty paedo what did this? Did he take Ayesha?'

'No,' Logan said. 'I mean, I don't know. But there's no evidence to suggest that—'

'Bet it fucking was him. Dirty fucking bastard. You better get fucking round there before I do.'

'You're going nowhere,' Logan told her. 'You're staying here, you're phoning Ayesha. That's it. You got that? Stay here, and stay out of my bloody way.'

Kathleen grimaced at him. She started to respond, but the word snagged at the back of her throat and she erupted into a fit of coughing that doubled her over and made her vision go black.

When it cleared, a few seconds later, the DCI was no longer in the room. And nor, for that matter, were the letters or the laptop.

'Christ's sake, are you still here?' slurred a voice from downstairs, as the house's front door opened, then slammed closed again. 'I thought you'd fucked off hours ago.'

DS Hamza Khaled stud ied the area immed iately around the car, then turned his attention to a little further along the street. He tapped his fingers on the steering wheel, then picked up his coffee cup, only to find it empty.

'Well?' an impatient Tyler urged .

'Hang on, hang on,' Hamza said , then he shrugged . 'Bird ?'

'Nope.'

Hamza tutted , and went back to looking around .

'I've said bush.'

'Is that a question or a statement?' Tyler asked .

Hamza shot him a sid eways look. 'It's a statement. I've said bush alread y.'

Tyler raised an eyebrow. 'Have you?'

The DS sighed . 'Is it bush?'

'No,' said Tyler, shaking his head . 'You've said bush.'

'Fuck's sake,' Hamza muttered . 'Did I also say how much I hate this game?'

'You might've mentioned it, aye.'

'Bin!' Hamza cried . 'Bin. It's got to be bin.'

'No.'

'Blue bin, then! Because I know you're a picky bastard at this game. Blue bin. Got to be. Final answer.'

'It's not a blue bin. Or any bin,' Tyler told him.

Hamza threw his hand s into the air. 'Right. Well, I give up, then. What is it?'

Tyler interlocked his fingers behind his head and reclined triumphantly. 'Bag.'

'What?' Hamza sat up straighter and looked around them. 'What bag? I d on't see a bag.'

'One blew past when I was taking my go,' Tyler told him, which d rew outrage and ire from his superior officer.

'You can't use that! How was I meant to get that?' he d emand ed .

'You're meant to be able to see it!'

'I could see it.'

'Aye, but not now!' Hamza objected .

Tyler shrugged . 'The game's called "I Spy". It's not called "I Spy, and Will Continue to Spy Until Such Times as You Manage to Guess What I'm Looking At", is it? I spied it, I said it, I win. That means it's me to go again.'

Hamza, groaned , looked up at the car's ceiling and exhaled from the very bottom of his stomach. As social cues went, it was pretty on the nose.

Tyler, however, chose to ignore it.

'I Spy, with my little eye,' he began. 'Something beginning with… boss?!'

Hamza frowned , then jumped in his seat when a set of large knuckles rapped on the wind ow besid e him. He pressed the button that slid the wind ow d own, then the frame was filled by Logan's face as he squatted d own next to the car.

'Anything?' he asked , shooting a look in the d irection of the Donlons' house.

'Nothing, boss,' Tyler said . 'Quiet as a mouse.'

'Right, we're knocking it on the head ,' the DCI told them. 'Back to the station. Something's come up. You can give me a lift.'

He walked around to the other sid e of the car, stood waiting for a moment, then pulled open Tyler's d oor.

'Well, shift your arse then, Detective Constable,' he barked . 'If you think I'm squeezing myself into the back seat, you've got another blood y thing coming.'

'Oh! Aye! Sorry, boss!' Tyler said .

He tried to jump out of the car, but the seat belt had other id eas, and reined him back in. He tried again, this time unfastening the belt before giving up the front seat to the more senior officer.

'There you go, boss,' he said . 'I was just keeping it warm for you.'

Logan regard ed the passenger seat with a look of concern, like that well-intentioned remark might've just put him off the id ea. By then, though, Tyler was alread y opening the back d oor and starting to clamber insid e.

It was only the boom of a voice from a little further up the street that stopped them both climbing in.

'This a private gathering, or is anyone invited?'

They turned to find a moustache bristling its way towards them, attached to the face of the very man Hamza and Tyler were supposed to have been looking out for.

'Ronald,' Logan said, greeting him with a nod.

Ronnie Sr. stopped long enough to press the button on a key fob. A little way off down the street, his car locking mechanism gave a bleep-bleep.

He was dressed like an artist's impression of a gamekeeper—all tweed, checked shirt, and big Wellies. A flat cap on his head completed the look, and a long, tan-coloured bag slung over his right shoulder could realistically only hold one thing.

'Been shooting?' Logan asked.

Ronald jerked his shoulder upwards, shaking the bag and the shotgun contained within.

'Keeping the old hand in,' he said, then he laughed. 'And before you ask, yes, I have a licence! Feel free to check!'

'I will,' Logan said. He smiled, but didn't come close to meaning it.

'Ha! Quite right. Quite right, too!' Ronald said. He looked at Tyler, then lowered his head a little to stare in at Hamza. 'Are these two both...?'

'Detective Sergeant Khaled and Detective Constable Neish,' Logan said.

Ronald smiled at them both then looked to his left. From where they were standing, they had a clear, uninterrupted view of his front door—a fact that did not go unnoticed.

'Has the post been?'

'I'm sorry?' Logan asked.

'To the house,' Ronald said. 'I assume you've been sitting here a while? Just wondered if the postman has been yet?'

'Eh, not that we saw, no,' Tyler said, then he caught the look from Logan, flinched slightly, and pointed into the car. 'I'll just, eh, I'll go sit down, boss.'

'No, wait!' Ronald said. 'I'm just playing with you. I know you all have a job to do. And I get it. I do. Ronnie and Orla, they were sweethearts. Of course, he's going to be a suspect. But I assure you, he had nothing to do with this. He wasn't here when she went missing. He tells me that he hasn't heard from her since, and I believe him. But, you have to do what you have to do. I've been on that side. I've been in your shoes. I know the score.'

He thrust out a hand so suddenly in Tyler's direction that the DC almost instinctively tried to block it. Fortunately, he was able to resist the urge, but then felt compelled to accept the handshake. As soon as he did, Ronald clasped his other hand over it, pinning the detective constable's in place.

'I'd just like to say, though—to all of you, you two, Sergeant—how much the community appreciates what you're doing here. These last few months have been dark darks. So very dark, and yesterday... well, yesterday was the darkest of all.'

He continued shaking Tyler's hand, pumping it vigorously up and down while looking around at all three men.

'But you—the three of you, and your colleagues—you're going to bring the light back. I know it. I can feel it. And, I'm here if you need me. Anything I can do to help. Any advice I can give, local knowledge, whatever you think will help, just say the word. Anything I can do, just ask.'

'You could give me my hand back,' Tyler said.

'Hm? Oh! Sorry!' Ronald laughed, then released his grip.

He smiled and pointed at all three men, like they were long-lost friends of his, then doffed his cap in their direction.

'Now, if you'll excuse me, gents, I must leave you. I'm on dinner duty tonight, and Herself doesn't like it if I'm running late!'

He nodded curtly, snapped his heels together in a manner that struck Logan as distinctly Nazi-like, then went striding across the road, and along the alleyway, towards his front door.

'Well, I can't say for sure, sir,' said Hamza, leaning to look out through the open passenger door. 'But I *think* there's a chance he might've spotted us.'

Chapter 30

When Logan and the others got back to the station, Sinead was working her way through Orla Coull's diary, which had now been removed from its evidence bag.

'Palmer's team been?' Logan asked, eyeing the exposed journal as he shrugged off his coat.

'Hmm? Oh. Sorry. Yeah. They have, yeah,' Sinead said, eyes still fixed on the page she was reading.

'They get anything off it?'

Sinead finished the section she was on, before finally giving him her full attention.

'Nothing, no.'

Logan stopped, mid-shrug.

'What, nothing?'

'No.'

'As in… no prints? Not one print on it anywhere?'

'None, sir,' Sinead said. She stood up. 'But there is something you need to see. Inside it. Something Orla wrote.'

Logan finished taking his coat off, then tossed it onto the desk. 'OK. But first, Ben, get hold of the Uniforms. Put a shout-out for Ayesha Fulton. She didn't come home last night, and she's not answering her phone.'

'Aw, no. You don't think something's happened to her, do you?' Ben asked.

'Maybe, aye. Could be nothing, but I've got a bad feeling,' Logan told him. 'I'll give you her number. I want her found. Hamza, you're the tech expert. Have a crack at her laptop, see if you can get into it.'

'Will do, sir,' DS Khaled confirmed.

Tyler watched him take the laptop, then threw himself head first into the conversation.

'He's not just that, though!'

The others turned to look at him.

'What?' Logan asked.

'Hamza. He's not *just* the tech guy.'

'Tyler. Mate...' Hamza said, shooting the DC a pleading look.

'I'm just... I'm just saying, you're more than that,' Tyler said, wilting beneath the puzzled looks of the rest of the team. 'You're, like, you know... important, or whatever. To the team. That's all I'm saying.'

Logan regarded the detective constable for a few seconds, then sniffed. 'Well, that was a touching tribute,' he said. 'Are you quite finished, Detective Constable?'

Tyler's cheeks flushed red. 'Eh, aye, boss. Aye, I'm done.'

'Thank Christ for that. Now, everyone get to work. Where's Dave?'

'Out checking that necklace,' said Ben. 'His mate's mate, or whoever the hell it was, reckons it's a diamond. He's found a local guy to check with, though.'

'You really need to see this, sir,' Sinead said, shoving the open book in front of him.

It was the same tidy writing he'd seen when he'd flicked through the book earlier. The same as on the letters, too. His eyes scanned the page impatiently, trying to find some interesting detail to latch onto.

As with the other pages he'd glanced through, there were no days or dates on this one anywhere. Nothing to tether the contents to any particular moment in time.

'What am I meant to be looking for?' he asked.

Sinead didn't answer. She didn't need to. A word jumped off the page at him. He'd been looking around the centre of the page, a few paragraphs down, but the word that grabbed his attention was up near the top.

'Jesus Christ!' he ejected.

He looked away, then back to the page, as if checking that the word was real. That he hadn't imagined it.

It was still there when he looked back. Still sitting there. Still changing everything.

He stabbed a finger onto the page, drawing Sinead's attention to the word he'd spotted.

Steve.

'Is this…?'

'Paed o Steve, sir, aye,' Sinead confirmed. 'She goes on to write about visiting his caravan. Hanging on. "Having fun."'

'Fun? As in…?'

'She doesn't say they were in a sexual relationship, sir, but it's implied, yes.'

'Right, so Mr Boyd's been lying through his teeth to us, then,' Logan said, snapping the book closed. 'Time we brought the bastard in. Sinead, with me. You can show me where the caravan is. Hamza, Tyler, meet us there, in case he tries doing a runner.'

'See?' Tyler whispered to Hamza. 'What did I say about burning them doughnuts off?'

'Enough with the bloody chit-chat, you pair,' Logan bellowed, grabbing his coat again. He stormed past them as he rushed to the door. 'Fingers out your arses, people! And let's go nab this bastard!'

–

Logan's fingers wrapped so tightly around the steering wheel that it let out a worrying groan of complaint.

'You're sure?' he growled. 'You're absolutely certain?'

'It was right here, sir,' Sinead confirmed. 'The caravan was parked right here. In this layby.'

'Well, it's not bloody here now,' Logan pointed out.

He threw open his door just as Hamza's car rumbled to a stop behind his. Tyler's head popped out of the passenger side window like a dog enjoying the breeze on its face.

'Where's the caravan, boss?' he asked.

'How the hell should I know?' Logan snapped. 'Not here, clearly.'

He exhaled sharply, wasted a few second s looking the area over, then turned to ad d ress the other d etectives, who were all now getting out of the cars.

'Right, you pair, head back d own the Inverness road . Drop Sinead at the station. Sinead , put a shout-out. I want all eyes peeled for the bastard , and if he head ed that way, Hamza, Tyler, I want you two in full pursuit.'

'Oh, God ,' Tyler groaned .

'I'll head across the brid ge. He could 've gone that way,' Logan said , alread y marching back toward s his SUV, the engine still running and read y. 'Any questions?' he asked , but he d id n't leave any time for them to answer. 'No? Good .' He clapped his hand s at them, like he was chasing them away. 'Then let's get going!'

He jumped into the d river's seat of his BMW, glanced in the rearview mirror to make sure the others were getting a shifty on, then powered out of the layby and onto the main road . A flick of a switch activated the blue lights behind the front grille, and a heavy right foot shot the car forward , racing up the incline that led toward s the Skye brid ge.

This could be pointless, of course. Boyd could 've left at any point in the last twelve hours. For all they knew, he'd packed up and fucked off the moment Sinead and Tyler had left.

Although…

He stabbed the touchscreen d isplay on the d ash with an ind ex finger, found Sinead 's name in his contacts, and tapped again to call her.

She answered almost immed iately. 'Sir? You got him?'

'I wish,' Logan replied . 'The caravan. That layby. You passed it this morning on the way in, right?'

'Uh, yeah,' Sinead confirmed .

'Was he there then? Did you see it parked there?'

The DC hesitated before replying. 'Honestly, sir? I'm not sure. I wasn't exactly on top form, so—'

'Aye, he was there, boss,' Tyler said , his voice a little muffled by the sound of Hamza's engine. 'Definitely there. I clocked it on the way past.'

'Right. Good , that's something,' Logan said , then he blasted his horn and bellowed , 'Get out of the way, you slow-moving bastard !' at a hatchback pootling along the road ahead of him, before end ing the call.

The car in front swerved in closer to the sid e of the road , and he slid past it, engine roaring up the hill.

Und er normal circumstances, and d espite not really being a fan of such things, he'd almost have been impressed by the view as he reached the start of the brid ge to Skye.

The brid ge itself wasn't anything to write home about. There were no grand sticky-up bits. No towers, or stretching cables, or anything else that might make it look like some wond er of mod ern engineering.

It was a stretch of road , slightly humped in the mid d le, with a railing at either sid e to stop anyone falling off into the water.

Look left or right, though, and it was clear why the brid ge had been kept so unremarkable. How could even the most impressive of manmad e constructions hope to compete with the views stretching out across the loch on either sid e?

Had it been a d ifferent d ay, and a d ifferent situation, Logan might've slowed to appreciate the sheer, breathtaking majesty of it.

Focused on the chase as he was, though, he d id n't so much as glance at the land scape around him.

Which was why, just a few second s later, he was able to slam on his brakes and avoid hitting the man who stepped out onto the road in front of him, one hand held up in a 'stop' motion.

'What the hell d o you think you're d oing?!' Logan boomed . 'I could 've killed you, you blood y id iot!'

The wind ows were all up, but the volume of his voice meant it could be heard clearly by the man now approaching the front of the vehicle.

'Where the hell are you off to in such a fucking hurry?' asked Bob Hoon. He slapped his hand s on the BMW's bonnet, then proceed ed around to the front passenger d oor.

'None of your blood y concern,' Logan spat.

He moved to pull away, but Hoon was rattling the door handle, and while part of him would be more than happy to crush the bastard's feet beneath a back wheel, it would only slow him down in the long run.

With an exasperated sigh, he pressed the button that unlocked the door, waited until Hoon had got himself far enough inside that he wasn't going to fall back out, then he floored the accelerator.

'What the hell are you still doing here?' the DCI demanded. A warning sound began to chime from the dash, and he fired his unwelcome guest a savage look. 'Belt on before that bloody thing does my nut in.'

'Just went for a fucking wander. Is that all right with you?'

They crested the peak of the bridge at speed, and for a moment they both felt like they were lifting up off the seats. Hoon pulled his seat belt across his chest and clipped it as the car sped up on the downwards stretch of road.

The rest of the bridge and the road beyond were currently clear— no other cars to slow them down, but no sign of Stephen Boyd, either.

'You're not meant to be here, Bob,' Logan insisted. 'You were meant to go home.'

'Aye. Well, thought I might as well hang about. Knew you'd need me sooner or fucking later.'

'I don't need you, Bob!' Logan insisted. 'In fact, to be completely honest, you're the last thing I bloody need!'

'Well, is that no' fucking charming?' Hoon asked, shaking his head in disgust. 'And, aye, as a matter of fact, you do need me.'

'Like a hole in the bloody head, maybe,' Logan muttered.

'Who is it you're chasing?' asked the arsehole in the passenger seat. 'Wouldn't be a manky old shit-tip of a caravan, would it?'

Logan shot him a sideways glance. 'You saw it?'

'Might've done,' Hoon said, settling back in the seat. 'Might've done, aye.'

'So, it went this way?'

'Maybe.'

'For Christ's sake, Bob!' Logan barked.

Hoon smirked at him. 'Does this mean you're ready to start consulting?'

'Forget it,' Logan said, pushing the pedal all the way to the floor. 'I'll find the bastard myself.'

In the passenger seat, Hoon shook his head. 'You're no fucking fun anymore, have I told you that? Aye, he went this way. Take a left at the round about. First exit.'

'How do you know?'

'Because I've got fucking eyes, Jack,' Hoon said. 'I watched him go.'

'When?'

'Five, ten minutes ago,' Hoon said.

'Jesus. Must've just missed the bastard,' Logan muttered, then he dropped down a gear and the engine screamed at the sudden boost acceleration that was being asked of it.

Hoon gripped the handle above the door to stop himself from being thrown sideways onto the driver's lap when Logan hung a sharp, screeching left at the round about.

'Nicely done,' he remarked.

The comment, for reasons he couldn't quite explain, annoyed Logan immensely, but he chose to ignore it. These roads were narrow, with sharp, sudden bends that could bring you right up the backside of slower-moving traffic, if you weren't careful.

'What's he driving?' Logan asked.

'Focus, I think,' Hoon replied. 'Older model. And pulling that old fucking tank of a thing? He'll no' be making good time, put it that way.'

'Bet he's headed for the ferry,' Logan said. 'Get on that, off at Mallaig, then away he goes.'

'Makes sense,' Hoon said.

'Text Tyler. Let him know the score,' Logan ordered.

Hoon frowned. 'Who?'

'Just fucking do it, Bob! Tell him to get Hamza to turn around. And call ahead to the ferry, in case he gets there before we do.'

'He won't. No' in that thing,' Hoon said. 'He'll be lucky if it doesn't shake itself to bits halfway there.'

'Can you just pass the message on?' Logan asked.

'All right, all right. Fuck's sake.'

Hoon unlocked his phone, scrolled through the contacts until he found 'That Prick With the Hair', then fired off the text message as requested.

'There. Done,' he said. He looked from the road ahead to Logan. 'What is it we're actually chasing him for, exactly?'

'He's a suspect,' Logan said.

Hoon tutted. 'Aye, well, I guessed that much,' he said. 'I didn't think you were playing fucking Kiss-Chase. Why, though? What've we got on him? What's our fucking angle here?'

'*We* don't have an angle, Bob,' Logan replied. 'You're only here because I don't want to stop the car, and it's against the law to kick you out while I'm still moving. You're an unwelcome passenger, that's it. You're not a part of this investigation.'

'Bollocks!' Hoon said, grinning. 'That's shite, and you know it. Me and you, we're fucking *Tango and Cash*-ing the shit out of this!'

Logan shot him a look of exasperation. Shona would know what he was talking about, but the reference went right over the DCI's head.

Starsky and Hutch-ing? Now, *that* he would have got.

Logan banked around a bend, then onto another straight. There were four cars up ahead, bunched up together, taking their time.

'Sirens?' Hoon asked. Logan nodded, and with a flick of a switch, the car began to scream, its blue lights flashing across the trees and bushes that lined the road.

The cars ahead all slowed further, indicating left, pulling in closer to the grassy embankment at the side of the road. There was a delivery van coming the other way. Logan put his faith in the driver to stop, and swerved out onto the right-hand side of the carriageway, powering past the line of near-stationary cars.

Hoon lowered his window, thrust a hand out, then made a wanking motion to all the vehicles left in their wake.

'What the hell was that for?' Logan asked. 'They pulled in.'

'Aye, but they should n't have fucking had to,' Hoon countered . 'Did you see them creeping along there? If you can't d rive at a normal fucking speed , you should n't be d riving, full fucking stop.'

'By the way, d on't you even blood y think about putting in an invoice to Mitchell for this,' Logan warned . 'I'll d eny even speaking to you.'

'An invoice? Don't you worry about that, Jack,' Hoon said . He winked . 'I'm on a retainer.'

'You're *what*?!'

'Here, eyes front, eyes front,' Hoon urged , sitting up in his seat. 'Do you see what I fucking see?'

Logan faced forward again in time to catch the tail end of a caravan weaving through the last stretch of a wind ing chicane up ahead .

'That him?'

'The fuck should I know?' Hoon asked .

'Because you've got fucking eyes, Bob. Is that not what you said ? You saw it. You know what the blood y thing looks like!'

Hoon glared back at him, looking mortally offend ed . 'Well, pard on fucking me! I'm sorry a fucking nanosecond glimpse of the arse end wasn't enough for me to be able to say for sure if that's the—*Jesus fuck*!'

He gripped the hand le again as Logan d ropped a gear and slammed his foot all the way to the floor, calling on all the power the 4.4-litre V8 engine had to offer. They were both pushed back into their seats. The trees alongsid e the road became a blur, whipping past with a whoosh-whoosh-whoosh.

Logan skimmed the brakes when the road twisted and turned hugging the mid d le line, then accelerated out of the long left-hand bend that followed .

By the time he hit the next straight, the caravan was fifty yard s ahead , and closing fast.

'Right. There. That it?' he asked .

'Looks like the fucker to me,' Hoon confirmed . He narrowed his eyes, squinting at the vehicle ahead . 'Doesn't seem to be slowing d own, though.'

'No, I noticed ,' Logan said . He eased off the accelerator. It was one thing to get in close behind the caravan, but another thing entirely to plough straight through the blood y thing.

'Get alongsid e him,' Hoon instructed , hitting the button that wound d own his wind ow.

The seat belt alarm screamed from the d ashboard again, and a sid eways glance confirmed that Hoon had unclipped the buckle.

'What the hell are you d oing?' Logan d emand ed .

'Just get alongsid e the bastard ! I'll climb out onto the roof.'

Logan snorted . 'Aye, very funny, Bob. Get your belt on.'

'I'm not joking! I can totally fucking make that.' He pointed to various parts of the caravan as he spelled out his plan. 'I squeeze out of here, jump onto that bit, climb along the top there, throw myself onto the roof of his car, break a wind ow, grab the wheel. Bish–bash–fucking-bosh. Job d one.'

'Have you lost your mind ? You're an ex-d etective in his mid -fifties, you're not a blood y action hero!'

'What? The fuck are you talking about?' Hoon d emand ed . He jabbed a thumb backward s, like the past was right there on the road behind him. 'Have you seen half the shit I've been d oing lately?! I've been making James Bond look like Jimmy fucking Krankie!' He grimaced . 'I mean, to be honest, it's a fucking miracle I'm still alive. But this? This'll be a walk in the fucking park!'

He nod d ed forward to the caravan, which was now just a few car lengths ahead .

'So, pull up alongsid e him, hold the fucking car stead y, and you just watch me go.'

Up ahead , the car pulling the caravan swerved to take a bend . As it d id , the back of the caravan clipped the embankment. Logan and Hoon watched as car and caravan both went into a weaving skid , before momentum and gravity conspired to tip the whole back end up and over to the left.

Logan hit the brakes. The red lights that illuminated on the back of the caravan told him the d river of the car had d one the same, but by then it was too late.

The caravan rolled off the road , over the verge, and d own the embankment. The car, still attached to the front, was wrenched over onto its sid e, then onto its roof, before the towbar gave out, and both vehicles parted ways with a screech of rend ing metal.

Tyres howling, Logan brought the BMW to a stop just a few feet away from where the upend ed Ford Focus lay on its roof, with its slowly spinning wheels pointing toward s the sky.

'Or, you know,' Hoon muttered . 'We could always just hold our fucking horses and see if that happens.'

Chapter 31

Dave David son mad e a point of showing DI Ford e that he was returning the necklace to the Exhibits box when he wheeled his way back into the Incid ent Room.

'I want it on record that I brought it back,' he said , then he pointed it out to Sinead , so she could corroborate the story, too. 'If it goes missing, it's not my fault.'

'Valuable, then?' asked Ben.

He had a small stack of Rich Tea biscuits besid e a mug on his d esk, and was working his way through them by snapping them into quarters, and slipping up to half of each biscuit to Taggart, who sat und er the d esk, gratefully receiving them.

'Three or four grand , he reckons,' Dave confirmed .

'The local guy? Or your mate?' asked Sinead .

'The local guy. He used to have a wee jeweller's shop in Plockton. He's more up on watches and rings, but he says it's d efinitely a real d iamond . Bit less than a carat. Not the clearest, but d ecent enough.'

'Don't suppose he sold it to Ronnie, d id he?'

'No. Nothing like the stuff he d id , he says,' Dave replied . 'But that's where my mate came in. Well, not my mate, my—'

'We know who you mean,' Ben said , cutting the explanation short before he had to sit through it all again. 'He have an id ea about where it came from?'

'Found one similar online,' Dave confirmed . 'Shop based d own south.'

'What, Glasgow?'

'No, bit further south than that. Milton Keynes. Want me to send them a photo and see if it rings any bells?'

Ben nod d ed . 'Please. Aye,' he said . 'See what they can tell us. And Sinead , if you're d one on the phone, get it up on the board , will you? Assuming you're feeling up to—'

'I'm fine, sir,' Sinead insisted , getting to her feet. 'I'll note it up there now.'

'Right. Good . Aye,' Ben said . He snapped another biscuit in half, passed one part d own to Taggart, then d unked the other in his tea. 'And no word back from the others yet, I take it?'

Sinead glanced at her mobile. 'Nothing yet,' she said .

'Ah well.' Ben sucked in his bottom lip, spat it out again, then smiled reassuringly. 'I'm sure they've got everything well in hand .'

–

They heard the screaming as soon as they got out of the car. Neither Hoon nor Logan rushed to help, though. Screaming was an area they both consid ered themselves to have some expertise in, and this partic-ular variation, while shrill and insistent, wasn't giving them much cause for concern.

For starters, when it came to traffic accid ents, it was the people who weren't screaming that you had to worry about. The silent ones. The motionless.

The ones who were wailing, and flailing their arms, and shrieking, 'Help, help, somebod y help!' like the current occupant of the upturned Ford Focus, generally turned out to be fine.

Fragments of broken glass crunched und er their heels as they approached the car. The engine had cut out at some point d uring the roll, but the alarm was making itself heard , and the hazard s were blinking away like d isco lights.

They both stopped at the ed ge of the embankment long enough to take in the remains of the caravan. It was surprisingly intact, consid - ering. It was still recognisable as having once been a caravan, at least, and had n't simply d isintegrated on impact.

It lay at the end of a long trench it had carved into the grass, partly collapsed like some half-built Ikea furniture. Most of the caravan's contents—clothes, crockery, some pots and pans and a half-sized ironing board—had been shed during the roll down the slope, and now lay scattered across the freshly scarred ground.

'Glad I'm no' the poor bastard who'll have to clear that up,' Hoon remarked.

'Your retainer not cover that, no?' Logan asked, then they both continued to where Stephen Boyd was still shouting for help from inside his overturned car.

Both men used their feet to clear away some of the glass before kneeling next to the driver's side window and ducking enough to look inside.

Paedo Steve was still held in place by his seatbelt, though his arms had fallen down below his head, and now lay heaped on the inside of the vehicle's roof, along with some broken glass, a smattering of coins, and a couple of *Now That's What I Call Music!* CD album cases.

His deflated airbag was also hanging down, and a fine film of white had dusted his face like Elizabethan makeup powder.

'You all right there, Mr Boyd?' asked Logan.

'What?!' Boyd spluttered. 'What do you mean? No! No, of course, I'm not all right! I crashed! I'm upside down!'

'Aye. Aye, we noticed that, right enough,' Logan confirmed, very matter-of-factly. 'Are you hurt?'

'Yes!' Boyd squealed.

'You don't fucking look hurt,' Hoon pointed out.

'I think I staved my wrist!'

Hoon tutted. 'Hear that?' he asked Logan. 'Staved his wrist. What a fucking champion, eh? What a fucking legend amongst men.'

'Can you move, Mr Boyd?' Logan asked.

'I'm upside down!'

'That doesn't really answer his fucking question, does it?' Hoon spat.

'Bob. Do you mind?' Logan asked.

The cars they'd overtaken a few minutes earlier were now approaching, and Logan waved vaguely in their direction.

'Keep them away, will you?'

Hoon's eyebrows climbed further up his forehead. 'Oh, I'm on fucking traffic d uty now, am I? Will I just go ahead and pick up some fucking litter while I'm at it?'

'If you want to, aye,' Logan told him, then he turned back to the man currently hanging arse over tit in the car. 'Ignoring your sore wrist for the moment, how's the rest of you? Can you move your toes?'

A look of panic flitted across Boyd 's face—at least, that's what Logan thought it was, though it was hard to jud ge at that angle—but then he exhaled and nod d ed . 'Yeah. I'm wiggling them. I'm wiggling them now.'

'OK, I d on't need a running commentary, son,' Logan told him.

The DCI looked back along the length of the car, and sniffed . There was a d efinite and d istinct od our of petrol that had n't been there a few moments ago. No part of the vehicle was currently on fire, so it wasn't a massive emergency, but it was probably best to get the occupant clear, all the same.

'Right, so the good news is that you weren't going that fast when you rolled over,' Logan told him.

'Easy for you to say!'

'I mean, your car's fucked , I'm not going to sugarcoat it, but I think you're going to be fine. Although, the sooner we can get you out of there, the better.'

'I'm upsid e d own!'

'Aye, so you keep saying. You d on't have to stay upsid e d own, though, is my point,' Logan told him. 'Can you unclip your belt?'

Boyd turned his head to look at him. His face was turning quite a brood ing shad e of red , and his eyes were becoming blood shot.

'My belt? How will that…? Oh, my *seat* belt, you mean?' With some effort, he figured out how his hand s worked , and fid d led wi the clasp. 'No, it's not releasing! It won't let me go! I'm pressing the button, but—'

There was a thud as the belt unfastened and he land ed awkward l on the roof.

'Shit! Ow. Ow.'

'You're all right, son,' Logan said . 'You're d oing fine.'

He got up, and though it took a few firm yanks to unjam the top of the d oor frame from where it had come to rest on the pavement, he was able to pull the d oor open far enough for Boyd to crawl out.

'You OK? Nothing broken?' Logan asked, helping him to his feet.

Boyd waited a few second s to see if pain was going to strike, then shook his head. 'No. No, nothing broken.'

'Clearly, he hasn't seen his fucking caravan,' called Hoon.

He was stand ing at the front of a growing line of cars with his arms crossed, blocking the road. Further back along the straight, another car was racing up, blue lights flashing behind its front grille.

'That's Hamza and Tyler,' Logan announced. 'Get them to call this in.'

'What am I, your fucking secretary?' Hoon d emand ed.

Logan shot him a look as he escorted the d ishevelled and somewhat d azed -looking Stephen Boyd over to the BMW.

'You said you wanted to help, Bob,' he said. 'So quit your blood y whinging, and help.'

—

Half an hour later, Stephen Boyd sat in the back of an ambulance, being checked over by a couple of paramed ics. The Uniforms— Sergeant MacGeachan and Constable Coleman—had taken over traffic d uty, and were d irecting d rivers through a single-lane system they'd put in place alongsid e the upturned Focus.

Logan and Hoon stood at the top of the embankment, looking d own at the d ebris of the caravan. Tyler and Hamza were in the process of picking through it, though they were yet to find much of interest.

That, however, was about to change.

'I see his laptop!' Tyler announced. His head was jammed through a crack in one of the caravan walls, and his voice echoed around insid e what was left of the flimsy structure. He laughed at the boom it brought to his word s. 'I sound like Darth Vad er in this!I"am your father!"'

Up on the road sid e, Hoon shook his head. 'Fuck me. How d o you put up with that?'

Logan shrugged . 'Just washes over you, after a while,' he said , then he raised his voice. 'Tyler. Concentrate. The laptop.'

'Yes… my master,' Tyler said , still channelling his inner Sith Lord .

There was some grunting and groaning then. A bit of wheezing. An exhalation or two, as Tyler tried to stretch far enough into the wreckage to grab the computer.

Finally, his fingers were able to get purchase on one corner of the plastic casing, and he reeled the laptop in with a triumphant cry of 'Got ye!'

He extracted all his various parts from the semi-collapsed caravan, held the computer above his head , then d ucked as various bits of screen, motherboard , and hard d rive rained d own on him from above

'Shite!' he d eclared , opening up the laptop to reveal its smashed innard s. 'Think it might've got d amaged in the crash.'

'Here, let's have a look,' said Hamza. He leaned in closer, peered along the length of his nose at the shattered screen, broken plastic, and buckled metal, then nod d ed . 'God , yeah. Good eye, Tyler. You migh be right. It might've picked up a wee d ing or two d uring the smash, right enough.'

'Can you fix it?' Tyler asked .

'Maybe if you give me five years and a few hund red tubes of superglue,' Hamza replied . 'But there's no way it's powering on again.'

'Fuck me, Boyband strikes again,' Hoon remarked from up by the road .

Tyler looked up at the former d etective superintend ent—albeit briefly—then d own at the mangled remains of the laptop. 'This isn't my fault!'

Hoon eyeballed him. 'Oh, aye? You fucking sure of that, are you?'

Tyler was sure. At least… he thought he was. He *had* been sure, at any rate, up until right that moment. Now, though, with the way Hoon asked the question—the conviction with which he mad e the accusation—Tyler was starting to have some d oubts.

Before he could take all the blame, though, Hamza squeezed past him and peered in through one of the buckled seams of the caravan's walls.

'Here. Hang on. What's this?' the DS asked , reaching through the gap.

His arm emerged again a moment later, carrying a red d ish rectangle of rough stone.

'It's a brick,' Tyler said .

'Well, obviously. I know it's a brick,' Hamza said . He waved it in front of the DC's face. 'Does it look familiar?'

'Aye. Now you mention it, it looks like every other brick I've ever seen,' Tyler said , then the realisation hit him and he pointed to it with a gasp of excitement. 'Wait! No! It's the same one! Well, I mean, not the same one, but the same kind .'

'Exactly,' Hamza said . He held the brick aloft for Logan's benefit. 'You seeing this, sir?'

The DCI peered at it for a moment, then nod d ed . 'That looks suspiciously like the one some bastard lobbed through the station wind ow,' he said .

'Pretty much id entical, sir,' Hamza confirmed .

Logan put his hand s in his pockets and rocked back on his heels. 'Well, then,' he said , looking over to where Paed o Steve was still being checked by the paramed ics. 'It looks like Mr Boyd 's going to have even more explaining to d o than we first thought.'

Chapter 32

Sinead stood in the kitchen, stretching her back as she waited for the kettle to boil. The day was wearing on, and while her morning sickness had long since passed, her general levels of crankiness were now once more on the rise.

She was becoming familiar with the cycle now, the end less rotation of irritation and nausea that accompanied her every waking moment of late.

The mid wives assured her that the magical part was coming. That she'd soon be radiant and glowing with the promise of the new lives she carried inside her.

Right now, she'd settle for not having swollen ankles and backache, and for every trip to the toilet to no longer require Olympic levels of concentration and effort.

The kettle clicked off. She poured herself a cup of hot water, then dropped in a slice of the slightly dry, withered lemon she'd picked u at the little supermarket down the road.

After stirring it around a bit, she took a sip, confirmed that it was *exactly* as flavourless and disappointing as she'd been expecting, and then she returned to the makeshift Incident Room, where Ayesha Fulton's laptop sat open on the desk.

Ben and Dave were both on the phones, either spreading the word about Ayesha's disappearance, or following up on leads. Sinead wasn't sure which, and didn't have the energy to listen in long enough to figure it out.

She groaned with relief as she sat down, but took care to not do it loud enough that the others might hear, otherwise Ben would insist that she never stand up again, and remain seated until such time as the babies were born.

He meant well, of course. They all d id . It was just a shame that their good intentions had to be so blood y infuriating.

But then, she thought, that might be the hormones talking.

The login box on the screen sat taunting her. Technically, of course, she should n't have been trying to access the computer. They had no warrant, and there was nothing to ind icate for sure that Ayesha was even missing.

DI Ford e had tasked her with trying to get into it, though, and had mad e it very clear he'd take all responsibility for any complaints or grievances that arose. She'd suggested that it might be better to wait for Hamza to come back, so he could have a crack at it, but Ben had encouraged her to give it a whirl.

It was one way of keeping her sitting at the d esk, she supposed .

She took a sip of her hot water and tried to will some hint of lemon flavour into it, to no avail. Then, with a crack of her knuckles, she typed 'password ' into the password box.

The little white rectangle on the login screen gave a shake, like it was shrugging the suggestion off.

She tried again, this time typing the d igits '1-2-3-4.'

Another shake. Another rejection.

This was going to be hard er than she thought.

Sinead d rummed her fingers on her mug. She sucked air in through her teeth, trying to d ecid e on what her next strategy would be.

Potentially, the password could be anything. A name. A d ate. An incomprehensible string of characters. A sentence, even. The sky was the limit.

Except, it wasn't. Not really. It might've been the hormones talking again, but realistically, people were id iots. Realistically, people were all too pred ictable.

She typed the same four numbers as last time, but this time chucked a '5' on the end before hitting the Enter key.

There was no shake this time. No d enial. Instead , a little circle spun around for a few second s, then the screen changed to show a cluttered desktop with a photo of Ayesha and Orla set as the background wallpaper.

Sinead let out a little laugh, but it was a dry, mirthless thing, that almost sounded more disappointed than amused.

'Predictable idiots, the lot of us,' she muttered, then she set down her mug, leaned in closer, and began to click her way through the contents of the computer.

It was twenty minutes later when she made the discovery that would change everything.

And it was right around that time when, from under the desk, Taggart let out a low growl of warning.

'What's up?' Sinead asked, leaning back in her chair to look down at the dog.

He was still lying down, facing the door, the fur on his neck standing on end. The growl wasn't like him. There was something threatening about it, she thought. Or something scared.

'What's the matter, Tag?' she asked.

Taggart got to his feet, but kept low, like he was preparing to pounce. Sinead followed his gaze to the door, and was about to ask him again what the problem was when she heard it.

Or rather, heard *them*.

Voices. Angry. Shouting.

And lots of them, too.

'What the hell's going on out there?' asked Dave, finishing up his phone call.

'Don't know,' Sinead said. She stood up, closing the lid of the laptop. 'But we'd better find out.'

–

'What the hell's this?' grunted Logan, bringing the BMW to a sudden stop at the back of a small but vocal group of people that had assembled around the entrance to the police station.

Hoon contemplated the gathering for a moment, then declared them to be 'some shower of arseholes, by the looks of it.'

From the back seat, both men heard Stephen Boyd let out a groan. He'd seen crowds like this before. More than once, in fact.

'You know these fucks?' Hoon asked, turning to look into the back.

It was Logan who answered. 'I do,' he said, unfastening his belt. 'Some of them, anyway.' He began pointing out the faces he recognised. 'That's Ayesha Fulton's grandmother and her partner. I told them to stay at home. That's Merry Donlon, Ronnie's mother. And ... Christ. Orla's parents.'

'Orla? As in the dead girl?'

'Aye,' Logan confirmed. 'Fuck.'

He took a breath, then opened the door, ordered the other two men to wait where they were, and stepped out into the car park. The crowd was twenty or so strong, and a handful of those at the back turned at the sound of the DCI's door closing.

The others, however, remained focused on the police station, and began to jeer and boo when the front door was opened, and a startled-looking Sinead poked her head out.

'Right, enough with the bloody racket,' Sinead snapped. 'What are you all doing here? What do you want?'

There were a few replies—'Justice!' 'The truth!' and that sort of thing—though none of them was shouted with any real sense of conviction, and Logan got the impression that, like most angry mobs, this one hadn't really thought things through.

The one exception was Orla's mother. Sarah Coull didn't shout. She didn't have to. Her voice carried through the crowd like a siren's call.

'I want my daughter to be alive,' she stated, holding Sinead's gaze. 'That's what I want. But I can't have that, can I? You can't give me that. So I suppose what I want is for you lot to have taken all this seriously.'

'I promise you, we are taking things seriously, Mrs Coull,' Sinead said, but she was drowned out by support from the crowd.

'Yeah, now you are, maybe!' one man bellowed.

'All just a smidge too bloody late, though!' added another.

The accent was a dead giveaway. Logan's eyes were drawn to the voice, and soon spotted the speaker's distinctive purple hair standing out among the crowd . Hugo was here, too, then. Of course he blood y was. Any excuse for a bit of attention.

'And now we've got another girl missing!' a woman in the crowd cried . 'Our kid s aren't safe. None of us are safe!'

Sinead raised her voice, trying to make herself heard . 'Listen. Please, I know how worrying this must be for you all, but you have to believe me that—'

'You've got that paed o in there, ain't you?'

That was Kathleen Fulton talking. Logan recognised the slurred speech and ravaged throat.

'What's the sick fucker d one with Ayesha?' she rasped . 'Bring him out here so he can fucking tell us where she is!'

There were some more shouts of support then, though perhaps a touch less enthusiastic than they had been for Sarah Coull. There may be a truce right now, but in a town this size, Logan was sure that almost every member of the protest would've had some sort of run-in with the Fultons in the past.

DI Ford e appeared in the d oorway behind Sinead and held up h hand s for silence. The crowd , though, completely ignored him and continued with its chorus of complaints.

Logan raised an arm and waved to the other d etectives to catch their attention, then leaned into his car and pressed d own in the centre of the steering wheel, blasting the horn. He kept his hand on it until everyone had turned to face him, then kept it there a little longer until he was sure they were all sick of hearing it.

'Right, then,' he boomed when he finally released it, and the sound fell away into silence. 'I'm going to say this once, and once only. So, I suggest you all shut your mouths, pin back your ears, and pay attention.'

He swept his gaze across the crowd , eyeballing all the members of it, like he could implant his will d irectly into their brains without having to say another word . From the d isd ainful looks and hostile glares they fired back at him, though, it was clear he was going to have to stick to d oing things the old -fashioned way.

'I get why you're here,' he said . 'I d o. You're angry. You're scared . And you want answers.'

234

'Aye, you're fucking right we do!' spat Kathleen Fulton's junkie boyfriend.

'Obviously, you didn't hear the part when I told you to shut your mouth,' Logan said. 'I'm warning you, open it again, and you're under arrest.'

'What for?' Kathleen demanded. 'You can't arrest him just for talking.'

'No, but I'm sure I can find a list of other things to do him for,' Logan said. 'Do the pair of you want to turn out your pockets?'

From the way they both shrunk back, it was clear that they very much did not want to do that.

'No. Thought not. Then shut up,' Logan said. 'And that goes for all of you. We're here to do a job. We're here to find out who killed Orla. We're here to find Ayesha. That's why we're here. That's what we're going to do. But, you lot? You lot are getting in the way of that. Whatever you might think you're doing—whatever you think this wee hissy fit is going to achieve—you're wrong. This—you lot, here, now—this will not help us find out what happened to Orla. This will not bring Ayesha home. This will slow down the hunt for a killer, and put another young woman's life at risk.'

He left them to dwell on that for all of five seconds, then followed up before they had a chance to say anything stupid.

'So, I'm going to ask you nicely, just this once. Go home. Please. Leave us to do our jobs, and I give you my word that—'

'Here, wait a fucking minute,' Kathleen Fulton ejected. She pointed to Logan's car, and to the man currently sitting on the back seat. 'There's the dirty paedo bastard in there!'

Gasps rang out through the knot of townsfolk. The revelation rippled through them like some sort of seismic event, and a few of the braver ones surged towards Logan and the BMW, dragging several of the more reticent members along in their wake.

Shite.

Logan stepped forward to block their path, but there were too many of them to intercept. They swarmed around the car, slapping at the back windows, faces knotted up with hatred and rage for the man cowering in the back.

235

'Right, fuck this!'

The front passenger d oor was thrown open without a thought for those on the other sid e of it. A frothing, wasp-faced woman in her mid -thirties was sent spiralling to the ground , accompanied by a barked 'serves you fucking right' from Hoon as he erupted from insid e the car.

Hugo had grabbed the hand le of the rear passenger sid e d oor, and was rattling it furiously in an attempt to get it open.

Hoon stud ied his d yed hair and facial piercings for a moment, ther shoved him away with one hand . 'The fuck are you meant to be?' he asked .

Hugo hissed at him—actually hissed , like a movie vampire—and mad e another lunge for the hand le. Hoon waited for him to come within reach, then grabbed his nose ring and plucked it out with a sharp d ownward s tug.

'Argh! My nose!' the lad wailed . 'You tore right through my nostril!'

Hoon d id a d ouble-take, then threw a look across the car to Logan. 'What sort of accent is that meant to be? Is he related to the fucking Queen? And you brought that on yourself, by the way.'

He flicked the little silver hoop away as Hugo began to wail and clutch at his face, then turned on the crowd .

Not *to* the crowd . *On* it.

'I swear to fuck, everyone better back *the fuck* off!' he roared . His face twisted with a fury that had stopped even the most d eranged o Glasgow hard men in their tracks so many times over the years. 'The next one of you sticks of d og shite I see touching this fucking car, I'm putting my thumbs through your eye sockets and playing your brain like it's a fucking Xbox controller. And I know that might sound like an exaggeration, but I assure you, it's not. I'm *underplaying* what I'll fucking d o to you. I'm toning it d own so as no' to upset any of you. You just wait and fucking see.'

It could 've gone two ways, Logan knew. The threat could 've thrown fuel on the fire, escalated things further, and turned the situation uglier than it alread y was.

And yet, that didn't happen. For all its mob mentality, for all its blind rage, the crowd could sense the danger that radiated from the man now facing them down.

'Better,' Hoon announced. Logan opened his mouth to interrupt, but Hoon silenced him with a raised hand and a 'Jack. Please' then continued addressing the mob. 'Right, so, I don't actually know what the fuck's going on,' he admitted. 'Your man in the back there, I've got no idea who the fuck he is. Is he a horrible paedo? Maybe. Did he kill that lassie? Might've done. Has he got the other poor cow hogtied in a fucking dungeon somewhere?'

'Jesus Christ, Bob!' Logan hissed.

'We don't have a fucking clue,' Hoon pressed on. 'But are we going to find out? Aye. Are we going to hang this prick up by the fucking eyelids until he shites out every creepy wee nonce secret he's got rattling around in that warped wee head of his? You bet your arse we are.'

There was some enthusiasm from the crowd for that idea. A lot of nodding. Some murmuring of approval.

'Or, I should say, he is,' Hoon said, nodding to Logan. 'Me? I'm with you lot.'

Logan frowned. What the hell was the man on about now?

'Bob?' he muttered. 'What are you doing?'

'You fuckers might have come here to kick off and start shit,' Hoon said. 'But as of right now, you're no' a fucking mob. You're a search party. You say you want to find that lassie? Fine. Fucking prove it. Everyone who wants to make themselves useful, line up against that fucking wall. Anyone who wants to keep being an arsehole and getting in the way better fuck off home, sharpish.'

Nobody moved. Not at first. It was only when Hoon stamped a foot, clapped his hands, and bellowed a command to 'get a fucking move on!' that at least half the crowd fell into line along the front wall of the car park, backs straight, eyes wide and eager to please.

The remaining number, without the more vocal element, quickly drifted away from the car, until only Sarah Coull remained. She stood staring into the back seat of the BMW, at the man sitting there who was refusing to look up and meet her eye.

'Um… come on, Sarah,' her husband muttered, but she whipped her arm away when he tried to touch her, and glared at him until he backed off.

It was only when Merry Donlon took her arm and offered a smile of support that Orla's mother turned her back on the car.

Then, gripped by some sudden burst of rage, she turned to the window and spat on it, then fell against Merry like her strength had left her, and allowed herself to be led out of the car park, and off down the street, with her husband scuttling along a safe distance behind her.

While everyone was watching the show, Logan approached Hoon. From the corner of his mouth he asked, 'What the hell are you playing at?'

'Doing you a favour, you ungrateful fucking savage,' Hoon replied. 'I just killed you two fucking birds with one stone. Get rid of me for a bit, and get shot of this lot. You should be down on your fucking knees thanking me, Jack.'

Logan grunted, which was about as close to a display of gratitude as Hoon was likely to get. 'Aye. Well, keep them out of my hair, but for Christ's sake, Bob, stay out of trouble.'

Hoon grinned. 'Come on, Jack. You know me.'

'Aye. I do.' Logan sighed. 'That's the problem.'

Hoon winked, then jabbed a finger at Hugo, who was still nursing his bleeding nose.

'Right, you. Little Lord Fuckelroy, you attention-seeking prick, fall in, or fuck off. It's no skin off my nose, either way. Pun totally fucking intended, by the way.'

Keeping his hand pressed against his torn nostril, Hugo looked from Hoon to Logan, then back again. And then, with a nod, a gritting of teeth, and a clumsy salute, he joined the others in the line by the wall.

A moment later, Hamza's car pulled up behind Logan's, and both detectives riding in it opened their doors and stepped out.

'Maybe I'm wrong, boss,' Tyler said, watching as the mob continued to morph into a posse. 'But I can't help but feel that we might've just missed some excitement…'

Chapter 33

Ten minutes later, Stephen Boyd had been successfully brought inside, hurriedly processed, then slung in the holding cell for safekeeping. All this was followed by some well-earned cups of tea for the team, and a quick catch-up in the Incident Room.

'That does look like the same brick, right enough,' said Ben, looking over the rocky rectangle retrieved from the wreckage of Boyd's caravan.

The broken parts of the one that had been lobbed through the station window sat on the desk beside it, and there was no denying the similarity. Same shape, same colour, same manufacturer, and used for the same purpose.

'So, do we think Paedo Steve is the window smasher? Or do we think someone did his window in, too?' Ben asked.

'Not sure, boss,' Tyler announced. He held up something else they'd been able to retrieve from the crash site. 'But Paedo Steve's got a security camera. If we're lucky, it might answer that for us.'

'Brilliant!' Ben cheered. 'Then, after we've cracked the case of the broken window, we've just got the murder and the kidnapping to go, and we've done the lot!'

Tyler's smile faded a little. 'Was that sarcasm, boss?'

'Aye, son. Very much so,' Ben confirmed. He winked at the DC, then addressed the team at large. 'Quick update on Ayesha for you all. Phone network says her phone's off, possibly dead. Last ping on it was last night on the street outside her house, around the time you saw her, Jack.'

'She hasn't used it since?'

'No. Hasn't accessed her bank account, either,' Ben said.

Logan groaned. This wasn't sound ing good. 'You put a shout out, aye?'

'I d id. All eyes are peeled for her. Got Uniform coming across from Inverness to help with the search. I mean, assuming Hoon and his new gang of pals haven't found her by then...'

'What should I d o with this, boss?' asked Tyler, still hold ing up the camera. 'Am I back burnering it for now?'

Logan glanced at the camera, then shrugged. 'Hamza, take a quick look, will you? See if you can get into it and look it over. Might be hand y for when I go through and talk to him.'

'Or someone else could d o that!' Tyler hurried ly interjected. 'I mean, like we were just saying, it's not exactly top priority, is it? Should n't be wasting a sergeant's time on that sort of thing. Dave could d o it.'

'Oh, cheers for that,' Dave David son piped up.

Hamza glared long and hard at Tyler, then sighed. 'I mean, I suppose someone else *could* d o it. It should be pretty straightforward,' he ad mitted. 'It's just checking a memory card.'

'Aye, and we've got*two* technical geniuses on the team now,' Ben d eclared. 'Sinead was able to crack that laptop!'

'Just crack it?' Logan muttered. 'Tyler managed to smash one to bits.'

Sinead and Ben both looked confused by the remark.

'Sir?' Sinead asked.

'Doesn't matter. What's he on about?'

'The password !' Ben said, replying for her. 'The security. She was able to bypass the whole lot!'

'See!' Tyler said, nod d ing meaningfully in Hamza's d irection. 'You d on't even*need* to d o that stuff now! Sinead can d o it!'

'You bypassed the security?' Logan asked.

Sinead shrugged. 'I typed one-two-three-four-five. It was hard ly hacking the Pentagon.'

'Still, though!' Tyler cheered. 'That's brilliant! Isn't it, Ham?'

'Aye,' Hamza said, keen to shut the topic d own. 'Brilliant.'

Tyler tried to continue gushing out praise, but Logan spoke over him.

'Find anything on there?' he asked Sinead.

'I did, sir, aye.'

All ears pricked up at that, with the exception of Taggart's, who was fast asleep under the desk.

'And? What is it?' Logan asked. 'What did you find?'

Sinead opened up the laptop lid. The screen had locked, so she punched the numbers into the password field again.

The screen changed to show a rectangular window taking up half the display. Orla Coull filled the frame of the video, a little white triangle over her face inviting the viewer to press play.

'I think, sir,' Sinead said, tapping the icon. 'That you'd better see it for yourself.'

—

They all sat staring at the laptop, not speaking. Not daring to. Not yet.

It was DI Forde who eventually broke the silence, though not with anything particularly insightful.

'Bloody hell,' he muttered, then he looked around at the others, as if to check they'd been watching the same video clip he had. 'We all saw that, aye?'

'Play it again,' Logan instructed.

He hadn't moved since Sinead had started the video. Or rather, he hadn't moved much. Only his eyebrows had shifted, first creeping up his forehead, then bunching together into a knot as it became clearer what he was watching.

The rest of his expression had remained fixed. Static and stoic.

And haunted by what he'd seen.

Sinead scrubbed the video timeline back to the start. Orla Coull flailed around in close-up, her anxious and furtive hand movements now appearing cartoonish and comedic. Her tears rolling back up her cheeks, before her ducts sucked them back in.

'Make notes,' Logan instructed.

Tyler looked around the group. 'Who, boss?'

'Everyone.'

A tap of the laptop's touchpad set the vid eo playing again, and they all watched and scribbled as Orla Coull—some younger version of her, some living version—shared her secrets.

It sound ed like a confession. Looked like one, too. It was there in her eyes, in the way she could n't look at the camera for more than a second at a time, in the way that she sat almost completely still throughout her speech, rarely shifting on the end of the bed on which she sat.

And it was there in her voice, and in the shad ows of her eyes. Shame.

'I, um, I can't remember exactly when it started ,' she began, as if answering a question someone had asked before the camera started record ing. 'I was… twelve, maybe. Or, no. Eleven? It was before high school. Primary seven, so… yeah. Eleven. Mum was away. Two or three nights. Work, I think. Can't really remember.'

She scratched her arm. Slowly. Deliberately, the touch of her nails leaving marks on her skin.

'That's when it started ,' she whispered . 'That's when he first started coming into my room.'

They listened to the rest of it, Orla's revelations accompanied by the sound s of pen nibs scratching on paper. By gasps, and tuts, and muttered obscenities.

And by a stern, solemn silence from the d etective lead ing the case.

And then, just a minute or two later, it was over. Orla Coull's shame had been laid bare once more.

'So, this was on there, was it?' Logan asked , still staring at the image paused on the screen. 'This was on Ayesha's laptop?'

'Yes, sir,' Sinead confirmed . 'Attached to an email that Ayesha sent a few weeks back.'

All eyes turned toward s her.

'An email?' Logan said . 'Sent to who?'

'To Leonard Coull, sir,' Sinead said . 'Ayesha sent that clip to Orla's father. No message. No subject, just the attachment.'

'Did we hear back from Hugo Hend erson's mobile provid er yet?' Logan asked , still keeping his anger in check, though just barely.

'Oh, aye! We d id , boss!' Tyler said . 'It's in the group inbox. There was only a text, not a call. Hugo was telling the truth.'

'So Leonard Coull was lying,' Logan conclud ed .

'"Disgusting little man",' Sinead said . 'That's what his wife called him.'

Logan rose to his feet—slowly, inexorably, like some great sea monster rising from the d eep—and the rest of the room seemed to shrink back from him, as if sensing his wrath.

'I want him brought in here. Now,' he said . It was not a request. It wasn't even an ord er, in fact. It was simply a statement of how things were going to be.

The others nod d ed , jumped up, started to move. It was only Ben who d ared point out the logistical issues.

'There's no room for him. Unless we're d oubling him up with Stephen Boyd .'

'We'll keep Boyd in the cell,' Logan said . He gestured to the laptop. 'After this, I want a crack at Leonard first. Everything else can wait.'

'*Or*, we could go with my plan,' Ben said .

'Which is?'

Ben leaned back in his chair, making the most of his big moment. 'The bank.'

'The bank?'

'It's shut d own. But the build ing's still there. I had a wee snoop in the wind ow, and the furniture's still insid e, too. No bugger's cleared it out yet.'

'And ?' Logan pressed .

'And ...' There was a jingling sound as Ben held up a bunch of keys. 'Guess what I persuad ed the land lord to let us borrow.'

'The bank?' Logan said . 'You're borrowing a whole bank?'

'Aye, well, no point d oing things by halves, is there?' Ben said . He tossed the keys to Logan, who snatched them from the air. 'Now,' the DI said . 'Go get the bastard !'

243

Leonard Coull looked surprised to find DCI Logan and DS Khaled on his front step. At the sight of them, he sidled out through the front door and quietly closed it behind him, cutting off the sound of sobbing from the living room.

'I'm sorry, it's not a good time,' he whispered. 'Sarah's very upset. Merry's with her now, trying to calm her down, but I'm not sure seeing you two here will—'

'We're not here to see her,' Logan told him.

'You're not?' Leonard's eyes flicked between both detectives. Neither of them was smiling. Neither of them was anywhere close. 'So, uh, so why are you here? There, uh, there hasn't been news, has there? Developments?'

'Oh, I'd say there's been a development. Wouldn't you, Detective Sergeant?'

'I'd say there's been a development all right, sir, aye,' Hamza confirmed. 'Quite a big one.'

'You're going to have to come with us, Mr Coull,' Logan told him.

Leonard swallowed. He smiled —or grimaced, maybe—a hopeful, desperate baring of the teeth that he hoped might win him some favours.

'Is it urgent? Can it wait? Like I say, Sarah's very upset, and —'

'There are two ways we can go about this, Leonard,' Logan said, shutting his objections down. 'You can come with us on a voluntary basis, or we can place you under arrest.'

'Under arrest?!' the man on the front step spluttered. 'What do you mean? What for?'

'For the sexual assault and murder of your daughter,' Logan said.

Leonard Coull staggered back against the door, grabbing for the wall to support himself, as his face collapsed in shock, and the bottom fell out of his world.

'The decision is yours, Mr Coull,' Logan told him. 'So, which is it to be?'

Chapter 34

'How are you feeling now, son? I hear that was quite the crash you were in.'

DI Forde's smile was a patient, avuncular thing. It made him look like a kindly uncle, or a well-meaning grandparent, and not a highly experienced detective just trying to sweet talk a suspect into opening up.

Stephen Boyd's reply was considerably less good-natured. 'Fine. Though, I could sue.'

'Oh?'

'Yes. It was you lot who ran me off the road,' Boyd claimed.

Ben sat back in the one of the chairs he'd had Tyler bring through to the station's kitchen, and arranged his features into a look of outrage.

'God. I didn't realise. You should. Sue, I mean,' he said. 'That's not bloody on. DC Neish?'

'Boss?'

'Remind me to get Mr Boyd all the necessary forms when we're finished here, will you?'

'Will do, boss,' Tyler said, despite the fact he had absolutely no idea what paperwork the DI was referring to.

'You could be onto a tidy sum there, Stephen—do you mind if I call you Stephen?'

Boyd shrugged to indicate he couldn't care less. Ben thanked him, before continuing.

'You could be onto a nice big payout there, Stephen. A healthy chunk of change,' the DI said. He winced. 'Course, it won't be easy spending it if you're in the jail.'

'Yeah, well, there's no danger of that, because I haven't done anything!' Boyd said, leaning forward and spitting out those last few words for emphasis.

'Oh, I hope you're right, son,' Ben said. His gaze flitted briefly to a box file sitting on the desk beside him. He ran a hand across the top, then gave it a pat. 'I really hope you're right.'

'You sure you don't want a solicitor, Stephen?' asked Tyler. 'I know we've asked this already, but we need you to say it for the recording.'

'I don't want a solicitor. I don't need one because, again, I haven't done anything! I'm a victim here.'

'Of the officer you say ran you off the road?'

'Of everyone!' Stephen declared. 'Of this whole fucking village. You saw that crowd out there. They hate me. They'd rip me apart, given half a chance.'

Ben couldn't argue. He'd seen mobs turn ugly before, and the one outside had been moments away from it. If they'd managed to drag Boyd from the back of the car, there's no saying what they'd have done to him.

'People are upset,' Ben explained. 'There's one girl dead, and another missing. So, the people here—the ones who were outside—they're scared. Folk aren't themselves when they're scared. But, it'll all calm down. Ultimately, that lot out there, they just want the same as Detective Constable Neish and I do. As we all do. We want to bring that missing lassie home, and catch the person who killed Orla Coull.'

Paedo Steve sat back and shrugged. 'I wish I could help, but like I've said, time and time again, I didn't know Orla. I didn't know her, I don't know what happened to her, and I sure as hell didn't kill her!'

Ben nodded. 'That's right. You did say that, didn't you? That you didn't know her.'

Boyd watched as the DI opened the box file, withdrew a hardback notebook, then set it down on the table between them.

'The only problem with that, son,' Ben continued. 'Is that Orla Coull says otherwise.'

'What?' Boyd sat up straighter in the chair. 'What do you mean? What are you talking about?'

Ben smiled and gave the book a pat. 'We'll come back to that,' he said .

'She's lying! If that's what she's… it's not true, she's lying!'

'We'll come back to it,' Ben repeated , his smile falling away just a fraction. 'First, though, we want to clear a few things up.'

'Why d id you run away, Stephen?' Tyler asked .

'What?'

'This was your home. That's what you said last night. This place was your home, and you weren't going to be d riven out of it.' The d etective constable shrugged . 'What changed your mind ?'

Boyd tapped a finger on the table. Dum-d um-d um-d um. Dum-d um-d um-d um

'Well, I knew what was coming, d id n't I? That lot. I knew they were going to blame me for what had happened .'

'You must've suspected that last night,' Tyler pressed . 'Why not go then? Why wait until tod ay?'

'Did something happen, Stephen?' Ben asked .

Boyd stared back at them. He almost said something—both d etectives saw the thought forming—but then he just shook his head .

'For the record , Mr Boyd just shook his head ,' Tyler d eclared .

'For the tape, please,' Ben urged .

Boyd sighed and leaned closer to the microphone. 'No. Nothing happened .'

'Nothing triggered your change of heart?' the DI continued . 'Nothing mad e you d ecid e to load up and roll out like that?'

'Nothing in particular. No.'

'OK. Interesting. Interesting,' Ben said , crossing his arms and leaning back.

He looked d own at the notebook sitting on the table between them, like he was about to return to that topic. When he d id n't, his question caught the suspect off guard .

'Did you put a brick through our wind ow, Stephen?'

Boyd blinked . He spent a good few second s d oing nothing but, in fact. Then, at last, he shook his head .

'What? No.'

'You d id n't put a brick through our wind ow?' Ben clarified .

'No. I d id n't put a brick through anyone's wind ow.'

Ben nod d ed to Tyler. The DC bent, rummaged und er the d es for a moment, then prod uced two evid ence bags, each containing bricks. One of them was broken in half, but otherwise, they appeared id entical.

'Then here's a funny coincid ence, Stephen,' Ben told him. 'This here? This was thrown through the front wind ow out there last night. Right blood y mess it mad e, too.'

'And then I got hit by a car,' Tyler ad d ed , which earned him frown of confusion from the suspect.

'How's that connected ?'

'Doesn't matter,' Ben said , cutting in. 'The point is, *this* brick— which, I d on't know, to my untrained eye, looks exactly like*that* brick—was found in your caravan earlier. Now, I'm sure there's a very rational explanation for it, but we've been struggling to come up with it, so we're hoping you can help us out, Stephen.'

It was Tyler's turn to fold his arms, mirroring Ben's posture. 'Well, Stephen?' he asked . 'Can you explain?'

Across the table, Boyd 's gaze shifted from one brick to the other, then d iverted to where Orla's journal sat taunting him with its secrets.

'No,' he ad mitted . 'No, I can't explain.'

'Oh,' said Ben.

'Well,' said Tyler.

'That is unfortunate, isn't it, Detective Constable?'

'Aye, Detective Inspector,' Tyler agreed . 'That's very unfortunate, ind eed .'

–

Dave David son sat at the d esk in the Incid ent Room, humming to himself as he scrolled through yet another of the vid eo clips retrieved from the camera in Stephen Boyd 's caravan. There were d ozens of d ifferent files, d ating back over a week. Some of them lasted only a few second s, while others stretched to a few minutes.

The camera, it seemed, was motion activated. It had been carefully angled so that it would only start recording if anyone approached the caravan, and wouldn't be activated by cars passing on the road beside it.

That was the theory, anyway, though the reality was somewhat more complex.

A bird or insect flew past? It fired up.

A strong wind shook the caravan? It fired up.

It rained? It fired up.

There was a lot, Dave was discovering, that made the bloody thing fire up, from swaying branches to motes of dust, and working his way through all the clips was taking longer than he'd expected.

'Sorry... can you not do that?' Sinead asked.

She was sitting on the other side of the desk, still going through the contents of Ayesha's laptop.

Dave looked up from his screen, his broad face pulling into a frown. 'Do what?'

'That humming.'

'Humming?' Dave's eyes flicked down, like he might be able to see the sound coming out of his mouth. 'Was I humming?'

'Yes,' Sinead said.

'What, like a tune?'

'Well, I think so. Sort of. Yeah.'

'Sorry, didn't realise.'

'It's fine,' Sinead assured him. 'Don't worry about it.'

'Right...' Dave looked even more confused now. 'It's fine as in, you don't mind me humming?'

Sinead quickly shook her head. 'No. God, no. If you hum, I'll probably cut your lips off,' she said. 'I mean, it's fine, there's no apology necessary.'

Dave laughed and tapped a finger to his head in salute. 'Message received and understood,' he said.

He sat back in his wheelchair, turned his attention to the screen, then gave it all of five seconds before he started beatboxing.

Sinead's eyes went wide, flashing *DANGER!*

'Sorry,' Dave chuckled. 'Could n't resist. I'll shut up.'

Across the d esk, DC Bell laughed. 'Thank God. I genuinely thought I was going to have to kill you,' she confessed. 'Thanks. And sorry. I know I'm being a pain in the arse. It's just… it's amazing how annoying things are when you're pregnant.'

'What sort of things?' Dave asked. 'Besid es humming, obviously. We've established that one.'

'Just… things,' Sinead said. She shrugged. 'Just all things. And everyone.'

'Ouch! I won't ask you to help me look over this stuff, then,' he said, d ouble-clicking on another vid eo file. 'I'm not even a third of the way through, and I want to chuck the laptop into the sea.'

'What end d id you start at?' Sinead asked.

Dave's forehead furrowed. 'Eh?'

'Well, I mean, it should be organised by d ate, right?' Sinead ventured. 'Did you start with the old est, or the newest?'

Dave stud ied the screen, and the list of files he'd worked through. 'Shite,' he said. 'Old est.'

'Newer stuff is probably going to be more interesting,' Sinead remarked.

The uniformed constable swiped a finger across the touchpad, scrolling the list all the way to the bottom.

'Probably not the last few,' Sinead suggested, pred icting his next step. 'They'll just be from the crash. I'd check the timings. See what you've got from sort of mid -afternoon.'

Dave checked the list, then shot a look across the d esk. 'Blood y hell, you are quite good at this stuff, aren't you?' he said, then he d ouble-clicked a file and leaned in closer, waiting for it to load.

A few second s later, he watched a car pull into the layby behind Stephen Boyd 's caravan.

He watched a woman emerge and come storming over, her face bunched up in rage.

He saw a hand going into a carrier bag. Watched a rough red brick being pulled out, an arm being d rawn back, a projectile being hurled.

'Eh, Sinead,' Dave said. He turned the laptop towards her, letting her see the events unfolding on the footage. 'I think we might've found something.'

–

Ben had not been lying. The bank building had been sitting untouched since its closure a few months back, as the fine film of dust covering every surface would attest.

After some searching around, they found the manager's office, and Logan sat with Leonard Coull in an adjoining waiting area while Hamza prepped the room for the interview. A large, square, metal vault door stood at one end of the waiting room, ever so slightly ajar. Hamza had taken a quick peek inside on his way past, and had looked disappointed that there weren't any big sacks of cash sitting in there.

That had been five minutes ago, and both men sitting in the waiting area were growing impatient.

'I don't know what this is all about,' Leonard insisted. It was not the first time he'd said those words since Logan had told him to sit down, nor was it the first time that Logan completely ignored them.

Let the bastard stew for a while. Let his stress and worry do the detectives' work for them. That way, by the time the interview started, he'd already be halfway to a confession.

'I've done nothing wrong,' Leonard insisted, his voice becoming higher pitched and more desperate with each protestation. 'I don't understand what all this is about!'

The door to the manager's office opened, and Hamza emerged. With a nod, he declared the room was ready, and Logan bounded to his feet, eager to start putting pressure on the snivelling, red-faced man currently cowering on a chair in the corner.

'Right, Leonard, through we go,' he instructed, pointing to the door.

Leonard leaned over a little so he could get a better view of the office. He peered into the room for several seconds, like he was terrified of what might be lurking in there, then he slowly eased himself up off the seat and went shuffling through the door ahead of Logan.

Hamza had given the place a quick tidy, which had largely involved sweeping most of the dust off the manager's desk. Now, tiny white motes of it hung in the air, buffeted around on invisible breezes, carried this way and that around the office-turned-interview room.

'Take a seat,' Logan said, pointing to the chair closest to the door.

There were two other chairs on the other side of the desk—the side the manager would've sat on while crushing hopes and ruining dreams—but Logan elected to remain standing while Hamza made himself comfortable across from Orla's father.

Ayesha's laptop sat with its lid closed on a small folding table Hamza had positioned on his side of the desk. The tabletop wasn't much larger than the computer, so there was roughly an inch of space visible around the edges of the laptop. Logan had no idea what purpose the table would've served back when the bank was active, but right here and now, it looked like it had been designed specifically for the purpose of supporting the computer.

Leonard Coull didn't seem to have noticed it. Or, if he had, he'd thought nothing of it.

The contents of that device might lead to him being jailed for the rest of his life, and the poor bastard had absolutely no idea.

'Sarah's going to be worried sick,' Leonard said. 'She's already upset, and now she's going to be climbing the walls, wondering where I've gone!'

'Oh, I don't know, Leonard,' Logan said. He pulled the window blind closed, before turning back to the men sitting at the desk. 'From what I saw yesterday, I doubt she'll even notice you're gone. She might even be relieved, in fact.'

Leonard swallowed. He held Logan's gaze for a moment, but any thought of defiance soon left him, and he lowered his head without offering any argument on the matter.

'What was it she called you? A disgusting little man, wasn't it? That doesn't strike me as someone likely to be concerned by your sudden disappearance, even if there is a killer on the loose.' The DCI shrugged. 'Still, best keep her in the loop, I suppose. DS Khaled, message DC Bell, will you? Ask her to pop round and pay Mrs Coull a visit. Let her know we've brought her husband in for questioning.'

'Will d o, sir.'

Panic flashed behind Leonard 's eyes. 'Wait, no. No, d on't d o that. She'll get the wrong id ea. Don't d o that, please.'

'Too late, I'm afraid ,' Hamza said , as his phone gave a whoosh to ind icate his message had been sent.

'We'd better get through this sharpish, Leonard , so you can get back home and explain everything to her,' Logan suggested . 'Don't want her getting "the wrong id ea", like you say. So, how about we skip all the niceties and get right d own to business?'

Leonard Coull ran the back of his arm across his forehead , wiping away an oasis of sweat that had pooled there.

'What d o you mean?' he asked . 'What d id you bring me here for? What d o you want to know?'

'What I want to know, Leonard ,' Logan began. 'Is what possessed you to sexually assault and murd er your d aughter? And what have you d one with Ayesha Fulton?'

Chapter 35

'OK. OK, fine. You want to know why I ran? You want to know why I was leaving?'

DI Ford e smiled patiently at the man on the other sid e of the table.

'Oh. OK, so we're jumping back to that now, are we?'

The d iary—and the lack of information they'd shared with him on the subject—was taking its toll. Boyd could n't sit still in his seat now, and was repeated ly running his hand s through his hair like it was some invasive parasite he was d esperately trying to rid himself of.

'I was more interested in the brick right now, but I'll take what I can get. And , your reason for clearing out *is* one of the questions we've been repeated ly asking you, Stephen, so yes. Please. We'd love to know the answer, would n't we, Detective Constable?'

'Love to, boss,' Tyler confirmed . He waved his pen around . 'I'm read y to write it d own, and everything.'

Boyd leaned closer, and prod d ed the tabletop with an ind ex finge 'Because I knew, all right? I knew what was going to happen. I knew they were coming for me.'

'You knew who was coming?'

'Them. That lot! Everyone!' Stephen cried , waving emphatically toward s the d oor. 'They'd d ecid ed it was me, that I'd killed that gi and snatched the other one. They'd got it into their head s.'

'And how d id you know that?' Ben asked . 'Did someone contact you?'

'Yes. No. I mean, no. Not exactly.'

'You d on't seem very sure, Stephen,' Ben pointed out. 'Did someone contact you, or d id n't they?'

Boyd had another go at his hair, first with one hand , then the other. Then, when it continued to cling stead fastly to his head , he settled for peeling a sliver of a thumbnail off with his teeth.

'It was that other girl,' he began, the word s slow and reluctant. 'The missing one.'

'Ayesha.'

'Yeah. Yeah, her. Her... whatever. Parents? Grand parents, I think someone said , one of them posted in the Facebook group.'

'Facebook group?' Tyler asked .

Boyd nod d ed . 'It's, like, a local community page thing. It was set up when Orla went missing. Don't know who by. Someone who thought it'd help, I suppose. People share upd ates there. Sightings, theories, any news.'

'And you're a member of this group?' asked Ben.

'Yeah. No.'

'You're at it again, son,' the DI pointed out. 'Straight answers are going to be better for you.'

'I have a fake profile,' Boyd explained . He glanced at the d etect-ives, checking their reaction to this revelation. If they were shocked , though, they were keeping their card s close to their chest. 'If I was on there und er my real name, they'd rip me apart. So, I created a fake account, and joined that way.'

'Why?' Ben asked . 'You claim you d on't know the girl. Why d o you care?'

'Well, because I'm not a fucking monster!' Boyd replied . 'Like, just because I d on't know her, d oesn't mean I d id n't want her to turn up safe.'

'Be in your best interests, too, I'd have thought,' Tyler ad d ed . 'If they're all blaming you, better to keep an eye on what they're saying.'

'Well, yeah. Yeah, that, too,' Boyd ad mitted . 'And it's a good job I d id , because otherwise, I would n't have seen the other girl's grand -parents ranting about me on there, saying I'd grabbed that other girl. Whipping people up. Getting them mad . You can look for yourself, it'll still be on there. Dozens of them, all blaming me. Saying someone had to d o something. Saying the police weren't going to get me, so it was high time someone d id .'

'And that's when you ran?' Ben asked .

Boyd snorted . 'Well, would n't you?'

Ben consid ered the question for a few moments, then shook his head . 'No.'

'No?'

'I'd stay. Show them I d id n't have her. Clear my name.'

'Running makes you look guilty,' Tyler ad d ed .

'Bullshit! Running makes me look scared ,' Boyd snapped . 'And you know what? I was. I am!' He took a d eep, stead ying breath, and when he spoke again, he sound ed calmer, less d esperate. 'I haven't d one anything. I haven't hurt anyone. I d on't care what you say, I d id n't know Orla. I d on't know the other girl, either.'

'In her d iary, Orla suggests you were having a relationship,' Ben said .

'Well, she's talking shit,' Boyd countered .

'Your name comes up several times. She obviously thought very highly of you, though started to complain you were getting a bit possessive near the end .'

'This is absolute bollocks! It's fantasy. I d id n't know her, all right?' His head tick-tocked between both officers, his expression becoming a wild and d esperate thing. 'I've never even spoken to her!'

'Yes, well, I'm afraid —' Ben began, but Boyd cut him short.

'I've changed my mind . I want a lawyer,' he said .

'Ah, come on, Stephen, we're making great progress here. The last thing we need is a solicitor coming in and slowing things d own. We're just starting to get somewhere.'

'You're not listening.' Boyd leaned in closer. His ind ex finger extend ed again, and he prod d ed the d esk to punctuate the next fe word s out of his mouth. 'I want a lawyer,' he spat. 'Get me a lawyer, or I'm leaving here right now.'

Before either d etective could offer any argument, there was a knock at the d oor that led through to the makeshift Incid ent Room.

'In you come,' Ben called , and Sinead opened the d oor just enough to meet the DI's eye.

'Sir? There's something you should see,' she said .

Ben dismissed her with a nod, then crossed his arms again and sat back. Beside him, Tyler mirrored the movement. Both of them regarded Boyd with an air of hostile curiosity.

'Well, then, DC Neish, kindly escort Stephen back to his cell while we sort out legal counsel, will you?'

'Will do, boss,' Tyler said.

Ben got to his feet, returned the diary to the box file, then tucked it under his arm. 'Don't get too comfortable, Mr Boyd,' he suggested. 'This conversation is far from over.'

–

Once Boyd was safely back under lock and key, Tyler and Ben sat down at Dave's computer and watched the second most shocking piece of video footage they'd seen that day.

They saw a silver Vauxhall pulling up behind Paedo Steve's caravan, watched the woman getting out, and then whistled quietly through their teeth as she hurled a brick straight through the caravan window. They heard shouts from Boyd —angry, shocked —and saw the woman retreating in the car's direction, but not yet climbing in.

At the far left of the screen, Boyd threw open the caravan door and emerged onto the top step of the little metal staircase Tyler and Sinead had climbed the night before.

His face, when he stepped out, was a picture of anger. At the sight of the woman, though, it quickly changed to one of surprise.

They both stared at each other for several seconds in total silence, then she climbed back into the car, pulled on her seatbelt, and drove off.

A few moments later, with Boyd still standing there on the step, the video came to an end.

'Thoughts?' asked Sinead, perching herself on the edge of the desk.

'I think he's going to need a new window,' Ben replied.

'He's going to need a whole new caravan, by all accounts,' added Dave Davidson.

'What? Oh. Aye. Forgot about the crash.'

Tyler, though, had a bit more insight to share. He practically bounced into the air while jabbing a finger towards the screen. 'That's... Jesus Christ! That woman. That's her!'

'Who?' asked Ben.

'The bride, boss. At the wedding yesterday. Where the body was found. She was the woman getting married.'

Ben looked from the screen to Sinead, then to her husband. 'You sure?'

'Positive, boss. I'd recognise that crabbit-faced bastard anywhere!'

'There's something else, too,' Sinead said. 'Something bigger.'

There were blank looks all round. Dave grinned, and his wheelchair gave a *squeak* as he leaned forward and tapped the screen.

'Good bloody job I was here to spot it then, eh?' he said. 'Check the plate.'

Ben and Tyler both refocused on the screen. Tyler read the registration out loud. 'ER17...' he said, but DI Forde was already a step ahead of him.

'Hang on! WO! It ends in WO!'

'Bingo!' Dave declared.

'We think it might be the same car that was on the bank's CCTV camera footage,' Sinead said. 'Silver Vauxhall. Same last two letters.'

'But they're not local, are they? The wedding party, I mean. They're up from London or something, aren't they?'

'Essex, boss,' Tyler corrected.

Ben waved a hand as if to suggest this was the same thing. 'Either way, they're a long way from home.'

Sinead shook her head. 'They come up this way a lot. The groom told me. That's why they picked the castle to get married.'

'But we don't know if they were here when Orla disappeared?'

'No, sir,' Sinead admitted. She pointed to the screen. 'But, based on that footage, I reckon we've got someone in custody who might be able to tell us.'

Ben frowned, already deep in thought and planning his next move. 'Aye. Good work, you two. This is... well, I don't know what it is, but it's something.'

Tyler watched Sinead reaching for her jacket. 'You off somewhere?'

'Orla Coull's house,' Sinead replied. 'The boss has asked me to check in with Sarah Coull. See what she has to say about her husband.'

'Sounds delicate,' Tyler said. 'Want me to come?'

Sinead smirked. 'You did hear yourself saying the first part of that sentence, yeah?' she said.

Tyler nodded slowly. 'Aye. Fair point. Maybe best if I leave you to it. But just... be careful, yeah? If you need me...'

'You'll be the first to know,' Sinead promised, then she planted a kiss on his cheek, gave a little wave to the others, and went striding out of the room.

Tyler continued to watch the door, even after she'd left. This did not go unnoticed by DI Forde.

'She knows what she's doing, son,' he said. 'You up for having another crack at our guest?'

Tyler's gaze continued to linger for a few moments more, then he turned back to Ben and gave a nod. 'Aye, boss. Let's do it!'

Chapter 36

'How d are you?' Leonard Coull spat. 'How fucking*dare* you say that to me? I d id n't hurt Orla! I'd never. I could n't. God ! She was my d aughter, for Christ's sake!'

His anger burned red hot for all of ten second s, then collapsed into grief. Tears ran d own both cheeks, his throat tightening around the rest of his protestations.

'She was my little girl. My beautiful girl.'

Logan, who had been leaning on the wind ow led ge with his arms crossed , now stood up straight. 'Were you abusing her?'

'I beg your pard on?!'

Logan closed the gap in two big paces and slammed both hand s on the d esk so hard that Leonard —and , if he was honest, Hamza, too— almost jumped out of his seat.

'You heard me!' the DCI roared . 'Quit stalling for time. Your d aughter. Orla. Were you abusing her?'

'N-no! No, of course I wasn't! God , no, how can you even say that? I'd never—'

'Is that why your wife hates you, Leonard ?' Logan d emand ed .

'What? She d oesn't*hate* me! I mean, we've had our d ifficulties, but it's been—'

'Oh, no, she hates you. That's clear as d ay,' Logan insisted . 'That ship has long sailed .'

Leonard offered no further argument on the matter, but instead , just shook his head and looked to the wind ow, like he could see out through the closed blind s.

Logan caught Hamza's eye, and the DS picked up the cue.

'We want to help you here, Mr Coull.'

'Help me?! By saying this... this rubbish?! How are you helping me, exactly?'

'Well, first of all, we want to bring Ayesha home.'

'You think I d on't?'

'Things will go a lot easier once we know she's safe,' Hamza continued . 'Once she's back home, we can talk things through prop-erly. We can figure out our next steps.'

'I d on't know where she is!' Leonard squealed , which incurred another angry outburst from Logan.

'Well, Leonard , you'd better hurry up and tell us what you do know, or I'll go through you like a d ose of the shits. I'll be like a pint of Third World tap water. Even as I lock you up and throw away the key, your insid es'll be erupting out of you from both end s. So, enough's enough. Cut the shit. Tell us where she is.'

'You're not listening!' Leonard cried , leaping to his feet. 'I d on't know where she is. I d on't know what happened to her. I have nothing to d o with this. With *any* of this! I d id n't take Ayesha, and I certainly d id n't kill my d aughter!'

Logan glowered at the much shorter man. 'Sit. Down.'

'No!' Leonard shot back. But then, a moment later, he thought better of it and flopped back d own onto his seat. 'This is a mistake,' he whimpered . 'This is all wrong. I d id n't d o anything.'

'Did your wife know?' Hamza asked . He smiled kind ly. 'It's all right, you can tell us.'

'Did she know what?'

'About everything? Any of it?' the DS continued .

'The abuse,' Logan intoned . 'You molesting your d aughter. Did she know about that, Leonard ? Is that why you d isgust her?'

'I d on't *disgust* her...'

'She called you a "d isgusting little man", though,' Logan remind ed him.

'Well, yes, but... she d id n't mean it like... that wasn't what she...'

'Who phoned you?' Logan asked .

The sud d en shift of gears mad e the suspect's face scrunch up in confusion. 'What?'

'Yesterday. After Orla's body was found. Who phoned you? You said it was Hugo, right?'

Leonard swallowed. His face turned a shade or two paler. 'Uh, well…'

'Well, what? That's what you said, wasn't it? You said Hugo phoned to tell you Orla had been found.'

'Yes,' Leonard admitted.

'Right, well, that's very interesting, Leonard, because—'

'That's what I said.' Coull's eyes darted from one detective to the other, then down to where his fingers were tangling together on the desk. 'But that's not what happened. Not exactly.'

Logan pulled out the chair beside Hamza and lowered himself onto it. When he spoke, much of the rage was gone, replaced by something that sounded more like concern.

'Why don't you tell us what happened, then?' he said. 'Help us clear all this up.'

Coull rubbed his eyes with a finger and thumb, sighed shakily, then fired a pleading look in the DCI's direction. 'OK. OK. But first of all, you have to understand, it's not how it sounds.'

Logan said nothing. Just waited.

'It really isn't,' Leonard insisted. 'There's nothing… there's nothing wrong in it. In any of it. Nothing immoral—certainly nothing illegal.'

'You might want to get on with it, Mr Coull,' Logan urged. 'Because you're starting to protest too much.'

The suspect groaned, blew out his cheeks, then threw out a curve ball.

'It was Ayesha,' he said.

Hamza's pen scribbled a note in his pad. Logan continued to whittle away at Leonard with his stare.

'Sorry… what was Ayesha?' Hamza asked.

'On the phone. She called me. Hugo did get in touch with me, but by text. I hadn't actually seen it. Didn't spot it until later. But he texted. He didn't call.' Coull met the DCI's eye for a second, but did n have the nerve to hold it. 'Ayesha called. Ayesha told me. Hugo had already messaged her about it.'

'Why did you lie?' Logan asked. 'Why not just say that from the start?'

Leonard wriggled around on the chair. He was getting uncomfortable now. They were getting close to the crux of the matter.

'Because... Sarah.'

'Because Sarah what, Mr Coull?' Hamza pressed.

'Because she... didn't approve.'

Logan's chair gave out a little groan as he leaned forward an inch or two. 'Of...?'

'Our... friend ship.'

'Your friend ship? You mean you and Ayesha Fulton?'

Leonard nodded. It was quick. Furtive. The movements of a mouse, not a man.

'And tell me, Leonard,' began Logan, interlocking his fingers and leaning his elbows on the desk. 'What exactly was the nature of this friend ship...?'

-

'It was humiliating. Totally humiliating!'

Sarah Coull sat in the middle seat of her three-seater couch, her hands squeezed together between her knees, her eyes ringed with circles of red.

Through in the kitchen, Sinead could hear Merry Donlon keeping herself busy by making tea and some sand wiches. She'd tried to make her excuses and leave, but Sarah was having none of it, and had all but plead ed with her to stay.

She'd looked to Sinead for approval, then had excused herself from the living room, while making it clear to Sarah that she was 'only a holler away'.

She had then shut the kitchen door and immed iately turned on the rad io, and Sinead got the impression that this wasn't the first police interview Merry had tried to prevent herself from overhearing. One of the quirks of being married to a local inspector, the DC supposed.

'They were laughing about it. At him. And at me, of course,' Sarah continued . 'And , I mean, of course they were. Why would n't they? Of course they laughed . It was just so blood y pathetic.'

'I'm afraid I'm not completely following, Mrs Coull,' Sinead ad mitted .

'I told you! Him! Leonard ! And that… that *bloody girl.*'

'Ayesha? Ayesha Fulton?'

'Yes! It was all over town. Everyone knew about it!' Sarah insisted . 'I mean, they d id n't say as much to me—they would n't, would they? But I heard the whispers about a young girl and an old er man. The salacious gossip. And I saw the way people looked at me. Looked at him. Heard them muttering away. Sniggering.'

She covered her mouth with a trembling hand , the fingers pressing into her gaunt cheeks. The fire and the fury that Sarah had d emonstrated yesterd ay, and again at the police station earlier, were now absent. She had aged . Even in the couple of hours since Sinead had last seen her, the woman had grown old er and frailer.

'I confronted him about it. He d enied it. Of course he d id . What else could he d o? Own up to it? Ad mit he's having it away with a girl young enough to be our…?'

The last word proved too much for her to even attempt. She d rew in a d eep breath, shook her head , then went back to looking out through the front wind ow as she'd d one for most of the conversation.

'Is that why you called him a "d isgusting little man", Mrs Coull?' Sinead asked . 'Because of his relationship with Ayesha.'

Sarah d id n't speak, d id n't turn to look, just nod d ed . Just once.

'Nothing else mad e you call him that? Nothing else he'd d one that you were aware of?'

'Like what?' Mrs Coull d emand ed , snapping her head back to glare at the DC. 'What sort of thing? What's he d one?'

It was Sinead 's turn to take a d eep breath. Then, without any further hesitation, she went for it.

'Is it possible that your husband was sexually abusing Orla?'

Sarah Coull seemed to sink back into the cushions of the chair, like the question carried a physical weight she was unable to push back against. Her eyes closed for a moment, then she let out a sound that wasn't a laugh, but was somewhere in that neck of the woods.

'Well, of course he bloody wasn't!' she cried. 'Leonard is a lot of things, and not many of them good, but *abuse Orla*? I won't defend him on much, but by God, I'll defend him on that! No. No, it's ludicrous. It's ridiculous. He didn't. He wouldn't. He couldn't.'

Sinead flashed a thin, kindly sort of smile at the woman on the couch. The woman whose life had already been torn apart once that week. And now, here Sinead was, about to do it again.

She took out her phone and tapped to cue up the video she'd copied there.

'There's something I need you to look at for me, Mrs Coull,' the DC said. 'And I'm afraid it's going to be upsetting…'

–

'It was just… Ayesha and I, it was just a friendship, that's all. Nothing else. I swear!' Leonard insisted. 'There was nothing off about any of it.'

Tears were starting to well up again, and his voice was vibrating like the strings of a guitar in dire need of tuning. Hamza continued to smile encouragingly, while Logan sat back with his arms folded, looking like he wasn't buying a bloody word.

'She's eighteen, Leonard,' the DCI reminded him. 'You're, what? Mid-forties? Some people might consider that a bit *off*.'

'Well, they'd be wrong! There was nothing sinister, or, or, or *creepy*, or anything like that. She just… after Orla disappeared, she and I, we… we used to chat. That's all. Chat. About Orla. About how much we both missed her. Ayesha, she was upset, and her grandmother is… well, she's no bloody use. She needed someone to talk to.'

'And you were happy to provide a shoulder for her to cry on?' Logan said, making no effort to hide his disgust. 'Is that it?'

'It wasn't like that! She just… she needed someone to talk to. God, we both did! It helped me as much as it helped her. More, maybe!' Leonard replied, his voice rising in pitch and volume. 'But there was never anything more than that. Never. I swear.'

'Then why not just say it was her on the phone?' Hamza asked.

Leonard groaned like he'd been d read ing the question. 'To keep th peace. Because Sarah d id n't believe me,' he said. 'Because, no matter how much I assured her there was nothing between Ayesha and me, she d id n't believe it. She refused to.'

Hamza scribbled a note. 'She thought your relationship was sexual in nature?'

'I mean…' Leonard threw his arms into the air, then let them d rop back onto the d esk. 'I suppose so.'

'You *suppose so*?' Logan asked, his eyes narrowing.

'Yes. Yes, I mean… yes, she thought we were… that it was… our friend ship, she thought it was of… a sexual nature.'

'But it wasn't?'

'No! Of course not! That's what I'm saying. That's what I'm telling you!'

'Why d id n't she leave you?' Hamza asked.

Leonard had no real answer to that. He blew out his cheeks and gave a sad, resigned little shake of his head. 'I honestly d on't know,' he ad mitted. 'Though I suspect it's only a matter of time.'

Logan's next question hit the other man like a sucker punch. 'And what about with your d aughter? Was that relationship of a sexual nature?'

Leonard's features contorted in anger. He started to issue yet another d enial, but was stopped by the DCI hold ing up a hand to interrupt.

'Hang on, hang on. Before we go any further, Leonard, I think it's important we show you something.'

Coull's gaze followed Hamza as he reached for the laptop and placed it d own on the d esk. From where Leonard was sitting, he wasn't able to see the screen as the DS opened the case and typed in the five d igit password.

'What?' he mumbled. 'What are you showing me?'

'It's something that might make you consid er the next word s out of your mouth more carefully,' Logan told him.

He tipped Hamza the nod , and the DS started the vid eo. Logan stud ied every movement of every muscle on Leonard Coull's face as the screen was turned toward s him, and Orla began to speak.

There was shock at first. Confusion.

The corners of his mouth creased . His chin d impled . Tears came— not in some big, over-the-top cascad e, but in silence, one by one.

Before Orla had even mad e her accusations, Leonard buried his head in his hand s, covering his face as his should ers shook in great, heaving sobs.

'Please watch the vid eo, Mr Coull,' Logan said .

'What? Why?' Leonard replied .

He took his hand s from his face, and both d etectives were taken aback by the pained smile plastered there. The tears were still falling, but the shaking of the should ers came from some barely-contained laughter.

'Oh, you id iots,' he wheezed . 'You absolute blood y id iots!'

-

Sinead sat staring at Sarah Coull, the sound of Orla's 'confessions' still vibrating through the air. She sat back, her hand s on her knees, replaying Sarah's last few word s in her head to make sure she'd und er- stood them properly.

'An aud ition?' she mumbled . Her eyes fell on the laptop, and Orla's face frozen on the screen. 'That's… an aud ition?'

'Yes. From last year, I think,' Sarah explained . 'She d id them all the time. Her and Hugo and …' She hesitated before saying the next name, like it brought her pain to d o so. 'Ayesha. There were all sorts of, God , I d on't know Projects being d one online. Pod casts. YouTube vid eos. Whatever. They aud itioned for a lot of them.' She nod d ed to the screen. 'There are d ozens of these. More, probably. We haven't seen all of them, but since Orla went missing, we were trying to gather them all up. You know, just to… to see her. Her friend s have been send ing them as and when they come across any they've got saved .'

'So...' Sinead looked from the grieving mother to her dead daughter on the screen. 'This isn't real? None of what she says, none of it is real?'

'Of course it isn't! Like I said, Leonard's many things, but he never hurt Orla. Not in that way. Not in any way. She adored him. Trusted him implicitly.' Sarah rolled her eyes and coughed like there was something in her throat. 'Far more than she did me. She rarely told me anything. Nothing important, anyway. We didn't really have that sort of relationship. She went to Merry when she had her first period. Can you imagine what that was like? For me, I mean? How embarrassed I was when Merry phoned? How that made me look?'

She adjusted herself in her seat, and forced a smile.

'I was happy she had someone to go to, of course. And Merry was great about it. Very understanding. But, yes, that one hurt,' Sarah confessed.

She cleared her throat, wiped her eyes, then sat up straighter.

'But her audition stuff? She was happy to show us that. And that one you just played, she made a point of showing us that one. Given its content, she wanted to run it by us first. Make sure we were OK with it. I was hesitant, I'll be honest, but Leonard?' Sarah shook her head, and the smile she had fixed in place almost became genuine. 'He was just blown away by her performance. He was just so proud, he didn't care about the content.'

'It's, um, it's an impressive performance, right enough,' Sinead said. 'Very convincing.'

'Yes. Clearly,' Sarah said, and the barb did not go unnoticed.

Sinead got to her feet. 'Um, could you give me a minute?' she said, reaching for her phone. 'I should probably go make a quick call.'

Chapter 37

DI Ford e stood outsid e the cell d oor at Kyle of Lochalsh Police Station, hold ing up a laptop screen for the prisoner insid e to see. Stephen Boyd stood at the hatch, staring at the grainy grey footage with a look of quiet resignation.

'You probably d on't recognise the actual record ing, but I'm guessing you recognise the lassie with the brick,' Ben said .

Boyd said nothing. Not for a long time.

'No,' he finally muttered , which earned him a reprimand in gut from the man on the other sid e of the d oor.

'Aye, well, see, I know you're lying there, Stephen,' Ben said . 'Because we had a wee d ig around while you've been sat stewing in here. You and Ellie here, you go way back, d on't you?'

There was no response from the man in the cell. And then, out of nowhere, a nod .

'It was her, wasn't it? She was the girl,' Ben said . 'She was the fifteen-year-old .'

'Almost sixteen,' Stephen seethed .

'Right, aye,' Ben said . He glanced at the screen. 'Clearly, there's a bit of animosity there after all these years. What's the cause of that, then? Because she seems angry, and from the way you d escribed the whole thing to my colleagues, she's got no real reason to be. Accord ing to you, you were two teenagers in love who got a bit carried away with themselves. Based on that, and given everything that happened afterward s, it sound s to me like you should be the angry one. You're the one who went to prison. You're the one on the register.'

Ben tapped the laptop, drawing Stephen's attention back to it. He need n't have bothered. Boyd had n't taken his eyes off it the whole time.

'So, how come she's the one chucking a brick through your wind ow? Is there something you're not telling us, Stephen?'

Boyd rolled the next few word s around in his mouth, like he was feeling the shape of them with his tongue.

'I d umped her,' he said.

Ben raised an eyebrow. 'Sorry?'

'That's why she's mad. She's been furious at me for years. After I went to jail, I d umped her. Told her it was over between us. She refused to accept it. Kept trying to come in to visit. Just pretend ed nothing had happened. That I had n't said anything. Even when her family moved d own south to get away from everything—the scand al of it—she kept writing letters. Two, three a week.'

He backed away from the d oor and sat d own on one of the benches. Ben moved closer to the hatch so he could keep watching the other man's reactions.

'When I got out, she came to my house,' Boyd said. 'Just turned up one d ay. Took the train north. Said she was old enough now, that we could go back to the way things were. She had n't told her parents she was coming. They called the police, and I got hauled back in for questioning. And I thought, 'This is it. I'm going back insid e.' I'd d one nothing, but I was convinced of it. Just seeing her, just remembering it all, I thought… I can't be near you. I can't even look at you.'

'And she d id n't take that well?'

Boyd snorted. 'You could say that. She lost her mind. That's how it felt, anyway. Started telling people we'd been having sex for years. Said I'd groomed her from the start. Said I'd threatened to kill her i she told anyone.'

He wiped his eyes on his sleeve, and stared d own at the floor between his feet.

'My, eh, my mum got really upset by it. I d id n't want her seeing it, so I left. Went to Lond on for a while. Thought she would n't find me there. Big city, and all that.'

'*Camden Steve*,' Ben said, realising the significance of Boyd's self-appointed nickname. 'Seems a strange move if you were trying to get away from her, though. Lond on's a hell of a lot closer to Essex than Tain is.'

'I know. I know, I can't really explain it,' Stephen ad mitted. 'I think... I think I thought that it would let my mum get on. You know? Like, I'd remove the whole problem. And maybe Ellie would find me d own in Lond on, but at least it would n't be on my mum's d oorstep. You know? At least she would n't have to d eal with it anymore.'

'And d id she?' Ben asked. 'Ellie. Did she find you?'

Boyd shook his head. 'No. I mean, not that I know of. But... I d on't know. Being d own there. Being that close to her, I was always on ed ge. And it d id n't stop her from harassing my mum. Phoning. Turning up. Send ing the police round. My mum could n't tell her where I was, because she d id n't know. I was too anonymous, I suppose. Too well hid d en.'

'So you came up here?'

'So I came up here,' Boyd confirmed. 'Got a shitty caravan, posted a few photos on social med ia to give her somewhere else to look, and then just waited for her to turn up. Did n't take her long. She's been up here a d ozen times in the past five years. Used to come round and spill all this stuff about us getting back together. About how we were meant to be together forever. How everything that had happened had just mad e us stronger.'

'And what d id you say?' Ben asked.

'I said, "fuck off, you lunatic, and leave me alone",' the prisoner spat. 'Eventually, it seemed like she'd got the message, because she d id n't come back for about eight, nine months. When she d id, she had a guy in tow. Brought him round to the caravan.'

'She brought him round? To see you?'

'Mad e it look like an accid ent,' Boyd said. 'Pretend ed they were stopping to take some photos, and then acted surprised when she saw me, like she'd never been there before.'

'And you d id n't call her out on it?' asked Ben.

Boyd shook his head. 'No. Why would I? Last thing I wanted to d o was kick it all off again. I was polite. Shook the guy's hand. Wished them both well. I hoped maybe that would be it d one. That I would n't hear from her again. That she'd moved on. Properly, I mean. But then, she send s me a wed d ing invitation. For the castle. And I knew then, she had n't moved on.'

'Might've just been burying the hatchet,' Ben suggested .

Stephen raised his head just long enough to look at the laptop in Ben's arms. 'Did that look like she was burying the hatchet? She wants to ruin my life. Even more than she alread y has, I mean.'

'Aye, well, to be fair now, I d on't think she forced herself on you. It takes two to Tango, son,' Ben reasoned .

Boyd jumped to his feet. 'So, what, you think all this is fair? You think I should suffer forever for one stupid mistake?'

'I d id n't say that,' Ben replied .

Insid e the cell, Stephen sighed . 'You know I d id n't d o this, d on you? You know I d id n't kill that girl, and that I d on't know where the other one is.'

'I'm afraid I d on't know any of that, son,' the DI told him. 'What I d o know is that Orla's d iary names you in it. Several times, in fact. So either you, or it, are lying.'

'I'm not lying. I'm telling you the truth!' Boyd insisted .

'Well, we'll get to the bottom of it just as soon as we can, Stephen,' Ben promised . He smiled , not unkind ly, and shut the lid of the laptop 'In the meantime, you sit tight, and I'm going to work on getting you that solicitor.'

–

By the time Ben returned to the Incid ent Room, the place was stand ing room only. Logan, Hamza, and Sinead had all returned from their respective interviews, joining Tyler and Dave, who were alread y hunched around the d esk.

There was a d istinct lack of enthusiasm from the officers, and the sense of d efeat would 've been absolute, were it not for the waggy-tailed positivity of the smallest team member, who d ashed around the room, licking hand s and sniffing hopefully for biscuits.

'Bloody hell. Who died?' asked Ben. He winced. 'I mean, aside from the obvious one.'

It was Logan who replied. By the sounds of him, it took a lot of energy and effort.

'The video. Orla Coull talking about her abuse.'

'What about it?' Ben asked.

'Dead end.'

Ben placed Dave's laptop back on the desk in front of where the constable sat.

'What do you mean, "dead end"? How can it be a dead end? You've got him bang to rights.'

'It's not real, sir,' Sinead said.

Ben frowned. 'What? She was lying?'

'Acting,' Logan explained. 'It was an audition piece for some bloody pod cast.'

Ben stared back at him for a while. Then, when that got him nowhere, he stared at Sinead instead.

'What the hell's a pod cast?' he asked.

'Doesn't matter,' Logan grunted. 'Point is, we're back to square one. Leonard wasn't abusing her.'

'Oh. Right.' Ben sat on the edge of the desk, then sucked in his bottom lip. 'Is it wrong that I'm a bit disappointed?'

Logan shrugged. It *was* wrong, of course. They should've been over the moon to discover that Orla Coull didn't suffer years of abuse at the hands of her father.

And yet, if she had, they'd at least be a step closer to getting justice for her. They'd at least be on track to solve her murder. As it stood, it didn't feel like they had made any progress at all, beyond losing another girl, and that could hardly be considered a positive development.

'So, we're back to Paedo Steve?' asked Hamza. He looked around at the others. 'He's our best bet, right?'

Logan gave a non-committal sort of grunt. 'Right now, aye,' he said.

'You don't sound convinced, boss,' Tyler said. 'We've got her diary though, right? He's named in there.'

'Aye, well lest we forget, we thought we had her on vid eo telling us that her father was sexually assaulting her, and look where that got us,' Logan reasoned .

'Her old man d id say she used to write a lot of stories, right enough,' Tyler said .

'But it's not a story,' Hamza countered . 'It's a d iary.'

'It's a d iary with no d ates. No times,' Logan said . He d rummed his fingers on the d esk, d eep in thought. 'And no fingerprints, either. Not one. So, it was wiped clean. In what world d oes a teenage girl d o that?'

'You think someone planted it, boss?' Tyler asked .

'I d on't know,' Logan ad mitted . 'And I d on't like not knowing things. It makes me irritable.'

'Here's a wee nugget of info for you,' Dave David son announced . 'Just came in a few minutes ago from that online place we thought might've sold Ronnie the expensive locket thing you found in Orla's room. What they've said is*preeeety* interesting...'

'Ronnie Senior bought it,' Logan said .

Dave's broad should ers took on a sud d en slope. 'Eh, aye. Aye, that's right,' he said . 'How d id you know that?'

'It's the only interesting answer. If Ronnie junior or Orla bought it, that's not interesting.'

'Fair point,' Dave conced ed .

'Orla, boss?' Tyler asked . 'What, d id you think she might've bought it?'

Logan shrugged . 'It was a possibility. She could 've bought it and not yet given it to him. But that still would n't have told us anything. Ronald senior buying it, though? That is interesting.'

'You think they were shagging, boss?' Tyler asked .

'Surely not?' said Hamza. 'She was seventeen when she d isappeared . He's, what? Fifties?'

'I will say, he d id always have an eye for the younger women,' Ben remarked .

'Hang on, hang on,' said Sinead , sitting forward . 'Sarah Coull. She said there's been gossip locally about an old er man and a younger woman. Connected to her family, and she jumped to it being Leonard and Ayesha. But what if it was Orla and Ronald?'

Logan stared blankly at a wall for a moment, and the rest of the team could practically hear the cogs spinning and whirring away.

'What about Ayesha?' he asked, breaking from his trance. 'Any word?'

It was Dave Davidson who piped up again. 'Nothing yet. Got a dozen officers from Inverness and Portree going door to door, checking the local haunts, and talking to public transport. Her name and photo are being released on social media and to the press soon, if they haven't been already.'

'They have,' Sinead confirmed. 'Just saw it popping up on the socials a few minutes ago.'

Logan sighed. It was all necessary, of course, but the press had already had a field day with Orla Coull's disappearance. Now they were sure to get wind of her murder, and turn up in their droves. They'd be crawling all over the place in hours. Just what he bloody needed.

'And Hoon?' he asked. 'Any word from him and his search party?'

'Nothing so far, no,' Dave said, and the others murmured similar responses.

'Aye, well, with a bit of luck they might've all fallen into the loch,' Logan said. 'The longer they stay out of our bloody way, the better.'

He stood up, stretched, then crossed to the Big Board and stared at it in silence for a while.

'Seeing anything, boss?' Tyler asked.

'Gaps,' Logan replied. 'A lot of gaps.'

Sinead got to her feet behind him. 'Sorry, I should've been updating it,' she said, but Logan waved for her to sit down again.

'It's not urgent,' he said, then he checked his watch and muttered something about the time below his breath. 'We should grab something to eat. Get our second wind. Maybe even knock it on the head for the night, and come at it fresh in the morning. We'll bring Ronald Donlon in first thing and give him a going over.'

'Actually, Jack...'

All eyes turned to DI Ford e. He rocked on his heels, enjoying his big moment.

'There's one other thing I think's worth mentioning.'

Logan gave a curt nod of encouragement. 'Right, well, spit it out, then, Benjamin.'

'I had a very interesting chat with Stephen Boyd a few minutes ago.'

'Paed o Steve?'

'The one and only,' Ben confirmed .

'What's he saying about the d iary?'

'Denying all knowled ge,' Ben said . 'But that's not the interesting thing. Remember the car parked outsid e the bank the d ay Orla cleared out her account?'

Logan frowned , searching his memory banks. 'Silver Vauxhall. Partial plate.'

'Aye. We've got it.'

Logan turned to face him, and seemed to grow a little taller. 'It was Boyd 's car?'

Ben shook his head , looking quite pleased with himself. 'Too obvious. You'll never guess.'

'Then d on't make me blood y try,' Logan snapped . 'Whose car is it?'

'It's the brid e's.'

'The brid e's?'

'From the wed d ing,' the DI clarified .

'Aye, well, most brid es are from...' Logan began, then he realised what Ben was getting at. 'Wait. *This* wed d ing? Yesterd ay? That mouthy bitch from the castle?'

'That's her,' Ben confirmed . 'Turns out, she was the lassie Stephen Boyd had it away with. Been harassing him since he got out of prison. Mad e his life hell, he claims. Says she was out to ruin him.'

'We also reckon she's the one who put the brick through the station wind ow,' Sinead ad d ed .

'So, it's her fault I got hit by that car?' Tyler cried .

'Nud ged by that car,' Hamza corrected . 'Nud ged .'

276

Logan's gaze flitted and leapt across the board, filling in the gaps with this new information. If the diary was a plant, then someone had set out to frame Stephen Boyd for Orla's abduction and murder. For anyone looking to cover their tracks, he was an obvious target to direct suspicion towards.

But what if all this wasn't just about someone covering their tracks? What if everything—the whole thing—was a way of getting back at Boyd? What if Orla was just a piece on a game board? A pawn to be sacrificed?

How deranged would someone have to be to do that? How filled with bile and hatred?

Logan thought back to the woman he'd met the day before. The encounter had been a brief one, but there was nothing about her that made him immediately dismiss her as a suspect.

If the others were right—if she'd put a brick through the window of the polis station because they'd rocked up and ruined her wedding day while trying to solve a girl's murder—then she ticked a lot of boxes in the 'potential murderer' checklist.

'Is she still in town?' Logan asked.

'Not sure, sir,' Hamza replied, and he was already reaching for his phone when Logan gave the order to 'hurry up and find out.'

'We bringing her in, Jack?' asked Ben.

'If she's around, aye,' Logan confirmed.

'I don't get it, boss,' Tyler said. 'Does she have any connection to Orla? Has she got any motive for killing her?'

'Not that we know of,' Logan admitted. 'But, by the sounds of it, she's got a motive for setting Stephen Boyd up to take the fall. Maybe he's her intended victim, not Orla.'

Tyler nodded slowly, processing this. 'I don't know, though, boss,' he answered. 'I mean, she seems like a bit of a cow, but that's proper mental, something like that. Abducting a girl you don't know, then murdering her on your wedding day to get back at an ex-boyfriend from a decade ago? Seems a bit convoluted.'

'Where would she have kept her, though?' Dave wondered. 'Not easy to hide someone for six months, especially if you don't live in the area.'

'Maybe she d id n't stay in the area,' Sinead suggested . 'She might've gone back d own to Essex with them.'

Logan clicked his fingers and pointed at no one d etective in partic- ular. 'Get her photo circulated d own there. See if anything pings up.'

'Might be worth checking the maternity units too, sir,' Sinead suggested . 'If she had the baby d own there...'

'Aye. Good thinking,' Logan said , then all eyes went to DS Khaled as he hung up the phone. 'Well?' Logan asked . 'She here?'

'No, sir,' Hamza said . 'Left this morning.'

'Bollocks!'

'But, bit of a lucky break. Before they left, they told the recep- tionist they were flying out on honeymoon tomorrow morning from Inverness. She's not sure what hotel they're staying at tonight, but it's near the airport, which narrows it d own to a hand ful.'

'OK. OK, good ,' Logan said . 'Find out where she's at, then get Uniform round there.'

'We bringing her in to Burnett Road , Jack?' asked Ben.

Logan shook his head . 'No. Bugger making that d rive. They can bring her here. That should give you and me a couple of hours.'

Ben frowned . 'A couple of hours to d o what?'

Logan reached for his coat. 'You and me *Mustang*, are going to take up your old pal's offer of popping round for d rinks.'

Chapter 38

Ellie Tonks, née Baker, stared d own at the plate on the table in front of her with a contempt she wasn't bothering her arse to conceal.

She had n't complained to the waitress—it wasn't her fault—instead saving all her ire for her husband . They had been married for just over twenty-four hours, but he was starting to think the 'husband ' title should alread y be prefixed by 'long-suffering.'

'What the hell's this?' Ellie d emand ed , using a finger to flick the plate an inch or two toward s him across the restaurant table.

'It's your d inner. Isn't it?'

'Very funny, Gavin. Hilarious,' Ellie hissed . 'I gave you the benefit of the d oubt. I thought maybe the menu was just shit, but the food would be good , but look at that*Look at it*.'

'It looks fine,' Gavin replied .

'Fine? Oh. That's all right, then,' Ellie said , crossing her arms. 'That's OK. As long as it's *fine*. That's all I need , isn't it? That's all I d eserve on my honeymoon. Not good , but fine.'

'We're not on honeymoon until tomorrow,' her husband protested .

In hind sight, he'd ad mit this was a mistake. She all but lunged for him, and for a moment he thought she was going to slap him. Instead , she snatched up a fork and struck the table with the bottom of the hand le, making a bang that d rew the attention of the closest d iners.

'No, Gavin, we're on honeymoon *now*! The honeymoon has started . And this…' She gave the plate another shove. 'This isn't good enough. It isn't. It's a fucking joke.'

Gavin lowered his voice, and injected some lightness into it, in the hope that both these things would prove contagious.

'It's an airport hotel, babes. It's just for tonight.'

'I know it's a fucking airport hotel, *babes*,' she shot back, spitting out that last word like it was toxic. 'But why are we at an airport hotel? The airport's barely out of town. We could 've been in a *nice* hotel, eating *nice* food . Not this shit.'

'Keep your voice d own,' Gavin plead ed . 'People are staring.'

'I d on't give a shit!' Ellie replied , very much not keeping her voice d own. 'Let them stare. Let them see how you d on't care about our honeymoon. About *your wife*!'

'Jesus Christ, what's got into you?' Gavin asked , find ing a bit of backbone. 'You're behaving like a child .'

'A child ?! A fucking *child*?! Oh, well, I'm sorry, Gavin! I'm sorry that having the most special d ay of my life ruined has turned me *childish*. I'm sorry that having my wed d ing gatecrashed by a d ead bod and the cast of *The Bill* has mad e me behave in such a fucking juvenile way.'

'It was my wed d ing, too!'

'Oh, d on't start that. You d id n't give a shit! You'd have held it a a registry office, with us in jeans, if you thought you could get away with it.'

'*And*?! That would 've been better!' Gavin pointed out, his tone coming close to matching hers. 'You d on't get corpses washing up at registry offices in Essex!'

Ellie's hand s tightened around the cutlery. Were she not so fixated on her husband 's stupid , smug face, she might've noticed the commotion over by the entrance. She may have seen the high-vis yellow jackets of the two men now talking to one of the waiters.

'Sometimes, I d on't even think you wanted to get married , Gavin!' Ellie said , and anyone listening in—which was everyone within earshot at this point—would 've been forgiven for thinking the wobble in her voice was entirely genuine.

Even Gavin appeared to buy it, slipping his hand s on top of hers to comfort her. Or possibly to prevent her from stabbing him in the throat with her knife and fork.

'Hey. Hey. Babes. Listen to me. Don't talk like that. Don't even think that. That's crazy!'

'Don't call me crazy!' Ellie hissed, and her husband quickly tightened his hold on her hands.

'I'm not saying that, babes! Course you're not crazy. Course you're not! That ain't what I'm saying! I'm saying, me not wanting to marry you? You, the most beautifullest, most specialest girl in the world? *That's* crazy. I'd have to be crazy to not want that.'

She eyeballed him for several seconds, her breath wheezing in and out through her nose as her rage slowly subsided. Her hands relaxed, and blood returned to her fingers, gradually colouring her knuckles again.

'You would,' she agreed. 'You'd have to have been mental.'

'Right?!' Gavin laughed, as much with relief as anything else. He risked taking his hands away, and indicated the plate of food that had triggered the argument. 'And you're right about this, too, babes. It's our honeymoon! We should be celebrating!'

'That's all I was trying to say,' Ellie told him. 'It's our honeymoon. We *should* be celebrating!'

Gavin took out his phone and opened a web browser. 'Give me two minutes, babes,' he said. 'I'll find us somewhere nice. Somewhere a bit posh.'

'A *bit* posh?' Ellie asked, a thin, carefully plucked eyebrow rising.

'Proper posh, I mean!' her husband hurriedly corrected.

Ellie nodded, smiled, and sat back in her seat. While Gavin looked for somewhere better to eat, she helped herself to a couple of the chips off his plate. She blew on them, then popped them in her mouth and chewed.

Despite her protestations of just a few moments before, she had to admit they tasted pretty good. Not as good as her actual dinner was going to taste, of course. And not as delicious as the victory she'd just won. But decent. *Fine*.

The wedding had been a disaster, granted. Her honeymoon had started badly. But now, at least, things were finally on the up.

'Mrs Tonks?'

Ellie looked up into the face of a man in a police uniform. He did not, judging by his expression, share her current elation.

'Yes?'

The entire restaurant was watching now, not just those close enough to have heard the argument. Not a glass clinked. Not a fork scraped on a plate. Silence hung in the air alongside the smell of hot oil and onion rings.

The constable tucked his thumbs into his high-vis vest.

'I'm afraid I'm going to have to ask you to come with me.'

—

Ronald Donlon was surprised to see Logan and Ben come traipsing in through the front door. Running a bed and breakfast, you no doubt got used to strangers coming wandering into your house, but it would be harder if you were ex-polis, Logan thought. They were, by nature, a shower of suspicious bastards.

And that suspicion was clearly visible on Ronnie Sr.'s face when the detectives rocked up. Still, he quickly wiped it away, and grabbed Ben by the hand, shaking it enthusiastically.

'Mustang! Look at you! I'd say you haven't changed a bit, but we both know I'd be talking shite!'

Ben laughed. 'Aye, well, you're no' exactly fresh out of the bloody wrapper yourself these days, Ronnie!' Ben said. 'Good to see you! When Jack here told me you'd invited us over for a drink, I couldn't say no.'

'Ha! Some things never bloody change, then!' Ronnie replied. He released Ben's hand, slapped him a couple of times on the upper arm, then turned to Logan. 'And Detective Chief Inspector. Good to see you again. And so soon! I wasn't expecting you tonight, I have to say.'

'Aye, well, no saying we'll be around much longer,' Logan told him. 'Things are moving pretty quickly on the case.'

Donlon's eyebrows rose. 'Oh?'

'Aye, we're making progress,' Ben confirmed. 'We've got the bastard in our sights. So, we thought...' He held up a bottle of whisky they'd bought at the supermarket on the way over. It was cheap stuff. No need to go overboard. 'Might as well celebrate.'

Ronald considered both men and the bottle of Scotch. He nodded, and as he did, he broke into a broad, beaming smile. 'Typical Mustang. No messing, no nonsense. Right in there, and straight down to it. I was right, outward appearances aside, you've not changed one bloody bit!'

He shot a slightly wary look at the kitchen door, then lowered his voice and beckoned for them to follow.

'Come on. Through here. We'll get a few cheeky halfs inside us before the wife starts mumping and moaning.'

They followed him through to a small square study, roughly ten feet wide and long. One whole wall was taken up by lines of wooden bookcases which ran from floor to ceiling, sagging beneath the weight of the volumes they held.

There was a bay window at the far end of the room that looked out onto the garden. A desk had been built into the space, and Ronald sat in the high-backed leather chair that had been tucked beneath it, then indicated for the detectives to take a seat on the ancient and battered, two-seater leather couch that was somehow holding itself together in the corner.

Before he sat, Ben handed over the whisky. Ronald held the bottle by the neck, and read the label, nodding with false approval.

'Lovely. This is… I've never tried this one. Tell you what, if it's all right with you, I'll hang onto it for later.' He tapped the side of his nose, and rolled his chair over to a globe-style drinks cabinet. 'Special occasion, and all that. We should be on the good stuff.'

He flicked open the top of the globe, reached inside, and produced a half-full bottle of golden liquid. It sloshed around as he gave it a shake, before he presented it to them like a sommelier showing off the house's most exclusive tipple.

'Bowmore. Twenty-five years old. Sweet, smoky, and with just a hint of peaty aftertaste. It's an exceptional malt. Fitting for an occasion such as this.'

'Lovely!' said Ben, rubbing his hands together. 'Better than that shite we brought.'

Ronald chuckled as he produced three glasses from inside the cabinet. 'Yes, well, polis wages. I know what that's like. Best move

I ever mad e, getting out. Cashed in my pension, put it into this, paid for itself ten times over alread y.'

He placed the glasses d own on the coffee table between them, and poured the first two d rinks. The smell of the Scotch was swirling tantalisingly around in the air when Logan put a hand over the final glass.

'None for me, thanks.'

'What? What d o you mean? Come on, man!' Ronald teased . 'Get a wee nip of this insid e you. It's good stuff. And d on't worry, I'm not going to ad d it to your bill!'

'Honestly. I'm fine,' Logan insisted .

Donlon groaned . 'Oh, God . You're not one of them, are you?'

'Maybe. Depend s what you mean.'

'A teetotaller.'

Logan shook his head . 'Alcoholic.'

'Oh. Well. I suppose that's not so bad , then,' Ronald said , after a moment's thought. He gave the bottle a little shake. 'Sure I can't tempt you? Not even just the one?'

'No. Thank you,' Logan replied . 'I'll have a cup of tea if one's going, though.'

Donlon looked d own at one of the filled glasses on the table, presumably sizing that one up for himself. He looked genuinely crest-fallen when he screwed the lid back on the bottle, returned it to the cabinet, then got to his feet.

'Tea. Right,' he said . 'Won't be long.'

They waited until he'd left the room, then both d etectives got to their feet. Logan looked through the paperwork on the d esktop, while Ben had a rummage around in the d rawers.

'Blood y hell. He is d oing well for himself,' the DI remarked when he came across a stack of bank statements showing the guest house's turnover. 'They're getting two hund red quid a night for some of these rooms!'

'That's not helping us,' Logan pointed out, and Ben moved on to the next d rawer.

The paperwork on top of the desk wasn't giving much away. It was mostly bills—electricity, broad band, all the usual suspects. At the bottom of each bill, he'd written the word 'PAID', along with the date, and the last four digits of the card used to make payment.

The bills were organised first by supplier, then by payment date, so you could look back and see a complete picture of the last six months of phone usage and leccy bills.

If Logan had been harbouring any doubts that this man could be a murdering psychopath, they left him then. It took a certain kind of mind to try and enforce such a level of order on something as mundane as a Sky TV monthly statement. If the bastard wasn't a killer, then it was probably just a matter of time.

'Letters. Jack. Letters,' Ben whispered, producing a small bundle of envelopes from the bottom drawer.

'From who?' Logan asked, craning to get a look.

Ben glanced back at the door, then quickly whipped the first letter from its envelope. It was typed, not hand written, and as he scanned the first few lines, his initial excitement faded.

'This one's from him,' he said. 'To the local paper, complaining about the condition of the roads.'

He fumbled it back into the envelope, then prised the next envelope open enough that he could read the start of the letter without removing it.

'Bugger. Same again. Moaning about the shortage of public toilets this time.'

'Keep looking,' Logan said. 'But be quick.'

However quick DI Forde was, it wasn't quick enough. Behind them, a throat was cleared. The bluntness of the question caught them both by surprise.

'Aye, aye. What the fuck are you pair of sleekit pricks up to?'

Hoon sauntered into the study, and pushed the door shut with the side of a foot.

'Bob? What the hell are you doing here?' Logan demanded.

'I'm fucking staying here,' Hoon told him. He spotted the whiskies on the table, and helped himself to a glass. 'Cheers, lads,' he said, before knocking it back in one go. 'Christ, that's good . Nice peaty aftertaste,' he remarked , then he pointed to the other glass that was half-filled with the amber liquid . 'This one going spare?'

'No, it's blood y not!' Ben said , grabbing the d rink before Hoon could swipe it.

'You're staying here?' Logan asked , still stuck at that part of the conversation. 'What d o you mean? Why here?'

Hoon shrugged . 'Decent reviews.'

'Bollocks. Since when d id you care about what other people think?'

'Ha! Aye, fair enough, you got me,' Hoon said . He jabbed a thumb back over his should er. 'You know the guy that owns this place used to be on the job? *And* his son used to go out with your d ead lassie.'

'I know! Of course, I blood y know!' Logan told him. 'Why d o you think we're here?'

Hoon consid ered the question, then clicked his fingers. 'That's why you're snooping around in his stuff. What, is he a suspect? You think he d id it?'

'Will you keep your blood y voice d own?' Logan spat. 'And piss off before he comes back with—'

'Tea's here!' Ronald announced , pushing open the d oor. He stopped when he saw the three men all on their feet besid e his d esk, then very quickly noted the two empty glasses on the coffee table.

'Fuck me! Bonnie Ronnie Donlon!' Hoon cried , throwing his arms wid e. 'Fucking get in here, you!'

Ronald barely had time to pass Logan his mug before Hoon wrapped his arms around him and pulled him into a bear hug.

'Um…' was all that Ronald had to say on the matter. Logan could n't really blame him. A Surprise Hooning was a d ifficult thing to d eal with.

'You two know each other?' asked Ben.

'Aye. Fucking hell, aye! Course we d o!' Hoon cheered , finally releasing the other man from his grip. 'I mean, not personally. Barely in passing, really. Just by reputation, if anything. I d on't think we've ever met, but… fuck me!' He slapped a hand d own on Ronald 's should er, and from the look on Donlon's face, it almost paralysed him.

'Bonnie Ronnie Donlon. That's what they fucking called you, wasn't it?'

'I, uh...' Ronald shook his head. 'I don't think so, no. Not that I ever heard.'

'No? Well, they fucking should've,' Hoon countered. 'They missed a fucking sitting goal there. Face like that? Bet the lassies were fucking creaming themselves every time you stepped in the room. Nips like fucking bullets, I bet.' He leaned in a little closer and lowered his voice to a salacious murmur. 'That how you scored a wife that fit? I mean, Bonnie Ronnie Donlon or not, you're fucking punching there, pal. She is tidy.'

From the look on his face, it seemed that Ronald didn't know whether to be insulted or pleased about the comments, so he played it safe by changing the subject.

'Well. It's like a polis reunion in here, isn't it?' he said, with a forced joviality that didn't suit him in the slightest. 'We have met, actually, Mr Hoon. A number of times. You were usually shouting, if I recall. And, of course, I read with interest news of your...' His gaze flicked up and down, like he was getting the measure of the former detective superintendent. '...fall from grace.'

For a moment, there was something dangerous behind Hoon's eyes. Something raw, and primal, and ancient that made Ben hold his breath, and Logan prepare to intervene.

But then, to both detectives' surprise, Hoon sniffed, shrugged, and let out a little laugh. 'Wasn't so much a fall as a headlong fucking dive from the upper atmosphere,' he said. 'The world's first-ever fucking base jump from grace.'

Logan cleared his throat. 'Aye. Right. Well, it was good seeing you, Bob. We'll, eh, we'll catch up later, all right?'

'What? No. Fuck that! Polis reunion!' Hoon said. He held up his empty glass and waggled it suggestively in front of Ronnie Sr.'s face. 'This was fucking good stuff,' he declared. 'Any chance of a top-up?'

Chapter 39

Tyler and Hamza strolled along the street from the Kyle of Lochalsh Police Station, letting their noses guide them in the direction of the nearest chip shop. It had been raining on and off for most of the day, and while it was currently dry, they both got the sense that another downpour wasn't far away.

As they walked, the street lights clicked on around them, pushing back the growing darkness. Summer had started to wane into autumn, and the nights were drawing in. It would be getting dark by half-seven, pitch-black by nine. And then, another day would be over, with very little concrete progress made.

Without meaning to, or even realising they were doing it, both detectives had instinctively fallen into step as they made their way along the street, adopting the same slow, plodding saunter they'd both mastered back in their Uniform days. Old habits, it seemed, were hard to break.

'So. Any more thoughts?' Tyler asked, voicing the question he'd been holding in for far too long now.

'About what?'

'Shut up. You know what,' the DC replied. 'About the interview. About the new job.'

'Oh. That.' Hamza shook his head. 'No. Well, I mean, lots of thoughts, aye, but no decisions.'

'I think you should stay,' Tyler said.

Hamza smirked. 'I got that impression, right enough.'

'You don't want to be stuck doing bloody, I don't know, Windows updates, do you?'

'I had to install a printer and a router this morning,' Hamza remind ed him.

'Yeah, but—'

'And then get everyone connected to both.'

'Yes, I know, but—'

'And explain to DI Ford e how to print. Again.'

'Well, aye, that's true, but you haven't *just* d one that, have you?' Tyler said . 'You, eh... what else've you d one tod ay?'

'Went to get chips?' Hamza said .

'No. Proper, I mean.' Tyler looked worried , like this conversation was not going the way he'd intend ed it to go. Then, he clicked his fingers and his face lit up. 'You interviewed Leonard Coull!'

'That was mostly the boss,' Hamza countered .

'We went looking for Paed o Steve!' Tyler said , seizing on another non-techie task they'd carried out.

'We d id n't find him, though.'

'Well, no, but that's not the point!' the DC insisted .

Hamza sid e-eyed him. 'What is the point, then? What are you saying?'

'I'm *saying...*' Tyler chewed his bottom lip. They walked on in silence. 'OK, I d on't know what I'm saying, exactly, but just... I d on't think you should go. I think you should stay. We need you, mate. Sinead 's going to be off on Maternity Leave. I'll be off for a while, too. You can't leave. The team need s you!'

Hamza stopped . It took Tyler a few moments to realise before he turned back.

'What about what *I* need ?' the DS asked . 'Or Amira. Or Kamila? What about that? Because, trust me, mate, you think this job is hard now? Wait until you've got kid s at home.'

'We've got Harris,' Tyler said .

'Aye, but he's old er. And he d oesn't mind getting bounced around . You can't d o that with a baby, never mind with two of them.'

'We'll manage,' Tyler insisted .

'Will you? How? What makes you so special? What makes you think you'll be any d ifferent to Logan, say?' Hamza asked . 'Because the job killed his relationship with his daughter. And I've seen it happen to dozens of others, too. We both have. Break-ups. Divorces. Broken families. The job does that. We've seen it. Over, and over, and over again.'

He looked up as a few flecks of rain began to fall, and let the droplets wash over him for a while.

When he lowered his head again, he looked a little embarrassed by his outburst. Thrusting his hands into his jacket pockets, he set off along the street again, with Tyler following a half-pace behind.

'I love the job. I do,' Hamza said. 'I love that we get to make a difference. Not always. Not often enough, maybe. But we do. Sometimes we do. And that feeling? When we really, honestly, truly manage to help someone. When we manage to make the world a better place, even just for a few minutes. That's almost worth everything else. It's worth the late nights, and the not knowing when you'll be home.'

The rain was becoming heavier now. Hamza lowered his head, tucking it into his shoulders, steeling himself against the sudden arrival of an icy-cold downpour. Somewhere, far off in the distance, thunder pealed.

'But is it worth my relationship with my wife and daughter?' He shook his head. 'No. No, it isn't. Nothing is.'

He picked up the pace, leaving Tyler hurrying to catch up.

'Now, come on. The chippie can't be far. The sooner we get there, the sooner we can get back.'

And, with the speechless detective constable trailing behind, Hamza pressed onward into the strengthening storm.

Chapter 40

'Bud ge up, you fat fuck.'

Logan slowly turned his head to the left and glowered at Hoon, who was trying to insert himself into the three inches of space between the d etective and the arm of the couch.

'It's a two-seater, Bob,' he intoned . 'Maybe you should go sit somewhere else? Your room, for example. Or, better still, your house.'

'Ah, quit your fucking whinging and shift up,' Hoon insisted , forcing his arse into the narrow gap, and leaving Logan with no option but to shuffle closer to DI Ford e.

'Careful, Jack. You'll be sitting on my knee at this rate,' Ben remarked . 'And I d on't think my old bones could hand le all that weight.'

'Can we stop suggesting I'm fat?' Logan asked . 'I'm not over-weight.'

'No, but you are fucking enormous,' Hoon pointed out. He wriggled uncomfortably on his sliver of couch. 'Don't know what it's like d own your end , Benjamin, but I feel like fucking Baby Bear here, wed ged in next to Dad d y.'

'Again, you d on't have to sit here!' Logan stressed .

'I could go get another seat through,' suggested Ronald , who had been quick to claim the d esk chair when Hoon had started eyeing it up.

'No, d on't you fucking stress yourself, Ronnie,' Hoon said . 'You've d one enough. Ignore this moaning fuck.'

'I'm not the one moaning!' Logan cried .

Hoon winked at their host and waggled his glass, which had once more found itself empty. 'Just you worry about keeping the fucking d rink coming. Everything else'll sort itself out.'

He leaned forward and held out the tumbler while Ronnie Sr. refilled it. Hoon watched him pouring, nod d ing with encouragement every time it looked like he was about to stop.

Once the glass was almost completely filled —and the bottle now close to empty—Hoon raised it in a toast. 'To the fine lad s and lassies of the fucking polis,' he d eclared . 'Present company exclud ed .'

Ben and Ronald both raised their glasses, and murmured som confused , uncertain version of the toast. Logan just sat sullenly in the mid d le of the couch, and took a big slurp of his tea.

'How are things going, then?' Ronnie asked , once they'd all taken a d rink. 'You said you were making some progress on the investigation?'

'We've got Stephen Boyd in custod y,' Logan said .

'Ah. Yes. Should 've known. He was always a suspect, of course,' Ronald said . 'But we—I mean, the police—could n't pin it on him. Could n't make any connection between him and Orla. Not for want of trying.'

Logan watched the other man carefully. 'Aye. Well, we struck it lucky there,' he said . 'We found a d iary.'

'A d iary? Whose? Boyd 's?'

'No. Orla's.'

Ronald froze with his glass almost to his lips. He stared at the DCI over the rim for a moment, then took a larger than usual gulp.

'Orla had a d iary?'

'Aye. Well, I mean, it looks that way,' Logan replied . 'It was in her bed room. Stashed und er a d rawer.'

'Oh. Wow. Wow, wow, wow. Well. That is...' Donlon blew out his cheeks, like he had no id ea where that sentence had been head ed 'And it mentions Stephen Boyd ?'

'It d oes, aye,' Logan confirmed .

The man in the chair swirled his whisky around in his glass. 'In, uh, in what sense?'

'Going by what she wrote, they were in a sexual relationship.'

'Fucking hell, seriously?!' Hoon spat. He leaned forwards, momentarily blocking Logan's view of Donlon, so he missed their host's initial reaction to this news. 'I mean, don't get me wrong, I heard some gossip today that makes a lot more sense now.'

He sat back, but by then Ronald's expression had settled into a sort of mild surprise, that could have been genuine, but could equally have just been well-rehearsed.

'What sort of gossip?' asked Ben, leaning forward to see past Logan.

'I heard she was at it with some older guy. Aye, shagging him, like. Talk of the town, apparently,' Hoon said. He shifted his gaze in Ronnie Sr.'s direction. 'You heard anything about that?'

Donlon was quick to shake his head. 'No. No, of course not. People knew that Orla and Ronnie... they were a couple. They were together. Nobody would dream of saying anything like that to me.'

'Because they're scared of you?' asked Hoon.

'Because it wasn't true!' Ronald countered. 'They were together. They were boyfriend and girlfriend. She was a nice girl. She wouldn't cheat on Ronnie. Not with *him*.'

'Who would she cheat on him with, then?' Hoon asked.

Logan tried very hard not to look at his old boss then. The bastard was interviewing him. He had barged in here, and he was interviewing Ronald Donlon right before the detectives' eyes.

'Nobody!' Ronald insisted. 'She wouldn't. She wasn't. She was a kind, loving girl, and the last thing she'd do would be cheat on Ronnie.'

'Aye, well,' Hoon took a sip of his drink. 'That's no' what everyone's saying. They reckon she was getting pumped by some older guy on the regular. But, I mean, you'd know the facts of the matter better than me.'

'Yes. Yes, I would,' Ronald said, and there was a venom there that none of the other men could miss. 'No way she was seeing that child molester. No way.'

'Speaking of your son, one thing that struck me as interesting, Ronald,' said Logan, jumping in before Hoon could continue. 'Is that he's not mentioned anywhere in the case files.'

'Well, he was away. He was in Manchester.'

'Aye, I get that, but he was also her boyfriend at the time. There's mention of him being away, but then… nothing. No interview to try and determine her emotional state in the weeks running up to disappearing. He wasn't questioned on any other friends she might've had, or where she might've been going.'

Ronald adjusted himself in his chair. 'Well, we all thought—the police thought—that she'd just left. She was an adult. They didn't think anything had happened to her, so they didn't feel the need to carry out a full missing persons investigation.'

Logan nodded. 'Aye. Aye, makes sense,' he said. He took another drink of his tea, then shrugged. 'Except, they spoke to her friends. Ayesha. Hugo. A few others from school. They asked them questions. But not Ronnie. Not your son. Why's that, do you think?'

Ronald regarded the three men on the couch in silence, finally realising what was happening here. This wasn't a friendly 'polis reunion'. This was an interrogation.

'Because I asked them not to,' he admitted. 'That's what you want to hear, isn't it? I used my influence to keep my family's name out of the investigation as much as possible.'

'Why?' asked Ben. 'Why do that?'

'Isn't it obvious? Because I didn't want it getting dragged through the mud! Ronnie was seventeen years old. Seventeen, and his girlfriend goes missing. The press turn up, and of course they start digging. Poking their noses in. Asking about Ronnie and Orla's relationship. Did they argue? Had anyone seen them fighting? Raking up bloody muck where there wasn't any!'

'Aye, sounds like them, right enough,' Logan admitted.

'He was freaking out. He was terrified. You know what the internet's like. Point a finger, and suddenly it's trial by social media. And it stays there. Guilty or innocent, all that stuff, all those comments, all those bloody judgements, they stay there. Online. Forever.'

He knocked back his drink and shook his head as he swirled it around in his mouth.

'No. No, I wasn't having that. Ronnie had nothing to do with it. The police, they were easy. They knew he wasn't involved. They agreed that it wasn't fair to treat him as a suspect. They knew it could n't have been him, but the press? Oh, no. Those bastard s were d etermined to paint him as the villain. And that wasn't right. It wasn't fair that they focus on him. It wasn't fair that they mad e him suspect number one. You'd have d one the same. All of you, in my shoes, you'd have d one everything you could to keep your child 's name out of the papers.'

Logan realised where this was going. 'You pointed them toward s Stephen Boyd . You gave them his name.'

Ronald d id n't reply. He d id n't even look at the d etective. Instead , he just reached for the bottle of Scotch and emptied what was left of it into his glass.

'It wasn't fair they focus on my Ronnie,' he said again, then he sat up straighter, really starting to get into the swing of it. 'And now look, here we are. It turns out that maybe I was right all along! Maybe Boyd d id kill her. If they were... seeing each other, maybe I had him pegged from the start!'

'A minute ago, you said there was no way they were seeing each other,' Logan remind ed him.

'Yes, well. But you said it's in her d iary. Maybe I d id n't know her as well as I thought. And the same goes for Ronnie, too! Maybe he had the wrong id ea about her. I mean, yes, they were boyfriend and girlfriend , but they were kid s! It's never really serious at that age, is it?' Ronald scoffed . 'It's not like it was ever going to go anywhere.'

Logan took that as his cue to reach into his coat pocket. Having Hoon and Ben jammed up against him d id not make this particularly easy, and they both complained about his excessive elbow action before he finally pulled out the evid ence bag he'd been reaching for.

'Interesting you should say that, Ronald . That they weren't serious.' He sat the evid ence bag on the table, with the heart-shaped pend ant insid e it plain to see. 'That looks pretty serious to me.'

'Fuck me. That's a bit fucking bling for a seventeen-year-old , isn't it?' asked Hoon, leaning over to peer at the jewellery.

'That's what I thought,' Logan agreed .

He was back to watching Ronald like a hawk, stud ying every twitch, every movement of his face. Donlon was looking d own at the locket in the evidence bag like it was an unexploded bomb, or something noxious and toxic.

Something to be afraid of.

'You know about this, Ronnie?' asked Ben. 'You ever seen this before?'

'Uh… no. No, don't think so. I don't remember.'

'You don't remember?' Logan sounded incredulous. 'It's a gold er heart with a diamond on the front. It was bought less than seven months ago. You'd remember it. So, either you've seen it, or you haven't.'

Donlon raised his eyes to meet Logan's intrusive gaze. 'Then I haven't,' he said.

'You've never seen this?' Logan asked, picking up the bag. He opened the seal and tipped the locket into his hand. 'You're sure about that?'

Ronald took a moment to adjust himself in his seat before responding. 'I'm not one-hundred percent. But I don't recall seeing it.'

'Right. Well, then I'm confused, Ronnie,' Logan said.

'No fucking change there then,' Hoon muttered. When Logan drew him a sharp look, the former detective superintendent shrugged. 'Sorry, can't help it. It's just instinct.'

Logan sighed, almost imperceptibly, then turned his attention back to Ronald.

'I'm confused because, according to the website this was bought from, you're the one who bought it.'

Donlon held the detective's stare. His eyes flitted down to the pendant, just for a moment, then he frowned. 'Really? That's strange.'

'I thought maybe someone might have had access to your credit card,' Ben said.

Donlon grasped for the lifeline with both hands. 'Yes! Yes, that could be it. That could explain it.'

'It cost almost five grand,' Logan said. He pointed to the desk at Ronald's back. 'The way you organise all those bills there. The way you keep on top of it. I find it hard to believe you would n't have noticed that popping up.'

Ronald twisted his chair around until he saw the stack of paperwork on the d esk. When he turned back, his face had d arkened .

'Were you going through my things? What the hell is this? Mustang? What the hell's this about?'

Ben's smile was a weak, watered -d own thing. 'Just… I'm sure there's a perfectly good explanation for all this, Ronnie. That's all we're trying to find .'

'It was ad d ressed to you, too,' Logan continued . 'The online store sent us a copy of the invoice. "Ronald Donlon Sr" is what it said on it.'

'He's got you by the fucking baw hairs there, pal,' Hoon said .

With a click, Logan opened the locket, then set it d own on the table, turned to make it easy for Ronald to read the writing.

'Can you tell me what's inscribed in there?' Logan asked .

Donlon d id n't look. Not yet. He sat in his chair, his hand s gripping the armrests, his face a brood ing shad e of crimson-purple.

'Tell me what you see, Mr Donlon,' Logan insisted . 'I want to hear you say it.'

His eyes d id n't move. His gaze d id n't shift. He answered , all the same.

'Ronnie and Orla.'

'Impressive,' Logan said . 'You d id n't even have to look.'

'That's quite a fucking trick,' Hoon said . 'Can you tell what number I'm thinking of, too?'

'I remember now,' Ronald said , and there was a calm, icy cold ness to it. 'I haven't seen it before. Not d irectly. Orla asked me to buy it. She wanted to give it to Ronnie for his birthd ay.'

Logan snorted . 'She asked you to buy him a five grand locket so that she could give it to him for his birthd ay?'

'She was going to pay the bill every month,' Ronald said .

'And why could n't she ask her parents?'

'She d id n't want to. Her mother can be a bit of a d ragon, as I'm sure you've seen,' Ronald said .

The red ness was d raining from his face now, returning him to a more natural-looking colour palette. He sat up a little straighter, his confid ence stead ily growing.

'She knew Sarah would lose the rag. She'd always been able to talk to Merry and me, so she came to me,' he said .

'And you said yes?' Logan asked . 'Despite the fact that, as you said yourself, they were kid s. It was nothing serious, yet you agreed to fork out five grand so Orla could give your son this locket—a woman's locket—for his birthd ay?'

'It's not a woman's locket. It's... what d o you call it?' Ronald waved a hand , searching for the right word .

'Bisexual?' Ben suggested .

'Well, not that, exactly, but something along those lines. Gend er-neutral, I think she said .'

'Looks a bit fucking girly to me,' Hoon said .

Donlon pulled a smile that was ninety percent grimace. 'Yes. Well, times change, I'm told .'

Logan consid ered the locket on the table for a moment, then picked it up and snapped it shut.

'So, to recap, your story is that you agreed to pay five grand for a piece of expensive jewellery that a girl you ad mit you d id n't really know all that well asked you to buy for her to give to your son, d espite the fact that you d id n't consid er their relationship a serious one?'

It took Donlon a few moments to reply, like he was checking the story for holes before agreeing to it.

'Yes. Basically.'

'And you somehow forgot all this until a few moments ago,' Logan continued .

That one caught him off guard a bit. He shuffled in his chair, swallowed , then shrugged . 'I just... I'd never actually seen it. It was marked on the envelope where it came from, so I just hand ed it straight to Orla.'

'We'll be able to see evid ence of her paying you back, aye?' asked Ben, and there was a hopeful note to it, like he was the one now grabbing for the lifeline.

It slipped through his grip a second later, when Donlon shook his head .

'She went missing before the first payment was d ue,' he said . 'I actually wond ered if maybe that's why she'd run away. If I'd been conned .'

'But you d id n't think to mention that to the polis at the time?' Logan asked .

'I assumed she'd turn up before long.'

'Right. Fair enough,' Logan said . He returned the necklace to the evid ence bag, then stashed it back in his coat pocket.

'Watch your fucking elbows,' Hoon protested .

With a grunt of annoyance, Logan rose to his feet, and both Ben and Hoon almost rolled together in the space he'd just vacated .

'It's an interesting story, Ronald ,' the DCI said . 'Very d ifferent to my version. You want to hear that?'

'Not particularly, no,' Ronnie said . He stood up, should ers back, head high. 'What I want is for you to leave. All of you. Get out, right now.'

'Well, tough, because I'm going to tell you anyway,' Logan said . 'In my version of the story, you bought that locket for Orla. You're the Ronnie inscribed insid e.'

'And why on Earth would I d o that?'

'Because the two of you were in a relationship,' Logan said .

'Oh, d on't be rid iculous! I'm old enough to be her blood y father!'

'To be fair, you're no' a kick in the arse off being old enough to be your wife's father, too,' Hoon interjected . 'But I d on't see that fucking stopping you.'

'Did you know she was pregnant, Ronald ?' Logan asked .

He d id n't. He d id n't know. Either that, or he was the greatest living actor of his generation. Everything about him changed in an instant. His bravad o fell away. His nerve collapsed . Logan watched the arse falling right out of the other man's world , and witnessed his d esperate attempts to hold himself together.

'Pregnant? Orla?' he said , his voice becoming d ry and hoarse, like all the moisture had left his throat. 'Orla was pregnant? I d on't... I can't... How?'

Hoon got to his feet, formed a circle with thumb and forefinger, and began sliding the index finger of the other hand in and out of it.

'Well, I'd imagine from the old ...'

He whistled in time with his finger action, and Donlon watched him for a while, like he was completely mesmerised by the in and out movement.

'I take it this is news to you, Ronnie?' asked Ben, using the arm of the couch to push himself up into a standing position.

Ronnie Sr. turned to look at the DI, but didn't speak. Instead, he made a few vague 'um' sort of noises and stared, wide-eyed and slack-jawed.

'I think you fucking broke him,' Hoon remarked.

'No,' Ronald ejected, the word popping out of his mouth like the cork from a champagne bottle. 'No, no, I didn't know that. She never told me. She... she never said.'

'And what about your son? Do you think she told him?'

Ronald sat back down in his chair again, using the thumb and index finger of one hand to massage his temples. 'No. I mean, not that he's said. And he would've. If he knew. He would've.'

'Right, well, maybe we should —'

'Get out,' Donlon told them. 'All of you. Get out of my house.'

'Ronnie, come on now,' Ben began, but the other man was having none of it.

He leapt back to his feet, face twisting up in rage, breath swirling from his nostrils like he was a charging bull.

'All of you out. Now. None of you are welcome here. If you have bags, get them, because you're not staying here another night. Not in my home. Not when you come in here spilling this bullshit. Poking around in my things. I'll be putting in a complaint. Mark my words on that. You've got no right to go snooping through my personal affairs. Not without a warrant.'

He drew in a series of big, gulping breaths, like he was trying to swallow back his rage.

'Lest you forget, gentlemen, I know how all this works. So, unless you're going to arrest me—and, let's be clear here, you've got absolutely no evid ence with which to d o so—then I am ord ering you to leave my home.'

'You're just going to make things hard er, Ronald ,' Logan said . 'We're going to get the evid ence we need . We're going to bring you in for this.'

Donlon stood as tall as he could , and stepped in closer so his face was just a few inches below Logan's.

'Yes, well, Detective Chief Inspector,' he said , the word s slid ing out through his gritted teeth. 'Good luck with that.'

Chapter 41

The police station reeked of chips and vinegar when Logan and Ben returned. To their surprise, they'd managed to shed Hoon along the way. With them both turfed out of the B&B, Hoon had announced he was going to go spend the night with a mate of his who lived in a bunker across the bridge on Skye.

The detectives had chosen not to question this, and just counted their lucky stars, instead.

The walk back to the station had felt almost positive after that, but that all changed the moment they stepped in through the front doors.

'Oi! What the hell's this?' Logan demanded, gesturing around the greasy wrappers scattered across the kitchen table. Taggart lay on his back on the floor, his legs in the air, apparently deep in some sort of food coma. 'You lot been to the chippie?'

'Had to, boss. We were starving,' Tyler said. 'And Sinead needs to keep her energy levels up.'

'I didn't want anything,' Sinead reminded him.

Tyler winced. 'Aye, but we offered. That was the main thing. And we got you that bag of salad from the shop.'

Logan glared at her with a mix of horror and contempt. 'Salad? Jesus Christ. Are you punishing yourself for something?'

'Just couldn't face more chips,' Sinead explained. She gave her stomach a rub. 'They don't half give me heartburn these days.'

'You have my sympathies,' Ben told her.

Hamza, who had been finishing up what looked to have been a generously filled chip butty, gave his hands a wipe on the paper it had come wrapped in, then scrunched it into a ball.

'How'd you get on?' he asked. 'Any joy with Ronald Donlon?'

'No big confession,' Logan said . 'He knows we're onto him, though. Denied any relationship with Orla, but I'm not buying a word of it.' He turned to DI Ford e. 'You?'

Ben sighed . The look on his face said it all. 'No,' he ad mitted . 'No, I'm not buying it. There was something going on there.'

'Good . So now we need to prove it,' Logan said . 'He's a wily bastard , and clued up. We can't blund er through this. We d o it by the book. We turn over every stone, but we d o it properly. If that bastard killed her, I'm not having him wriggle free on some blood y technicality. That clear?'

'Got it, boss.'

'Clear, sir.'

Sinead nod d ed . 'Und erstood .'

Logan looked around the kitchen. 'Where's Dave?'

'Next d oor, boss, manning the phones.'

'Any word on Ayesha?' Ben asked .

'Nothing, no,' Hamza said . 'If we d on't find her soon...'

He d id n't bother finishing the sentence. They all knew how it end ed .

'Aye, well, we'll just have to make sure we d o,' Logan said . 'I want Uniform watching Ronald Donlon's house tonight. If the bastard so much as takes out the bins, I want to know about it.'

'Won't you be there anyway, boss?'

'No. He kicked me out.'

'Oh. Wow. You must've annoyed him,' Sinead said .

Logan blew a burst of air out through his nose that might just have been the start of a chuckle. 'Aye. I d id that, all right,' he said . 'See if there's anywhere else for me to stay, will you?'

Sinead nod d ed and reached for her phone. 'Will d o, sir. Should n't be too d ifficult. The wed d ing party was taking up everywhere last night, and they've mostly left.'

'Speaking of which,' Logan began. 'The brid e. Any news?'

'She's on her way in,' said Hamza. 'Uniform's bringing her here. She's not best pleased , by the sound s of it.'

'No. No, I'd imagine not,' Logan said .

'Her husband's following in his own car,' the DS continued. 'I think they're still hoping they make it back for their flight tomorrow.'

'What time's the flight?'

Hamza puffed out his cheeks, then looked to Sinead with a raised eyebrow.

'Not sure,' the detective constable replied, her phone pressed to the side of her head. 'Late morning, early afternoon, I think. I wrote it on the Big Board.' She turned away as the phone was answered, and pressed a finger into the opposite ear. 'Hi, yes. I was wondering about your room availability for this evening...'

Logan ran his tongue across the back of his teeth, and rocked on his heels, considering his next course of action.

'Let's leave her until tomorrow morning,' he said. 'The bride, I mean.'

'What, and deliberately make them miss their flight?' asked Hamza.

'Bit harsh, boss,' Tyler added.

'Well, for all we know at this stage, we might be charging the woman with murder,' Logan reminded them. 'But, if she's got anything to tell us, the fear of missing out on her honeymoon might just be the encouragement she needs to share it. We'll use it as motivation. I'll do the interview. Hamza, you'll sit in with me.'

'Good call, boss,' Tyler said. 'He's really good at doing interviews, isn't he?'

Logan looked from Tyler to Hamza, then back again, the lines of his brow deepening. 'Is there something going on that I should know about?' he asked. 'Because you pair are acting fucking weird.'

'Nothing, sir,' Hamza said, then he glared at Tyler until the DC shook his head.

'Nothing going on, boss. I was just saying... he's good.'

Logan looked unconvinced, but decided not to push the matter. 'Fine. Whatever.'

It was decided that Ellie Tonks, upon her arrival, would be placed under arrest for the bricks-through-windows incidents, and kept in the cell overnight. This would almost certainly not be the start to her honeymoon that she'd been hoping for, but should soften her up a bit for her interview the next morning.

The only problem with this plan, of course, was that the station's one and only cell was currently occupied by Ellie's former boyfriend.

'We'll just have to let him go,' Logan said. 'All we've got on him is that diary, and I'm becoming less and less convinced by that. Tomorrow, I want a full comparison between the handwriting in the book and the letters Orla wrote. I think Ronald Donlon planted it as an insurance policy.'

'Didn't her dad think the writing was hers?' Hamza asked.

'Aye, but at a glance, and not side by side with anything else. Could easily be mistaken,' Logan said.

'Donlon would've got to know plenty of shady bastards in his time, too, boss,' Tyler pointed out. 'Might know a forger or two.'

'Worth a check,' Logan agreed. 'Someone better go break the good news to Stephen Boyd, and tell him he can go home.'

'Eh, did you not completely destroy his home, boss?'

'Oh. Shite. Aye,' Logan said. He sucked in his bottom lip, then shrugged. 'I'm sure he'll find somewhere. And, for the record, I didn't destroy the caravan. He destroyed it himself. I was nowhere near the bugger. Well, I mean, I was near-ish, obviously, but he's the one who lost control. If he didn't want to roll his house down a hill, he shouldn't have been speeding in the bloody thing.'

Despite his objections and protestations, a pang of guilt clearly hit the DCI a moment later, and he asked Sinead to try finding Boyd a room for the night, too. After scribbling down the details for Logan's hotel room—he was in the same hotel as Ben, and they were prepared to make allowances for the dog, given the circumstances—Sinead got straight back on the phone.

'Better try and get him somewhere none of us are staying,' Logan suggested. 'Be a bit awkward meeting the bastard at breakfast.'

Sinead nodded, then retired to the other side of the room to make some calls. Logan gave Taggart a nudge with the side of a foot.

'Right, you, up,' he said, and the dog flipped over onto all four paws, his chip-induced nap abruptly coming to an end. 'Everyone else, go get some rest, then be back here early. Hamza, you and me are having that chat with the bride. Dave and Sinead 'll dig into Ronald Donlon. Tyler, I've got a mission for you, too.'

'Oh aye, boss?' Tyler asked , a touch warily, like he d id n't like the sound of where this was going. 'And what's that?'

'Merry Donlon. I want you to bring her in.'

'What, arrest her?'

'No. Of course not. Why would you be arresting her? Don't take her here, take her to the bank. It's less official. Tell her it's for background on Orla, or something, but when you've got her, see if she can tell us anything about her husband . I get the feeling he's lifted his hand s. If we can get her to confirm that, we've got reason to bring him in.'

'No bother, boss,' Tyler said . 'I can d o that. I'll work my charms on her.'

'Jesus, no, d on't d o that,' Logan said , looking the younger d etective up and d own. 'We want her to talk, not throw up in her mouth. Just talk to her, and see how you get on.'

He looked around at the team. Down at his feet, Taggart snuffled around on the floor, hunting for any stray leftover chips.

'Any questions?' he asked .

'No, sir.'

'None, boss.'

'All sound s good to me, Jack.'

Logan nod d ed . 'Right, good . Now then, Detective Constable, Detective Sergeant, how about you point DI Ford e and me in the d irection of this chippie?'

Chapter 42

The next day dawned to a sky slicked with grey, and a series of hotel breakfasts of varying size and quality.

They regrouped at the station, then each set about their designated tasks for the morning, interviewing, researching, and —in Tyler's case—trying to attract the attention of a woman almost twenty years his senior.

For once, his luck was in. Merry Donlon was out front, loading her car with cleaning equipment when he pulled onto the street. She was dressed in a black fleece, tight grey leggings, and a pair of sporty looking trainers, and Tyler got the impression that she was either planning to go for a run, or had just come back from one.

She bent to pick up an old -style cylinder vacuum cleaner, and her fleece lifted , just for a moment, just long enough for Tyler to catch a glimpse of a blackening bruise around her kidney area.

He brought the car to a stop behind her, and she straightened and eyed him with suspicion when he shut off the engine.

'Hello!' called the detective constable, getting out of the car.

Merry looked him up and down, finished shoving a Hoover into the boot, then turned fully to face him. 'Can I help you?'

'Eh, aye. Hopefully. Detective Constable Tyler Neish.' He produced his warrant card and held it out to her. 'I'm, eh, I'm with the police,' he added , unnecessarily.

'So I see,' Merry said , relaxing a little. She closed the boot, gave her hands a wipe, then nodded towards the house that Tyler and Hamza had been scoping out the day before. 'Ronald's away out, if you're looking for him. Fishing, I think. He was off early.'

Tyler looked at the house, his gaze flitting from window to window like he might see someone looking back at him. 'Is he?' he asked. 'Right. Well, I'm not actually looking for him.'

Merry's body language changed, like a switch had been flicked. She stood taller, arms folded, brow creasing, more in anger than confusion. 'Ronnie? We keep telling you, he had nothing to do with any of this. He doesn't want to talk, and you can't make him.'

'Oh. No, no, sorry,' Tyler said, flashing the woman one of his better smiles. 'It's you I was hoping to have a quick word with.'

'Me? What for?' Merry asked.

'I was just hoping you might be able to give me a bit of background on Orla Coull,' Tyler said, reciting Logan's suggestion from the night before almost word for word. 'Her mum—and your husband, in fact—mentioned that she was able to talk to you. Both of you, you and Ronald. I was just wondering if maybe she said something to you before she went away, or… I don't know. Mentioned being in trouble in some way?'

'No. No, nothing like that,' Merry said, her body language softening again. 'Believe me, I've thought about. I've thought back, but… no. There was nothing.'

'Right. OK. Just…' Tyler glanced back over his shoulder, perhaps looking for support, or for someone to feed him his next line. 'It'd be useful if you could come in for a quick chat about it all.'

'Does it have to be now?' Merry asked. 'I've got a lot to do this morning.'

'It'll only take twenty minutes. Promise. If that,' Tyler said. 'We can get a cup of tea, have a wee blether about it, and then you can get on. It'd really help us. It'd really help Orla and her parents, too.'

Merry looked into the back of her car. She looked back at her house. Finally, she looked at Tyler, and gave him a nod.

'Twenty minutes,' she said. 'That's your lot.'

—

While Merry Donlon was proving to be quite accommodating, Ellie Tonks was being anything but. She cursed and swore and hissed like an animal when she was led out of the cell by Sergeant MacGeachan, and d elivered to the kitchen-come-interview room, where Logan and Hamza sat waiting for her.

'This is a fucking joke! You people are fucking id iots!' she snarled , struggling against the hand cuffs Sand ra had been forced to secure her with. 'I'm going to have all your jobs! I mean it, all of you better start looking for new careers, because you've fucked this one!'

At the table, Logan and Hamza both took a sip of their tea, and waited for Ellie to burn herself out. For someone who had spent a sleepless night on a thin mattress, though, she appeared to be brimming with energy, and a minute later, when her ire showed no sign of slowing, Logan was forced to intervene.

'You've got...' He checked his watch. '...just over five hours until your flight. It's possible you can still make it, but not if you keep ranting at us. Because not only are you wasting precious minutes, but keep talking to me like that, and I'll be inclined to really take my time over these questions. Really d rag them out. You've seen me d rag them out, haven't you, Detective Sergeant?'

'Oh, yes, sir,' Hamza confirmed . 'I've seen you *really* d rag them out.'

'And that would not work out in your favour, Mrs Tonks,' Logan said . 'Seems to me, you've had something of a shite start to married life. Be a shame to miss the honeymoon, too.'

Ellie's eyes narrowed to slits. When she spoke, the word s hissed out through the sid e of her mouth.

'You fucking...' she began, but then she plonked herself d own on the chair, her hand s still cuffed behind her back, and eyeballed the two men across the table.

'Sleep well?' Logan asked , which almost set her off again.

She swallowed d own a fit of rage, before shaking her head and hissing, 'No, of course not.'

'No. No, they're not great bed s, I'm afraid ,' Logan said . 'Still, you'll have somewhere nicer tonight, all being well. Tenerife, I hear? I'm told it's lovely. Never been. You ever been, Detective Sergeant?'

'I've never been, sir, no,' Hamza said . 'But I hear it's nice this time of year.'

Logan clasped his hands and sat forward in his chair. 'So, let's see if we can manage to get you there, will we, Ellie? Let's see if we can salvage something for you from this car crash of a wedding weekend. Would you like that? Would you like to make it to your honeymoon?'

'Well, of course I fucking would.'

'Good. Then we're on the same page,' Logan said, smiling across the table at her. 'Here's how that happens. We ask questions, you answer them, quick as you can. No pissing about, no lying to us, no bullshit. We ask, you answer. Make sense?'

With some reluctance, she nodded.

'We can, of course, arrange for a solicitor to be brought in, Mrs Tonks,' Hamza added. He looked at his watch and winced. 'Though that might hold things up...'

'Just get on with it,' Ellie barked. 'Tick-tock.'

'I like this attitude. This is a positive start,' Logan said. He nodded to Hamza to open his notebook, then launched straight into it. 'Did you put a brick through the front window of this station?'

Ellie held his gaze, unflinching. 'Yes. Next question.'

The abruptness of it took both detectives by surprise.

'Well? Come on!' Ellie spat. 'You said you wanted to rattle through it, chop-chop!'

'Right. Aye. OK,' Logan said, recovering quickly. 'Why?'

'Because you're all cunts,' she said, quite matter-of-factly. 'And because you completely fucked up my wedding.'

Logan's voice lowered into something not far from a growl. 'A girl's body was found, Mrs Tonks. A teenager. Murdered.'

'Yes, I know. Boo-hoo. How sad,' Ellie said, twisting her face into a mockery of grief. 'But that doesn't change the fact that you lot trampled all over my big day. You could've dealt with it all differently, you could've tidied her away without making a fuss, but oh no. You've got to come windmilling in, upsetting everyone. Spoiling everything.'

She shrugged, and her handcuffs rattled against the back of the chair.

'Should I have done it? Should I have thrown that brick? No. Of course not. I was angry. It was stupid. I regret it. Mostly. So, I'll pay whatever the fine is, I'll take the slap on the wrist, and —' She pushed out her bottom lip and put on a baby voice. '—I pwomise not to do it again.'

Hamza sat with his pen still poised over the paper. He side-eyed Logan, who seemed equally as stunned by the woman's performance.

Their momentary silence only made her worse.

'Well, come on, then!' she cried, jerking around in the chair. 'You said we were in a rush. I'm doing my bit here. You two hurry the fuck up and do yours!' Her bottom jaw jutted out, showing all her lower teeth. 'I swear to God, if I miss my flight because of you two sitting there staring like a couple of gormless idiots...'

Hamza's pen began to scratch across his pad. Logan, who had sat back in surprise at Ellie's outburst, now leaned forward again.

'Right. Thanks for owning up to that, Mrs Tonks. We'll deal with that in due course. Moving on—and due to time constraints, I'm not even going to phrase this as a question, because we already have you on video. You also put a brick through the window of Stephen Boyd's caravan.'

'Yes. Because he raped me as a child, so I think that's fair enough, yeah?'

'Mr Boyd doesn't quite see it that way,' Logan said.

'So? The law did,' Ellie shot back. 'Having sex with a fifteen-year-old is illegal. Even up here. Yes? *Yes?*'

'It is,' Logan confirmed, though he wasn't pleased by the 'even'.

'Well, then. Case closed. He had sex with a fifteen-year-old. He broke the law. He's a dirty paedo.'

'He claims that you spent several years trying to rekindle the relationship,' Logan told her.

'I don't give a fuck what he claims,' Ellie said, leaning in closer like she was mirroring the detective sitting opposite. 'He's a rapist.'

'*Statutory* rapist,' Logan said.

'Oh, and that's fine then, is it?' Ellie demanded.

'That's not what I'm saying.'

'No? Because it sounds like that's what you're saying. That it's fine to have sex with children, as long as they're up for it. That's OK in your book, is it?'

'Of course not,' Logan insisted. 'Nobody's saying that, Mrs Tonks. We just want to know why you attacked his caravan.'

'And I told you why,' Ellie said. 'Next question.'

'You invited him to your wedding,' Hamza said.

Ellie turned on him, eyes blazing. 'And? So?'

'So... seems a bit odd. If you hate him that much. If you just think of him as someone who raped you. Inviting him to your wedding just seems a bit... weird.'

'It was just the evening reception,' Ellie replied, as if this somehow made it less strange. 'Which you lot also fucking ruined. Thousands of pounds, down the drain. We'll be claiming for that, by the way. We'll be sending an invoice for the whole thing. Let's see if you're still fucking smiling, then!'

'We're not smiling now, Mrs Tonks,' Logan pointed out.

The woman was a horror, and it was taking everything Logan had not to lose the rag with her. But, to her credit, she was answering his questions fully, honestly, and with a turn of speed they could barely keep up with.

He didn't care about the bricks through the windows. Not really. It was nice to think she was going to be charged with something, but that wasn't the point of calling her in.

She was glaring at them both, waiting impatiently for them to continue. Logan decided to strike while the iron was visibly pissed off.

'You were here six months ago, Mrs Tonks,' he said.

That caught her off guard. She blinked a few times, like she was struggling with the question's cognitive load, then scowled back at him.

'So? I've come up here lots of times.'

'And one of those times was six months ago,' Logan said. 'We know, because we have your car on CCTV.'

'Right. Fair enough,' Ellie said. 'So? What's that got to do with anything?'

'The footage was taken the day Orla Coull disappeared.'

'Who the fuck is…? Wait. The d ead girl? That's her, isn't it? That's the d ead girl.'

'That's right, Mrs Tonks,' Logan confirmed . 'And , see, here's a funny thing. Not only d id she turn up d ead at your wed d ing, the last time anyone saw her alive she was leaving the local bank, having just cleared out her account. And your car was sat out front with the engine running. That strikes me as one hell of a coincid ence. How about you, Detective Sergeant?'

'One hell of a coincid ence, sir,' Hamza agreed .

Logan interlocked his fingers, and fixed Ellie Tonks with his most piercing of stares.

'There's only one problem with that, Mrs Tonks,' he said , but before he could reveal what that one problem was, the d oor to the makeshift Incid ent Room was thrown open, and Sinead came running through with a hand over her mouth, mumbling a frantic apology.

They all watched as she ran out through the other d oor, then, through the station's thin walls, listened to her chucking up her guts in the bathroom.

'Sorry about that,' Logan said .

'She's pregnant,' Hamza explained .

'I could n't give a shit,' Ellie retorted . 'What's the "one problem with that"?'

'What? Oh. Aye. Right,' Logan said . 'The problem with that…' He tried the stare again, but the sound of Sinead 's morning sickness stole some of the gravitas from it. 'Is that I d on't believe in coincid ences.'

Chapter 43

'Sorry, it's a bit d usty,' Tyler said , lead ing Merry Donlon through the waiting area of the bank.

'It's fine,' Merry said . 'Strange being back, actually. I worked here for a bit.'

'Oh? Doing what?' Tyler asked .

Merry stared at the back of his head for a moment, then said , 'I was a bank teller.'

'Oh. Right. Aye. Course. Makes sense,' Tyler said , grinning sheepishly. He stopped at the open vault d oor, and peered insid e. Like Hamza before him, he appeared d isappointed by the lack of riches lying within.

'They cleared it out,' Merry told him. She pointed to another, regular-sized d oor a few metres further along the same wall. 'And the fire hazard of a stationery cupboard , too, though we were able to nab a few bits and bobs before upper management came swooping in.'

Tyler looked back over his should er at her, and she quickly rushed to clarify.

'From the stationery cupboard . Not the vault.'

'Ha! That's a relief,' the DC said . 'I've not brought my hand cuffs.'

He opened the d oor that Hamza had told him to watch out for, leaned insid e to check it was the right place, then stepped back to let Merry go ahead of him.

'This is it. Manager's office,' he announced . 'You ever get to go into this room when you worked here?'

Merry shot him a curious look. 'Aye. Most d ays.'

'Oh,' said Tyler, a little d eflated . 'Right. Cool. Eh… well d one.'

'Uh, thanks?' said Merry, leading the way into the room. She pointed to one of the two smaller chairs on the side of the desk closest to the door. 'Will I just sit here?'

'No. Go ahead. You take the big chair,' Tyler urged, smiling at her like this was some sort of special treat.

Merry hesitated, but then walked around to the other side of the desk, and sat down in it. She let out a little yelp of surprise when it leaned back on her, then laughed as she righted herself.

'Bloody hell. Thought I was a gonner!' she said. She fumbled down in the workings below the seat, and locked the tilt mechanism in place. 'There. That's better.'

Tyler sat in one of the chairs opposite, and pulled it in closer. A block of wood, about the size and shape of a Toblerone, sat on the desk. A brass plaque on the front read 'Manager'. He held it up for her to see, smiled, then set it in front of her, like he was crowning her the new boss.

'Do I get the salary and bonuses that go with it?' Merry asked.

'Sadly not,' Tyler told her.

'Ah, damn. Shame,' she said.

She smiled, and he suddenly got the distinct impression that she was flirting with him. He cleared his throat, grinned awkwardly, then slapped an out of time drumbeat on the edge of the desk.

'Right. Aye. So,' he said, his mind going completely blank on what he was meant to be asking. It came to him in a flash a moment later, and Merry jumped in fright when he cried, 'Orla!' at quite a high volume.

'Orla,' Merry echoed, and her smile fell away. 'Poor Orla. Bless her.'

'Aye. Aye, it's a real shame,' Tyler said. 'Horrible. You two were close?'

Merry shrugged. 'I mean... she was a nice girl. "Close" is stretching it. But she was always polite. Always chatty. And ... yes. Sometimes, I got the impression that she couldn't talk to her mum about some things. Sarah can be... uncompromising. So I think she saw me as a bit of a softer touch.'

'And how did she get on with the rest of the family?' Tyler asked.

Merry's eyes narrowed, but only for a moment. 'Well, she was my son's girlfriend, so… pretty well.'

'Right. Aye. Right,' Tyler said. 'And, um, and your husband? He and her get on OK?'

There was a pause, just a brief one, before Merry replied. 'I mean, Ronald is Ronald,' she said.

'How do you mean?'

'He doesn't really *do* friends, as such. He's friendly, he gets on with people, but he's quite solitary. He was polite to her, of course. He was always happy to see her, but they were never close, if that's what you mean. Ronald rarely gets close to anyone. From his perspective, she was someone who visited the house. Just another person who happened to be in his orbit.'

'And that's all?' Tyler pressed.

This time, the narrowing of Merry's eyes lingered for a little longer. 'Yes. That's all. What else would it be?'

'What? No. Nothing. Just wondering, that's all,' Tyler replied. 'And things were good with her and Ronnie. Junior, I mean. Your son.'

'Yes. Very. Or, so he thought, anyway.'

Tyler sat forward. 'How do you mean?'

'Well, she ran off, didn't she?' Merry replied. 'Without so much as a word to him. I'll be honest, we were a bit disappointed in her for that. But, of course, now, with everything… who knows what happened to her? Poor girl.'

'Aye. We're doing our best to find out,' Tyler promised. 'Did, eh, did your husband mention that a couple of my colleagues went to see him last night?'

Merry, who had been shifting her revolving chair ever so slightly to the left and right during the interview, now sat perfectly still. 'No. He didn't say,' she said. 'About?'

'Just much like this, really,' Tyler said, keeping things light. 'Bit of background. We're talking to everyone.'

'Right.' The chair gave a creak as she resumed her movement. 'I see. Well, no, he didn't mention. Although, he did mention that a couple of guests decided to check out early. Any connection?'

Tyler winced. 'Maybe, aye,' he admitted. 'DCI Logan was staying with you. He can be a bit... abrupt sometimes. It's possible your husband took offence.'

Merry considered this for a moment, then laughed. 'Yes, well, Ronald isn't exactly known for his diplomacy, either. I'm sure the detective chief inspector wasn't entirely to blame.'

'Oh, I don't know,' Tyler said, chuckling along. 'He can be a real belter sometimes.'

'Must be a senior officer thing,' Merry said. 'Ronald can be very quick to—'

She stopped herself, just in time, and tried to laugh off the lapse of judgement.

'Very quick to what, Mrs Donlon?' Tyler asked. 'Anger?'

Merry looked away, looked back, then became fascinated by the desktop, like she'd never seen anything quite like it before. She ran a hand across it, tracing the contours of the wood with her fingertips.

'Anything you say is between you and me,' Tyler assured her. He gave her a moment to think on that, before continuing. 'Does he get angry?'

'Everyone gets angry sometimes,' Merry said. 'Believe me, when it comes to a shouting match, I give as good as I get!'

'And what if it comes to anything else?' Tyler asked.

Another pause. Longer this time.

'I don't know what you mean.'

'Does he ever hit you? Your husband?'

'Of course he doesn't!' Merry cried, her voice piercing and shrill. 'That's... how dare you? Of course he doesn't. Ronald's an ex-policeman, for God's sake. He's a good man!'

'The two don't necessarily go hand in hand, I'm afraid,' Tyler told her.

'Yes, well, Ronald is good. He's not perfect, no—show me any of us who is—but he's a good husband, and a good father, and I won't have his name dragged through the mud.'

Tyler held up his hands in apology. 'Of course. No. You're right, sorry,' he said. 'That was out of line. If you say he isn't violent, he isn't violent.'

317

'Right. Good .' Merry sniffed , then shrugged her should ers, one after the other. 'Thank you.'

'But if he *was*, then you could tell me. That's all I'm saying,' Tyler explained . 'If you say he's not, he's not. But if he*is*...'

'He isn't.'

'Right. OK, then. Good . I'm glad to hear that,' Tyler said . He smiled and nod d ed , like the subject had been d ropped , but then rallie one last time. 'But if that changes, or if you d ecid e that's not the case, then you can tell me. All right?'

Across the d esk, Merry sighed . She looked up to where a circle of d arker paint on the wall above the d oor suggested a clock at once been, then checked her watch instead .

'Are we d one?' she asked .

'Just about,' Tyler said . He fixed on another of his better smiles, and fumbled around in his pockets until he found his notebook. 'Just a few more questions, if you d on't mind ...'

–

Ellie Tonks sat at the table in the kitchen/interview room, her head thrown back, her should ers shaking with laughter.

Logan and Hamza both nursed their now half-empty mugs of tea, and waited for the outburst to pass.

It took a while, and had it not been for the pressing issue of the honeymoon flight, Logan got the impression it would 've gone on much longer still.

'Seriously? You seriously think I'm involved in this?' Ellie cried . Literally cried , in fact, as laughter tears came cascad ing d own her cheeks. 'You think I... what? Killed her? Is that it? You think I kid napped some rand om kid , kept her hostage for six months, then killed her on my own wed d ing d ay? Why would I d o that? I d id r even know her.'

'No, but you know Stephen Boyd ,' Logan told her. 'And you've mad e it very clear what you think of him.'

'What's that got to d o with anything?'

There was a soft knock at the d oor lead ing through to reception, then Sinead sheepishly popped her head into the room.

'Sorry, sir. Mind if I…?'

'In you come, Detective Constable,' Logan told her.

He and Hamza both offered her comforting smiles as she tiptoed through the room at speed , apologised again at the other d oor, then scurried into the Incid ent Room.

'This is a fucking joke,' Ellie said . And , to be fair to her, it was hard to argue.

'Aye. Sorry about that,' Logan said . He frowned . 'Where were we?'

'Me hating Stephen. What's that got to d o with anything?'

'Right, aye. Well, you see, Mrs Tonks, someone seems to have gone to great lengths to make it look like Mr Boyd was romantically involved with the victim before she d isappeared .'

'Oh, I bet he was, the d irty bastard !'

'Not from what we can gather,' Logan said . 'The only evid ence we had to suggest otherwise is in the process of being d isproven. We called round to her friend s and family last night, and none of them believes she was seeing him. And yet, someone tried to make us think she was. Who would d o that, d o you think, Detective Sergeant?'

'Someone who really hated Stephen Boyd , sir, I'd reckon,' Hamza replied , neither man taking their eyes off the woman sitting across the table. 'Someone who wanted to make him suffer.'

'They'd have to be angry at him,' Logan reasoned .

'Furious.'

'Furious enough to horse a d irty great brick through his wind ow?'

'Definitely, sir. Definitely that furious.'

Ellie laughed again, but there was no real humour behind it this time, just something bitter and raw.

'You really think I killed some kid to… what? Teach him a lesson? You really think I'd ruin my wed d ing d ay for that child -molesting piece of shit? Not to mention risking ruining the rest of my life! You seriously think I'd d o that?'

'I d on't know, Mrs Tonks,' Logan told her. 'You strike me as impetuous, hot-head ed , irrational, vind ictive, uncaring, and —pard on my French—a pain in the fucking arse. Are you a murderer? I haven't decided yet. But, like I say, I don't believe in coincidences. And ye here's your car out front the day Orla went missing, and here's you getting married the day she turns up dead.'

'Well, you know why the car was there! You know I didn't have anything to do with her disappearing!' Ellie snapped. She took in their blank expressions, then rolled her eyes. 'The video. I sent you the video.'

Both detectives' chairs creaked as they shifted their weight forward.

'The video?' Hamza asked.

'What bloody video?'

'God. You lot are more fucking useless than I thought!' the suspect seethed. She jerked her arms, rattling her handcuffs. 'Get me my phone,' she instructed. 'Get me my fucking phone, and I'll show you.'

—

Sinead sat at her laptop, massaging her temples, trying to rub away the headache that was building there. It was shame, mostly, she thought—the blood-rushing embarrassment of having to race through an interview with a murder suspect to chuck up her guts.

Still, at least she'd made it to the toilet.

Mostly.

'Huh.'

Sinead and DI Forde both looked up from their computers, and across to where Dave Davidson was squinting at his screen.

'Everything all right?' Ben asked.

'Hm? Oh. Aye. Just reading something,' Dave said.

'Something interesting?'

'Not sure yet. Give me a couple of minutes.'

Ben and Sinead locked eyes, shrugged, then turned their attention back to their own research.

They were interrupted again just a few seconds later when the door was thrown open, and Logan came charging in brandishing an iPhone in a sunshine yellow case.

'Sinead ! Ben! Anyone!' he boomed . 'The case file. The original case file—was there any mention of a vid eo taken outsid e the bank?'

'A vid eo? No, sir,' said Sinead . She glanced up at the Big Board to d ouble-check, then shook her head . 'Not that I saw anywhere.'

'Why?' asked Ben. 'What's happened ?'

'Her. The brid e. In there,' Logan said , hold ing up the phone. 'She sent an email.'

'How'd she manage that from her cell?' Ben wond ered .

'No! Not now, then. Back at the time. When Orla went missing. There was a shout out for information. For anyone who'd seen her to come forward .'

'And she'd seen her?' Sinead asked , looking over at the d oor that led to the kitchen. 'She had her on vid eo?'

Logan crossed to Dave and beckoned for the others to join him there.

'Dashcam,' Logan said . 'They were parked outsid e the bank while her man went into the shop. When the shout went out, she thought she remembered seeing something. Checked her camera, and emailed it in.'

'She hear anything back?' asked Ben, ad justing his glasses so he could better see the screen of Ellie's phone.

'No. Not a cheep,' Logan said . 'But watch this.'

He hit play, and then leaned back, letting the others get a better view of the screen, which currently showed a view of the street along from the bank.

At first, nothing much happened . A couple of cars d rove past. Some music was playing on the rad io, and they could hear Ellie singing along to it below her breath.

And then, from the left of the screen, Orla Coull entered . She was carrying a rucksack on her back.

She was hold ing an envelope thick enough to contain a few hund red quid in cash.

And she was not alone.

'Hold on,' said Sinead . She bent closer to the screen, then turned to the DCI. 'Is that…?'

'Aye,' Logan intoned . 'Aye, I think it is.'

–

Tyler was trying very hard to think of a way to steer the conversation back onto Ronald Donlon Sr., and his relationship with Orla Coull, when his phone rang.

'Sorry,' he said , taking the mobile from his pocket. 'Do you mind ?'

'No. Course not,' Merry said .

Tyler flashed her a grateful smile, then stood up, turned away, and pressed the phone to his ear.

'All right, boss? Everything all right?' he asked .

He listened to the reply, then slowly looked back over his should er. Merry sat watching him, her hand s clasped in her lap, the swivel chair shifting ever so slightly to the left and right. He smiled , just a touch too broad ly, then turned away again.

'Yeah. Yeah, she's here,' he said . 'She's here now.'

He listened intently to the voice on the other end of the line, and hoped the volume was d own low enough that Merry could n't hear what was being said .

'Aye, no bother at all, boss,' he said , keeping as much light and cheer in his voice as he could . 'We're grand . We'll be here. See you in a bit.'

He rubbed his forehead , then end ed the call and returned th phone to his pocket. Before he turned , he d rew in a breath, and pulled on the most convincing smile he could conjure up.

'Sorry about that,' he said , taking his seat across from her.

'Everything all right?'

'Aye! Aye, everything's grand !' Tyler said . 'Just… DCI Logan wants a wee word .'

'What about?' Merry asked .

'Dunno, he d id n't say!' the d etective constable chirped . 'He just said …'

His gaze fell on the d esk between them. Something was d ifferent about it. Something was missing. Something was…

He realised , too late, what it was. The solid wood and metal 'Manager' nameplate caught him a glancing blow across the temple, send ing him sprawling sid eways out of the chair and onto the carpet.

Rolling, he hissed as his wrist twisted beneath him, and then he was on his back, wid e open, looking up as Merry swung the solid Toblerone-sized block d own again. Again. Again.

He kicked out. Cried out. Threw his arms up to block the attack. Pain ricocheted through his wrist. He twisted to avoid another strike, but it caught him hard on the sid e of the head , and the floor beneath him became a soft wet swamp, sucking him into it, swallowing him d own.

Tyler tasted blood . Choked on it. Breathed it in.

And then, an arm swung d own. A bomb went off insid e his skull.

And the whole world was flushed away into d arkness.

Chapter 44

Logan, Hamza, and Sinead were in the process of throwing on their jackets when Dave piped up from his laptop.

'Here we go!' he announced, looking over at the DCI. 'You said Merry and Ronald Donlon met through her brother, right?'

Logan nodded. 'Aye. He and Ronnie knew each other through work.'

Dave laughed. 'I bet they did. Merry Donlon, formerly Merry Lewis. Brother of Nicholas Lewis, who did an eighteen-month stretch for... wait for it... forgery.'

'Bloody hell, seriously?' asked Ben.

Dave shrugged. 'Well, technically he was done for "Uttering", but that's a stupid bloody word for it, as we all know. But, aye. Merry Donlon's brother is a convicted forger.'

'She must've planted the diary,' Sinead realised. 'It's her. It's been her all along.'

'Right, let's get round there,' Logan barked, leading the way out of the room.

Sinead and Hamza hurried after him. Taggart jumped up to follow, then whined when the door was closed in his face.

'Sorry, boy,' Ben said, patting his knees to call the dog over. 'Looks like you're stuck here with us useless bastards.'

'Oi!' Dave protested. 'Speak for your bloody self!'

–

Logan charged out through the front door of the station, and almost collided with Hoon coming the other way.

'Fucking hell!' the former detective superintendent spat. 'What's this, the annual migration of the fucking wild ebeest? Watch where you're going.'

'Christ. You,' Logan grunted, striding past him with the other two detectives rushing to keep up. He clicked his fingers and pointed back to Hoon. 'Actually, you might be useful. Come with me.'

'And just since when the fuck did I start taking orders from you?' Hoon watched the others go marching off.

'Jack? I said, since when the fuck did ...?' He tutted, then broke into a jog. 'All right, all right, hold your fucking horses, I'm coming.'

The bank was less than a minute's walk away. Easier to run to than to take the cars. Sinead quickly fell behind, but when Hamza slowed, she waved for him to go on.

'Just hurry,' she wheezed.

Hoon slowed to a stop beside her. 'She's fine. I've got her. Go do whatever the fuck it is you're going to do.'

He caught Sinead by the elbow, his voice softening from its usual angry bellow.

'You all right? You're no' going to drop these fucking sprogs now, are you?'

'No. I've got months left,' Sinead said.

She leaned one hand on the wall of the building beside her, and begrudgingly allowed herself to be supported by Hoon on the other side while she got her breath back and swallowed down her sickness.

'Thank fuck for that. I delivered a baby once. Never a-fucking-gain.'

He looked ahead down the street. Logan and Hamza were almost to the corner, the downhill slope granting them an extra burst of speed.

'What's the big fucking rush, anyway?' Hoon asked. 'They opening a new fucking cake shop, or something?'

'It's Tyler,' Sinead said.

Hoon frowned. 'Who?' he asked.

Sinead shot him a withering look, then pulled her arm free of his grip. 'He's interviewing a suspect. We think she's the killer. He might be in trouble,' she said, walking on.

'Fuck's sake. Is there a time when that bastard's *not* in fucking trouble?' Hoon asked, keeping pace with her. 'I swear to Christ, the boy's a fucking jinx. I mean, impressive hair, if you're into that sort of thing, but fuck knows what else you see in him.'

He walked, and Sinead waddled down the hill until they reached the corner. The bank was up ahead on the right, and Sinead let out a little worried groan as she spotted it.

'His car's not there. It should be there. Why's it not there?' she asked.

'How the hell should I know?' Hoon replied. He flinched when he heard the words coming out of his mouth. 'Don't stress. I'm sure he's just off joyriding somewhere, or away buying sweets with his pocket money. You know what kids are like.'

Ignoring the rising tide of nausea, Sinead picked up the pace. She reached the front of the bank just as Logan and Hamza emerged. Once again, a full-on collision was only narrowly avoided.

'I swear you're doing that on purpose, you fucking galoot!' Hoon ejected.

Sinead looked past the DCI. Hamza already had his phone out, punching in digits.

'What's wrong?' Sinead asked. 'Where is he?'

'Not there. He's gone. They're both gone,' Logan said, and there was something about his tone, and about his face that made Sinead's heart skip a beat.

'What is it?' she demanded. 'What's happened?'

Logan looked down at her. 'There, eh, there's blood,' he said.

'Blood? What do you mean? What blood? Whose blood?'

'We don't know,' Logan said.

'Aye, but you can take a pretty good fucking guess, though,' Hoon interjected. Again, he winced, and forced a smile when he turned to the shaking, wide-eyed Sinead. 'But I'm sure he's fine.'

'We've got to find him! He could be hurt. We need to find him!'

Logan caught her by the shoulders and fixed her with a solemn stare. 'We will. I promise,' he said, then he let her go and turned to

DS Khaled , who was talking into his mobile. 'Hamza, with me. We'll go track d own Merry Donlon. Sinead , you just head back—'

Whatever he was going to say, she chose to ignore it, and plunged on into the bank without another word . Logan moved to follow, but Hoon blocked his path.

'It's fine. I've got her. You pair fuck off and find him.'

Logan glanced into the bank, then met Hoon's eye and nod d ed . 'Look after her,' he instructed .

And , with Hamza hurrying behind him once again, Logan turned and set off up the hill.

–

DC Tyler Neish was not d ead . Not this time. Everything hurt far too much for that to be the case.

His tongue was stuck to the roof of his mouth, and his face was wet with sweat, or blood , or perhaps a blend of both.

It was warm. Stiflingly so.

And it was d ark. Disorientatingly, terrifyingly d ark.

He brought up a hand and gingerly brushed his fingers against the worst of the pain. His hair was caked with blood . That part of his skull was a d ifferent shape, and not one he was particularly fond of.

After a few moments of cautious prod d ing, he mad e a d iscovery. The realisation came to him all at once, and all of a sud d en.

He was lying d own.

He was lying d own somewhere warm, and*impossibly* d ark.

Or had he gone blind , maybe? Could that have been it? It would certainly explain the absolute absence of light in the room, and the fact that his eyes were not, even several second s after coming round , making any effort to ad just.

'Hello?' he called , and his voice was a thin croak that echoed strangely around him.

Very strangely, in fact.

A little maggot of d read started to wriggle around insid e his guts.

Stifling. Dark. Echoing.

In a bank.

'Fuck.'

Despite the fact he was lying on it, it took Tyler several second s to fully find the floor. From there, it took him another ten to figure out a way to get up off it.

Over the course of the previous minute, the pain had d ropped a place or two d own his list of immed iate concerns. Now it came roaring back to the top spot, and he d ropped back to his knees, coughing and wheezing, almost grateful for the d arkness, as it meant he d id n't have to see the room spinning around him.

After another couple of aborted attempts to stand , he fumbled around until he found some metal shelving, and used it to haul himself up to his feet.

He paused at the top, letting the hammering in his skull subsid e, stealing his breath back, gulp by gulp.

'Right, then,' he muttered , feeling his way along the shelf.

The word s were intend ed to reassure himself, and calm his growing panic. To try and trick himself into thinking that this was all in hand . That none of this was a problem.

But the way they bounced around in the d arkness d id nothing to set him at ease.

Keeping his left hand on the shelf, he reached out with the right, searching blind ly as he shambled along.

What he hoped to find was a light switch. That would be nice. Although…

He stopped and patted himself d own for a while, hunting out his phone. Even when he realised he d id n't have it, he rechecked all the pockets one by one, just in case he'd missed it the first time.

He had n't.

Shite.

His shuffling resumed , his right hand waving vaguely away at nothing.

Maybe she'd just turned the lights out before locking him in the office. Aye, there had been a wind ow, but maybe he'd been uncon-scious for a while. Maybe it was now d ark out.

Very d ark.

Impossibly d ark.

His fingertips brushed against the d oor.

The metal d oor.

'Oh, great. The bitch put me in the vault,' Tyler whispered , though he barely heard the word s above the jackhammer of his own heartbeat.

He ran both hand s across the d oor, searching the smooth metal for a latch or a hand le. He found neither.

DC Tyler Neish was alone. Trapped . Locked in an airtight vault.

He wasn't d ead . That much, he knew.

But as he clawed and hammered at the unmoving d oor, he knew that it was only a matter of time.

–

Logan's BMW screeched to a halt outsid e the Donlons' house, lights flashing, but sirens muted so as not to warn Merry they were coming. Not that it mattered , of course. The chances of her having returned straight home were slim, to say the least.

He and Hamza both jumped out before the engine had even rumbled to a stop. They set off d own the alleyway toward s the house, and after three solid thumps on the front d oor went unanswered , Logan put a should er to it, forcing his way insid e.

The silence of the house was d eafening. It screamed at them, letting them know the place was empty. Letting them know that, whoever they were looking for, they would n't find them here.

But they had to try.

'Hello?' Logan bellowed . He barged into the kitchen, while Hamza checked some of the other rooms off the hall. 'Tyler? Merry? Ronnie? Anyone here?'

There was a smugness to the way the house absorbed the echo of his shouts. An *I Told You So.*

A sud d en movement out in the hall mad e the DCI go racing back there, only to find Hamza hurrying up the stairs, shaking his head .

'Nobod y d own there,' he announced . 'I d on't think they're here.'

'Shite!' Logan spat. He checked in Ronald's study, found it empty, then marched out into the garden just as Hamza came down the stairs two at a time. 'Anything?'

Hamza shook his head. 'No,' he said, following the DCI outside. 'Empty.'

They slammed the door, and set off back towards the BMW. As they drew closer, the car parked just ahead of it caught Hamza's eye.

'Here, wait,' he said, hurrying ahead so he could see the vehicle's number plate. 'This is her car. I had Dave pull the plate on the way over. This is it.'

He peered into the boot, then pulled the handle to open it. An old vacuum cleaner fell out and clattered to the ground at his feet, forcing him to skip back to avoid it.

'It's cleaning stuff,' Hamza said, spotting the mops, buckets, and various chemicals in bottles all stashed in the back of the car. 'It's a lot of cleaning stuff.' He picked up one of the bottles and read the label. 'Industrial strength, too. You think she was planning cleaning a crime scene?'

Logan shook his head. 'No. Maybe. I don't know. She said she'd been sorting out her mother's... shite!'

Hamza frowned. 'Her mother's shite?' He looked into the back of the car. 'Aye, you'd want rubber gloves for that, right enough.'

'Her mother's house,' Logan said. 'She said she'd been working on her mother's house for the last year. Sorting it out after she died.'

'Sounds like the perfect place to stash someone. Where is it?'

Logan grimaced. 'I don't know. She didn't say. Just... Skye somewhere. Across the bridge.' He pulled open the driver's door of the BMW. 'Get on the phone. Get Ben and Dave on it. See if they can find out.'

'Or...' Hamza nodded along the street. There, walking towards them with a carrier bag of shopping, was Ronnie Donlon Jr.

'Oi! You!' Logan roared, stabbing a finger in the teenager's direction. He crooked it, summoning him over. 'Here. Now.'

Ronnie stopped.

Ronnie stared.

Then Ronnie threw down the bag, turned on his heels, and ran.

'Oh no, you fucking don't!' Logan hissed, sliding into the car.

Hamza set off running after the lad, dodging clear when the BMW roared past him, siren screeching. The shopping bag exploded beneath one of the vehicle's front wheels, spraying the ground with milk, and eggs, and a fizzy puddle of Irn Bru

The road was straight and clear up to the corner where Ayesha Fulton's house stood. As fast and determined as Ronnie was, there was no way the bastard was outrunning a BMW X5.

He howled in fright and threw himself out of the vehicle's path as Logan went racing past him. The SUV went into a controlled spin, wheels smoking as the whole thing spun to face Ronnie, who now stood there in the street, clutching his head and staring back in mute terror as Hamza ran up behind him.

'Cut your shit, son!' Logan barked, throwing open his door. 'And get your arse in the bloody car!'

–

'Oh. Oh, God.'

Sinead stood in the doorway of the manager's office, her eyes locked on the puddle of red liquid on the floor, and the wooden nameplate sitting in the middle of it, the blood pooling in the grooves of the letters.

Tyler's blood.

'Look, there's no saying he's badly hurt,' said Hoon, looking over her shoulder. 'I mean, aye, it looks like he probably is, but... you know. He might not be, is the point I'm trying to fucking make. He might be fine.'

His gaze returned to the puddle.

'Unlikely as that seems.'

The sight of the blood —the smell of it—became too much for her. She turned away, one hand over her mouth, the other leaning on the wall to support herself.

Hoon danced back out of spewing range, his hands raised like he was getting ready to fend off an attack. Sinead swallowed three or four times in quick succession, shook her head , then wiped her watery eyes on her sleeve.

'I'm fine. I'm OK,' she said .

'You sure? Because you d on't fucking look OK. You've gone the colour of God zilla's bellend .'

Sinead scowled at him. 'What colour's that?' she asked , but Hoon just pointed at her face in response.

She shoved past him, head ed for the d oor, one hand slipping und e the curve of her belly to support the weight. 'I need to go help,' she said . 'I need to go find him. He's hurt!'

Hoon d arted ahead of her again and blocked her path, halfway across the waiting area. 'Listen. Wait. Hold your fucking horses. You're in no fucking fit state to go running around looking for him. So how about—'

'Shh!' Sinead hissed . 'Shut up.'

'Don't fucking *shush* me, Princess. I'm trying to fucking help you here!'

'Quiet! Shut up!' Sinead urged , jamming a finger against her lips and hold ing up the other hand for silence. 'Listen.'

Against all his instincts, Hoon bit his tongue, and listened .

But not for long.

'The fuck am I listening for?' he whispered , then Sinead slapped him on the arm, silencing him again.

And then he heard it. Soft. Faint. Muffled .

A voice crying out.

Crying for help.

Slowly, in near-perfect unison, Hoon and Sinead both turned toward s the bank vault.

'Tyler? Tyler, is that you?'

There was a pause, then the voice came again, like the DC was shouting from somewhere far off in the d istance.

'Sinead ?! Sinead ! Aye, it's me, it's me!'

Sinead rushed to the vault d oor. Hoon hung back, pinching the brid ge of his nose, and muttering a quiet 'for fuck's sake.'

'Tyler, I'm here!' Sinead called . 'Are you all right? Are you OK?'

'I think I'm in the vault,' Tyler called back. 'It's proper d ark, and the d oor's metal.'

Sinead grabbed the big lever hand le that was fixed to the d oor. 'Don't worry, we're getting you out,' she assured him, then she pulled .

The hand le d id n't bud ge. She tried again, and when it failed to move a second time, she shot Hoon a plead ing look.

'All right, all right, hang on,' he said , coming over to join her. 'Out the fucking road , and I'll d o it.'

He spat on his hand s, stretched , then grabbed the lever by its hand le and pulled . His muscles strained . His face turned purple. His breath, at last, fired out of him as a gasp.

'Fucking Hell. No, that's stuck.' He rapped his knuckles on the d oor. 'Sorry, Boyband , you're fucked , pal.'

'There's a keypad ,' Sinead said . 'Look. It must be a lock.'

Hoon inserted himself between her and the pad , stud ied it for a moment, then punched in four d igits. The screen turned red and let out a bzzzzt of warning.

'What d id you d o?' Sinead d emand ed . 'What number d id you put in?'

Hoon shrugged . 'Fuck knows. I just pressed a few at rand om to see what happened .'

Sinead hit him with a flurry of light slaps, d riving him out of the way.

'Well, d on't just mess about with it. It might d ead lock, or some-thing. Go and find someone who knows the cod e.'

Hoon stared back at her. 'Where the fuck am I meant to find them?'

'Go to the station!' Sinead snapped . 'Ben arranged for us to get access to this place. Whoever gave him the keys must know the cod e!'

'What's happening?' Tyler called . 'I can't really hear much in here. It's really warm, too. Like… it's *really* warm. Is it warm out there?'

'No. Not really,' Sinead said .

She watched as Hoon ran a hand along the joint where the thick metal d oor met the housing, feeling for moving air. When he shook his head , Sinead 's face crumpled , but she managed to keep her voice stead y, so as not to show her fear.

'It's all right, Tyler. It's all right,' she promised .

Hoon went hurrying out of the room, and Sinead ran a hand d own the cold , solid front of the vault.

'Hang in there,' she said . 'We're going to get you out!'

Chapter 45

'It's up here. Take a left, then follow the road d own to the water,' said Ronnie Donlon Jr. from the back seat of the BMW.

He looked at both d etectives sitting up front, as Logan jerked the wheel and steered the car onto a long, narrow d riveway running between two rows of pine trees.

'What's this about?' he asked . 'Why won't you tell me?'

The Beamer round ed a bend , and there, d irectly in front of them, was a d etached two-storey house, with board s on the wind ows, and an unmarked polis Volvo aband oned near the front d oor.

The build ing stood d own by the ed ge of the loch, though the trees around it would mostly mask it from anyone stand ing on the d istant shore opposite.

'Whose car is that?' Ronnie d emand ed . 'What's going on? Tell me what's going on!'

'You, shut up, stay there, and d on't say a word ,' Logan replied , shutting off the engine. 'Hamza, call it in. I want Uniform here, pronto.'

He threw open his d oor, then looked d own when Hamza grabbed him by the sleeve of his coat. 'You, eh, you not going to wait for backup, sir?'

'No time,' Logan said . 'No saying what's going on in there.'

'Shite. OK. Wait there, wait up,' Hamza said . He quickly rattled off a text with a Google Maps reference embed d ed , then jumped out of the car. 'Stay,' he told Ronnie, before catching up with Logan near the front d oor.

'Get back to the car, Sergeant,' Logan said . 'Wait for backup.'

'With, eh, with all d ue respect, sir… bollocks to that,' Hamza said . He nod d ed furtively toward s the d oor. 'Like you said , no saying what' going on in there. I'm not letting you go in by yourself.'

Logan fixed him with a particularly d evastating glare, but Hamza stood his ground .

'If you're going in, I'm going in,' the DS reiterated , and Logan chose not to waste any more time arguing.

'Fine. If Ayesha's in there, and if you see a chance, you get her out. You get her safe. That's priority one.'

Hamza nod d ed his und erstand ing. 'Got it.'

Logan took a d eep breath. 'Right, then,' he said . He reached for the front d oor hand le, pushed it d own, then winced as the hinges creaked to announce the d etectives' arrival.

Right in front of them, half-hid d en by the gloom, came an explosion of movement. Logan brought up his arms, shield ing his face, then d ucked to allow a startled -looking pigeon to go fluttering out through the d oor, and up toward s the overcast sky.

'I think I just shat myself,' Hamza whispered .

They were in a wid e hall, with four d oors running off from it, and a set of stairs lead ing up to the floor above. Hamza pointed upward s, and Logan reluctantly gave a nod .

Light came in through the front d oor, but the board ed wind ows meant it d id n't make it far into the house before being overwhelmed by the d arkness. Hamza quietly unzipped one of his jacket pockets, took out a small torch, and held his finger on the power switch as he crept his way up the stairs.

Logan, meanwhile, began a search of the ground floor. The closest d oor led to a small room with a toilet and a wash hand basin, both in matching shad es of avocad o green, and both d otted with spots of black mould .

He approached the next d oor, moving slowly, carefully, trying not to announce his presence any more than he alread y had . If Merry was in here, she knew they were there, too. But that d id n't mean he had to let her know *exactly* where in the house he was.

The second door was fully closed, so he had to turn the handle to open it. He pushed it inwards with the flat of his left hand, his right clenched in a fist, ready to block, or to swing.

A cupboard. That was all. A few boxes, some old coats, and a pull-along shopping trolley in a dark red tartan fabric.

Somewhere close by, a floorboard groaned. Logan turned, searching the hall, but saw nobody. The creaking came again, and his eyes went to the ceiling. Hamza. Just Hamza.

Or so he hoped.

Setting his sights on the third door, Logan snuck across the hall, and reached, once again, for the handle.

-

Upstairs, the darkness was thicker. Richer. The shadows shifted around in it, like the walls of the house were alive.

He'd delayed as long as he could, but couldn't put it off any longer. Hamza flicked the switch of his torch and swept it across the upstairs landing, making sure that he was alone. The beam picked out the faded pattern of old floral wallpaper. He caught sight of himself reflected in the cracked glass of a landscape painting, and was shocked by how frightened he looked.

Hardly surprising, he told himself. He didn't exactly have the best record when it came to poking around in abandoned old houses, as the scar on his back would testify.

'I could be sitting at a computer,' he whispered, so quietly then even he could barely hear it. 'I could be sitting in an office with a cup of tea, waiting for software to install. But, oh no.'

He took another look around, less panicky this time.

There were three doors upstairs, all standing open to reveal empty rooms that had presumably all once been bedrooms.

The first one had been stripped of everything but the carpet. There were some mushrooms sprouting from the floor, and the smell of damp forced him to quickly back out again.

The second room was fungi-free. Some light filtered in through a gap at the edge of the window board, like it had been prised off at one corner and not yet reattached. Other than that, though, there was nothing in there worth noting.

He crept across to the third room, poked his head and his torch insid e, and checked it out. Once again, he saw nothing of any interest.

'Shite,' he whispered.

Then, just as he was about to leave, he spotted a cupboard in the corner, set into the wall. It was narrow—two-third s the wid th of a normal d oor, maybe—but the only possible hid ing place up here that he had n't yet checked.

The floor was sagging a little besid e the d oor, so it felt soft and spongy beneath his feet. He held his torch raised by his head, read y to strike with it if some bugger should come leaping out of the cupboard at him.

He gripped the hand le, stead ied himself, then pulled.

It wasn't a cupboard. That was the first thing he noticed. It had been, once upon a time, but now it served a d ifferent purpose.

Hamza gripped the lad d er that rested against the wall behind the d oor, and shone his torch up through the open hatch in the ceiling, revealing nothing but roof insulation and d ust motes.

Bollocks.

He looked back to the bed room d oor. He should shout Logan. Wait for backup. What he d efinitely should n't d o was climb up there, unarmed and alone.

He thought of Ayesha. A young girl, missing and alone.

He thought of his own d aughter. Of how he'd feel. Of what he'd d o if she were the one missing.

After that, the choice was easy.

Jamming the torch between his teeth, Hamza placed both hand s on the lad d er, and began to climb.

—

Sweat soaked Tyler's back. It soaked his front, sid es, and most of the rest of him, too, but it was his back that was bothering him most. He had alread y untucked his shirt, but it had n't helped much, so he pulled it open at the front, pinging buttons in all d irections, and took the whole thing off.

'You OK?' Sinead asked . 'How you hold ing up in there?'

It was hard to tell through the d oor, but she sound ed worried . She was trying not to, of course. Most people who heard her would n't pick up on it. They'd think she was fine.

But Tyler heard it. Tyler knew.

'Fine, aye,' he replied . 'Bit hot. Air's feeling a bit... thin. But fine.'

'Good . We're going to get you out,' Sinead promised him. 'Are you sure there's not a hand le? There should be one, I think, in case of emergencies.'

Tyler ran his hand s over the d oor again. Smooth metal, mostly, with what felt like a rid ged vent somewhere near the top. He'd consid ered trying to climb through it, like Bruce Willis in *Die Hard*, but from what he could tell it was only about nine inches wid e by six high, so it'd be a hell of a squeeze to even get his head through, let alone all the rest of him.

'Can't find one,' he told her.

'OK. It's fine. Don't worry. Help will be here soon.'

'I think Merry Donlon might be the killer,' he told her. 'Call it a hunch.'

He heard her laugh. Something about it mad e his eyes sting, and his throat tighten. He d id n't bother wiping his tears. There was nobod y here to see them, after all.

'Think you might be right,' Sinead confirmed . 'But right now, that d oesn't matter. Right now, all I care about is getting you out.'

'Aye, that'd be nice, right enough,' Tyler agreed . He waved a hand in front of his face. 'Christ, it's hot. You've got no id ea how hot it is in here. Should it be this hot?'

'It's fine. You're going to be all right. Try not to panic, OK?'

Tyler coughed , wheezed , then nod d ed .

Then, when he remembered that she could n't see him, he respond ed out loud .

'I'm not panicking,' he said , although this wasn't entirely true.

There was d efinitely an element of panicking going on. Although, strangely, not as much as in that escape room a couple of d ays before. At least in here, Logan could n't wring his neck if he proved to be useless.

Just as well, too. Right here and now, with blood congealing on his head , and sweat pooling in the crack of his arse, he consid ered himself to be pretty blood y useless ind eed .

'Talk to me, will you?' he said .

'About what?' came the reply.

Tyler slid d own the d oor. His head was aching now. His chest felt tight.

'Anything. I d on't know. The babies. Talk to me about the babies. We're going to be good parents, aren't we? Me and you? We're going to be good .'

–

Outsid e the vault, Sinead pressed a hand against the metal, like she might be able to reach through and pull him out. She took a moment to stead y her voice before replying to him.

'We're going to be great,' she said . 'It's not going to be easy, though.'

'We'll make it work,' Tyler replied . 'It'll be perfect.'

Sinead laughed at that, then sniffed back tears. 'No, it won't!'

There was a suggestion of something in Tyler's reply. Shock, maybe. Or ind ignation.

'What? What d o you mean?'

'It won't be perfect. It can't be. Nothing ever is, and there's no point pretend ing otherwise,' she told him. 'But we'll love them. More than anything. Both of us. Harris, too. We'll be a family. Not perfect. Just us.'

There was no reply from insid e the vault. Sinead knocked on it, but the thick metal absorbed all the sound .

From somewhere beyond the d oor, muffled and d istant sound ing there came a sud d en crash.

'Tyler?' Sinead cried . Then, when he d id n't respond , she raised he voice to a full-volume shout. 'Tyler, what's happening? What's wrong?'

'Nothing! Nothing, I'm all right, I'm all right!' her husband replied. 'Was just taking my trousers off and fell. I'm fine, just really hot.'

Sinead relaxed. Not all the way, but a little.

'Don't d o that to me,' she scold ed. 'Jesus, I thought you'd d ied!'

She turned as the d oor to the waiting room opened. Taggart shot through first, tail wagging, tongue lolling around like it was trying to break free of his mouth. Ben stumbled in next, pulled along by the d og's lead, struggling to keep his footing.

'Don't shite yourselves, the fucking cavalry's arrived!' announced Hoon, bringing up the rear. 'I've got the cod e! We'll have the d ozy prick out of there in no time.'

Sinead slapped a hand on the d oor. 'Tyler, you hear that? We're getting you out! We're getting you out!'

'Seriously?' Tyler yelped, and even though he sound ed far away, the relief in his voice was unmistakable. 'Thank God. I d on't know how much longer I can last in here! Should I stand back, or cover my ears, or what?'

'We're no' blowing the fucking d oors off, son,' Hoon shouted to him. 'It's no' the fucking *Italian Job*. We're just putting in the number and opening the d oor.'

'What is it?' Sinead asked. 'What's the number?'

'It's five, three, nine…' Hoon stopped and scratched his head. 'Wait. Hang on. Five, nine…' He caught the d angerously wid e-eyed look from Sinead, then grinned. 'Just kid d ing. Five, three, nine, eight.'

Sinead punched in the numbers. The panel flashed red. A buzzer offered a short, sharp reprimand.

'That d oesn't sound good,' said Ben, still struggling to contain the excited Taggart, who was pulling so hard on the lead that his front two legs were bicycling in mid -air.

'That's not it,' she said.

'Aye, it is,' Hoon insisted. 'Five, three, nine, eight. That's what the bastard told us it was. You must've put it in wrong.'

'I d id n't put it in wrong! It's four numbers!'

'Here, let me have a fucking try,' Hoon said, practically should er-barging her out of the way. He whispered along as he thumbed each of the numbers in turn. 'Five, three, nine, eight. There.'

The panel turned red . There was no angry buzzing this time, but the light stayed on, two word s flashing over and over on the d isplay.

'It says, "Security Lockd own,"' he said . He put his hand s on his hips, chewed his bottom lip for a moment, then tried the hand le.

Just like before, it d id n't bud ge.

'Huh. Numbers must be wrong,' Hoon d eclared .

'Oh, you *think*?' Sinead cried .

'What's happening?' asked Tyler. His voice sound ed even more d istant. Even further beyond their reach. 'Why is it taking so long?'

Sinead fired Hoon a scathing look, then took a moment to inject some levity into her voice before replying.

'Nothing to worry about. It's just… we're just working on it, all right? Just stay calm.'

'Am I stuck?' Tyler asked . 'Tell me honestly, Sinead . Am I stuck in here?'

'Just… for now. Just for now. Not for long,' she told him. 'We're getting you out soon.'

At the far end of the waiting area, Taggart's d etermination proved too great for Ben's arthritic fingers. The d og pulled free, yanking the lead from the DI's grasp. Ben mad e a grab for him, but the pup was too fast. He ran around in two wid e circles, then mad e a beeline for the d oor that stood a few metres along the wall from the vault.

'I d on't know how much air's left in here,' Tyler called .

Hoon stepped in closer to the vault d oor, sighed heavily, then cleared his throat. 'You're all right, son,' he said . 'We're going to get you out of there, even if we have to pull this fucking d oor off its hinges. You're going to be OK, Boyband . I know I treat you like you're a useless, hopeless, gormless, clueless, clumsy, id iotic fucking jebend of a horse's cock. And rightly fucking so—'

He caught yet another of Sinead 's fiery looks, and flashed her a smile of apology.

'Sorry, force of habit,' he ad mitted , then he raised his voice and ad d ressed the man in the vault again. 'Just you hang in there, son. All right? Your Uncle Bob's on the fucking case. Everything's going to be—'

He and Sinead both looked to their left as Ben pulled open the door to the stationery cupboard, and a naked Tyler rolled backwards into the waiting room with a strangled 'Fuck me!' of surprise.

Taggart pounced on him immediately, all slobber and tongue. Tyler waved one arm to fend him off, used the other to shield his eyes from the bright light, and wished he had another with which to hide his modesty.

Still holding the door handle, Ben peered into the cupboard, where an ancient boiler system hummed away against the far wall. The inside of the door had been kitted out with a metal heat shield, which now shone with dozens of sticky, sweaty handprints, and the imprint of at least one bum cheek.

'It's a heating cupboard,' the DI remarked.

'For fuck's sake!' Hoon spat. He thumped a fist against the vault door. 'He's no' even fucking in there!'

But Sinead didn't care. She ran over to him as fast as her extra cargo would allow, dropped to her knees, and hugged him. Taggart squeezed in between them, back end flailing, tongue lashing and lapping at any exposed bit of skin within reach.

Which, in Tyler's case, was quite a lot.

When she left him go, he lay down on his back again, covered his crotch with both hands, and looked up into the faces of the dog, the two detectives, and whatever the hell Hoon was these days.

'I, eh, I don't suppose we can agree to keep this between ourselves, can we?'

Ben chuckled, winked, and three of the four of them all shook their heads.

'Absolutely not a chance in hell,' the DI told him.

'Funny,' Tyler said, blowing a strand of blood ied hair from his eyes. 'I had a feeling you might say that...'

Chapter 46

Hamza saw the bucket first. It was tucked into the loft insulation so the top was almost level with a narrow floored area, and from the smell of it, he could already tell what was inside.

He took the torch from his mouth and shone it around the attic, shivering lightly in the cold. There were ropes hanging down from the apex of the loft space. Discarded junk food wrappers. A pile of filthy rags bundled up against the eaves, where the sloping roof met a few haphazard sheets of plywood laid across the beams.

A bundle the size of a person.

A bundle the size of a girl.

'Shit,' he whispered.

He was still on the ladder, half in the loft, half out of it. His legs weren't up for moving, but he forced them to take him up a step, then another, until he could pull himself up on one of the support struts and feel around with his feet until he found a solid place to stand among the wads of fibreglass insulation.

All the while, he kept the beam on the torch on the someone-sized bundle of rags on the floor.

'Hello?' he said, but his voice was shaking so badly that he didn't think it would make it all the way to the other side of the attic.

He cleared his throat, picked his way across a couple of beams, and tried again.

'Hello? Is anyone there?' he asked.

The light from the torch picked out a shape, half-hidden by the filthy fabric.

A bare foot, blood congealing on the injured sole.

'Oh, no. No,' Hamza whispered , and sud d enly all thoughts for his own safety were forgotten.

He mad e his way to the flooring, estimating the d istance between each beam, then bound ing the gap with his heart in his mouth.

His guesses were good . His footing was sure. He stumbled on the last step, and land ed on his knees on the ed ge of the raised plywood flooring. The whole roof space seemed to shake with the impact. Trickles of thick, gritty d ust fell from overhead , colouring his d ark hair and skin with shad es of grey and white as he picked himself back up.

'Hello?' he said again.

The shape beneath the rags d id n't respond . The oval of torchlight shook as he creaked the last couple of steps, took hold of the d irty material, and braced himself for the worst.

–

The kitchen, like the bathroom and cupboard before it, was empty. Not cleaned out—there were open boxes of cereal, empty crisp bags, and torn-open biscuit wrappers scattered around , not to mention a sink full of d ishes steeping away in cold , manky water—but d evoid of any human life.

Logan put a hand on the kettle. Cold . He waved the same hand above the rings of the cooker hob, but felt no heat there, either.

There was a knife block on the worktop, besid e a pile of crusted -up baking trays. One of the knives—one of the larger ones—was missing. He checked the sink for it, but d id n't d are explore the murky grey water too thoroughly, for fear of what might be living in there.

He flicked the water from his hand , looked around for somewhere to d ry it, then conclud ed that wiping it on any of the d ishcloths or rags lying around the kitchen would only make him more d irty, not less.

He gave the hand a wipe on his coat, instead , and then froze when something hard and metallic was pressed into his lower back.

'Please,' Merry Donlon whispered from two feet behind him. There were two clicks as hammers were drawn back. 'Don't do anything stupid.'

'I'm not the one pointing a shotgun at a police officer, Merry,' Logan said. He put his hands on the worktop directly in front of him, ostensibly keeping them in plain sight, while at the same time bringing them within grabbing range of the knife block. 'The only one doing anything stupid here is you.'

He considered the knives. One lunge, one grab, one quick turn. Could she get a shot off before then?

Logan sighed inwardly. Aye. Aye, of course, she bloody could.

'Hands up. Back away from there,' Merry instructed, sensing his intentions. She prodded him harder with the end of the gun. 'Out into the hall. No funny stuff.'

She didn't sound upset. If anything, she sounded more in control than the other times he'd spoken to her. Mind you, having a gun in her hand probably helped immensely with the balance of power.

At the same time, though, the situation should 've been making her nervous. And yet, here she was, as calm and collected as could be.

In a lot of ways, of course, this was good —the main way being that nervous people were much more likely to accidentally pull a trigger.

And yet, there was a coldness there that Logan hadn't been expecting. He'd thought all this might turn out to be an unfortunate series of escalations that Merry had got herself all tangled up in. That maybe she wasn't a bad person, just a scared, misguided one who'd done bad things.

But there was no fear in the woman who jabbed the shotgun into the base of his spine again, and calmly instructed him once again to back out the room and into the hall.

Once out there, she stepped away, and he turned slowly to face her so his back was to the front door. The shotgun was the one they'd seen Ronald Sr. with, Logan guessed, but she held it like she knew how to use it. And, more importantly, like she was prepared to.

'How about you put the gun down, Merry?' Logan asked. 'Let's talk about this.'

'Talk?' Merry let out a shrill laugh. 'And let me guess what you're going to say. Is it, "you're und er arrest", maybe? Is that what you want to talk about?'

'I mean, it's not off the table, I'll be honest,' Logan ad mitted . 'But I want to hear your sid e, too. Make me und erstand all this.'

Merry ad justed her aim, so the shotgun was pointed at his chest, rather than the centre of his stomach. She wasn't a large woman, and the weapon looked oversized for her. But she held the butt pressed tight against her should er, and had planted her feet to brace herself against the firing kick.

Logan realised that, right now, as it stood , she intend ed to shoot him.

He thought about d od ging sid eways, throwing himself at her, grabbing for the gun. But he wasn't exactly a small target, and his chances of crossing the four-foot gap between them without getting one or more holes put through him were slim.

'No,' she said .

'No?'

'I won't tell you "my sid e". My sid e is none of your concern.'

'Well, I mean, if not mine, Merry, then whose?' Logan asked her. 'Right now, you're looking at going to jail for a very long time. And if you pull that trigger, a whole lot blood y longer. See, everyone's looking for you now. Everyone knows. There's no going back from this, Merry. You might think that killing me will let you go back to your normal life, but it won't. There is no normal for you to go back to. Do this, shoot me, run, and how far d o you think you'll get? In a stolen polis car, no less.'

Her grip shifted on the gun, just a fraction. Her feet shuffled , searching for a new footing.

'Right now, you're in trouble. Big trouble. Trouble with a capital T,' Logan said . He nod d ed to the weapon in her hand s. 'But d o this? Kill a police officer in cold blood ? And you're not just in trouble, Merry, you're fucked . Totally, absolutely, comprehensively fucked . And I know you d on't want that.'

Logan smiled . Not much—not enough to seem patronising and risk riling her—but enough to appear sympathetic to her current situation.

'So, how about you put d own the gun, we go back to the station and get a cup of tea, and we'll sit and talk this out?'

–

Hamza lifted the ragged fabric away, and almost screamed at the sight of the girl's face. Her eyes were open, staring back at him, pupils constricting in the sud d en light. A gag was tied around her head , pulled between her teeth, cutting into the flesh of her cheeks.

Her hand s were bound together at the wrists, fingers interlocked , and then wrapped in thick tape to form one solid ball. She pulled her hand s in closer to her chest and screwed her eyes shut, like she was bracing herself for something terrible to happen.

Something *else* terrible to happen.

She was hurt. She was scared .

But she was alive.

Hamza angled the torch away so it wasn't shining right into her face.

'It's OK. It's OK, I'm with the police,' he told her. 'I'm here to help, OK? I'm here to take you home, Ayesha.'

Down on the floor, the mention of her name mad e her risk opening one eye. It swam around , trying to find focus, then settled on the shad owy outline of the man kneeling above her.

She whimpered , but allowed her head to be lifted while Hamza worked the knot of the gag.

'Don't scream, OK?' he whispered to her. 'Just stay quiet, and we'll get out of here. We'll get you back home.'

He waited a second or two after he'd untied the gag to make sure she und erstood , then removed it and tossed it asid e. Ayesha let ou a gasp, then her head , should ers, and soon her whole bod y began to shake, as her face screwed up, and tears began to fall.

Hamza put his arms around her and pulled her in close to him, hold ing her while she sobbed .

'You're all right. You're OK. I've got you,' he told her. 'I've got you. We're getting out of here, all right? You and me, we're getting you out.'

She nod d ed , her breath hot against his should er. Hamza looked d own at her feet, which she'd curled up behind her now. Both soles were scratched and cut, like she'd recently walked over broken glass.

Still hold ing her, he stretched out one of his legs, and used the heel of his shoe to part the rolls of loft insulation enough that he was able to see the beam nestled between them.

Carpet gripper strips had been attached to it, the jagged pins pointed upward s.

'Wow, she really thought this through,' Hamza muttered , sound ing almost impressed .

He looked at the feet of the girl still sobbing away on his should er.

He looked at all those short but oh-so-sharp nails.

Ah, bollocks, he thought.

And with that, he reached for his shoelace.

Chapter 47

Merry Donlon, it seemed , was still not up for confessing, d espite the fact that the gun she currently had pointed at DCI Logan implied a certain level of guilt.

Logan shrugged , though he was careful not to be too sud d en about it.

'Fine. Why d on't I tell you what I think happened ? And you can tell me how close I am,' he said . He d id n't give her time to even think about this, much less object. 'I think Orla Coull came to see you. I think she told you that she was pregnant. She had n't told her mum, but then she d id n't tell her mum when she started her period s, either. She told you. Her boyfriend 's mum. An ad ult she thought she could trust.'

Merry said nothing to that. Nor d id she flinch away from it. She just stood there, gun pressed to her should er, sights set on the unmissable target of the d etective's chest.

Logan took the risk. Took the leap.

'It was your husband 's, wasn't it? The baby,' he said .

No protest.

No outrage.

No shock, or surprise.

'Did she tell you, or d id you figure out yourself?'

Merry's face showed some emotion then. Not much, and what was there was hard to d efine, but a crack had appeared in her steely facad e.

'She told me. She told me, but she d id n't have to. I alread y knew." She wrenched her mouth into a smile. A raw, painful, unamused sort of smile. 'How could I not? It was going on und er my own roof. In my own bed !'

'What did she want?' Logan asked. 'Why did she come to you? Why did she tell you?'

Merry's voice wobbled a little. Another crack in the armour. 'Help,' she said. 'She wanted my help. She wanted rid of it. I told her to go to the doctor, but she didn't want to abort. She wanted to give it away. To see out her pregnancy, then farm it out to someone else.' Her voice became a whisper. The gun trembled worryingly in her hands. 'People were going to find out, but she said she didn't care. She was legal age. They'd done nothing wrong, she said.'

Merry laughed. It was a harsh, scraping rasp, and one of the worst sounds Logan had ever had the misfortune to hear.

'Done nothing wrong! Can you believe that? She cheats on my son, fucks my husband in my own bed, and then comes to me saying they've done nothing wrong!'

'Aye, that must've been tough,' Logan said.

'Oh, don't! Don't pretend you care!' the woman with the shotgun spat. 'Do you have any idea how hard I worked to get where I am? A nice life. A lovely house. Do you know what it took to get here from where I started? From the family I was born into?' She jerked her head, indicating the house around them. 'It wasn't always like this, you know? She got this later. I grew up in shit and filth. And look at me now!'

Logan looked, very deliberately, at the state of the place around them.

'Not here! My house. My son. My family!' Merry hissed. 'I built up all that, and then... what? I'm supposed to let some little slut who can't keep her legs closed come along and mess it all up? Undo all my hard work? No. No, I couldn't. I wouldn't let her.'

'So you killed her?'

'I helped her. I did what she asked. I brought her here to hide. To see out the pregnancy. I was going to do the place up for her. For them. Just for a while. She was on board with it. She went along with the plan, wrote a note for her parents, made it look like she'd gone off somewhere.'

Merry drew in a breath. It was a deep and unsteady gasp that brought tears to her eyes.

'She was going to stay here. We were going to d eliver the baby, leave it somewhere, and then she'd come back. That's what we planned . That's what she agreed to. That's what she agreed to go along with!'

Logan thought back to all those bruises and injuries on Orla's bod y. That wasn't someone who'd gone along with a plan.

'She changed her mind ,' he said .

'Stupid bitch! It could 've worked out. It could 've been fine, but oh no. Oh, no, she wanted to leave. She wanted to go back home. She wanted to ruin everything, tear my family apart, d estroy everything I've worked so hard for!' She sniffed loud ly, then shook her head 'You d on't get it, I can see that. You d on't know what it's like in a town this size. How important your reputation is.'

'Aye, well, I think you can safely say it's pretty much fucked now,' Logan pointed out, then he raised his hand s higher when she swung the shotgun up so it was pointed at his face.

'Shut up! Just… stop! Shut up!' she warned . 'I had to keep her here. I had to make her stay! I d id n't… I d id n't want to d o those things, bu she d id n't leave me any choice. It was her fault. Hers, not mine! She changed the plan. She was going to ruin everything!'

'What happened to the baby?' Logan asked .

Merry's jaw tightened . Tears pooled in her eyes. She shook her head , just a fraction. 'It d oesn't matter,' she told him.

Logan closed his eyes, just for a moment, as if offering up some silent prayer.

'And what about Orla?' Logan asked . 'How d id she d ie?'

'It wasn't me. I d id n't d o it,' Merry insisted . 'She fell. She was trying to get out, and she fell.' Her eyes d arted left and right, like she was watching events playing out in front of her. 'Then she was in the water. And she wasn't moving. She wasn't trying to swim, or shout, or d o anything. So I just… I watched . I watched her floating away. I watched her going und er. I just watched her.'

'And what d id you feel about that, Merry? What d id you fee watching that young girl d ie?'

The woman with the gun let out a breath. 'Relief,' she whispered . 'Relief, that it was over. That she was gone. And then she has to go and turn up again and ruin everything.'

Her anger was building. Her memories seemed to be distracting her now, her attention no longer so tightly focused on Logan. Maybe he could chance making his move now. If he rushed her, he might be able to get in too close for her to get off a clean shot.

From overhead, there came a soft thump. Merry's eyes flitted upwards for a fraction of a second. When they settled back on the DCI, her concentration had crystallised once again.

'Who else is here?' she demanded. 'Who's up there?'

'Like I said, Merry, it's over,' Logan told her. He brought one hand down just far enough to push out an ear. 'Can you hear that? Listen. Do you hear those sirens?'

She couldn't, he knew, because nor could he. Still, from the way her eyes widened, the deception seemed to be working.

'That's the cavalry coming, Merry,' he continued. 'Now, either they're going to turn up here and find you pointing a gun at a senior police officer, or they're going to turn up and find you sitting quietly in the back of my car. I know which one's going to look best.'

He risked bringing his arms down, then held a hand out to her like an offer of help.

'Come on, Merry. Give me the gun. Let's not do this anymore.'

She looked at the hand, then down at the weapon she was holding. It suddenly appeared alien to her, like she wasn't sure what it was, or where it had come from.

'That's it. Come on. Let's go and get that cuppa, will we?'

The butt of the gun moved an inch or two from her shoulder. Her finger relaxed on the trigger.

Then, from the foot of the stairs, there came a creak. A high-pitched scream of fright as Ayesha saw the scene playing out in the hallway.

Merry reacted. Panicked. Pulled the gun close, pulled the trigger hard.

And thunder and blood filled the air.

Chapter 48

Despite having absolutely no right whatsoever to involve himself, Hoon had designated himself the driver, and was powering Hamza's Volvo across the Skye bridge while Tyler hastily redressed himself in the back seats.

Sinead sat up front, her feet wedged into the footwell, both hands gripping onto any and all available hand rails as Hoon raced towards the roundabout at the end of the bridge, showing no signs of slowing down.

'Jesus, Jesus, Jesus!' she wailed, knuckles whitening as Hoon hung a left so quickly the car threatened to tip up onto two wheels.

'Fucking relax, will you? You're making me tense!'

'*I'm* making *you* tense?' Sinead cried. 'I'm not the one driving like a bloody lunatic!'

'Fuck me, is she always like this?' Hoon asked. He adjusted his rearview mirror to address Tyler in the back, then grimaced when he got an eyeful of something he shouldn't. 'Jesus! Put that thing away before I fucking arrest you!'

'You can't arrest him. You're not in the police,' Sinead snapped.

'I can still make a fucking citizen's arrest, I'll have you know!'

'What, for getting dressed in a car?'

'He flashed his cock at me!' Hoon shot back.

'What? No, I didn't!' Tyler protested. 'I've got my trousers on! Was it not my thumb?'

'Well, I don't fucking know, do I?' Hoon cried. 'It's no' like I kept looking. I caught a wee fucking glimpse and looked away.'

'Stop!' Sinead said.

'We're just having a fucking discussion, sweetheart, no need to—'

'It's back there!' Sinead told him. She pointed over her shoulder. 'The turn-off. The house. It's that way!'

'Oh. Shite,' Hoon said. 'Everyone hold on.'

He dropped a gear, jerked the wheel, yanked up the electronic hand brake, and the car spun a one-eighty in the road, leaving a spiral of tyre marks on the tarmac, and hammering the already bloodied Tyler against the side window.

'Ow! Jesus! A bit of warning!' he protested.

'I said, "everyone hold on." What the fuck more do you want?' Hoon spat.

And then he shoved his foot to the floor, and the engine roared them onwards.

–

Logan clutched his left arm, just above the elbow, the sound of the gunshot still ringing in his ears.

'I'm fine! I'm fine, relax! Everyone just relax!' he implored. His gaze was fixed on Merry Donlon, but the words were meant for everyone. 'Everyone just stay calm, all right? It's just a graze, Merry. Just a graze. This can all still be fixed.'

He heard the padding of a footstep behind him, and the creaking of a floorboard.

'Hamza, do not move!' he warned. 'Merry and I have got this under control. Merry and I are both fine. Aren't we, Merry? We're both good.'

She was shaking now, as the fear and adrenaline she'd been holding back came crashing through the dam all at once.

He'd been lucky. The first shotgun blast had gone wide, punching a hole through the door of the cupboard, but leaving him relatively unscathed. He didn't fancy taking his chances on a second one, though.

'Detective Sergeant Khaled is going to take Ayesha out of here, Merry. All right? But I'm staying here. I'm not going anywhere.'

'Sir,' Hamza protested.

'It's not a discussion, Sergeant. Take her outside. Intercept the backup. Tell them not to come in. Tell them Merry and I are having a chat, and we'll come out when we're done.'

Hamza opened his mouth to object again, but then he saw the fear etched on Ayesha's face, and knew the call was the right one.

'I'll come back,' he said.

'No. No, you won't. We'll come out when we're good and ready. Right, Merry?'

She didn't reply, just stared up at him like he was something from a nightmare, only kept at bay by the gun she held trained on him.

Behind the DCI, over by the foot of the stairs, Hamza took Ayesha by the arm, and hobbled her towards the door.

'Don't,' Merry warned. 'Don't move. Move, and he dies.'

'Ah, come on, Merry,' Logan said. 'Don't make this worse. Let them go. It'll be better for you if you do.'

'Nobody's going anywhere,' she told him. Her voice cracked, becoming piercing and high-pitched. 'Everyone stay where they are! Everyone stay where they are, and shut up, and let me think, or—'

From the other room—through the door that Logan hadn't checked, came a sound the DCI had been too afraid to even hope for.

A baby's cry. Sharp. Shrill. Urgent.

Merry's gaze was drawn to it. Just for a moment. Just for long enough. Logan threw himself at her, grabbing for the gun, but pain erupted up his arm and through his shoulder, throwing off his aim.

He missed, she staggered back, and he was staring directly down the barrel of the firearm as her finger tightened on the trigger.

'Mum?'

She let out a sob that didn't sound all the way human. It was a broken-hearted squeak, a primal, animalistic grunt. Sadness, and sorrow, and shame, all wrapped up in that one, desperate noise.

A breeze blew in through the front door at Ronnie Jr.'s back. He looked around —at Ayesha, at the detectives, at his mother with the gun in her hand —like he was trying to make sense of it all. Trying to find a way of excusing it. Trying to find an explanation for it all beyond the terrible, awful, obvious one.

'Mum? What's going on? What is this?'

Merry shook her head. 'No, no, no, no,' she whispered. 'No, Ronnie, no, you can't be here. Not here. You can't, you can't, you need to go. You can't be here!' The words bubbled and boiled inside her, becoming a scream. *'You can't be here! You can't see this!'*

'He has seen it, Merry,' Logan said. 'And he can see you sorting it. He can see you fixing things.'

He held out his right hand again, and tried not to worry about the amount of blood on his palm. There'd be time for that later.

Hopefully.

'Give me the gun, Merry,' he pleaded. 'Your son's scared. Give me the gun, then go give him a hug.'

She gazed over at Ronnie Jr., and wept at the fear in his eyes. He looked at her like he didn't recognise her. Like he didn't know this version of this woman standing there in this hallway.

'I'm sorry,' she told him. 'I'm so sorry.'

And then, with a jerk of her arms, she spun the shotgun so the muzzle was pressed to the underside of her chin, screwed her eyes shut, and thumbed the trigger.

The gun fired, but not before Logan had slammed his bloodied hand against the barrel, throwing it sideways. Plasterboard rained down from the ceiling above them. With a twist, and a push, Logan separated Merry from the spent weapon, and they both landed heavily on the filthy floor.

'Mum, Mum!' Ronnie yelped, racing over and dropping to his knees beside her.

She covered her eyes, buried her face in her hands, and turned her body away, unable to look at him. Unwilling to see the hurt and confusion on his face.

'I'm sorry!' she wheezed, through raw, throaty sobs. 'I'm sorry!'

'All right, nobody fucking move!' boomed a voice from the doorway.

Logan sighed, and turned to find Hoon standing there, blocking Tyler and Sinead from entering.

'Aye,' the DCI intoned . 'About blood y time, too.'

From the room next d oor, the baby continued to cry. Sinead elbowed Hoon asid e, d rawn in by the sound .

'Detective Constable.' Logan grimaced through the pain as he pointed to the d oor further d own the hall. 'Perhaps you'd be good enough to d o the honours?'

Chapter 49

Once the squad cars and ambulances had arrived , and everyone was busy d oing their thing, Logan took a moment to congratulate Hamza on a job well d one.

'You d id good in there, Sergeant,' he said .

'Thanks, sir,' Hamza said . He was half-sitting, half-leaning on the boot of Logan's BMW, the boot lid open above him like a canopy, keeping the d rizzle off him. 'You d id n't d o too bad ly yourself.'

'I got shot,' Logan said .

Hamza smiled . 'Aye, well, there's that, I suppose. I got hund red s of wee nails in my feet, if that makes you feel any better?'

Logan looked d own at Hamza's feet, and realised he was stand ing in his socks. He looked over to where Ayesha was being examined by a paramed ic and saw that she was wearing the sergeant's shoes.

'Aye. It d oes, weird ly,' Logan said .

He motioned for Hamza to scoot over, then sat next to him. The back of the BMW d ipped und er the ad d itional weight.

They both sat in silence for a while, watching the scene unfold ing. Merry Donlon was in the back of a police car. Ronnie Jr. had insisted on going with her, and when one of the Uniforms had told him he could n't, Logan had intervened . Might as well let the lad spend some time with her now. He wasn't going to have many other opportunities.

Sinead and Tyler were stand ing at the back of the other ambulance, waiting as the paramed ics prepared the bed . Sinead was hold ing the baby she'd found kicking away in a crib in the living room of the house. She bounced from foot to foot with it, calming it with whispers and coos, while Tyler just stood there grinning at her. Mesmerised by her.

'Good practice, I suppose,' Logan remarked .

'Aye,' Hamza agreed.

'Maybe he won't be a total disaster.'

'I think he'll be good,' Hamza said.

Logan nodded. 'Aye. Aye, I think you're probably right.'

He looked up and closed his eyes for a moment, letting the fine mist of rain wash over him. Then, when he felt sufficiently cleansed by it, he opened his eyes again and gestured around at the orchestrated chaos of the driveway.

'Don't get this in the tech team,' he said.

He stared ahead, but from the corner of his eye saw the look of surprise on the detective sergeant's face.

'Tyler told you?'

Logan shook his head. 'No. He didn't say a word. I mean, it was obvious you'd mentioned it to him, he's not exactly subtle. But he didn't tell me.'

'Then how did ...?'

Logan did turn to face him then. 'They asked me for a reference before they offered you the job.'

'Oh. Right. Aye.' Hamza scratched his head and smiled sheepishly. 'And what did you say?'

'I said, "over my dead fucking body,"' Logan told him. He sighed 'And then, I deleted that, and said that Detective Sergeant Hamza Khaled is one of the finest officers I've ever worked with, and that he would be an asset to any role, either in the polis or out of it.'

Hamza looked up, then down, then away in general, like he couldn't figure out where his eyes were supposed to be pointing.

'Right. Right, well... wow. Thanks, sir.'

Logan clenched a fist, and bumped him lightly on the thigh with it, then stood up. 'I'll get someone to come check out those feet,' he said. 'If you're leaving us, then you're leaving in one bloody piece.'

–

Three hours later, Logan and the others stood in the car park of the Kyle of Lochalsh Police Station, suitcases loaded, and keys in hand.

Taggart was already secured in the back of Logan's Beamer, and both rear side-windows were marked with nose and tongue prints, as he tried to get an eyeful of everything going on outside.

Their work—this part of it, anyway—was done. Orla's baby and Ayesha would both be at Raigmore, already being checked over, already being cared for.

Tyler should've been there, too, after the hammering he'd taken from Merry Donlon, but—following a check-up from the paramedics, and a rare display of injury-related understatement, he'd insisted he was fine.

Before the ambulance had headed off, Hamza had been able to talk to Ayesha. She wouldn't talk to Logan. Wouldn't talk to anyone else, in fact, besides the man who had found her.

She'd gone to Merry Donlon the night Orla had been found. Orla had told her months before about the affair with Ronnie Sr., and Ayesha had kept it secret when she'd thought that her friend had left of her own free will.

When she'd turned up dead, though, Ayesha had gone to Merry to break the news of the affair. Merry had acted surprised. She'd thanked Ayesha for bringing it to her, then asked her to wait outside until Merry joined her, so they could discuss it further in private.

That, Logan realised, was when he'd seen her outside with Ronnie Jr. He'd told her to go home, but instead, she'd hung about for Merry, and gone off in the car with her to discuss things, not knowing what fate the woman really had in store for her.

'How did Ronald senior take the news?' asked Logan. He'd been getting his arm bandaged at the time, and it was felt that—given the men's relationship—Ben should be the one to tell Merry's husband everything.

'I mean, he wasn't over the moon,' the DI replied. He was standing by the passenger side of Logan's BMW, clearly itching to get off. 'He's shocked by... well, by all of it. By his wife being a killer. By him having a daughter. I think it's fair to say that it all caught him off guard.'

'And their son?' asked Sinead. 'How's he?'

'Fucked in the head, I'd have thought,' Hoon chimed in. He was leaning against the driver's side door of Hamza's car, having declared the detective sergeant's feet injuries too serious for him to drive with. He spun Hamza's keys around on his finger, and shrugged. 'But then, aren't we all?' He pulled open the door. 'Especially in this fucking job.'

'You're not in this job, Bob!' Logan reminded him, but Hoon just extended a middle finger, climbed into the driver's seat, and blasted the horn.

'Get a fucking move on!' he shouted, glowering at Hamza and Dave Davidson. 'Or I'm leaving without you.'

'It's my car!' the DS protested, but he opened the back door so Dave could clamber in.

'Cheers!' Dave said. 'Mind shoving my chair in the boot?'

'My feet are full of holes,' Hamza reminded him.

Dave grinned. 'Aye, well, my legs don't work. Guess who wins.'

Up front, Hoon let out a cackle, then started the engine. Hamza wrestled Dave's chair into its folded position, then opened the boot.

Tyler hurried over and lifted it in for him.

'Thanks,' the DS said.

'No bother, Sarge,' Tyler replied. He turned to Logan. 'He did really well today, didn't he, boss? That was proper good, wasn't it? Saving the girl, and that. He should maybe get a medal or something.'

'Tyler,' Logan intoned.

'Boss?'

'Shut up,' the DCI said.

'Aye, but I was just saying, boss, that—'

'I know what you were just saying, son. And I agree. God help me, I agree with you,' Logan told him. 'DS Khaled did good out there. He always does. And that, in my book, means he's earned the right to make his own decisions.'

There were some confused looks from DI Forde and Sinead. Logan was a little surprised by at least one of those. Tyler, it seemed, had kept Hamza's secret well.

'What the hell are you on about, Jack?' asked Ben.

'Doesn't matter,' Logan told him. 'Just get your arse in the car, Mustang.'

'Aye, about time, too!' Ben said , opening the d oor. 'Some of us have got a hot d ate tonight!'

He winked , rubbed his hand s together gleefully, then climbed into the car. Once he'd shut the d oor, all of the d etectives, to some extent or another, shud d ered at the thought.

'Right, so, I guess we'll see you all back at the office?' Sinead said , opening the d river's d oor.

'Not blood y likely,' Logan told her. 'Some of us have been injured in the call of d uty. I think that earns us an afternoon off, d on't you, Sergeant?'

Hamza smiled . 'You won't hear me saying no to that, sir.'

'Does that includ e me, boss?' Tyler asked . 'Since, you know, I nearly had my head caved in by a murd erer.'

'Aye, son. I'm sure, in this instance, we can extend it to you, too.'

'Nice one, boss!'

Hoon blasted the horn again, bellowed , 'Fucking hurry up, I'm missing *Bargain Hunt!*' then revved the engine.

'Good luck, Sergeant,' Logan said , turning to Hamza.

Hamza opened the front passenger sid e d oor, then nod d ed back at him. 'Thank you, sir. I appreciate that.'

'Wait!' Sinead called , so sharply that everyone stopped to look at her. 'What about Ellie Tonks? The brid e. She's still in the cell, isn't she? Should n't we let her out? She might still make her honeymoon.'

Logan sucked in his bottom lip, thinking back to his interview with the woman, and her complete d isregard for the d ead girl in the water. She really was a horrible bastard .

'Och,' he said , smirking as he climbed into the car. 'I'm sure the Uniforms'll find her soon enough.'

And then, with everyone load ed up and buckled in, DCI Jack Logan led the convoy out of the car park and head ed back east toward s the city.

And then, on the very first few metres of the very first straight stretch of road , Hoon flew past him into the lead .

Epilogue

Hamza said his good byes to Dave, plead ed with Hoon to d rop the ca safely at the Burnett Road station, then hobbled up the path toward s his front d oor, wincing at the pain in his band aged feet.

He'd got his shoes back, at least, though between the band ages and his socks, they were too tight to properly tie.

Amira was watching for him from the living room wind ow. She gave him a wave, then retreated into the room. He'd texted ahead from the car, partly just to let her know he was on his way back, and partly because, given Hoon's d riving, he wasn't sure he was ever going to see her again.

The front d oor opened before he reached it. Amira winced at the way he was moving, then came out to take his bag off him and help him up the step.

'Careful, take it easy,' she told him.

'I'm fine. Don't worry. They're just flesh wound s,' he told her. 'Just six or seven hund red flesh wound s.'

'Sound s lovely,' Amira said. She closed the d oor behind them, then gripped his arm again, hold ing him stead y. 'Rough d ay at the office?'

Hamza shrugged. 'I've had worse.'

'Dad d y!'

Kamila came racing along the hall at the sound of his voice, waving a sheet of paper she'd carefully coloured with crayons.

'Careful, Kammi, d ad 's sore,' Amira said, but Hamza shook his head and d ropped to his knees, read y to catch his d aughter's full-speed flying hug.

'It's fine. It's fine. This makes me better, d oesn't it?' he said, giving Kamila a squeeze.

She giggled , hugged him back for all of half a second , then wriggled free so she could present him with her drawing.

'I did you this! Do you like it?'

'Let me see it, and I'll tell you,' he said , taking the picture from her.

It showed a figure, done in brown crayon, with a flapping red cape. He was holding a trophy of some sort above his head , while three other figures cheered on.

'That's you,' Kamila said , pointing to the superhero standing proudly in the centre. 'That's me, that's Mummy with the big tummy.'

'Oi! I heard that!' Amira said .

Kamila smirked . Her finger traced across the page until it found the fourth figure. It stood a little apart from the family, but was joining in with their celebration, nonetheless.

'And that's the lady you saved from the bad people.'

'Oh! Oh, that's nice,' Hamza said .

He looked up and met his wife's gaze. She pulled a half-grimace of apology.

'Sorry. I might have mentioned something. Proud wife moment.'

Hamza rolled his eyes, but smiled at her. He turned back to his daughter, and admired her picture one more time.

'I love it,' he said . 'Can I keep it?'

'No,' Kamila said .

Hamza frowned . 'No?'

'No, I like it,' his daughter told him. She plucked it from his hands, pressed one of her fingers against his nose and went, 'Boop!' then turned and skipped off along the hallway.

'To be fair, it is a good picture,' Amira said , helping her husband to stand again. 'I can see why she wants to hang onto it.'

'True,' Hamza agreed .

They kissed , then hugged , and stood there like that for what felt like forever, yet not nearly long enough.

'What was it you wanted to tell me?' she asked , once the embrace was over.

'What?'

'Your text,' Amira said. 'You said you had something you wanted to tell me. Sounded important.'

'Oh. That. I wanted to tell you that… I just… I wanted to say…'

Hamza thought of his little girl, and of the drawing she had done. He thought of the other girl, Ayesha Fulton. Safe. Alive.

Because he'd been there.

Because of him.

He slipped an arm around his wife's waist, smiled at her, then shrugged. 'I just wanted to tell you that today was a really good day,' he said.

'Good. I'm glad to hear it.' She planted a kiss on his cheek, then pointed into the living room. 'I'll get the kettle on. You take a seat. Your feet must be killing you.'

Hamza looked down at his shoes, fat with the bandages hidden away beneath his socks.

'Do you know what?' he said, giving his toes a wriggle. 'I hadn't even noticed.'

And then he headed through to his favourite chair in the living room, took out his phone, and opened up his emails.

Do you love crime fiction and are always on the lookout for brilliant authors?

Canelo Crime is home to some of the most exciting novels around . Thousand s of read ers are alread y enjoying our compulsive stories. Are you read y to find your new favourite writer?

Find out more and sign up to our newsletter at canelocrime.com

Penguin Random House LLC
1745 Broadway
US-NY, 10019
US
https://www.penguinrandomhouse.com
1-800-733-3000

The authorized representative in the EU for product safety and compliance is

Penguin Random House Ireland
Morrison Chambers, 32 Nassau Street
D02 YH68
IE
https://eu-contact.penguin.ie

ISBN: 9798217269754
Release ID: 154078558